Dear Little Black Dress Reader,

Thanks for picking up this Little Black Dress book, one of the great new titles from our series of fun, page-turning romance novels. Lucky you — you're about to have a fantastic romantic read that we know you won't be able to put down!

Why don't you make your Little Black Dress experience even better by logging on to

www.littleblackdressbooks.com

where you can:

* Enter our **monthly competitions** to win **gorgeous** prizes
* Get **hot-off-the-press** news about our latest titles
* Read **exclusive** preview chapters both from your **favourite** authors and from brilliant new writing talent
* Buy **up-and-coming** books online
* Sign up for an essential slice of romance via our **fortnightly email** newsletter

We love nothing more than to curl up and indulge in an addictive romance, and so we're delighted to welcome you into the Little Black Dress club!

With love from,

The *little black dress* team

Five interesting things about Sarah Monk:

1. I once met the Queen. Unfortunately it was when my husband and I were making our merry way arm in arm to the champagne tent at Ascot, mindless of the fact that she and her entourage were trying to do a procession. Although her minder stopped Terry from crashing through it with a muscular arm, when he stopped dead the momentum made me swing past and land flat on my back on the floor in front of her madge! Oh, the perils of too much champagne on a hot day . . .

2. I have two much adored terrier dogs, Ruby and Freddie, the latter named after Freddie Ljungberg. The husband (a Londoner and Gunner) thinks this is in honour of him being Arsenal number 8 for many years, but for me it's more commemorative of those amazing Calvin Kline ads . . .

3. When I'm not writing, I love to cook. My favourite kitchen invention is a recipe for a white chocolate and raspberry cheesecake, where one of the secret ingredients is vodka, and I harbour an unnatural and overwhelming desire to be a contestant on *Come Dine with Me*.

4. I've written quite a few books, but I actually started my writing career penning lots of short stories for the legend that is *Just Seventeen* magazine.

5. I almost became an Opera singer but I had to make a choice, and my love of writing saved the world's ears from being tortured by my voice. Although I'm afraid I still massacre the odd jazz number when drunkenness and opportunity collide!

By Sarah Monk

A Romantic Getaway
Bittersweet

Bittersweet

Sarah Monk

little
black
dress

Cataloguing in Publication Data is available from the British Library

ISBN 978 0 7553 4512 0

Typeset in Transit511BT by Avon DataSet Ltd,
Bidford-on-Avon, Warwickshire

Printed and bound in Great Britain by
Clays Ltd, St Ives plc

Headline's policy is to use papers that are natural, renewable and
recyclable products and made from wood grown in sustainable forests.
The logging and manufacturing processes are expected to conform to the
environmental regulations of the country of origin.

HEADLINE PUBLISHING GROUP
An Hachette UK Company
338 Euston Road
London NW1 3BH

www.littleblackdressbooks.com
www.headline.co.uk
www.hachette.co.uk

For my husband
who (as he keeps reminding me) is my inspiration

Acknowledgements

Huge thanks to Claire and Sara and everyone at Little Black Dress, and to Amanda and all at Luigi Bonomi Associates. To DW for saving me from myself by eating all the chocolate biscuits. To BW, an angel in disguise. To EH for always sharing the floor *and* making us dance when we're down there. To GGG for being himself. To my IT and the ever gorgeous AH who've both put up with me for a scarily long time. To Jane, my friend and Cornish mum who always brightens my day when she calls Dave dad. And finally love and thanks to Terry, Freddie and Ruby who, despite the fact that it's their mission in life to stop me working, actually make it possible for me to do so.

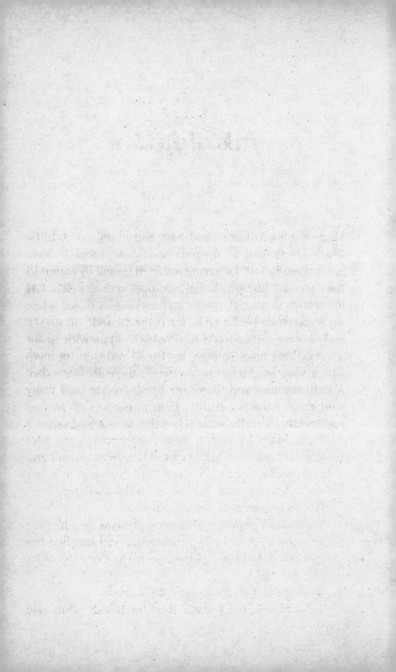

Being woken up by someone screaming was never a good thing.

What was far worse, however, was being woken up by someone screaming whilst three thousand feet up in an aeroplane.

Nell's life didn't exactly flash before her eyes, more parade, like a row of cancan dancers in the middle of the Moulin Rouge: manic music, arms linked in a row, each high kick smacking her hard in the face, harder even than the turbulence was booting her firmly up the bum every couple of seconds as the bloody plane dropped as terrifyingly stomach-lurchingly as a ride at a fairground.

'Holy Mary Mother of God!' she heard Ange utter breathlessly, and then felt her hand take her own and grip it hard, too hard, painfully hard. But Nell had no voice with which to ask Ange to ease up on the death grip.

Her voice was gone, frightened away.

The sudden plummet of the aeroplane as they literally fell into a pocket of violent turbulence had terrified her beyond belief, but the sudden summary of her life so far was far, far scarier.

'Where did it all go wrong?' she rasped.

'I don't know, but I blame it on the bloody pilot,' said Ange.

And then the free fall stopped and the screaming stopped; in fact the plane fell eerily silent as the pilot set them flying lower to get out of the pocket of turbulence that had assaulted them with all the vicious stealth and violence of a mugger in a dark alleyway.

Despite falling faster than the Dow Jones in a recession, Ange had somehow managed to hang on to her vodka and tonic without spilling a drop.

'Well that's a bloody miracle, so it is,' she laughed, taking a reassuring swig and then offering one to Nell.

Nell too took a swig of the strong drink and began to laugh.

And then the woman in the seat behind them began to cry.

Which set off a group of hungover girls in pink feather boas and matching T-shirts stating 'Hilary's Hens Hit Prague' who all began bellowing like a bunch of overtired toddlers.

The air stewardesses, finally released from their own seats by an announcement from the captain, who was confident he had completely recaptured control of his wayward plane, sprang into action with boxes of tissues and reassuring voices.

If she was honest, despite the laughter, Nell felt like crying too. Which she supposed was nothing new, as she had felt like crying most of the time over the last two days.

Initially she had been really looking forward to the trip to Prague.

Her boyfriend Marcus's father Charles was marrying his long-term Czech girlfriend Dita. Everyone had been invited to the city for a weekend of celebration. Nell loved the place, loved its history, its architecture, its shoe shops. She was also so tired, she really needed a break. She was moving in with Marcus when they got home, and had spent the last two weeks packing up her own house, the sale of which was due to complete on the following Friday. And work had been so manic lately; work was always manic. A break was definitely needed.

This weekend had turned out to be a break all right.

As in painful, and fractured.

It had all started when the two couples met up at Stansted airport.

Marcus and Nell, Justin and Ange.

Marcus and Justin were brothers.

Despite the fact that there was almost two years between them, they could easily have been mistaken for twins. Same height, same hazel eyes, same mouth, same brown hair, same dress sense, so much so that they often independently bought the same outfit and then laughed like drains when they turned up somewhere looking like Tweedledum and Tweedledee.

They had the same sense of humour, which was a bit of a crass cross between toilet and rugby songs, and the same likes and dislikes, except when it came to women, which explained why Nell and Ange were so different.

They were handsome, smart, funny, successful in their own way: Marcus as a manager for the same company as Nell, which was how they had met, although fortunately for a completely different department, which meant that they could easily keep work and home separate; and Justin as an underwriter for a large insurance company.

Unfortunately they also had the same capacity to make you feel when they got together that you were completely and utterly invisible.

As well as being brothers they were best friends, which was lovely really, unless you were their other half.

They had arranged to meet up in the airport bar, and by the time Ange and Nell, who hadn't seen each other since Christmas, had finished embracing each other and exclaiming their pleased hellos, the boys were already halfway down their first pint and ordering their second, and engaged in a conversation that had left no room at the table for anyone else to sit down.

Ange had simply raised her eyebrows at Nell and, linking arms, suggested a trip to the duty-free shop.

'I'm not in the mood to get leathered before we even hit the air,' she murmured, pulling Nell towards the exit.

'Shouldn't we tell them where we're going?' Nell looked back at Marcus and Justin, who, heads together, were guffawing over an anecdote Marcus had just told about a rugby game he had played at the weekend.

'You're kidding, aren't you? They won't even notice we're gone. And what's more, I bet you a pound to a penny they won't even notice when we come back.'

Ange was probably right. In fact if Nell was honest, there was no 'probably' about it. When they got together, the boys always went off into their own little world, a world that usually revolved around consuming copious amounts of alcohol and catching up on each other's lives in detail that was so minute it would be kicked out of Lilliput for being too small.

By the time Nell and Ange returned with their perfume and their chocolate bars the size of a small country, the boys were three quarters cut and raring to go the full pint.

Fortunately they managed to pull themselves together enough to be allowed on to the plane, where they promptly fell asleep for the entire journey.

'Thank heavens for small mercies,' Ange whispered across the aisle as they both began to snore, and Nell nodded as if she agreed but couldn't help thinking back to how she had imagined their take-off would be, hand in hand and half a bottle of champagne between them to celebrate their own forthcoming change in status from boyfriend and girlfriend to cohabiting couple.

And so she shared the champagne with Ange instead, whilst listening to Marcus snore, and thought how funny it was that for a girl who was so focused, so structured, so ordered, life never seemed to turn out at all how she planned it.

They had arrived at Charles and Dita's beautiful Prague home from home to find that an impromptu stag night was being held the night before the wedding. The lads were on the town. Meanwhile the girls were expected to take the luggage to their hotel and unpack, and then return to the house for a ladies' night in.

This on the whole didn't sound too bad, although they would have both preferred a ladies' night out, but visions of giving each other manicures and facials in order to look beautiful for the following day were sharply elbowed by the reality of Dita's choice of hen night, which was a movie evening. A Czech movie evening. Where no one could work out how to get the subtitles running, and the English contingent were far too polite and claimed it really didn't matter to them if they watched *Sliding Doors* and *Love Actually* in Czech, which was fine for Marcus and Justin's Great-Aunt Mabel because she could lip-read, but not so much fun for everyone else, apart from when Ange, who had seen *Love Actually* about thirty times and knew the words almost off by heart, began to speak the parts.

Her impressions of Martine McCutcheon and Hugh Grant were enough to send Nell into one of those fits of giggles where you just can't stop and people who don't know you and most definitely people who don't speak your language think you're laughing at them or being rude, and so Ange had to stop and the room fell into a bewitched silence for the Czech contingent and a bored silence for the English. After this Nell and Ange decided the only thing left to do was get drunk, and so they drank too much Czech vodka, which was fortunately pure enough to negate the hangovers they were expecting the following morning, and went back to the hotel and to bed early.

Justin and Marcus crawled in at four in the morning, full of not so pure Czech vodka, a rake of Czech, English and indeed multinational beer, and several shots of something that looked like a toad had crawled into the bottle and died. They both fell into bed, and once again began to snore.

Amazingly enough, they woke up the next day raring to go, no hangover in sight. Nell and Ange decided this was because they were still actually drunk, a state that continued and worsened as the wedding day itself progressed.

They had got stupidly drunk together – even more so than they already were – and danced with everyone in sight. Well, everyone but Nell and Ange, that was; Nell and Ange they had somehow managed to ignore for most of the day.

'You know what it is, don't you?' Ange had said, frowning as Justin positioned himself within the ample cleavage of a stunning Czech girl for a slow one.

'Enlighten me,' Nell had said drily.

'It's because it's a wedding. They're both petrified we'll be getting ideas ourselves.'

'And what? They're making themselves look as unattractive as possible by behaving like complete arseholes?'

'Well, I meant that that's why they're avoiding us, but I can see where you're coming from with that one as well.'

Nell watched Marcus stagger round the dance floor with a well-built German girl, trip over the bride on his way back to the table, grab hold of an elderly lady to stop himself from falling and then fall anyway, taking the poor old dear down with him. She decided that as much as she didn't want to do it, it was time for an intervention, especially when as soon as he got back to their table, he grabbed hold of some lethal Czech concoction called slivovitz and poured himself a very large shot of it.

As he raised the glass to his lips, Nell put a hand on his arm and asked him very gently, 'Don't you think you've had enough to drink?'

To which he replied, 'Doesn't the very fact that I'm getting myself another one answer that in the negative?' in that awfully haughty way only the very drunk can master.

It was two in the morning by the time Nell could persuade him to leave, and that was only because he no longer had the capacity to think for himself.

Justin was only slightly better, the two of them intertwined and staggering, bouncing off each other and the objects around them in hazardous oblivion.

Their father's best English friend and his well-built wife, who were staying at the same hotel, helped Nell and Ange wheel them back there, a feat that they wouldn't have been able to manage on their own, and there they literally toppled into bed like felled trees, beginning to snore even before they hit the pillow face down.

*

It was small consolation that their hangovers the following day were monumental.

Marcus wanted nursing and Nell was damned if she was in the mood to do it.

Fortunately, after she'd fetched the Lucozade and chocolate he was demanding from the nearby shop, he fell back into the sleep of the dead, and she was able to escape the drink-drenched confines of the hotel room, and out into the fresh air of Sunday morning.

What to do now?

Their flight wasn't leaving until late evening, and there was a lunch being held at Charles and Dita's house in the suburbs, but Nell wouldn't go on her own.

Sightseeing?

In Prague, great; doing it on your own, not so great.

Shopping? Better idea, but what would be open on a Sunday?

She decided she'd start with a walk, and set off down the road, determined at the very least to find a shoe shop that was open, but she'd only gone a hundred yards when she was hailed from the café on the corner.

'Thought I might spot you escaping from here. Is yours as sick as mine?'

'In the head,' Nell muttered, flopping down into the empty chair next to Ange and pulling her coat around her to keep out the breeze that was blowing.

Ange laughed and signalled for the waiter. 'Two coffees, please, young man, and you'd better bring us a very large cake as well.'

'You want piece of cake?'

'No, not a *piece*,' Ange explained carefully. 'The *whole* cake. The *entire* thing. Two spoons.'

Then she grinned at Nell and told her quite happily that Justin had thrown up four times already.

'. . . and he was talking in his sleep – well, not so much talking as yelling and calling for someone called Jelena. So I told him he can get Jelena to clear up his mess and fetch him sweet tea and bacon sarnies, and left him to it. Honestly, the cheek of them: act like twats all weekend, then, come Sunday, expect us to be Florence effing Nightingale . . .'

'I know.' Nell grimaced. 'They were so embarrassing yesterday, weren't they, and the people at the wedding were so lovely. What must they think of us?'

'Well, they most probably think the fellers are total eejits and that you and I are saints for putting up with them, that's what I say. I also think that when we've had our cake we should sod playing nursemaid and go and indulge in a spot of retail therapy.'

'Shoes,' said Nell, smiling for the first time that day, and then she frowned again. 'You don't think we should go for lunch at Charles and Dita's?'

'Goodness no, girl! Don't you think we've done our duty for this visit? We may as well salvage something good from this bloody weekend. And talking of good . . .' Ange nudged Nell in the ribs as the waiter returned to their table bearing an obscenely large amount of cake.

'Wow, you're right, that does look good. Do you think they'd take back the spoons and bring us a trowel each?'

Ange grinned. 'I say sod the spoons and hold on to my hair.'

Ange and Nell had known each other for five years, ever since Nell had started dating Marcus. Ange had been engaged to Justin for about six years now. At thirty-one, she was four years older than him and often referred to him as her outgrown toyboy.

The two girls had always got on really well; always

wondered when they did meet why they didn't do it more often. They placed their excuses firmly in the fact that Nell lived on the outskirts of Hemel Hempstead and Ange in Battersea, and even though they were only separated by the river when they were at work, Ange worked 24/7. A complete workaholic, my Ange, her mother would tell friends and family with a proud tinge to her voice, little realising when she boasted about how well her daughter had done for herself that it was to the detriment of many other things in her life.

It didn't help that Nell too spent most of her waking hours at work. She also wasn't that good at girlfriends. Her godmother, Maud, told her it was because she was too nice. She wasn't a doormat, but because she gave people the benefit of the doubt, always replied to messages, was there whenever she was needed and didn't take offence if she was not, people sometimes thought she could be walked over. And because she wasn't a doormat but people still tried to walk all over her anyway, Nell walked herself away from them.

And Nell's office wasn't exactly the place to meet lifelong friends. Everyone was far too competitive, more likely to stab you in the back than pat you on it. If some-one at work invited you out for drinks after, it was only so they could get you drunk and steal your ideas. If they asked you to join them for lunch, you could guarantee a partner in crime was raiding the files on your computer whilst you were chowing down at Pret A Manger.

Ange wasn't like that. Ange was different.

Nell liked Ange's caustic wit, her honesty; she was fresh and fun and feisty, she spoke her mind, and did as she pleased, but under the spiky exterior, Nell knew there was a big marshmallow.

As for Ange, she genuinely liked Nell. In Ange's line of

work it was rare to meet someone as genuine as her. Everyone always wanted something from you. Ange was in A & R for a large record label. It was funny how many people in this world wanted to be a singer, longed for recognition, a record contract, gold discs and a slot on *MTV Cribs*. She had got to the point where she told people she was a dinner lady. Funny how no one ever questioned this lie.

Nell was real. Nell was the kind of person you just knew that if you called her at two in the morning from a lay-by in the middle of nowhere, with a flat tyre and a bad attitude, she'd turn up with a smile, a jack, a spare, a cake, a flask of coffee and a hug.

And today, whilst both were furious with their respective other halves, each was pleased that it gave them the chance to spend some girlie time together.

They wandered the city arm in arm, darting in and out of shops, buying things they couldn't afford, didn't need, but couldn't resist. They guiltily but gleefully eyed up the handsome Czech men with their Slavic cheekbones and hooded eyes, and got wolf-whistled several times, much to Ange's delight.

'I should go out with you more often.'

'Yes, you should, but it's not me they were whistling at.'

'Utter bollocks!' Ange retorted.

Ange envied Nell.

With her shining black curls dyed a bright flame-red and dove-grey eyes, Ange was an attractive girl, but being a normal healthy size fourteen, she was always on a diet in search of the elusive size ten, a diet that seemed to consist of eating everything and anything and then complaining about the fact that she'd done it, as if the very act of contrition for her gluttony would burn off the extra calories.

Ange thought that she was average in looks and above average in size. Justin had, in unkinder moments, been known to burst into the bathroom whilst she was in the tub and pretend to harpoon her with his snooker cue: not very good for a girl's self-esteem.

Nell, however, was far from average. She wasn't conventionally beautiful, but Ange had come to the conclusion that this was what was so attractive about her. She had chestnut-brown hair to her shoulders, straight when she'd had time with her GHDs but naturally slightly wavy, big golden-brown eyes, full lips, fifties-film-star cheekbones, and a nose that she always protested she hated because it was too long and too big, and perhaps it was a little, but not on Nell's face; on Nell's face it looked perfect.

The irony was that Nell also envied Ange.

She thought that Ange was incredibly pretty, with the kind of cleavage that Nell could never hope to achieve without the help of plastic surgery, but it was her confidence that Nell wished she could emulate. Ange was always so certain about everything. No fear, a slogan that could have been written for her rather than a T-shirt.

Spending time with each other was fun and easy.

It particularly helped that they both loved to shop.

Laden with bags, Ange easily managed to overrule Nell's half-hearted suggestion of 'Don't you think we should go back and check on them?' and persuade her into a late lunch in a little restaurant near the river.

'I live my life by my own set of rules,' she told Nell firmly, 'and rule number three on my list is never let your man rule your life.'

Nell smiled. 'What's rule number one?'

'Well you see, rule number two is never tell anyone what rule number one is.' Ange shrugged enigmatically.

'Rule number four?'

'Oh, I can tell you that one, no problem. Rule number four is that when men drive you to drink, don't stop the car before you reach the bar.'

And sitting down at a terrace table, she waved for a waiter and ordered a bottle of wine.

An hour later and they were putting the world, or rather their world and the men who were ruining it, to rights.

'Do you know what really gets my goat?' Nell took a slug of her wine, feeling the rhubarb-tinged white tingling on her taste buds. 'When once in a blue moon with no R in the month they do the washing-up, or the washing, or hoover or something, doesn't matter what, just something trivial and domestic that we do every day with no thanks, and they look at you like a kid who's just got a gold star for their homework and is expecting a big fat pat on the back and a bag of sweets for it.'

'Oh I know, that totally does my crust as well.' Ange rolled her big grey eyes. 'I do the washing-up every bloody day; he does it once a year and expects praise. If I only did it once a year I wouldn't get praise, I'd get called a lazy slut.'

Nell laughed. Ange had a way of saying it like it was.

'Thing is,' Ange continued, 'you can't rely on a man to look after you any more, and if women have realised that, why haven't men woken up to the same fact?'

'What do you mean?'

'Well, how things used to be, yeah, men and women, it was an exchange, wasn't it? I hesitate to add the word "fair" because that's a calculation that could take some working, and my maths and my social politics aren't that good, but the bottom line was that they looked after us, so we looked after them. The weekly wage in exchange for the necessities of an easy life: cooked food, clean shirts, clean underpants, house that isn't caked in dust and grime. Now we go out to work, but they still expect the same. They want someone who will earn enough money to take the pressure off, to help pay the bills and the mortgage, to ensure decent holidays, and still provide a home-cooked meal and clean sheets to snuggle down in at the end of the day.'

'They want Superwoman!' Nell nodded her agreement. 'What was that thing Jerry Hall said, about cook, whore and mother? Well, you can add bank manager to that just to update it.'

'Although,' Ange conceded, 'I suppose we can't blame it *all* on men. People expect more from life nowadays. Fifties Stepford Wife didn't want new shoes every other week and a fortnight in the Maldives at Christmas. Higher expectations need higher incomes, which means a woman has to work. It's not just want, it's necessity. You never used to have to pay out twenty years' wages in advance just to buy yourself the smallest house in Britain.'

'Yeah. Most girls nowadays want to marry a footballer and live in a mansion, and never have to lift a manicured fingernail again.'

'It's the modern-day great expectations.'

'I'd settle for a bit of respect,' Nell said wistfully.

'Respect for what, though? You earn respect how nowadays?'

'By being good at what you do? Though nowadays nobody knows what the hell they're supposed to do any more. Nothing is ever enough. You learn how to cope with life, how to live your life, from the previous generation. If everybody's lost, how on earth can anyone lead the way?'

'If you had a daughter, what would you teach her?'

'That's a hard one, Ange.'

'I know, but we're sitting in the sunshine in a foreign country, half cut. If you can't wax philosophical now, when can you?'

'I'm not sure that I can, actually. It's kind of a biggie. Thinking about what advice you'd give your own kids to set them up for life. It's hard enough to even imagine having my own kids.'

'But you do want them? Kids?'

'Well, I've never really thought about it in great detail, but I think I've always just assumed that I will, yeah. Not that Marcus would be keen.'

'No?' Ange asked in surprise.

'Nah!' Nell hiccuped and leaned in on Ange's shoulder. 'He'd have to share his toys. Heaven forbid, one day they might even want to have a go on his PlayStation.'

Ange nodded. 'Him and Justin used to fight like crazy when they were younger.'

'Not like that now, are they?'

'Nope. Thick as thieves.'

'As tight as arseholes,' Nell added. They both shrieked with laughter, and then Nell swallowed the laughter as rapidly as it had erupted from her and suddenly looked mortified. 'Oh my Lord, he is an arsehole, isn't he, Marcus, a complete arsehole?'

Ange's own laughter hiccuped to a halt. 'Does that mean that when you picture your kids they don't have Marcus's eyes?' she asked carefully.

Nell thought for a long moment. 'Only if they're using them as marbles,' she said, and started to cackle again.

Ange's face joined in the laughter, but her eyes were showing a different emotion.

Concern.

'If I had a kid? Now there's a thought . . .' Nell was musing, waving her half-full glass so that the wine sloshed dangerously close to the edge of it. 'If I had my own daughter, I suppose I'd probably say to her that life is too short. It's hard to find which way you want to go, but if you end up on the wrong path, which happens far too easily, for heaven's sake don't keep going in the hope that you might just end up somewhere nice, instead of where you actually wanted to be, because it's more than likely that you'll end up somewhere horrible, like a swamp, a stinky, smelly swamp.' And with that, she upended her glass and drained it to the dregs.

Ange's eyes blinked wide in surprise. 'Is that how you feel about your life, Nell?'

Nell thought for a moment. The obvious answer was no, of course not, but she somehow couldn't get the words out.

'Well, the silence tells me everything I need to know,' Ange said, signalling for the waiter. Then she put her hand over Nell's and asked her gently, 'Are things all right between you and Marcus at the moment?'

Nell shook her head. 'Shit,' she slurred.

'What's happened?'

'Well, we went to this wedding yesterday and he was a total something starting with W that I'm too much of a lady to say . . .'

'I know that, Nell, that's why we're here now. I meant in general.'

'In general?'

It was as if Nell had suddenly sobered up.

'Yeah, in general. Are you two okay?'

The silence that followed this question seemed endless, but Ange was patient.

Eventually Nell answered. 'In general, I really don't know.' She frowned down at her wine glass, and then her eyes flicked up to Ange. There were no more signs of laughter. 'Have you ever noticed that life has a habit of gaining momentum without you even noticing? You just keep on going, trying to keep up. It's only when you stop that you wonder where you are and how you actually got there in the first place.'

'You're not okay, are you?' Ange said, frowning.

Nell shrugged, sighed, shook her head, then wrinkled her nose. 'Yeah, sure, we're okay, we're fine. He just really annoyed me yesterday, but hey, what's new? I'll get over it.'

'You sure?'

Nell didn't answer, but she nodded; and then, more as if to reassure herself than Ange, she nodded again more vigorously.

'Are you sure?' Ange repeated.

'Yes. But I think we should probably forget about that second bottle of wine, 'cause I might just change my mind.' She managed a smile that didn't really have any heart in it.

If truth were told rather than just thought and not said to anybody, the honest answer would have been that she was coming to the slow realisation that there were many things about Marcus that not just niggled her, but that she actively disliked. But how could she admit this to Ange when she'd only just dared to think it herself?

Ange looked at her watch and then startled Nell by jumping to her feet, eyes wide.

'Hell and damnation!' she shrieked, pulling on her coat and then throwing Nell's at her. 'Definitely sod the wine, and get the bill as well . . . and do you know the Czech for I need a taxi, like, yesterday? It's nearly five o'clock!'

The hotel room smelled like a drip tray, and Marcus was sulking. If there was one thing Nell hated, it was an atmosphere. What on earth was the point of spending time together when one of you had a face like a gargoyle and wasn't talking, the only communication being sighs and furrowed brows and pointed looks. He was annoyed that she had left him to fend for himself for the day, the fact that he had spent most of it comatose in bed obviously not enough for him to allow her that freedom.

For once Nell refused to be beaten into an apology for leaving him. As far as she was concerned she had done nothing wrong, and she and Ange had had such a wonderful day, she was determined he wasn't going to take the shine off her new shoes.

They packed their bags in a silence that was as stifling as the room. The one good thing was that since Marcus wasn't talking to her, he couldn't ask her to pack for him.

When they finally made it downstairs, to Nell's surprise Justin and Ange, on the other hand, seemed to be okay.

Justin had apparently recovered enough earlier in the day to get up and head out in search of food, only to find himself in a bar opposite the hotel, where he decided that Guinness was the best thing for an empty stomach and an aching head. The Guinness had been cold and the young Czech barmaid had been attractive and friendly. He was therefore in a jovial frame of mind, and Ange, high on shopping, was happy to have him so, despite his previous behaviour. The two of them were full of jokes and banter, which only served to highlight the deep, dark funk that Marcus had sunk into.

Things went from bad to worse when they finally got to the airport.

They were late, the flight was oversubscribed, and they had been bumped. Well, two of them had.

'Two seats left, four bums to fill them,' as Ange so succinctly put it.

Of course it was 'imperative' that Marcus got on the flight. Justin too. They both cited important work commitments the following day. They were both lying, of course. Ange and Nell too said they had things they couldn't afford to miss at work. They were telling the truth, but it was like one of those game shows where nobody knows who's being honest, and the two with the worst poker face aren't going to win a penny.

Nell had never had a good poker face, mainly because she'd never played the game. Ange, on the other hand, could win a seat on the last flight out of a hurricane zone if she put her mind to it, but she had no intention of leaving Nell, and Marcus had absolutely no intention of not getting on that plane. It was obvious from the voice and the stance that out of all of them he didn't care who went as long as it was him.

And so, after much argument, Ange decided to be altruistic.

'Okay, so you and Nell go. Justin and I will stay here and catch the next flight.'

'You don't mind staying?'

'If you really need to get home, then go for it.'

'Great, then you stay here with Nell, and me and Justin can catch the flight.'

'That wasn't what I . . .' Ange started to protest, but the boys were already gathering their bags.

'Thanks, girls. You're stars, both of you.'

Ange was so angry, all she could do was mouth like a goldfish as Marcus and Justin turned to the impatiently waiting girl on the check-in desk and thrust their paperwork at her once again.

Nell put a hand on Marcus's arm. 'You're seriously going to get on that flight and leave me here?'

'Oh come on, Nell, it's not a problem, is it? I need to get back. I feel like shit . . .'

Nell bit back the retort of 'Well, who's bloody fault is that?' as Marcus, frown deepening, added, 'And I've got a meeting with Andrew Mathis in the morning, and you know what he's like.'

'Well, I've got a meeting with Nicolette and the entire project board.'

'Nicolette? You can let that cow handle it on her own for once. Might do her good not to have you there. Might do you good too. You let the bitch walk all over you.'

Nell turned and walked away.

Whatever else Marcus was intent on saying fell out of his mouth in a silent exhalation of surprise. Nell never walked away from anything. She had gone to sit on a plastic airport seat with her back to him. For a moment he contemplated going over to her, but then Justin grabbed his wrist.

'Come on, bro, or they won't let any of us on the flight. They're calling last orders.'

Marcus turned to his brother and nodded.

Ange, who had finally found her voice again, wasn't as

restrained as Nell. 'I always knew you were a selfish, useless prick, Justin Bennet, and you keep doing everything you can to prove me right, don't you?'

Justin responded with a backward wave, and then when Ange threw 'Arsehole!' after him, very loudly, he turned and blew her a kiss, which infuriated her even more, as he'd known full well it would.

'If he thinks I'm going to stand here and wave him off, he's got another thing coming,' she stormed, marching over to Nell.

'They've gone?' Nell asked without even looking.

Ange nodded.

'Shall we hop on a flight to the Seychelles or something instead?' Nell said, the sadness in her voice negating the humour in the sentence.

'I've got a better idea,' Ange said, sitting down next to her and taking her arm. 'Let's grab a cab, head back into the city and party until we drop.'

'Sounds great, but we don't have time.' Nell looked at her watch. 'By the time we've stashed our bags, got a taxi and driven back, we'd probably squeeze in one drink and have to turn around and come right back here again.'

'Bar?' suggested Ange. 'Unless you have a better idea.'

Nell thought for a moment.

She felt a little shell-shocked, to be honest, though she didn't like to say so because it sounded so melodramatic, but that was the right word for how she felt at Marcus's behaviour.

It had happened, though, and Nell would deal with it, because that was how she worked.

So did she have a better idea?

'That I do.' She nodded, taking Ange's arm. '*Shops* and then bar.'

'You mean we didn't buy enough this morning?' Ange

said, kicking her straining suitcase, which was at least two kilos heavier than it had been on the outward journey.

'Can a girl ever buy enough? Especially when she's tempted by those two little words all girls love to hear . . .'

'*Two* little words?'

'Duty-free.'

'Ooh yes, duty-free. Shall we check in and head through to where the real bargains are lurking?'

Unfortunately when they got through to the departure lounge, there was a sight far more distracting than cheap perfume. The far wall of the airport was made of glass so that people could sit and watch the planes take off, and through it they could quite clearly see Marcus and Justin sprinting for their plane. Without verbal agreement the girls paused by the window, and as they watched what should have been their flight taking off without them, they imagined Marcus and Justin settling back in their seats with a hair of the dog and matching self-satisfied grins.

'Do you know, for a moment there I almost wished engine failure on them,' Nell mused as the plane became a speck in the distance.

'Before or after take-off?' Ange grinned evilly.

Whilst 'nice Nell' had definitely meant the former at the time she made the comment, she was changing her mind three hours later when they checked the boards only to see that their flight hadn't been called because it had been delayed. Indefinitely.

Nell and Ange spent the night crying (not literally – moaning would be a more apt description) and sleeping (quite literally) on each other's shoulders in the airport departure lounge.

Nell didn't do crying. She thought about it, and sometimes she felt like it, but that was as far as it got. No actual tears falling. Not if she could help it.

But now, with the realisation that her life was, as Ange would put it, 'a sack of shit', came another just as startling.

Marcus, her boyfriend of five years, the man she had just sold her own house to move in with, was an arse.

Nell felt her eyes fill with hot tears and blinked them away furiously.

'The Brothers Grim,' Ange had christened them at midnight.

At three in the morning they became 'Stupid, selfish, thick-headed, egotistical morons.'

At eight they were 'Sons of the spawn of the devil of selfish hell and devious damnation who should be boiled in oil and burned in the fires of Beelzebub for all eternity . . . especially that absolute shithead Justin.'

And finally at midday the following day a simple 'Utter pricks' was all she could manage to mumble.

Now, almost a day late in leaving, they were finally on the plane and found themselves wishing to God that they weren't.

It suddenly hit Nell as hard as the turbulence had.

'I don't want to go back,' she announced in a voice loud enough to make her non-wailing neighbours turn and stare.

'We're in the middle of the bloody ocean! Whatchya gonna do, Nell, ask the pilot to turn around and go back to Prague? It took us bloody long enough to get ourselves out of there. What do you want to be going back for?'

In her agitation, Ange's usually faint Irish accent came to the fore.

'That's not what I meant,' Nell said, shaking her head. 'I don't want to go back home.'

'Well, I'm not so keen to see those eejits myself either,' Ange huffed, taking an angry swig of her drink. 'I never thought Justin was a gentleman, but I never thought he was such a selfish bastard either. I had a really important meeting today. I'm dreading switching my mobile back on. My boss Tony is the nicest man you'll ever hope to meet, until you upset him. He's like the girl with the curl, only he's a boy, of course; at least I think he is.'

'Ange!'

Ange stopped mid-soliloquy and blinked in surprise at Nell.

The one thing Nell always let Ange do was talk without interruption. There weren't many people in Ange's life who would actually do this; in fact if she thought about it, it was probably just Nell and her own mother.

'What would you say if I said that I don't want to go back at all? I don't want to go back to London, I don't want to go back to work tomorrow, and most of all I don't want to go back to Marcus.'

'I'd say the turbulence has knocked you a touch.' Ange tapped her head with a finger as if to demonstrate.

'Well, I'd say if it has, it's knocked some sense into me . . . Ange, have you ever woken up one day, looked at your life and suddenly wondered how on earth you managed to get where you are? Do you ever feel like your life's a runaway bus that's hurtling you along a road you never wanted to take in the first place, and you're just holding on to your seat and doing your best to make the ride more comfortable?'

'And now you think it's time to grab the steering wheel?'

Nell nodded. 'Do you think it's possible to go back to the bend in the road where you took the wrong turning and go the right way instead?'

Ange shook her head. 'That's the problem with the journey we're all on, Nell. You can't ever go back, you can only go forwards.'

'But you can change direction,' Nell said, more to herself than to Ange. 'When were you happiest? What's your best memory?'

Ange frowned. 'I'm Irish Catholic, it's against our religion to have happy memories. I'll just have to share yours.'

Nell closed her eyes and thought. Thought really hard. For such a seemingly frivolous question had suddenly become of the utmost importance.

When had she been happiest?

One thing for sure was that her mind certainly wasn't instantly flooded with memories filled with Marcus.

And then they came to her, floating in on a salt-and-vinegar cloud of nostalgia.

Memories of sunshine and blue sky, of the smell of sea-weed and the sound of gulls, of ice cream and sandcastles, of hot chips and sunburned faces, short shorts and brown legs, and tea taken on a rug in a garden full of flowers and birdsong and laughter.

And of a face, smiling and kind and witty and weathered and wonderful.

Nell opened her eyes, and found that she was smiling. 'Cornwall,' she said emphatically.

'Cornwall?'

She nodded.

'And Maudlyn.'

'Maudlin?' Ange repeated, her eyes crossing in confusion. 'I thought we were talking about happiness here.'

'We are.' Nell grinned. 'We absolutely are.'

Aunt Maudlyn.

Not actually Nell's aunt, but one of those people in your life who take on the honorary title, and also one of the rare few who over the years earn the right to keep it.

Maud was Nell's godmother and her mother's oldest friend, and at one time her closest too, despite the fact that they were poles apart in terms of personality. They had met in the first year of high school, and instantly formed a bond because of their unusual names, the opposite of which would have suited their personalities far better.

Maudlyn was full of the joys of life and living.

Nell's mother Joy was as miserable as a party that no one turned up to.

Okay, so maybe that was a bit of an exaggeration, but she wasn't exactly the spontaneously happy type. She had never been that way, solid and sensible to Maud's naughty firecracker. The two girls' friendship had been a source of much amusement to their peers when at school, and yet it had endured for a very long time.

And whilst the two women had eventually allowed their many differences to let them grow apart, Nell and Maud had remained as close as ever.

Nell had needed Maud.

Her parents were Mr and Mrs Sensible. Her life with them had been lived to a strict schedule of school, homework and certain suitable extracurricular activities. Friends had been viewed as a distraction from their goal for her to be a doctor, and when her science grades weren't quite up to the mark, they had encouraged her to go into banking as a safe career.

Nell, sweet, eager to please two people who, whilst blinkered, were kind and affectionate in their own way, had usually done as she was bid. And when she needed to escape, it was to Maud that she turned.

Maud was also seen by Nell's parents as a distraction, full of love and indulgence, and prone to turning up unannounced to whisk Nell away for mad days out and with unsuitable presents – one year she bought her a pair of donkeys called Tristan and Isolde. For Nell it had been love at first sight; for Joy and Jeremy, Nell's father, it had been apoplexy at first sight.

All three, donkeys and Maud, had been evicted from their neat suburban four-bed detached with an alacrity that both annoyed and impressed Maud, who had always thought that Jeremy Everson was a bit of a wet blanket.

Both donkeys had fortunately gone on to live a long and happy life in Maud's cottage garden, where they had a ball eating every flower that ever tried to grow there. Maud just shrugged after the swallowing of her prize begonias and said that flowers would always grow again, and at least the donkeys were the best alternative to a lawnmower she had ever had.

From that point on, however, Maud was never welcomed to Norwich quite so warmly or so often. This didn't deter her; she just took to turning up unannounced. She would phone Nell's school and say that she was her mother and she needed to take Nell to the doctor/dentist/ optician/speech therapist/ a family funeral, and then arrive at the gates in her little white car and whisk Nell away for a wild day out, which they would both return from feeling guilty but gleeful.

Happy memories.

More to come, hopefully.

Lots more.

They finally arrived back at Stansted as dusk was falling.

It was raining, that horrible fine kind of drizzle that is barely noticeable at first, until you suddenly find that you're soaked to the skin.

'Right, you phone yours,' said Ange, when they had reclaimed their baggage, 'and I'll phone mine, and that way we might actually get one of them to come and fetch us.'

'You wouldn't rather we made our own way back?'

'Absolutely bloody not,' Ange exclaimed. 'It's the least they can do after abandoning us in Prague. We can find ourselves a decent restaurant and have some proper food after all that airport and aeroplane shit and wait for them to get here.'

Nell, however, wasn't surprised when she went straight through to Marcus's curt message.

'Wait for the tone, you know what to do.'

Nell had always thought that 'Leave a message if you must but I won't call back if I don't want to' would be more appropriate.

She hung up before it reached the end.

'Voicemail,' she sighed.

'Same!' Ange announced, shaking her head in disgust. 'I bet the lazy toad's half asleep on the sofa with a can of lager waiting for the football to start.'

'There's football on tonight?' Nell asked, her stomach stirring with acid.

'You betcha.'

'Well that explains everything, then.' Nell dropped her bags on the wet floor and closed her eyes, shaking her head in disbelief.

The way Marcus had practically fought to get that plane seat . . . She could picture them both now, using every means possible to make sure that they were the two to get on the plane and she and Ange were the ones to stay and wait.

There was a game on.

Nothing was more important than a football match.

Not even her.

She threw her phone back in her handbag in disgust, only for it to bleep at her straight away.

'Maybe that's him calling back?' said Ange hopefully. The boys had, after all, in a pretty useless attempt to placate as they sprinted for the last two seats faster than a Ferrari on a test circuit, promised a lift home from the airport if they phoned when they landed.

'Message,' explained Nell apologetically.

'Marcus?' Ange whispered as Nell went through to her voicemail to retrieve it.

Nell shook her head, her frown deepening. She knew before the first message even started playing that it would be Nicolette. Wimping out of calling her boss directly, Nell had left a message with reception to say that she was stuck at the airport and didn't know when she would be able to make it in. Nicolette never checked her messages.

'Boss,' she mouthed back at Ange.

Having heard all about Nell's boss before, Ange pulled a face that made her look like a halibut who had just been

booted up the dorsal, making Nell laugh despite the acid
tones that were currently assaulting her eardrums.

'Nell, this is Nicolette, where the bloody hell are you?
The meeting starts in half an hour. Call me . . .'

The phone dropped. The next message played in.

'It's Nicolette. The meeting starts in ten minutes. If
you're not here in five there'll be hell to pay, I can tell you.
In fact, if you're not here in five, don't bother coming in at
all . . .'

The phone dropped again and then the automated
voice announced the next message, three hours later.

No introduction, just a shrill voice shrieking, 'Where
the hell were you today? I can't believe you, you know
how important today's meeting was. You're totally out of
order, not even a phone call . . . I'm appalled . . . usual
irresponsible manner . . . come and go as you please . . .
this is the end of the line . . . gross misconduct . . . instant
dismissal . . .' On and on she went, voice rising
hysterically with every second.

Nell knew they were just empty threats. She could
hear the fear underneath the indignation, and she knew
that Nicolette would be in a total and utter panic. Nell had
carried this project, whilst Nicolette had taken all the
plaudits for her hard work. She wouldn't have been able to
cope with this morning's meeting on her own; she didn't
have a clue. That was why she was so angry that Nell
wasn't there, because it would have made her look like the
total idiot she was. There was some considerable comfort
in this as Nell was forced to listen to the dressing-down
she knew would have been overheard by everyone else in
the office.

'What did she say?' Ange asked, her voice laden with
sympathy.

'You mean you couldn't hear her?' Nell rolled her

eyeballs. 'Well, basically she said that if I wasn't there by eleven I could take a hike . . . not bother coming back at all.'

'She threatened to sack you?'

Nell nodded.

'Can she do that?' Ange frowned.

'Not really, but she could push the buttons of the people who can. Not that she would. If she got rid of me, she might actually have to do some work herself.'

Ange looked at her watch. 'Well you missed that deadline by a good few hours. What now? Are you going to have to phone and grovel?'

Nell nodded. 'Probably should,' she said, her lips pursing. 'Although . . . alternatively, I could phone and tell her to get stuffed and not bother going back at all . . .'

Ange, who had been casting glances round for signs to the taxi rank, immediately snapped her attention back to Nell.

'Did you really just say that, or was I imagining it?'

'Well, I could.' Nell shrugged.

Ange smiled hopefully. 'You could, yes. The question is, would you?'

'I'm fed up with people treating me like shit, of people thinking I'm going to put up with it.'

The next thing Nell knew, she was being hugged to within an inch of her life, and when she was finally released, she saw that Ange was grinning broadly.

'At bloody last,' she exclaimed. 'You know, I've always thought you were a great girl, Nell Everson, but sometimes I've just wanted to grab you and shake you . . . Sorry, that sounds awful, but you do know what I mean, don't you?'

Nell nodded. 'I know. I'm a doormat.'

'You are *not* a doormat. You're just so nice, people take advantage.'

'They do, don't they?'

'And now?'

Nell cocked her head to the side, her smile lopsided, her eyes kind of sad. 'I've had enough, Ange: this weekend, that phone call . . .'

'The final lump of ice that broke the vodka glass?'

'Well . . . have you ever seen that film with Michael Douglas? You know, the one where he just snaps.'

'Please don't tell me you're going to rampage round the streets of London with a machine gun?'

'I might . . .' Nell smiled weakly, as if a little shell-shocked herself. 'I wouldn't shoot anybody with it, though. I'd probably just stick it where the sun don't shine . . .'

'And Marcus?'

'Well he's just one big arse, so there's plenty of room for it,' Nell replied, even managing a small laugh.

She suddenly looked so lost and sad that Ange had to hug her again. 'So what now?' she said, letting her go and trying to look positive.

'Go back in, and hop on a plane to somewhere hot?'

'Sounds wonderful.'

'Does, doesn't it, but being serious? Well, I'm not sure what I want to do, but the odd thing is, I'm extremely sure about what I don't want to do.'

'Well that's a place to start.'

'And so is the train station. Come on, you.' Nell tucked her hand through Ange's arm. 'If we're not heading for the Bahamas, I suppose we'd better get ourselves back to London.'

They bought coffees and shared a pretty disgusting chicken sandwich, which had Nell marvelling at the fact that anyone could actually go wrong on making something that was essentially so simple, and then Ange took the taste of the disgusting sandwich away with some of her duty-free chocolate and fell asleep on Nell's shoulder.

As the train shuddered along the uneven track, Nell, who was tired but wide awake, couldn't help but think about the flight home, or, more accurately, the conversation they had had after they thought they were dropping out of the sky and heading for earth faster than a plane ever should.

Funny how she had instantly thought of Maud when trying to recall her happiest moments. Any memory that made her smile or laugh out loud normally involved Auntie Maud, although right now, thinking of her actually served to make Nell feel guilty. She hadn't seen her since Christmas, and then it had only been a flying visit squeezed in between visiting the folks and being called back into work early. In fact, thinking about it, it had been a while since she had spent any decent amount of time in Cornwall.

They usually made a point of speaking on the phone at least once a week, taking it in turns to call. It had been Maud's turn last week, and Nell had heard nothing, but she'd been so busy she hadn't even thought of it until now. She hoped everything was okay. She could do with one of their chats. Maud always helped her cut through the clouding that confused minds so that she could see straight.

What would she say to her now, knowing Nell's frame of mind? She knew exactly what Maud's advice would be, because it was always the same.

'Think about what's right for *you*, Nell.'

So what was right for Nell? Part of her problem was that she had always had other people telling her what was right for her, so it was very hard to decide for herself.

'Cut and run, cut and run, cut and run,' said the train

on the track, its rhythm echoing Nell's own heartbeat.

Could she? Could she actually follow her own feelings for once?

Ange had blamed the pilot.

Nell could blame the pilot; she could blame Marcus, she could blame Nicolette and the whole bunch of horrible people she worked with, she could blame her parents if she really wanted to, but she knew deep down that there was only one person to blame for where she was today. Herself.

'Do you want to come back to mine?'

They were on the station platform, each ready to head for their different tube lines.

Nell shook her head firmly. 'As tempting as that offer is, I think I have a few things I need to sort out.'

Ange nodded her understanding. 'You give him what for, Nell.'

'That's the thing, Ange. I don't know if I want to.'

'Don't back out now. He deserves it. Justin's going to feel the wrath of Ange, I can tell you. Little shit.'

'That's not what I meant.'

'Nell?'

'If he doesn't know himself, then I'm not going to tell him.'

'You're just going to let him get away with it?'

Nell shook her head. 'No, I'm just going.'

Ange's jaw dropped. 'You're going?' she repeated, as if she'd heard wrong.

'Yeah.'

'You were serious, then? About quitting it all. Your job . . . *and* Marcus . . .'

Nell nodded a more positive affirmative than she felt.

'Wow. And I thought you were just going to give them

all the boot up the arse they need to start treating you better. What are you going to do, Nell?'

Nell shrugged. 'Not totally sure yet, but not knowing what I'm going to do with the rest of my life is a damn sight more inviting than carrying on with it the way it is.'

Ange bit her lip and nodded her agreement. Despite her own turmoil, Nell noticed that she was blinking really hard and very rapidly.

'You going to be okay?'

Nell nodded determinedly.

'Well if you need me, you ring me, okay? Sod that, just ring me anyway. Promise?'

Nell nodded again, and then smiled and reached out to hug Ange. The hug was welcomed and returned threefold.

'What about you, Ange, you going to be okay?' Nell asked when she was finally released.

'You mean Justin? He's an idiot, but I've always known that . . . although . . .' she paused and frowned and started blinking furiously again, 'I think this is the first time I've actually admitted that to myself quite so easily. Justin is an idiot.' She said it again as though repeating it might make it go away, and then she sighed and shook her head. 'Oh Lord, Nell, why do women get so easily mixed up with morons?'

'Rose-tinted glasses?'

'Not strong enough. I was thinking more along the lines of blinkers or blindfolds.'

'Maybe you should quit too?' Nell smiled.

'Mmm, maybe I should,' Ange mused, and then, pursing her lips determinedly, she winked at Nell. 'Now I hate to say it, but I've got to run. I'm meant to be watching the next Coldplay rock the back room of the worst pub in Hackney in exactly half an hour. Not what I want to do after the last twenty-four hours . . .'

She pecked Nell on the cheek and, gathering up her bags, turned to leave. 'Take care, kiddo, and call me, okay, or I'll just worry, and I don't do worry.'

'I'll call, I promise,' Nell said, watching her friend hurry towards her exit. 'Oh, and Ange . . .'

Ange turned back round. 'Yes, love?'

'Justin may be an idiot, but he just happens to be the luckiest idiot I know . . .'

5

Nell stood and stared in through the window. The curtains weren't drawn, despite the fact that it was getting dark already, and the light on inside meant that she could see everything through the haze of the net curtain that was meant to afford privacy but only worked in daylight.

She could see Marcus in his sitting room. He was watching a football match on his pride and joy, the forty-two-inch wide-screen television he had bought with his last bonus, despite promising Nell in a drunken moment that he would take her to Rome with his next big pay-off.

In his boxer shorts, two-day-old socks and a T-shirt that had a picture of a shark on the front and the slogan 'Bite Me', he was sprawled on the sofa, one of those big padded leather things with a button on the side you could press so that you could turn it into a recliner. Despite this, he still had his feet up on the coffee table.

She hated Marcus's furniture: big, black and heavy, the height of eighties chic. Why he was still so enamoured of the style in this century, she could never work out.

Her own furniture had been elegant, understated, timeless. It had taken her a long time to choose everything for the little terraced cottage she had owned in Hemel Hempstead, bought before it had become too expensive for someone of her age to even contemplate looking at in this area without a trust fund to fall back on.

It had only taken her a few weeks to get rid of it all.

She had sold everything to move into Marcus's world, taking nothing with her except her very personal possessions.

He already had everything in the house that they could possibly need, he had explained to her with exaggerated patience, and her furniture would not fit with his. He was right about that: her things next to his would look incongruous, awkward, fragile; they would not fit.

Perhaps they never had.

And so there had been no compromise; well, there had been actually, but all on Nell's side. Nearly everything she owned had gone. Her house was empty, three packing cases all she had left to show for eight years.

Well, three packing cases and the equity she was holding in a high-interest-rate account at her bank.

The plan was to use this money to pay off Marcus's mortgage, for his house to become their house. It had made sense that way, he had said.

The way she felt at the moment, it made sense to bugger Marcus's mortgage and, as the ad said, hire a big yacht and sail around the world.

How could your feelings for someone change so quickly?

She had loved him so much in the beginning; he had been charming, fun, attentive.

It was only now she realised that she had been holding on for the man he had been, but that the man she had fallen in love with had never actually existed, except for those first few months of woo to win. This lump on the sofa, this man who would leave her in a foreign country and let her make her own way home from the airport for the sake of a football match, this ignorant, boring, boorish idiot was the person he actually was.

Nell stopped herself there.

She was sounding bitter.

Bitter was not what she wanted to taste.

It was better to say that it had been good at the start, but that complacency had set in so quickly, and now it seemed as if complacency had sunk into a rut of indifference.

It had quite simply run its course.

'Relationships,' Nell sighed to herself, 'so easy to fall into, so difficult to climb back out of.'

She could see him in there now, reclining on his leather monstrosity, the television on, the football match, the remote on the arm of the sofa next to him, a bottle of beer on the table to the side.

She pictured herself in there with him, and suddenly realised that if she were, then nothing within this scene would change apart from her presence. Marcus would still be reclining in his socks, beer to hand; the football would still be on, he would still be shouting at the TV. The room would not be altered in any way, still all exactly the same as she could see it now. The only difference would be her, sitting there next to him like a leaf on a lily pond, barely making a ripple on the surface.

His sitting room really was awful.

'Bland and soulless,' Nell muttered to herself, still looking at Marcus.

She hated grey paint on walls.

She hated black wooden furniture.

She hated leather sofas.

She hated net curtains.

Her gaze moved from decor to occupant, and she realised that the pained frown she was sporting remained in place.

Maybe the truth of it was that she hated him too.

She shook her head.

Hate was such a strong word.

She didn't hate him . . . but she didn't think she loved him either.

As she inserted her newly cut key into the lock, she found she was holding her breath, but if he heard her he showed no signs of it, his legs, visible through the open doorway from the hall into the sitting room, still propped up on the coffee table.

He barely looked up as she entered the room, merely muttering, 'All right?' His eyes stayed glued to the little men in black shorts and red shirts on the screen.

Nell didn't answer.

He still didn't look up, but after a moment he said those three little words every girl who's been abandoned at an airport in a foreign country wants to hear.

'Cup of tea?'

Unfortunately, it wasn't an offer, it was a request.

'You want tea.' It wasn't a question, rather a statement of disbelief.

No 'hello', no 'welcome home', no 'how are you?', nothing. Just a request for waitress service.

'Yeah. Actually, nah. I think I'll have another beer.'

Nell remained where she was for just one second, then she put down her bags, went to the kitchen, opened the fridge, pulled out a bottle, walked back into the sitting room and put it down next to Marcus, whose eyes were still glued to the TV screen.

Then she picked up her bags and walked out the way she had just come in without so much as a word. But as she stomped back down the street tugging her suitcase behind her, she found that there was something she had wanted to say for such a long time it came out in a scream.

'Screw you, Marcus Bennet! SCREW YOU!!!'

*

Nell later found out from Ange that it took him until after the end of the match interviews to even realise that, like Elvis, Nell had left the building.

It only took him one huge celebratory swig from the bottle, however, to realise that what she had actually handed him wasn't beer but Tabasco sauce.

Nell felt so empowered marching out of Marcus's house and his life that for a while she forgot she had no home to go to. At least not a home that had any of the usual stuff you needed to live in it, like a bed, or something to cook food with, or even something to eat it off once you'd cooked it.

When it dawned on her that her victory march actually had no destination, the buzz she had felt fizzled out like flat champagne.

The sale of her house was due to complete on Friday and she had been supposed to be moving in with Marcus straight after the wedding in Prague. Today, to be precise. It had seemed to her before this a rather romantic notion: to celebrate Charles and Dita's wedding and then come back to their new home together. But now . . . Well, as two people's lives together had just symbolically begun, hers and Marcus's had come to an abrupt and somewhat unexpected end.

It was her choice, but it was still a total shock.

If someone had asked her a year ago whether she and Marcus were for ever, she would have answered an unhesitating yes. Strange how easily the rot set in when you didn't repaint your windows, as Aunt Maud, who was used to having to paint her own windows regularly due to sea salt, would have put it.

Nell tried to think back to see if she could pinpoint a time, a moment when she had suddenly stopped loving him. She must have stopped loving him; if she loved him, she could never leave him. She was that kind of girl: loyal, affectionate, totally monogamous.

'I am a doormat,' Nell said aloud to herself.

'I am a homeless doormat,' she added, thinking sadly of her beautiful little house in Hemel Hempstead.

She had never been able to bring herself to live in the city. Initially this had been a lot to do with the cost of houses, but even if she had been able to afford it, she wouldn't have wanted to head inside the M25. It meant a long commute at the end of the day, but for her it was worth it. She far preferred a view of green to grey, and the only views of green in London came with a hefty price tag way beyond her means.

Nell had fallen in love with her house the first time she had seen it. Not quite a new build, it had been a modern version of a two-up two-down, but it had a quaint cottage feel to it, and a pretty little garden that was a magnet for local birds, one of the local birds being Nell herself, who thought there was nothing better than sitting in the back garden with some sunshine, a deckchair and a good book. If she closed her eyes and listened to the birdsong, she could almost imagine that she was in the middle of the countryside.

She had sold the house easily, with a mixture of reluctance and regret, and excitement and hope. How quickly things changed.

It had been her pride and joy.

And now it had been stripped.

Naked and vulnerable. A bit like me at the moment, she thought, although the naked is obviously metaphorical, because if I was marching down the street with no clothes on, I'd soon have a place to go, a place with bars on!

Unable to face the shell of former domestic bliss, and unable even to face the commute that would get her to this empty shell, she booked herself into a nearby hotel and assuaged the strange emptiness inside her with too much room service and in-room movies until late into the night. She got up in the morning and used the hotel gym, swam in the pool, and ate far too big a breakfast, considering how much room service she'd eaten the night before. Then, when kicking-out time came at eleven, she simply took her weekend case, still with the clothes for the wedding, and wandered the streets of London, wheeling it behind her like a lost tourist. Simply because she didn't know what else to do.

For Nell, walking was therapy.

Admittedly she wasn't usually pounding the pavements; green fields were much more of a balm to a ragged mind than city streets. She wasn't usually weighted down like a baggage yak either. Still, it would help burn off some of the Czech dumplings she had stuffed herself with over the weekend. Strangely enough, the thought of the dumplings managed to bring a smile back to her face. They had been delicious. Nell got passions for food. Something would catch her palate and that would be it, nirvana, to be chased and consumed whenever possible. She also loved to cook, not that she had the time, but she collected recipes like some people collected stamps. She had hundreds of them. All the stuff that she had kept was in a couple of large boxes in Marcus's spare room, waiting to be unpacked . . . well, at least they had been waiting to be unpacked; she supposed now that they were waiting to be collected, because even this morning, with the reality of what she had chosen to do well and truly sinking in, she was as determined to go as she had been the previous day.

Not quite sure where she had been going whilst her feet and her mind were on autopilot, it was thus that she found herself wheeling past the car showroom. By this point the novelty of being footloose around London was beginning to wear off, but it wasn't just her aching feet that drew her in there. It was the 'Star Car'. You know, the one they put up on a podium with ribbons and things on. The ribbons and balloons and stuff just weren't fair. Nell couldn't resist them. What was it with girls and pretty shiny stuff?

The fact that the Star Car was a purple Mini might also have had something to do with the way she was so easily suckered into the verbal embrace of an enthusiastic salesman.

Auntie Maud had owned a Mini when Nell was young,

It was a white Mini Clubman. She had called it Cyril, and had bundled her god-daughter into it as often as her parents would allow and carried her off on adventures. Some of the best memories of Nell's childhood were of her and Maud whizzing dangerously fast down narrow country lanes in Cyril. Nell had loved that car. Her heart had sung with happiness every time it had pulled on to the neat driveway of her parents' suburban home, because to her it represented Maud the Magnificent, sunshine and beaches and ice cream, chasing pretend villains, on secret missions.

And now here, gleaming in the afternoon sunshine, was a Cyril. A *purple* Cyril.

And Nell's favourite colour was purple.

Cyril had represented something else to Nell and Maud: freedom.

And now freedom was Nell's new agenda.

Freedom from trudging the streets of London like a little lost girl.

Freedom from her aching feet.

Freedom from everything.

It was too much of a cliché to refuse.

'Ten per cent deposit, nought per cent finance and ready to go in twenty-four hours,' a voice in Nell's ear had tempted her.

She hesitated for a fraction of a second, and then turned to face the besuited salesman and smiled sweetly.

'Fifteen per cent off for cash, no finance, and ready to go by the time we've signed the paperwork.'

As evening approached, Nell pulled the newly christened Cyril Junior into the car park of what had been her local supermarket. Inside, she bought a pillow and a king-size duvet, some linen with huge cheerful coloured flowers on it, a portable television that was on special offer, and a whole smorgasbord of her favourite foods, which included cold-water prawns, a loaf of crusty bread, some salted butter, a bag of rocket and lamb's lettuce salad, a box of Mr Kipling's French Fancies, a tub of mascarpone ice cream, two persimmons, and a very large bar of Cadbury's fruit and nut.

As she squeezed everything into the boot of her new friend and drove off into the sunset, she found that she was smiling, and then the smile turned into laughter, a rather manic laughter.

Leaving your life as you knew it behind you like trash screwed up and thrown into the waste bin.

It was like free-falling.

Oh so scary, but fabulously, breathtakingly exhilarating.

High on adrenaline, she found herself turning up the radio and singing along, a smile on her face, laughter bubbling on her lips.

Her empty house could have been the thing to shatter her mood. It was so strange to see it stripped of everything that had made it into a home. It not only looked and felt different, but it sounded different, smelled different. The new owners would be collecting the keys on Friday, but tonight she would sleep there herself, say a second and final goodbye.

But first she had to say a final goodbye to something else.

She looked at her watch. It was seven thirty; even the diehards would have gone home by now. She dialled the all-too-familiar number, and listened as it clicked through to answerphone.

'Hi, this is Nicolette. I'm either out of the office or on another call at the moment. Please leave a message and I'll get back to you.'

Nell took a deep breath.

'Hi, Nicolette, this is Nell. Just to let you know that you don't have to sack me, because I'm sacking myself. Yes, you heard me, I quit. Goodbye.'

She could have elaborated. It was so tempting to add more, maybe a nice rhyming couplet to the end, such as 'I quit, you shit', but if there was one thing Nell was determined to hang on to whilst booting everything else out of her life, it was her dignity.

Although she was rather proud of one she had come up with before she called, but had managed to stop herself from saying: 'You shall abuse me no more, you corporate whore.' Perhaps she should send that one in a card.

Then she set up camp in the sitting room, with her duvet and her pillows and her bag of goodies, watched back-to-back soaps, and fell asleep with *Pretty Woman* on and her face covered in ice cream and chocolate.

*

Nell woke early, realised she hadn't got any towels, so showered and then blow-dried not just her hair, but her entire body. Then she dressed, and cleared away last night's mess, eating the remainder of the French Fancies and a persimmon for breakfast. After that she folded up her makeshift bed and put everything in the new car.

When she went back inside and walked round every single room, and saw the house standing empty, a blank canvas, as it had been when she first moved in herself, ready and waiting for its new owners to arrive on Friday, she knew she was finally ready to leave. It was time to move on.

She went outside and closed the front door of the house for what would be the final time.

'Bye,' she whispered, and without even thinking to look to make sure no one was watching her, she leaned her face to the front door and kissed the door knocker. 'Thanks for having me.'

Then, feeling a little self-conscious as the previously empty road suddenly seemed to fill with early-morning joggers and dog-walkers and people picking milk bottles off doorsteps, she dropped her last set of keys through the letter box, scurried to the car and folded herself inside. With a turn of the key, she brought the engine roaring into life.

Once again Nell felt that same free-falling kick of adrenaline as she left the past behind in its entirety, and revved off down the road in her new Mini, into her new future.

A future uncertain.

And full of promise.

And then she heard a voice calling her name.

For a moment there was one word in Nell's head.

Marcus.

But then she realised that although the voice was familiar, it certainly wasn't his.

Putting on the brakes, she looked in her rear-view mirror to see Ange running up the road behind her, a loaded bag sliding from each shoulder, frantically tugging on a suitcase that couldn't keep up, its small wheels bouncing and catching on the uneven surface until the case twisted to the side and Ange in her panic to catch up was forced to drag it along, the material scraping on the tarmac.

When she reached the car, she was so out of breath that for a moment all she could do was stand panting by the driver's door.

Frowning, Nell flicked the switch to wind down the electric window.

'Ange, what on earth are you doing?'

'Sharing your happy memories.' Ange shrugged, her eyes hopeful. 'Putting on my rollerskates and grabbing on to the coat tails of your adventure in the hope that I'll come flying along behind you . . .'

'You want to come with me?'

Ange nodded.

'But what about Justin?'

'Over.'

'Over?' Nell's eyes widened further in surprise.

'Over,' Ange repeated firmly.

'Your job?'

'Quit.'

'You quit your job! You love your job.'

'I know.'

'So why . . .'

'I want to scare myself.'

As she finally began to understand, Nell stopped frowning and began to smile.

'You mean you didn't get enough of that on the plane?'

'That's the thing, Nell, I don't think I did . . . In fact, I have to confess that in a weird kind of way I rather liked it.'

Nell nodded slowly. 'I know. There's nothing like thinking you're going to die to make you feel alive again.'

7

Maud Pemberton was too striking a figure to be trying to slide inconspicuously through the village. For a start, she was one of the least inconspicuous people you could hope to meet. Always present at every public event, and with an opinion to accompany her appearance, she was both loved and feared in equal measures by everyone from Perranporth to Padstow.

She was also very tall, and as she strode swiftly down the steep, narrow cobbled street that was the main thoroughfare through the large fishing village of Polporth, her silver-grey hair was shining intermittently in the lamp-light like a beam from the nearby Pol Rocks lighthouse.

She had always been proud of her hair. A handsome woman rather than a beautiful one, she had felt that her glorious gleaming gold mane was her best asset, that and the ability to bend at the knees for an inordinately long time when standing next to a gentleman friend who wasn't quite as blessed in the height department as she, as most of them invariably had been, although she paid for it now with her grumbling joints.

Now that the glorious gold had turned to what Nell called 'sexy silver', it was still a magnificent piece of human architecture. Still worn as long as it had been in her youth, when allowed to flow free, which wasn't often nowadays as Maud was rigorous with her hair pins, it hung in an undulating curtain to mid-back, and was so soft and lustrously silky it should by rights have had its own shampoo commercial, despite the fact that Maud often forgot to buy shampoo and ended up scrubbing a squirt of Fairy Liquid through it.

What Maud was doing out in Polporth before the sun had even risen was nobody's business but her own. Suffice to say that like Nell, when she was troubled she liked to walk. She also had a head for mischief, usually tempered by a kind heart unless something or someone got her back up. And yesterday, several somethings and someones had managed to do just that.

Maud had therefore set out to exact revenge in her own way, and mission accomplished, she was ready to make her way back home. Usually she would walk out of the harbour, along the beach and up the steep path cut into the side of the cliff, but today she chose instead to take the only road that led out of the village for a little way, and then walk up the private road that branched off it to the house.

Halfway up, she paused to watch the sun begin to rise over the ocean, reassuring herself that she wasn't simply stopping because she was suddenly out of puff. She had seen the same sunrise a thousand times over the thirty years she had lived on the cliff above Polporth, and she swore she would never tire of it. Today it seemed even more poignant, even more breathtakingly beautiful, even more of a twenty-four-hour miracle. It was a sight to behold, the sun pulling herself dripping gold from the ocean, setting the sky alight with a red and orange fire.

And as Maud watched, she felt a little of her own self returning, enough to make her legs feel less heavy for the rest of her climb home.

'Today is going to be a better day,' she told herself, her favourite motto, ignoring the old saying singing in her head over and over: 'Red sky in the morning, shepherds' warning.'

She let herself into the darkened house, and immediately noticed that the light on the answer machine was blinking to indicate a message. It had been empty when she left the house two hours ago.

Who else would be up this early?

Pressing play, she listened as the machine spilled out a long, convoluted, breathless and slightly manic message from Nell, but by the time it had finished, she was smiling again.

Nell was coming to visit.

How wonderful.

She'd just known today would be a better day, and there was no better way for this to be proved than by a visit from her beloved Nell.

Such was her haste to get away, Nell sped all the way down the M4, Ange shrieking with horrified excitement every time she saw a police car, Nell slamming on the brakes at the last minute to pootle past in genteel fashion like a pair of old grannies on a Sunday outing, until the law were a distant speck in her rear-view mirror and her foot would go down on the accelerator again.

M4 to M5 to A30, the little car sped on like a purple bullet, Ange singing. 'Go Wild in the Country' over and over again. They stopped for coffee and the loo twice, filling the little car even further with sweets from the service station shops, which they shared along with much laughter on the way, both ignoring the intermittent bleeps of their mobile phones as they were chased by technology on their escape.

It was a journey that lasted for five hours, five hours they both knew had cemented their friendship for life.

When Nell announced, 'We're nearly there,' Ange, however, for probably the first time in her entire life, felt shy.

'Can we have another pit stop first, please, Penelope?'

'As long as you promise never to call me Penelope again, or let on that you know my real name.' Nell wrinkled her nose at Ange, who grinned wickedly. 'And that you *also* promise to stop singing.'

'I've been singing out loud?' Ange looked surprised. 'I thought I was just humming it in my head.'

Maudlyn lived in an old mine worker's cottage perched on the edge of the cliff overlooking the sea, so close it almost had the look of a person peering into the water. The house was long and low, its crumbling white facade tarred by salt, its dark Delabole slate roof tiles green with weather, its window frames peeling. The general air was not of neglect but of use, well-loved use.

Nell pulled over into the lay-by half a mile away that afforded the first view of what to her had become a second home.

'Maud's place,' she murmured, suddenly aware that it had been nearly four months since her last visit.

'Amazing.' Ange nodded appreciatively. 'How long has your auntie lived here, Nell?'

'For ever.' Nell grinned, putting the car into gear again and pulling away. 'And just so you know, she's not actually my aunt – well, she is in every sense of the word except for the fact that she isn't the sister of either my father or my mother.'

'Ah, I see. One of those aunties.' Ange nodded. 'Had a ton of those myself when I was a girl.'

'She's my godmother.'

'Fairy?'

'Definitely. Although if you asked my parents, they'd probably say gremlin.'

'Even better.' Ange grinned. 'What's she like?'

'The best,' Nell said simply.

'You know, I never thought to ask. Is there an Uncle Maud?'

Nell shook her head. 'Used to be, although I never got to meet him, I'm afraid. He was much older than her. It was a huge scandal at the time, apparently. Maud was only nineteen when she met him and I think he was in his fifties, but she was madly in love. He died about thirty years ago. Broke her heart at the time, but one of her favourite sayings is "Time heals all".'

'She never remarried?'

Nell shook her head. 'No. There's been the odd fling along the way, but never anyone else serious after Monty.'

'First love never ever dies,' sang Ange.

'Marcus was my first love.'

'Okay, first love never ever dies unless you get to a point where you decide you want to take it to the bottom of the garden and shoot it.'

As Ange got out of the car, a blast of sea breeze stormed in off the ocean like a fist, thumping her in the face, forcing her to inhale as it took her breath quite literally away from her. This was followed by a rack of coughing.

'Jeez,' she exclaimed as soon as she was able to. 'What do they put in the air down here?'

'Pure oxygen.' Nell grinned.

'Think I need a cigarette . . . Come on, Nell, don't look at me like that,' Ange said, noting Nell's look of concern as she delved into her bag, pulled out a Marlboro and lit it, inhaling as though it were lifesaving rather than the opposite. 'I've evolved from living in a city; my lungs don't work properly without some toxins.'

One puff and the cigarette went over the cliff edge.

'Jeez, why do you have this effect on me, Nell? Is it not enough that I've quit my whole life to come here with you? You want me to quit smoking as well?'

'You may as well be hung—' Nell began to quote, but Ange cut in.

'Like a donkey,' she said, grinning.

'For a sheep as a lamb.' Stifling her laughter, Nell finished the quote. 'But it's your body; it's your right to choose if you smoke or not.'

'Sure, but if you're going to look at me like I've just shot your dog every time I light up . . .'

'Well, you have said to me several times that you were going to quit,' Nell reminded her gently. 'A new start's a great time to do something like that.'

'I also said I was going to be a size twelve by my last birthday, and look at me now, still resplendent in Evans's finest.'

'You've got an amazing figure.'

'Sure, if you think Moby Dick's attractive.'

'Why put yourself down—'

'When there are plenty of other people out there willing to do it for you.' Ange finished Nell's favourite motto for her and sighed, lighting up another cigarette on autopilot and then realising what she was doing as Nell began to frown again.

'What are you, Nell, the vice squad? You need to loosen up a little bit, my lovely.'

Nell look shamefaced. 'I don't mean to nag, I just worry what it's doing to your lungs.'

'Oh, I've got a fine pair of lungs, so I have. Well, Justin used to tell me so anyway.' She laughed, pushing up her cleavage with her elbows. 'Do you know, I think that was the only thing that man truly liked about me.'

The second cigarette followed the first over the cliff edge none the less.

Nell's mobile phone had five voice messages and eight texts.

'You're going to have to talk to him sometime,' Ange said gently as Nell sat down on a rock and began to methodically erase them all.

'I know, but it doesn't have to be today, does it?'

'Absolutely not.' Ange nodded emphatically, sitting down next to her.

'How did Justin take it, you going?'

Ange bit her bottom lip and looked sideways at her.

Nell's mouth dropped open. 'You haven't told him!' It wasn't an accusation, just an exclamation of amazement.

Ange looked sheepish. 'Well, not exactly . . . He knows I'm here. He just thinks I've come away with you, you know, to be a friend, lend a shoulder when your hanky gets too soggy.'

'You mean you haven't actually told him that you don't want to be with him any more?'

Ange shrugged apologetically. 'Why sort things out when you can prevaricate?' she joked. 'You know what Justin's like. If I leave it long enough, he'll forget that he and I were ever an item anyway.'

'But you're engaged to the man, Ange.'

'Oh sure, he asked me when he was drunk. You know that doesn't really count, now does it?'

The first thing that Ange noticed as Maud excitedly flung open the front door to greet them was how friendly her smile was, and how tall she was. The second thing was her hair, thick and lush and shining as silver as the bangle Nell wore about her right wrist.

She was wearing a white artist's smock covered in sea-green paint, and there was paint in her hair, on her hands, on her tatty jeans, her old leather brogues and her smiling weathered face.

'Auntie Maud!'

'Nelly Belle!'

Maud pulled Nell into a hug that Ange could have timed on her watch, it went on for so long. Neither of them seemed to care about the paint. Ange saw that Maud was so tall that her chin was almost resting on Nell's head. Then, without a word of introduction, Maud released Nell and did the same to Ange.

She was thin. It was like hugging bones. But there was a warmth radiating from her that made it feel as if you were hugging something really cuddly.

'Oh, it's just so good to see you both!' Maud exclaimed happily, as if she had already met Ange a thousand times before and missed her too. 'Come in, my darlings, come in, come in, come in. I've just been repainting the summer house ready for the good weather.'

'The shed,' Nell mouthed to Ange.

'It is not a shed. Sheds don't have windows and card tables in them.'

'Ears on elastic,' Nell pretended to whisper.

'Or gin on optics, or a fridge for wine.'

Nell mimed someone drinking and crossed her eyes.

'And eyes in the back of my head.' Maud turned and winked at Ange.

The house was one of those Cornish long houses with no corridors, just each room leading on to the next. It was a decent size, although it could never be called huge, but Ange had never seen so much furniture in one place in her entire life. It was as though the house had swallowed another house and its entire contents whole, and then digested the bricks and mortar and just thrown up the furniture. Every single wall was covered in framed photographs, many of them of Nell at various stages of her life, and paintings galore. Each polished wooden floor had at least three rugs to a room, and if you were invited to sit down it would take you a week to choose where.

It was, however, elegance personified: the too many chairs were Queen Anne, the over-large sofas were crammed with the most exquisite embroidered cushions, the many artefacts on every surface from vase to bust were, Ange was sure, a treasure trove of antiquities, although like the exterior, everything was well used and a little shabby in places.

'It's like Aladdin's cave,' she exclaimed, her eyes agog.

'It's like Steptoe and Son,' Nell teased.

'And some day all of this will be yours.' Maud grinned at Nell, showing off straight white teeth.

'Heaven forbid!' Nell grinned back at her. 'You do know if you leave this lot to me I'll be on the *Antiques Roadshow* with a big For Sale sign, faster than you can say Ming Dynasty.'

Maud burst into peals of glorious laughter that to Ange sounded like the ringing of a melodious but very loud bell; either that or the honking of a tuneful goose.

She led them through the house to a large country kitchen dominated by an old wooden table big enough to seat eight comfortably, surrounded by an eclectic mix of chairs, and heated by an Aga that smelled deliciously of baking. Urging them to sit, she served them freshly baked biscuits the size of tea plates, and tea in little china cups as thin as paper, all the time asking questions about their journey.

The biscuits were heaven, but Ange contemplated the fragile china and, overawed, stuck out her pinky finger and longed for a good old-fashioned thick pottery mug that wouldn't break if she trembled too much with nerves.

Ange never got nervous, just blustered into every situation with her usual good humour as the wind in her magnificent sails, but for some reason Maudlyn rendered her as speechless as an über-fan meeting her hero for the very first time. There was something about the woman that was just so friendly and approachable, but there was something else that was absolutely terrifying. Ange couldn't quite put her finger on it, just likened it for now to a 'good headmistress' sort of quality: nurturing and guiding but all-powerful and really rather scary at the same time.

Maud, who had listened to Nell's early-morning phone message over and over and could only make out three words, 'I'm coming down', made sure that they were fed and watered and then asked one word and one word only.

'So?'

Nell knew this was her cue to explain, and nodded, taking the time to pour them all another cup of tea from the huge pot before offering an explanation in the most simplistic way she could.

'I've realised that my life has gone totally wrong and so I've quit it all.'

If she was shocked, Maud didn't show it. She simply nodded slowly.

'You don't seem surprised.'

'Well, I have often wondered how long it would take you to realise the guy was an idiot. I have to confess, I never thought it would take this many years.'

Nell's mouth dropped open. 'You didn't like Marcus?'

'Moron.' Maud nodded.

Nell's brow knitted into a piqued frown. 'Why didn't you tell me!' she stuttered.

'Because you seemed to rather like him for a while. I believe a girl should make her own mistakes. Besides, your parents are always trying to tell you what to do, so I'm hardly likely to join in, am I?'

'Mum and Dad really liked Marcus,' Nell mused, her nose twitching the way it did when something bemused her.

'Well, that says everything,' Maud huffed.

'So you're saying that for my next man I should find someone they hate and I will have bagged myself a good one?'

'Oh, I don't know about that.'

'No?'

'No, I rather think you shouldn't be thinking about the next man just yet, having been stuck with the last one for so long. You should take a break for a while, have some fun, flirt a bit, but don't get tied down again too soon. Find yourself first, my darling, and then start looking for someone else.'

'Cliché.' Nell grinned.

'Don't you just love 'em?' Maud winked. 'And what about work?'

'Killing me slowly.' Nell shrugged. 'Which is what Mum and Dad will do when they find out I've quit.'

'Which is why you've come here?'

'To hide behind your skirts. Either that, or borrow one to pitch as a tent and live in it. Do you know, I could swear you've grown since I last saw you . . .'

'I thought that was supposed to be my line, although they always say you get to a point where the child becomes the parent.'

'Well, if we're swapping roles, does that mean I get to drink too much and misbehave, and you have to be sensible for a change?'

The two smiled and hugged again, spontaneously, and then Maud, as if she were concerned that Ange might feel left out, turned and put a hand on her shoulder and asked her, 'What about you, Ange?'

'Me?' Ange almost squeaked as Maud addressed her direct gaze to her.

'What's your story?'

'I just came along for the ride.'

'As good a reason as any,' Maud said with a smile, and deciding that the inquisition could wait until they'd had a chance to settle themselves in, she offered to show them up to their rooms.

There were three bedrooms upstairs, the largest Maud's to the left-hand side of the stairs, and then two further rooms that used to run into each other before Maud modernised and put in an en suite in her bedroom and a new corridor.

The room at the far end of the house was Nell's. It had been hers for as long as she could remember, and was therefore filled with things that she and Maud had accumulated over the years: books, ornaments, photographs, treasures.

It had wooden floorboards and sloping ceilings and you had to duck your head to look out of the window. Nell liked nothing better than curling up on the cushions on the window seat with a book, and listening to the sound of the sea as she surfed a good story.

Maud had put Ange in the room next door. It was slightly smaller than Nell's because of the corridor Maud had installed, but Ange was still totally enchanted by the sloping ceilings. Never having been a particularly girlie girl – she had painted her bedroom dark purple at fifteen without asking her parents' permission – she was also surprised how much she liked the wild orchid wallpaper that rampantly climbed the crooked walls. But it was when she saw the view from the window that she was totally won over.

'I can see the sea.' She beamed ecstatically. 'Can I live here for ever?'

'Are you a neat freak like Nell?'

'Um, no,' Ange replied.

'That's like asking the Pope if he's into devil worship.' Nell nudged Maud and laughed.

'Then welcome to your new home.'

Having felt she was so tired she could sleep for ever, Nell was surprised to find that she woke really early the next day. She was even more surprised to find that Ange had done the same, and Maud, who was usually the early bird, was still snoring away in her darkened bedroom.

'What's the cunning plan today?' Ange asked as they breakfasted on toast and honey and Earl Grey tea in the kitchen.

'Well we're on holiday, aren't we? For now . . .'

Ange nodded enthusiastically.

'So I vote beach,' Nell said, peering out of the window at a blue sky that heralded a beautiful spring day.

'Sounds good to me. Should we wake Maud?'

Nell nodded. 'I'll take her a cuppa and see if she wants to come with us.'

She returned shaking her head. 'Said she's got something she can't get out of today, an appointment, dentist, so we should go without her and she'll see us for tea.'

'Tea?'

'You know, that thing we odd English do at four o'clock.'

'Oh, how quaint. I didn't know anyone still did that.'

'It's a tradition in Maud's house.'

'Earl Grey and cream scones?' Ange queried.

'Nope. Cupcakes and gin and tonic.'

'Tradition with a modern twist,' Ange mused. 'I like it.'

Ange couldn't get over the fact that if you walked to the end of Maud's long twisting garden and took the gate through the hedge that acted as a windbreak to her precious roses and apple trees, you found yourself on a path that led straight down the cliff to the beach.

'It's as good as tie-sided knickers,' she exclaimed as Nell led the way.

Nell turned and frowned in confusion.

'Instant access to something glorious,' Ange explained happily.

The wind was chilly but the sunshine was beautiful, so they set up camp behind some rocks for shelter and lay there and watched the world go by.

It was the last few days of the Easter holidays and so the beach was fairly busy for the time of year.

'This is the life,' Ange sighed as a pair of lifeguards jogged past one way and some surfers passed the other. 'I've never been to Cornwall before; I'm beginning to wonder why, if the view's always this good. Maybe I should take up surfing too . . .'

'It's a great way to get fit.'

'Really?' Ange pulled a face. 'Might have to pass, then, keep it as a spectator sport. Talking of getting fit, though . . .' She reached in the pocket of her abandoned jacket and pulled out a packet of cigarettes, and then a huge bar of chocolate, which she threw to Nell, who beamed in delight.

'You came prepared.'

'Thought you might not give me so much grief over the

odd ciggie if you're sitting there stuffing yourself with chocolate.'

'I can see why you got ahead in such a cut-throat business.' Nell tore into the dark purple wrapper.

'I always knew how to schmooze.' Ange nodded. 'Find a person's weakness and use it to your advantage. You know, I once signed up a band everyone was fighting over 'cause I found out the lead singer totally adored Krispy Kreme doughnuts and that was when you could only get them in America. Trusty FedEx and a box of raspberry glaze later, and he was signing on the dotted line.'

Ange was smiling at the memory of it.

'Think you're going to miss it?'

She shrugged. 'It's gone, so forget about it.'

'You can cut it off that easily?'

'Hell, yeah.' She nodded and lit a cigarette, then inhaled and leaned back on her towel, eyes closed in sybaritic bliss. 'Don't get me wrong, I loved it when I first started, absolutely loved it. It was so exciting, discovering new talent. But it's not what you think it's going to be . . .' She paused and bit her lip. 'After I left you at the station and went to watch that band, well . . . I just thought, I can't do this any more.'

'Were they that bad?'

'No, they were that *good*. So young and enthusiastic, and the sound . . . pure. Just pure.' Ange sighed. 'And I knew exactly what we'd do to them: pick them up, shake them up, style them to within an inch of their lives, rebrand them like cattle and then pitch them to the public as half the band they used to be but as marketable as a genetically modified peach that now looks perfect but doesn't taste half as sweet . . . and that excitement I usually feel when I find something new and amazing, well, it just wouldn't come.'

'And so you decided to get out?'

'Well, not that at that precise moment, no, but then Justin phoned.' Ange said this last with such a heavy sigh that Nell was certain he had done something really awful.

'What did he say to you?' she asked, her voice laden with sympathy.

'He asked me to pick him up a kebab on the way home,' Ange said bleakly.

'A kebab?' Nell's eyes crossed in confusion.

'Yep, a bloody kebab. The same thing he's asked me to pick him up after every gig I've been to in the past six years . . . and that's when I thought about you, poised on the brink of escape, and it suddenly came to me as clear as anything: there's nothing worse than letting life get too predictable.' Ange sat up again, flicking her ash in the sand so that it fell grey on gold, and then mixing the two colours with her fingers. 'So that's why I came running after you, and I'm bloody glad I did. Look at this place, Nell. Where would you rather be? London or here?'

Another muscled hunk jogged by, his wetsuit peeled to the waist and clinging to everything else. The two girls looked at each other and laughed.

'Here,' Nell said. 'Definitely here.'

'And isn't the fact that we are here exciting?' Ange continued, 'Aside from that . . .' she looked longingly after the man's firm backside, 'sweeping everything out of your life leaves so much room for possibility to come back into it.'

Nell's mobile phone beeped again.

She glanced at it, frowned, and dropped it back in her bag. 'You know that Marcus has called me ten times since I left?'

'Yeah?'

'Well, Nicolette has called me twenty-four.'

'And each call makes your heart sing with joy at her desperation.'

'I feel a bit bad, actually,' Nell confessed.

'Don't you dare, Nell Everson! That woman deserves every bit of shit you've dropped her in, riding your back like you're a donkey for the past three years.'

'Well, I was an ass to let her do it.'

'You were an ass*et* to her and that company and don't you forget it. You know what else really helps you get on in life? Respect, that's what, the respect of other people, sure, but first and foremost respect for yourself. You deserve some self-respect: you're a true star and don't you forget it.' She leaned across and unexpectedly plonked a kiss on Nell's forehead. 'And that's the last time I do mush, okay, so remember it well.' Ange stubbed her finished cigarette out against the rock and then buried it in the sand. 'Now, I'm just going to go and find somewhere I can get some more ciggies.'

'Try the pub,' Nell suggested. 'Across the beach to the town and just past the harbour.'

'What, no lecture? Just directions?'

'You're living on Brownie points at the moment,' said Nell, touching her forehead and mouthing, 'Thanks.'

Ange took her time. Probably getting in a swift glass of Chardonnay, Nell thought as she turned to follow the sun, but finally she returned with not just cigarettes but two plates of the lunchtime special of Chicken Madras with rice and naan, all wrapped up in foil, and a bottle of Pinot Grigio with two proper glasses.

'I never knew the Jolly Roger did takeaway,' Nell exclaimed in amazement as Ange produced it all from a carrier bag with a flourish and a fanfare of 'Ta-da!'

'They didn't until today, when I pointed out what a

good idea it would be. And I can't forget to take the plates back either, 'cause I also told them they should take a deposit for them.'

Ange had been brought up on the philosophy of 'you don't ask, you don't get'. Nell had been brought up to believe that it was rude to ask. It had made them into two very different people. But Ange was the one who got curry on the beach. Maybe, Nell thought as she tucked into the succulent Madras, she should take a leaf out of her book.

'That was amazing.' Nell sucked the last drop of sauce from her spoon and grinned at her friend.

'Good idea?' Ange queried.

'Brilliant. I hope you got a discount for furnishing them with business advice.'

'Oh, I got much more than that.' Ange grinned.

'Oh yeah, such as?'

'Well, the wine was free for starters.'

'And the rest?' asked Nell, sensing more.

'I'll tell you later.' Ange got to her feet. 'I'm in the mood for a paddle. Last one to the water has to snog a lifeguard!' and she was off and running, Nell jumping to her feet and skidding after her.

They made their way back up the cliff path to find that Maud had set them up for tea in her favourite spot in the garden, underneath the oldest apple tree, which grew like a king overlooking his subjects in splendid isolation in the middle of the lawn.

After tea, which Nell still managed to do justice to, even after most of the chocolate and their curry lunch, citing the fresh air as an extreme appetite stimulant, they sat around the kitchen table drinking gin and tonic and chatting about nothing much, until Maud, who felt she had let them off easy the previous day, decided it was time to get some proper answers.

It was wonderful that Nell had come to stay, Ange too; Maud couldn't have been more pleased, had wanted her here before but hadn't liked to ask as she knew how busy and full her life was, but to find that she was here now and had left everything that she had had behind her . . .

Her relationship she could understand. Her home, well, that was a shame but too late to do anything about it. But her job . . . Maud knew how much she hated it now, but it had after all been a really good job. In this day and age that was either extremely brave or downright idiotic. Heaven knew what her parents would say when they found out.

Maud knew Nell wouldn't have told them yet; in fact, knowing Nell as well as she did, she also knew that it was very possible that Nell wouldn't tell them at all and they'd end up tracking down the truth for themselves like bloodhounds on the trail of a missing daughter.

Maud wasn't completely surprised that Nell had gone AWOL.

She'd always known that Nell would rebel one day; anyone on that tight a leash would cut and run eventually, even someone as careful of others' feelings as her god-daughter.

Her concern was what had happened to make her do it now.

She had been careful to let details come in their own time.

Her philosophy had always been 'listen before you speak', because sometimes you got your answer without having to question, and Nell usually told her everything in her own time. It was a philosophy that usually paid off, but on this occasion a large hint was needed to start the ball rolling.

'It's so gorgeous to have you both here. Should I be thanking Marcus for making you come, or should I be heading up to London to kneecap him for it?'

'We had an NDE,' Ange said, adding more tonic to the gin Maud had poured her. 'A Near Death Experience. Bloody planes.'

'And we had an IBM.' Nell smiled that lopsided smile of hers where only one corner of her mouth went upwards; only people who knew her well were aware that this was an indication of sadness rather than humour.

'An IBM?' Ange and Maud both asked in unison.

'Inconsiderate Boyfriend Moment.' Nell was laughing but her eyes were serious. 'Have you ever had a moment of such clarity you feel like you've spent the last few years of your life sleepwalking? Do you know what I mean? Does that sound stupid?'

For a moment Nell saw a flicker in Maud's face that she didn't recognise, and then Maud sighed, long and heavy. 'No, not at all. I completely understand.'

'Well, that's what happened at the weekend. He was acting like a total arse.' She glanced at Ange. 'They were both acting like total arses,' she amended, 'and something inside me just snapped; well, not so much snapped as closed off. It was like one minute he was the best thing since sliced bread and the next he was . . . well . . . toast.'

As she said it, Nell realised with a jolt that the weekend already felt so far back, like a lifetime away, and yet it had only been days. This time last week, she had been looking forward to moving in with Marcus; now it was as though her time with him had never really existed. It was like a movie that had suddenly come to a rather unsatisfactory end, and now it was over, ejected.

Switched off.

She had once loved him so much it hurt.

Would her feelings flick back *on* so easily? Would she be here this time next week killing herself with regret at what she'd left behind?

'So you gave it all up?' Maud was prompting her.

Nell nodded. 'Do you think I'm an idiot?'

'Not at all. Brave . . .'

'Brave or stupid?'

'Brave,' Maud said again, more forcefully this time. 'The stupid thing would have been to stay in a job you hated with a man you were fast beginning to feel the very same way about.'

Nell had always been a sensible girl. She hadn't had any other choice; it had been drummed into her from a very young age by her eminently sensible parents.

Maud had determined early on that what Nell needed from her godmother was fun and frivolity, not that there was anything frivolous in the way she loved her; far from it: the love Maud had for Nell was as fierce and protective as that of any mother for her child, but she had vowed never to nag, never to niggle about homework when she came to stay, or keeping a tidy room, or putting money away for a rainy day, or thinking about her future.

With Maud, Nell always got to stay up late watching inappropriate television, eat the wrong kinds of food, waste her money on whatever fluff she fancied, scoff too many chocolate bars in one go, and live for the moment.

Sometimes, though, she needed a little bit of guidance, and right now, Maud felt sure, was one of those times. Nell had done one of the bravest things a person could. It was all very well to realise that your life was all wrong and complain about it; it was another thing completely to do something so drastic to change this fact.

And now Maud didn't want to see her drift into another unsatisfactory way of life simply because she needed to meet practical needs.

So it was now, whilst the two girls were so obviously relaxed, that Maudlyn chose to tackle her god-daughter on the subject of what she thought she might just be doing with the rest of her life.

'So . . .' she started again in her usual fashion, and then paused.

'So?' Nell repeated.

Maud had been trying to find a better way of putting it but couldn't, and so she said it anyway.

'So what are you going to do now?'

Nell shrugged and pushed herself further back into the oversized wooden chair, raising her feet and tucking them under her.

'Heaven knows. I don't suppose there's much call for an Information, Resource and Business Planning Facilitator in this neck of the woods.'

Maud smiled. The length and complexity of Nell's job title had always been a source of amusement between the two.

'You're staying here in Cornwall?' Maud tried not to sound too hopeful, but Nell nodded emphatically anyway.

'That's the only thing I am sure about. The minute I drove over the border I felt like I'd come home again. Which means I want to stay for a while, which really means that I need to get a job . . . so any suggestions gratefully received.'

'Well, the most common jobs down here seem to be artist, musician, writer or waitress.'

'Well, I can't paint, I can't sing, and I got an Unclassified in English Literature, so I suppose that leaves waitress . . . Are you sure there isn't anything else?'

'Lifeguard?'

'Better. If I could swim.'

'You can't swim?' Ange asked in surprise.

'Oh I can swim, just, I'd call it more of a flounder. I don't know if they'd let you rescue other people when you're barely out of water wings yourself.'

'Hotel receptionist? Shop assistant?'

'Possibilities, but not particularly tempting, although if needs must I wouldn't turn my nose up. I'm fed up with analysing and criticising and debating and paperwork. I wouldn't mind doing something a bit less mind-focused and more hands on . . .' Nell's brow knitted as she racked her brains for inspiration. 'You know, I'd be happy working for myself, I'm just not sure what I could do. I don't exactly have any skills that would translate well to being a one-man band,' and then her face fell as her own words registered.

'I don't have any skills,' she repeated in the same morose fashion as someone who had just discovered that they'd failed their exams.

'Well, if it makes you feel any better, you make a mean cupcake,' Ange mumbled through a mouthful of her third one of Maud's. 'Maybe you could be a baker, that's hands on.'

She was smiling as she said it, but then Nell began smiling too. To her it wasn't a total joke. In fact she kind of liked the idea.

'Not necessarily a baker, but something to do with cooking would be nice.'

'Chef?'

'I know that's the obvious when you say cooking, but I can't exactly picture myself feeding the masses.'

'You're not leaving yourself many options here,' said Maud.

'Catering, perhaps?' Ange suggested. 'You know, like dinner parties or something. Small dinner parties,' she added as Nell looked dubious.

'I'm afraid that when people want to eat around here without cooking for themselves, they go to the pub,' Maud said bluntly but not unkindly. 'Or the fish and chip shop,' she added, looking pointedly at Nell, who had a bit of a chip-shop chips fetish and normally made a beeline for the Good Cod the minute she hit town. 'They're not exactly dinner party people.'

'Well, if I'm staying, I'm going to have to come up with something. What about you, Ange?

'Staying. Definitely,' Ange said, 'as long as that's okay with you guys?'

'Not going back to London?' Nell asked in surprise.

'Not yet. Not for a while. I like it here.'

'So are you going to start looking for something? A job?'

Ange shook her head.

'Don't want to?'

'Don't need to,' she replied, and suddenly the slight smile playing about her lips blossomed into full grown. 'I got myself a job today. You're looking at the latest employee of the Jolly Roger. I'm going to be a barmaid.'

10

'A barmaid?'
The way Nell said it made Ange think of Lady
Bracknell and the infamous handbag.

'I just wanted to do something completely different for
a while, a lock-and-leave job.'

'A what?' Nell frowned in confusion.

'Well you see, the job I was doing before was great, but
it was a twenty-four/seven thing. If I wasn't actually at the
office, I was still working, or thinking about work, or more
to the point worrying about work . . . With this, I can do
my shift and when I walk out of the door I leave the whole
thing behind me. I'm hardly going to lie in bed at night
worrying about whether the lager's gone flat or we've got
enough Smoky Bacon crisps in, am I?'

Nell nodded slowly, thoughtfully. 'I see your point.'

'I'm having a brain break,' Ange added.

'Well, that's easy for you to do.'

'It is?'

'When you've already achieved so much.'

'I have?'

'Ange worked for Pumped Up Pimped Up Records.
She discovered Granny's Attic,' Nell said proudly to
Maud, who looked thoroughly confused.

'Granny's what?' She frowned as pictures of Ange with

a torch stumbling through a dusty attic full of antiques filled her mind.

'They're a rock band, went straight to number one with their first, second and third singles and platinum with their first album. Not to mention The Judas, and Jagged Little Pillocks, oh, and Dead, Deadly and Demonised, can't believe I nearly forgot them.'

'I can't believe that either.' Maud's faded blue eyes were getting wider with every name. It was obvious she had never heard of any of the bands that an always impressed Nell was reeling off in star-struck fashion.

'So you see, Ange has already had an amazing career.'

'Yes, and my amazing *new* career starts tonight,' Ange said happily, 'so I'm going to go and get myself into barmaid mode. You know, red lipstick, low-cut top. See you in a bit.'

'Can you believe that girl?' Nell shook her head in wonder. 'Goes for cigarettes and comes back with a new job. No wonder she's done so well for herself. She doesn't prevaricate, she just gets on with it.'

'You've had an amazing career so far too, Nelly.'

'No, Maud, I had an amazingly named career, but I never did anything that the whole world is going to remember.'

'Not many of us do. We can't all be Gandhis or Bransons.'

'So you're saying some of us were born to greatness, some achieve it, others have greatness thrust upon them, and the rest of us are supposed to be mundane and lump it?'

'Well, I wouldn't have put it quite like that, but I do believe we all have our place in life. Our own plan, our own purpose.'

'That's the thing. What is my purpose? My plan? I just don't know . . .'

'Why do you expect that you *should* know, darling? It can take a lifetime to work out what we want from life or what life wants from us, and sometimes you can get to the end of it and realise that you still don't know . . .' Maud sighed, and then smiled determinedly. 'If you really want to know what I think you should do, it's give yourself a break, and I'm not just talking a holiday, I mean in everything. Don't beat yourself up if you have a wander for a bit; you don't always have to stride along with a purpose. I'm sorry to roll out more clichés, but if you're too intent on the actual journey, then how the hell can you enjoy the view? Sit back and enjoy the wonders of God's creativity for a while without constantly wondering why you're a part of it.'

'Do you believe in God, Maud?'

'Do you know, that's a question I've asked myself a lot recently,' Maud replied, but Nell didn't get to hear whether she had come up with an answer, as Ange chose that moment to strut back into the room in a pair of knee-high boots, a leopard-print skirt that was too short and a touch too tight as well, and a cleavage-revealing blouse.

'I don't know whether to go for the Bet Lynch look, all hair, boobs and earrings, or the Liz McDonald look . . .'

'All hair, boobs and earrings?' Nell finished for her.

Ange grinned and nodded. 'There you go then, hair, boobs and earrings it is. My forte. Well, except for the earrings. Studs don't quite do it, do they?' she said, fingering her discreet earrings gently.

'You could borrow something long and flashy off Maud.'

'Thanks,' said Maud drily. 'And I always thought my taste in jewellery was expensive and tasteful.'

'I meant your charity bags. There's bound to be something in there.'

'Already looked,' Ange murmured, stroking the faux fur of the leopard-print mini. 'Where do you think I found this?'

'Now that actually was one of mine.' Maud grinned.

Nell's eyes almost fell out of her head as she looked from Ange to Maud in amazement.

'You wore that?'

'The sixties have a lot to answer for.' Maud nodded sagely.

Maud was reading the paper; Nell was channel-hopping Maud's five terrestrials, trying to find something to watch. That was one thing she missed about Marcus: his satellite television. He had over four hundred channels ... how sad was that? Or was the saddest thing that Nell missed them more than she missed him? She put down the remote as she realised with a jolt that it wasn't difficult to miss Sky more than she missed Marcus, because she didn't actually miss Marcus at all.

Maud looked up from her paper. Nell was obviously having a revelation of some kind, but if she wanted to share, Maud knew that she would.

After Nell had stared, wide-eyed, out of the window for a good five minutes, Maud folded up the paper and took off her glasses. 'Shall we go down to the Jolly Roger for a drink, see how Ange is getting on?'

It took Nell a second to switch back to the here and now, and then she smiled. 'Good idea.'

It was a fine night, warm and clear. The tide was out, so there was no sound of the sea crashing against the cliffs as they forsook the longer way round by the road and instead took the steep path that led down to the beach, which you could cross to the harbour and the village.

A third of the houses in Polporth were second homes

or holiday homes, the rest residents. The people of Polporth considered themselves lucky: in some parts of Cornwall the same ratio applied but the other way around.

Tonight the village was quiet, drenched in darkness, the Jolly Roger a beacon of light and music in an otherwise sleeping town.

It was common knowledge that Maud liked a nice glass of Scotch with a little bit of ice and some lemonade, and she was a regular face at the Jolly Roger and an old friend of the landlord London Tony, so named rather unimaginatively by the locals because that was where he had hailed from twenty years ago, and twenty years in Polporth still made you a newcomer. Nell had been in a few times when she'd been down to stay, but she was still a bit shy of the place. It wasn't somewhere she would ever walk into on her own.

Unlike Ange.

They arrived at the Roger to find that Ange was getting on just fine.

It was almost as though she had always been there. She was already a big hit with the closed-rank locals, who were chatting her up, buying her drinks and singing her praises, and even the notoriously spiky Marge, London Tony's second wife, younger and prettier than the first and jealous with it, was laughing and talking with her like they had known each other for ever.

And as for his sons, well, he had three of them, all of whom got on famously, and all of whom were now vying jealously with each other for Ange's attention.

London Tony had four children altogether. The eldest, Tony Junior, known as TJ, was a younger version of his father, without the beer belly and the bulldog tattoo. Second was Beth, a sweet, pretty girl with long hair the colour of soft brown sugar, an infectious laugh, and a scholarship to a posh school in Truro and four years studying art at St Martin's under her belt. Unlike her mother, she adored Cornwall and Polporth, and had returned as soon as she possibly could to work in the pub whilst she built up her collection and her money in order to open her own gallery.

She and Tony Junior were the product of Tony Senior's marriage to his first wife, Laura, who had loathed life in Cornwall with a passion that was far superior to any feelings she had for her husband, and had therefore left him and her children to run back to Bow.

The youngest of his children, twin boys, Liam and Ben, were the spitting image of their mother, Marge, but had their father's generous nature and sense of humour. Handsome in a belligerent, swaggering, shaven-headed way, they were, as Ange put it to Nell as she filled her in on her evening thus far, 'the cocks' of the Jolly Roger, and in more ways than one, she added with a knowing wink.

'You've been here two hours, Ange!' Nell exclaimed with a shocked grin.

'I know.' Ange shrugged. 'But it was my fault. I made the mistake of asking if they were identical in every way, and they obliged by showing me.'

Nell envied the ease with which Ange had fitted herself into the crowd at the Jolly Roger. She hadn't so much as had a drink in there and had already bagged herself not only a job behind the bar, but a whole bunch of new friends too. That was the thing about Ange: if she wanted something, she just went for it; she didn't worry about the 'what ifs'.

'Now, what can I get you, lover?' Ange said in a mock Cornish accent, leaning on the bar to show Nell her cleavage.

'I'll have a pint of vodka and my friend here would like a bottle of whisky with a straw.' Nell grinned, pretending to leer down Ange's top.

'Cherry on top?'

'And one of those paper parasols, please,' said Maud.

Ange brought Nell a vodka and tonic and Maud a large whisky with a splash of lemonade and exactly three chunks of ice.

'On the house,' she said magnanimously, and then, when Marge turned with flinty eyes, added quickly, 'Well, what I actually meant was on me.'

'Perfect.' Maud picked up her glass to admire it before drinking. 'Just the way I like it. Especially the fact that I don't have to pay for it myself. I have to say, Tony, Marge, I'm already very impressed with your new member of staff, not that I'm biased at all . . .'

'So how's it going?' Nell asked.

'Great.'

'You wouldn't rather be on this side of the bar drinking it instead of that side serving it?'

'Well, perhaps, but I'm still having fun, and I'm working. It's nice when the two can coincide.'

'I didn't know they could,' Nell said with feeling.

'Want me to ask Tony and Marge if there's anything else going here?'

'Not really my cup of tea, but thanks for the offer.'

'You'll find something, Nell.'

'Sure,' Nell said without too much conviction.

Maud had said not to worry, but they both knew that Nell couldn't help it. She had done nothing but. Even this afternoon, after they had spoken, she had scoured the local papers, then hooked up her computer and looked online, and seen nothing. She had lain on her bed listening to the sea and trying to think of anything that might appeal to her in the way of work, and yet still she was as clueless as when she had first arrived.

And as the first flush of freedom began to fade to a faint fizzle, she knew that panic would soon follow. It was the way she was wired. Where she worked and the people she worked with might have been driving her crazy, but the fact that she worked and did well at her job had given her a sense of satisfaction, of purpose.

But what could replace it?

Nine to five . . . well, in her case it had been eight until seven, but no matter what the hours, the regimented life just didn't cut it for her any more. Now that she had the chance to change, she knew that she didn't want to work in an office again.

She wanted something . . . something . . . oh hell, that was the bloody problem. She didn't know what the hell it was she wanted.

She took a sip of her vodka.

She had read a wonderful quote somewhere that went something along the lines of 'Worrying is just praying for what you don't want.' She wasn't sure who had said it, but no doubt it was a wiser person than she. Maybe it was one of those cases where you had to stop looking so hard before you could actually find something.

But could someone like her turn control of her life over to fate?

Something will turn up, she told herself, and then said it aloud with more conviction: 'Something will turn up.'

'Of course it will.' Ange appeared at Nell's elbow. 'And in the meantime, why don't you have another vodka?'

Whilst Ange and Maud slept off their hangovers, Nell spent the morning in Maud's kitchen, a favourite haunt of hers, where she indulged in a spot of baking therapy.

This meant that Maud and Ange came downstairs to the kitchen after their showers to a table laid with fresh coffee and freshly baked croissants, cherry muffins and melt-in-the-mouth madeleines.

'I think we should sleep in every day if this is what we wake up to,' Ange exclaimed.

'If we woke up to this every day we soon wouldn't be able to get down to the kitchen to eat it.' Maud's eyes were almost popping out of her head at the sight of so much food. 'We'd have to get the fire brigade in to crane us downstairs. Nell, can we freeze some of this . . .'

'You think I've gone a bit mad?'

'Well, put it this way, I have a charity breakfast for eighty next month and this one breakfast alone would solve my catering problems perfectly. Talking of which, what are you doing today, girls? I have my LLs.'

'Your what?' Ange frowned, bemused.

Nell grinned. 'Maud's Lunching Ladies.'

'What are they?'

'Exactly what it says on the tin. They're ladies who lunch and occasionally do sterling work for charity, such as breakfasts for eighty . . .'

'Never heard of them.'

'That's because the Polporth LLs are the only LLs in the whole country. They're unique.'

'Are they a bit like the WI?' Ange queried.

Nell shook her head as Maud's eyebrows scuttled up her forehead in consternation.

'Nothing like the WI,' she boomed.

'She got kicked out of the WI, so she formed her own posse,' Nell explained to Ange.

'I did not get kicked out,' Maud interjected.

'Okay, they asked you to leave.'

'Very nicely,' Maud added with a wicked smile.

'What did you do?'

'What didn't she do?' Nell answered for her. 'A very disruptive presence was, I think, the official line.'

'They thought some of my ideas for outings and fund-raisers were a little extreme, that's all,' Maud sniffed.

'So what are you and the LLs doing today?'

'We're having lunch at the Roger. Hardly extreme.'

'Ooh, so am I,' said Ange. 'Well, actually, I'm serving lunch at the Roger.'

'Want me to drop you down?' Maud offered.

'Yes please.'

'Mind if I tag along too?' Nell asked. 'Thought I might wander round the shops for a bit.'

'Come to lunch if you like.'

'Me, join the LLs? Thanks, Maud, but I think I'll pass on that one until I can join you for the early-bird discounts and pensioners' specials. Give me another forty years or so and I might be signing up for a spot at the table.'

'Cheeky mare.' Maud pretended to look affronted.

'We're not all zooming round on Zimmer frames sucking soup through straws, you know . . .'

After a long and happy afternoon wandering the eclectic shops of Polporth, it was the boats bobbing gently on the water and the aroma of food cooking in the Good Cod, the fish and chip shop on the quayside, that drew Nell down the road towards the harbour, and it was the For Sale sign that made her stop halfway there.

She remembered Ye Olde Tea Shop from times spent here when she was younger. It had been a real old-world place, a homage to chintz and bone china, run by the oddest couple of women she had ever seen.

Maud always insisted that they were lesbian lovers, and Nell had to confess she had been fascinated by them.

Elizabeth, the elder of the two, looked like Norman Bates's mother from *Psycho*, with her black hair drawn back tightly into the same bun every day, always in a black pencil skirt and white blouse, immaculate no matter what time of day you came across her. Nell imagined that in her younger days she would have been a bit of a glamour puss.

Claire, the younger, Nell had been sure was a witch, a white witch, if there were such a thing. Hair to her waist in flowing waves like the sea, and a similar colour too, because she streaked it with blue to match her eyes. She was always dressed in the most voluminous skirts, that billowed and swirled about her as she walked, and she wore so many bracelets on her wrists that she jangled all the time like wind chimes in a breeze.

A honking horn brought Nell back to the present. It was Maud, hanging out of the window of her ancient rusting Saab.

'Hellooo,' she called. 'I'm on my way home to start on supper. Do you want a lift back?'

Nell shook her head. 'No, thanks. I'm going to wander down to the harbour and wait for the tide to go out a bit more, then I can walk back up the cliff path.'

'Okay, darling.' Maud began to drive away and then turned back with a knowing smile. 'And no chips, Nell, it's your favourite beef stew and thyme dumplings tonight. Don't want to ruin your appetite.'

With Maudlyn's good-natured warning ringing in her ears, Nell couldn't help but feel a guilty thrill as she sat on the harbour wall and ate her chips fresh from the Good Cod. They were hot and satisfying as only chip-shop chips can be, and the slight drizzle and the chill in the air only served to make them taste even more wonderful.

The sound of the sea and the gulls circling above was the perfect seasoning.

It was four in the afternoon.

It seemed kind of surreal to be where she was.

'I shouldn't be here,' she said, and then, as only silence answered her, added, 'but I am.'

She knew exactly what she'd be doing right now if she'd stayed. Today was 12 April, the day of the big merger meeting, the culmination of exactly two years of hard work; well, hard work on her part. She had slogged her socks off to get this project right, while Nicolette had taken all the credit for the way it had run so smoothly. She had been the majestic floating swan to Nell's frantically paddling webbed feet. Today, this meeting was crunch time, and Nell knew that Nicolette would once again flounder without her.

Despite her too nice nature, she couldn't help a small smile of satisfaction spreading across her cold face.

And then the smile dropped as the enormity of what she had done finally hit her.

She had devoted two years of her life to this project and then she had just upped and left weeks before it would finally be completed.

'Penny for them?'

'My thoughts or my chips?' Nell grinned as Ange helped herself to a big handful of the latter.

'Well, I'd give you more than a penny for the rest of your chips – you know me and food – so the penny must be for what's going on in that head of yours that's stopping you from stuffing those before I can, and that's making your face look like you're eating razor blades instead of God's finest.'

'Just thinking about work.'

At the mention of the W word, Ange pulled a face. 'I thought we'd come here to forget the horrors of our past mistakes,' she said, helping herself to more chips.

'It might not have been the right job, but it was a good job: the money was good, the prospects were good. I'd worked hard to get where I was. I'd been there eight years, Ange, and I just quit. I didn't really think about it, I just did it.'

'Sometimes your gut instincts are the best ones to follow.'

'You really think so?'

Ange nodded firmly.

'Is that what you did?'

'I always follow my gut.' Ange grinned, patting her round belly and helping herself to more chips. 'Why worry? We're bright, we're young, we have the whole of the rest of our lives ahead of us. We both made something of ourselves before; we can do it again, and maybe this time you'll find something that actually makes you happy.'

'Thanks, Ange, that's just what I needed to hear.'

'Well, it's true. I'm not just mollifying you.'

'What about you? You enjoyed your job.'

'I know, but I'd been doing it for a long time. A change is as good as a rest, as they say, and besides, I can always go back to it if I want to. You never know, I might find some amazing undiscovered talent playing their little hearts out in the back room of some seedy pub, and I'll just pretend I didn't walk out and that I've been on a scouting mission the whole time.'

'Do you think you'll go back?'

Ange shrugged. 'Who knows? You ask me that now and my gut response is no. But in six months' time, a few years down the road, maybe. Ange rule number eighty-two. Never say never, because it seriously narrows your options.' She nodded sagely.

'How was work?'

'Fun. Funny. Tony and Marge went to the wholesalers, so TJ challenged Beth to a pickled-egg-eating competition. They ate seven between them before they realised that they were two years out of date . . . You've never seen two people turn so green.'

'So what are you doing here?'

'I was having a wander, looking at Polporth before I headed back to Maud's, and then I saw you sitting down here on your jack.'

'What do you think?'

'Polporth? Like it,' Ange said, sitting down next to Nell. 'Quaint. Sort of place that makes you think of sword fights and smugglers, and long skirts and cloaks and stuff. You know, secret assignations and long-running feuds and people running off with other people's wives or throwing themselves into the ocean lovelorn over lost liaisons.'

'Very poetic, Ange.' Nell applauded her, smiling.

'Well, it's a poetic kind of place. It smells of . . .' Ange paused dramatically, and sniffed the air.

'Fish?' Nell joked.

Ange shook her head.

'Adventure?'

'Nope,' Ange said emphatically. 'Sex.'

'And romance?' Nell added.

Ange shook her head. 'Nah, just raw sex.'

'That'll be the fish.'

'Nell! And I thought I was the crude one.'

Nell offered up the last chip. Ange took it, broke it in two and pushed one half into Nell's mouth and then the other into her own.

'Fancy a swift one at the Jolly Roger?' she offered, having already stayed on after work for a swift two herself.

'Maud would kill us.'

'For being late back for dinner?'

'Nah.' Nell kicked herself off the wall and stretched her legs, ready to walk back up the cliff. 'For going without her.'

The minute they walked in the door, Maud headed over and took Nell's hands in her own, lifting them to her nose and inhaling deeply.

'Salt and vinegar!' she announced, as Nell flushed with guilt.

Ange proffered up her own hands voluntarily.

Maud dutifully sniffed, but frowned in puzzlement. 'Chips?' she asked.

'Vodka,' Ange replied with a grin.

'Don't know which is worse,' Maud said, her frown barely masking the smile.

'If I promise you that I'm still starving, will you forgive me?' Nell pretended to look apologetic.

'If I promise you I'm starving, can I have another drink?' Ange asked hopefully.

*

Citing the excesses of the previous evening, Maud went to bed early, but when Nell went up an hour later her bedroom light was still on.

She stuck her head around the door. Maud was in bed with a book.

'You okay?'

Maud nodded.

'Can I come in for a sec?'

'Course you can.' Maud put the book down on her bedside table and patted the duvet next to her. 'Something on your mind?'

Nell sat down on the end of her bed. 'Sort of. Passed the tea rooms today. I hadn't realised it had closed.'

'Oh, quite a while ago now.' Maud nodded. 'Such a shame.'

'What happened to Claire and Elizabeth?'

'I'm afraid Elizabeth passed away last year. Claire carried on for a while without her, but her heart wasn't in it. The last I heard, she'd gone to run a gay bar in Ibiza, but I don't know if that's true or just wishful thinking.'

'Wishful thinking?'

'Yes. Isn't it a lovely image? Much better than a B and B in St Ives.'

'And it's been empty since?'

'Well, theoretically, yes, but I think it had squatters over the winter. Either that or the mice were burning candles, drying wetsuits out the windows and playing "Stairway to Heaven" on an out-of-tune guitar until three in the morning. Such a shame really,' she repeated. 'The place used to be the heart of the village in daytime. Elizabeth's special chocolate brownies were the talk of the county.'

'What would you say if I told you I was thinking of buying the place?'

Maud didn't actually say anything, but she did take off her glasses and sit back against the pillows.

'You're thinking of staying in Polporth?'

Nell nodded. 'I told you that.'

'You said stay for a while, Nell; buying property, well, that kind of hints at being here for longer than a while.'

'It does, doesn't it?'

'May I ask why?'

'You don't want me to?'

'That is most definitely not what I said, darling Nell. Would you answer the question, please?'

Maud in schoolmarm mode meant that there was something on her mind other than the news Nell had just imparted, but Nell knew when to humour her.

'Because it appeals to me, Maud. I like the thought of earning my living by feeding people my cakes and biscuits, of spending my days baking and brewing tea and washing up and scrubbing floors, and meeting new people all the time in summer when the holidaymakers come, and doing my own books instead of other people's, of being answerable to myself for my decisions and no one else, of buying a property that isn't just a home but a business too, and of buying property in this area when prices are actually lower than they have been for some time. I love the thought of taking a business that has been part of village life but has faded away and bringing it back to life again.'

Maud listened to her god-daughter, her smile and her pride growing with every word.

'You've really thought about this, haven't you?'

'Of course I have. You know me, I haven't just thrown away every value my parents hammered into me with a mallet. So what are you worried about?'

'Well, I was worried that you were just staying here

because it's the easy option at the moment. Because you have a home here, with me, and having just thrown away – no, sorry, Nell, that's not a fair choice of phrasing – having chosen to start your life again, left everything you know behind, perhaps the familiarity here makes it all seem less scary.'

Nell bit her bottom lip and nodded. 'Maybe that is part of it too. I'd be a liar if I said it wasn't lovely to be back in Polporth, to be staying here with you, to be able to see you as much as I want to, but there's so much more to it than that.'

'I can see that, Nell.'

'So what do you think?'

'Well, it's a tough economic climate at the moment. Can you afford to buy the place, spend the money on it that it needs and then survive if business takes a while to pick up?'

Nell nodded firmly. 'I've done my homework and my figures and I can do it. I'm certain.'

'Then I think it's a wonderful idea.'

'You do?'

'Oh, absolutely. Can't say your parents will agree with me, though.'

At the mention of her mum and dad, Nell, who had been looking excited and enthusiastic, totally deflated and started to look worried instead. 'They're going to go crazy, aren't they?'

'Probably.' Maud wouldn't lie. 'But although it would be lovely if they could be supportive, you are twenty-eight now, Nell. You are your own woman. What you do with your life is completely up to you. Besides . . .' She paused for a heartbeat until Nell looked up at her. 'How far is Polporth from Norwich?' She winked.

It was an old joke from when Nell was a teenager,

when she found her parents' regimen the hardest, and she used to escape to Maud's as often as she could.

'Not far enough,' they chorused the answer together.

Undeterred by the thought of her parents, who she could all too easily imagine turning pink then purple and then exploding all over their immaculate sitting room at the news, plastering the eau de Nil decor with guts and angst, Nell phoned early the next morning and managed to get an appointment to view Ye Olde Tea Shop at eleven that day.

She hadn't told Ange what she had been contemplating doing, just asked her to tag along when she went into the village, and Ange readily agreed, thinking that they were probably heading for the pub, where she was more than happy to spend both her working and her leisure time.

She hadn't told her, because she wanted Ange's famous gut reaction about the place, undiluted by her own thoughts and dreams and aspirations.

She had already been down and peered through the pretty sash windows. Obscured by months of dust and grub and spider's webs, she hadn't been able to see much, but her imagination gave her all the view she needed.

Would Ange see past the chaos to the potential too?

The agent was already waiting for them outside, standing under a large blue umbrella that had the company's name emblazoned upon it in gold lettering.

'Ah, Miss Everson, I presume?' He was too handsome, his smile too ingenuous, too salesman.

'Nell,' she replied, holding out a hand.

'Simon Porteous, from Benson and Masters. Pleasure to meet you. Have you had a copy of the brochure?'

Nell shook her head, and he handed her a copy and then offered another to Ange, who looked bemused but took it none the less, eyeing the estate agent's arse in suit trousers that were a touch too tight for comfort but perfectly cut for vanity as he led them to the front door and pulled out a large rusting key.

'This way, please, ladies.' He pushed open the door, which creaked in protest, and then stepped back to allow them both to pass through first.

The first thing that hit them was the smell. Must and sour milk, not a happy combination. A small mountain of junk mail was piled up behind the front door, which opened into a small hallway. To the right was a narrow corridor, which, according to the sign, led to the toilets. Straight ahead was a door marked Private, and through a glass-paned door to the left was the tea room itself.

They turned this way first.

The whole place had been opened up to form a large L-shaped room, with the kitchen in the kick of the L, closest to the door and cordoned off from the main room by a glass display counter.

The room was cold, that instantaneous kind of chill that makes your skin prickle with goose bumps. The tables and chairs were still in place, dark wood, old-fashioned, some with broken struts, others missing legs. Everything was caked in grime; the smell in the room was of damp and neglect.

But although Nell saw this, she also saw the open fireplace with its stone surround, the exposed stone walls, the original thick gnarled beams on the low ceiling, and she scuffed at the floor with her toe and smiled, for underneath the dirt was a grey slate floor.

'What do you think?' she asked Ange, her smile growing.

'What are we doing here?' whispered Ange in response. 'I thought we were heading for lager and chilling not decay and dusting.'

'Tell me what you think,' Nell urged without answering.

Ange dutifully cast a come-hither look at the young estate agent, who was too busy examining his cuticles to notice.

'Not bad, I suppose, although a bit too polished for my usual taste.'

'I meant this place, not the agent.' Nell laughed. 'Don't tell me you like him.'

'He's a man, isn't he?'

'Is that your only criterion?'

'Well, no, but it's a good starting point. What are we doing here, Nell?'

'Why do people normally arrange to view a property?'

'You're thinking of buying this place?' Ange's surprise was plastered very clearly on her expressive face.

'I'm seriously considering it, yes.'

Ange frowned and looked at the brochure again.

'Can you afford it? Have you seen the auction guide price?' Ange glanced over to make sure the estate agent was out of earshot. Fortunately he had found a dusty mirror and was busy rearranging the lock of hair that swept over his forehead.

'I've got thirty thousand more than that in the bank from the sale of my house, I've saved every single bonus the company ever gave me, and that was one thing where they were actually pretty generous, and I've still got some money that I inherited when my gran passed away. I was hoping if I could get it for about thirty grand below guide, then that would leave me sixty thousand to do all the work that needs doing, install the equipment, and bank-roll me for the first six months in case it's a slow starter.'

Ange's mouth had dropped open at the thought of Nell having such a large amount of cash so readily disposable.

'But Nell, you're rich.'

'Hardly. That represents eight years of paying a mortgage, and a sharp rise in prices. That's all my worldly goods, Ange.'

'Well, considering all my worldly goods fit in the two suitcases I brought down here with me, I stick with my first statement.'

'It's all relative.'

'Yeah, and I'm the poor relative.' Ange grinned.

'And so will I be if I buy this place. What do you think?'

'I think if I were you I wouldn't be in Cornwall, I'd be in Acapulco drinking cocktails and dirty-dancing with a waiter called José.'

Nell spluttered with laughter.

'But that would just be me going wild, blowing the lot, whereas this, well this is you, and it's an investment.'

'So you think I should do it?'

'Doesn't matter what I think.' Ange shrugged. 'It's what you think that's important. So the question should really be, do *you* think you should do it?'

'Heart's screaming yes, head's torn between "definitely" and "don't be so bloody stupid". I was hoping to get some of your gut instinct for a hit.'

'Well, that normally only works with musicians. I've never tried it with bricks and mortar before.'

'So you're feeling nothing?'

'Didn't say that.' Ange frowned thoughtfully, looked about, tried to see past the mess and the grime, picture the place touched by the gentle hand of Nell and feel what it would be like. Nell was a dab hand with a mop and bucket; in fact she was so keen on a cloth and a bit of Flash that she could almost list cleaning as one of her hobbies. She also made the best cakes Ange had ever tasted. It suddenly all made perfect sense to her.

'I think you could make this work.'

'You do?'

Ange nodded. 'Your baking is amazing. I'd stop by especially to buy something. Think of all those hungry tourists who'll be traipsing through here in the summer . . .'

As if fate wanted to prove a point, they both glanced out of the window in order to picture Ange's words, only to see a straggle of walking-booted, waterproofed people actually tramping down the street outside. They paused outside the tea shop, their eyes and smiles hopeful and relieved at the thought of a respite from the April showers with a pot of tea and a cream scone or two, only to crumple with disappointment when it sank in that the place was actually closed for business.

'There you go.' Ange grinned. 'Your first customers. Well, they would have been if we were here to open up rather than just look around.'

Nell nodded.

'And,' Ange added, trying to negate Nell's obvious remnants of reticence with her own sudden surge of confidence about the place, 'what's the one thing a girl will always want, through good times and bad, through boom and recession, through love and love lost?'

'Cake,' said Nell.

'Well, there you go then. I don't know about my gut instinct, but my greedy gut says, hell, yeah.'

12

It was a rowdy journey up to Exeter, where the auction was being held. Cyril Junior being deemed too small for a party of three, where one passenger declared her legs too long to sit in the back, which was very true, and the other declared her bottom too big, which wasn't so true but made them all laugh none the less, they were travelling in Maud's clapped-out old Saab, Nell in the back, not at all convinced they were going to make it that far, willing the rusting motor on with her mind, her feet trying very hard not to pedal whenever they went up a hill.

Ange was sitting in the front seat next to Maud and the two of them were singing along to 'Bohemian Rhapsody' on repeat play, falsetto voices and head-banging included, which was jolly disconcerting when they were travelling at seventy miles an hour up the A30, and even more so when they were stopped at traffic lights in Exeter itself, and even though it had been pouring with rain for the entire journey thus far, the sun had come out sufficiently for Maud to insist that they had the roof down.

And then, when the rain inevitably started again, still five miles from their destination, they couldn't get the roof back up, and had to stop at a McDonald's, where Maud and Ange, who didn't care that they were soaked to the skin, tucked into Big Macs, while Nell blow-dried herself with the hand dryer in the toilets, and tried not to feel the skin-prickling buzz that emanated from the knot of nerves and excitement forming in her stomach.

When Ange offered her the Big Mac they had bought her, Nell nearly threw up.

'Thanks, Ange, but I couldn't, my stomach's in knots.'

'Wondered why you were so long in the loo,' Ange teased.

Nell stuck her tongue out. 'My whole life could change today,' she said solemnly.

'You mean it hasn't already?' Ange squeezed her hand and the two girls shared a smile.

When they finally made it to the auction house, the queue was snaking out of the door and there wasn't a parking space to be found.

'Why on earth is it so busy?' Nell complained, her stomach tightening further.

Inside it was also packed with people.

'You'd think it would be quieter considering the state of the economy,' Ange muttered, elbowing her way past someone so she could grab some seats.

'I thought it would be.' Nell frowned, sitting down next to Ange. 'Surely all these people aren't bidding? I'm never going to be able to afford it if loads of people are after it.'

'Don't you worry, my love. 'Taint the property every-one's here for.' Their neighbour, an older woman, still in a raincoat and hat despite the warmth of the room, leaned across and whispered conspiratorially, 'More than half the folks 'ere won't be bidding. They's all just hoping to get themselves on the television.'

She pointed to the corner of the room.

Ange's mouth fell open, and then she dived into her

huge handbag and pulled out a lipstick, a mascara wand, a hairbrush and a compact and hurriedly began fixing her face.

Nell had been too busy trying to swallow her butterflies and Ange had been too busy fighting her way through the crowd to notice the camera crew, and the huge notices inside and out stating: 'Benson and Masters Auction House are delighted to welcome the *Grand Openings* team'.

'*Grand Openings*?' Nell frowned as she read the board behind the auctioneer's podium.

'*Grand Openings*!' Ange exclaimed, kissing her lips together. 'Don't tell me you've never seen it, Nell? It's the best programme ever. They go to auctions around the country and follow the progress of businesses that are for sale, like hotels and guest houses and run-down Indian restaurants. They did a hairdresser's one episode; that one was brilliant. The guy who bought it was so funny, like Graham Norton only camper. Then someone bought a riding stables where all the stables had woodworm and the menage was full of mole hills . . .'

'Don't forget the drag bar in Brighton,' interrupted their neighbour.

'Oh yeah, of course, the Queen Vic, that was a good episode. It was slap bang next to a Jehovah's Witness meeting hall who were objecting to everything they wanted to do, of course, and this huge fight broke out.'

'Satchels and handbags swinging like crazy,' nodded their neighbour. 'They had to call the police.'

'So anyway,' Ange continued, 'they watch these places being bought at auction and then they follow the property right from when it's purchased until it reopens. Hence the name, *Grand Openings*.'

'Sounds fascinating.' Nell yawned.

'It's really good,' Ange squeaked with the indignation of a firm fan, 'and you should see the guy that presents it, oh my sweet Lord, is that man gorgeous or what?'

'Gorgeous,' agreed their behatted neighbour with an emphatic nod. 'They did a garden centre once. Some posh tart bought that one; should 'ave seen the way she fluttered 'er falsies at 'im, and I'm not talking eyelashes 'ere, my loves, no I'm not.'

'And you should hear his voice.' Ange was positively drooling.

'Like thick Irish cream being poured over your cornflakes,' agreed the hatted one.

'He can pour himself over my cornflakes any day,' Ange growled lustfully, and the two women shared an appreciative sigh, sinking in their chairs under the weight of their lust but then instantly perking as the room hushed itself to welcome the auctioneer on to his podium.

'Hello everybody and welcome. As you can see, we're rather busier than usual today . . .'

Laughter throughout the hall.

'And that's because not only do we have some amazing lots in our auction today, but we also have the team from *Grand Openings* with us.'

A huge cheer echoed.

'And so to give you a bit of spin on today's proceedings, I'm delighted to introduce someone who might be familiar to many of you . . .'

'Tam!' breathed Ange and the hat lady together.

'. . . the one and only Oliver Gold!'

'It's the sidekick.' The two women sighed heavily with disappointment.

'The nice but ugly one,' they said in unison, as Oliver Gold took his turn to welcome everyone to the auction for the cameras.

'He's not ugly,' Nell whispered, rather taken with his spiky brown hair, chipmunk cheeks and cheery smile.

'He is when he's standing next to Tam.'

'Tam?'

'Tam McCavin!' chorused Ange and the lady in the hat, amazed at Nell's ignorance.

At the rather loud mention of his name, several women looked round hopefully.

'He's the presenter, love.' The neighbour proffered the piece of paper she had been clutching; it was a photograph. 'I'm 'oping I might get that signed. Look at 'im; in't he lovely?'

Nell looked at the photograph.

Tall, dark, handsome.

'Lovely,' she muttered unconvincingly, handing the picture back.

'Not your cup of tea, love?' asked the woman, looking surprised.

'Not really, I'm afraid, I prefer my men a bit less . . . conventional.' Nell tried to think of the right word so as not to offend such an avid fan. She obviously hadn't found the right word, because hat lady tutted and turned to show her picture to the woman the other side of her, who made far more appreciative noises and was offered a chocolate toffee eclair in return.

Maud, who had finally found somewhere to park the car, strode into the hall, looking about her for Nell and Ange. That was one good thing about being so tall: it was always easy to spot and be spotted, even in such a crowd.

'Room for a lanky one?' she boomed, spotting a single empty seat further up the row.

Hat lady reluctantly nudged her neighbour and they all shuffled up one so Maud could sit next to Nell.

'Took me an age to find a space. Thought I'd miss the

start. It was scheduled for eleven, wasn't it? What on earth is going on in here?' she demanded loudly, plonking herself down. 'Anyone would think we'd arrived at the circus, not an auction house.'

'Television crew,' Nell explained, pointing to the cameras, who had finished filming Oliver Gold's intro and were getting ready for the auction proper.

'Well, that explains it,' Maud sniffed. 'Some people would do anything just to get their fifteen minutes. Now have you got your paddle, Nell? Did you register? When I came in, the queue at the desk was back to the door.'

'All done.'

'She's number one hundred and twenty-three,' Ange explained, 'which is pretty apt, as my life rule number one hundred and twenty-three is: when you find something in life you really want, no matter how unobtainable you think it might be, you have to go for it.'

'Did you just make that one up to try and boost my confidence?' Nell whispered, as the auctioneer got back on his podium.

'Might have done.'

'Just remember, when it comes to your lot, don't do what people normally do and jump in at the last minute,' Maud told her. 'It's not unheard of for these people to place fake bids to get the property to an artificial level, knowing that someone keen may come in towards the end. Show them you're a strong and determined bidder from the start and it should keep the price in the realms of reality.'

Nell didn't feel strong and determined.

In fact she felt sick.

It didn't help having the television cameras scoping the room like searchlights.

It also didn't help that there were thirty-eight lots in the auction and Ye Olde Tea Shop in Polporth was lot number thirty-three.

By the time her lot came round, Nell's mouth was so dry she had no voice. She was dying for the loo, her butterflies had turned into elephants, and she was certain that everyone else with a paddle had been waiting for the same lot as her.

'You okay?' Ange nudged her. 'Ready to go?'

Nell nodded, and tried to swallow the ball of nausea that had risen in her throat.

'Just keep your head and you'll be fine,' Maud reassured her.

'It's not keeping my head that I'm worried about,' Nell rasped back. 'It's keeping my stomach from climbing out of my throat and sitting on my lap.'

Despite Maud digging her in the ribs with a sharp elbow, Nell was determined not to be the first one to begin the bidding. She also wanted the auctioneer to drop the price below the start-off point, and he wasn't going to do that if she shot her hand up the minute he opened his mouth.

It worked. He got to fifty grand under before someone five rows ahead of Nell stuck their arm in the air.

Ange squeaked in indignation that someone else had had the audacity to bid on Nell's lot. Already in her head the tea rooms were Nell's.

'Quick, stick your paddle up,' she urged Nell. 'Show him he's got competition.'

A camera-shy Nell spent most of her time trying to bid without being spotted, much to the camera crew's disgust, because all they could get in shot was a paddle on the end of an unidentified arm.

Bidding rose steadily, still easily within Nell's budget,

however, and then as it began to slow, a third person joined in.

'Ooh, it's a threesome,' shrieked Ange, bouncing in her seat in excitement and agitation. 'Bugger off, you idiot, you're just going to push the price up for no reason. Do you want me to go and swipe their paddle, Nell, do you—'

Maud reached across and pushed a boiled sweet in Ange's mouth, silencing her momentarily.

'You're doing great, kid,' Maud whispered. 'Keep on as you are, don't let auction fever get you too.'

The third person fell away at two hundred and twenty thousand, but the man who had placed the first bid continued determinedly. Nell, who had almost begun to enjoy herself, felt any vestige of pleasure begin to slip away as the price neared and then hit her set budget with the other bidder in pole position. She allowed herself another four thousand in an attempt to outbid him. Waited a heartbeat that seemed like a lifetime. And then watched in dismay as he outbid her again.

'Back with you, sir . . . Any more bids?' urged the auctioneer.

Ange was choking on her boiled sweet.

Nell raised her paddle again.

Twelve thousand over her budget.

'To the back of the room, now. It's with you. Sir? No? No? Then it's going once, going twice . . .'

Nell held her breath as she waited for the gavel to fall. It was going to be hers, it was going to be hers and then almost in slow motion the man lifted his paddle again.

'And back with you again, sir . . . Any more bids from the back of the room? The bidding sits at two hundred and forty-six thousand. Do I see two forty eight . . .'

Nell hesitated, her mind racing. If she bid again, it

would be eighteen thousand over the budget she had set herself, still well below the guide price as she had hoped, but her books were so finely balanced that it suddenly seemed a step too far, especially if that eighteen thousand pounds were followed by another two, and instead of the end of the bidding this was just the beginning of the real fight. She had seen it happen, bidding fever taking hold, people determined to win at any price. She wanted the tea rooms so badly this could easily happen to her, and if she went too far over her budget then she wouldn't be able to set the place up, or perhaps, heaven forbid, if it didn't take off as she hoped, afford to keep it. She had determined before they arrived at the auction that if she came to this point she would be strong, she would walk away if she had to . . .

Ange grabbed the paddle from Nell and thrusting it in the air yelled, 'Two hundred and fifty thousand!'

The room went quiet.

The auctioneer looked at the other bidder.

Nell, Maud, Ange and the lady in the hat, and the woman beyond her still chewing on a toffee, all held their breath.

Nell's opponent reluctantly shook his head.

And then the gavel fell.

'Sold at two hundred and fifty thousand, to . . . bidder one hundred and twenty-three.'

The camera crew finally got their shot as Nell leapt into the air and screamed with joy.

Lisa, the overworked researcher from *Grand Openings*, watched as the three women practically danced over to the admin desk. She waited until she could see that all of the paperwork had been completed to the auction house's satisfaction, and then, plastering on her best smile, strode over and put a hand on Nell's shoulder.

'Hi there. I'm part of the *Grand Openings* team, and you must be the proud new owner of Ye Olde Tea Shop in Polporth in Cornwall. Congratulations, you must be so pleased. My name's Lisa, by the way.' She held out a hand. 'Lisa Bryant, and you are . . .'

'Er . . . Nell . . .' Nell replied, a little fearful of what might be coming next.

Lisa registered the reluctance in the girl's eyes and forced her smile wider. 'Well, it's lovely to meet you, Nell . . .' She paused again, waiting for Nell to fill in the gap.

'Everson,' Nell squeaked. 'Nell Everson.'

'Well, congratulations again, Nell, a fight well won, don't you think, and what an opportunity for you because I'm absolutely delighted to tell you that the property you've purchased is one of the lots that we've been filming for our programme. Isn't that wonderful? So what we need to do now is just get your permission to carry on filming, with you on board, of course, and you and Ye Olde Tea Shop will be the stars of one of our shows. How great is that?'

As far as Nell was concerned, it was about as great as damp socks and athlete's foot, but before she could quaver a tentative 'Thanks, but I don't think . . .' a familiar Irish drawl cut in with 'Oh my word, that's wonderful, of course you can film, she'd be absolutely delighted.'

'Ange!' Nell hissed harshly and then turned apologetically to the girl with the clipboard.

'Look, I'm sorry, but all of this,' she waved a hand at the cameras, 'it's not really my scene . . .'

'You're kidding, aren't you, Nell?' Ange exclaimed, her face threatening disappointment. 'Think of the publicity this would give you.'

'Oh yes, absolutely, you'd get advertising money

couldn't buy.' Lisa the researcher smiled her brightest, most beguiling smile, a smile that hid her panic. They hadn't yet come across a purchaser who had refused to allow the programme access, and she had to confess that this had made them a little slipshod today. They had already shot the background footage of the tea rooms, and didn't have a back-up in the south-west area for this particular section of the show. If Nell said no, they would have to come back another time, and that wasn't in their schedule or their budget.

'I can promise you, the people who've already been on the show have all said what a wonderful boost it's been to their new businesses.'

'Oh well, yes, it would be, surely.' Ange, quivering at the thought of actually appearing on the show she loved so much, with the man she had lusted after for so long, nodded enthusiastically.

Seeing the desperation in both smiling, hopeful faces, and feeling her resolve begin to crumble, Nell looked round at Maud for help. 'Maud, what do you think? It might be a bit intrusive, mightn't it?'

Maud shrugged. 'Well, everyone has the right to privacy, but I'm sorry, Nell, I have to say Lisa's right, it would be a marvellous boost for the tea rooms as a business. I know it's not what you want to hear, but I think you might regret it if you say no.'

'And I wouldn't get to meet Tam McCavin if you say no either,' Ange pleaded with puppy-dog eyes, 'which *I'd* really regret. Please, Nell, please say you'll do it . . .'

Ange could sense weakness as Nell wavered. 'If I had the power to make it possible for you to meet one of your heroes, do you think I wouldn't do it for you?'

Ange had a point. If Lisa was standing there dangling backstage passes for a U2 concert and Ange was getting sniffy about the fact that she didn't like their music, Nell would be finding it pretty unbearable right now.

'Oh okay, okay, we'll do it.' Nell gave in, not particularly graciously, but Ange didn't care. Nell had said yes, she was going to meet Tam. She hugged Nell and then let out a whoop of utter delight.

Lisa resisted the urge to do the same and thrust pen and paper at Nell before she could change her mind.

'Oh that's wonderful. If you could just sign the release forms for me . . . they're to say that you're happy for us to film when we need to, and to release what footage we think is suitable for the show, and then we need you to do a really short piece to camera with Oliver just asking you a couple of questions, okay? Nothing to worry about, he'll lead you through it, he's a total pro and a total sweetheart . . .'

And with that, Nell was shepherded so speedily that she was in front of the camera before she even had time to blink, and Oliver Gold was asking his opening question.

'So, Nell, you've just won the bidding on our "you'd have to be barking to buy it" lot. How do you feel?'

13

'You'd have to be barking to buy it.'

Nell had never been described as barking before. She'd always been Captain Sensible.

Her eminently sensible parents had drummed it into her from a very young age: work hard, own your own home, set yourself up for life.

Well, now she had bought Ye Olde Tea Shop she could combine the two, work and home.

But had she been insane to buy it?

She'd been torn between hope and despair since the auction.

When she'd woken up this morning, knowing that all the legal side of things had been completed and she could collect the keys, she'd felt a buzz of adrenaline and excitement, but then using them to get into the shop . . . seeing the state of it again . . . She'd already known it was bad, but somehow now she'd been told she was an idiot it seemed even worse.

The camera crew were following her today as well, so despite the fact that the first job was 'Operation Clear, Clean and Cauterise' as Maud had chosen to nickname it, Ange had had her hair done and was wearing her favourite Calvin Klein jeans and a Betty Barclay top, just in case.

Maud, who had arrived with rubber gloves,

disinfectant and her own bucket, had been sent straight home again. She'd had a virus that had really knocked her out for a few days, and although she was feeling better, Nell was damned if she was going to let her run herself back down again by trying to deal with the hurricane of a mess that was Ye Olde Tea Shop. It was a fight, but she finally managed to persuade Maud that she was better off on the sofa with a blanket and a good book than on her knees on the kitchen floor with a scrubbing brush in hand.

Once she had gone, Nell had looked around her at the peeling paint, the broken furniture, the rubbish-strewn floor, the stink of something rotten hanging as heavy on the air as the cobwebs on the ceiling and in every corner, and felt her heart sink.

'I've thought of a new name already,' she morosely told Ange as the camera crew arrived and gingerly picked their way through the debris, noses wrinkling at the smell of sour milk that prevailed throughout. 'Ye Olde Disaster Zone.'

It hadn't seemed so bad when she'd first looked round with Ange and the estate agent; all she could see then was beyond how it was to how it could be, but when the *Grand Openings* director Ella Fitzsimmons arrived, she had been very cutting. She was also minus Tam McCavin, much to Ange's very vocal disappointment. Apparently they were just going to take some shots of the tea shop as it was now, and he would be doing a voice-over with incidental music later. Nell could just picture the music they'd use over that segment, probably something from *Jaws*, or the shower scene from *Psycho*.

Young and extremely attractive, Ella walked around the tea shop with the air of someone who had seen it all before and yet still couldn't quite believe her eyes, and then turned to Lisa, the researcher, and nodded her pleasure. 'Well done. This is perfect. You'd definitely have to be barking to buy this dump.'

Nell closed her eyes in despair.

What had she done?

Even Ange sneaking up behind Ella's back and pretending to stab her with a bread knife didn't bring the smile back to her face.

But then Oliver Gold the cheeky chipmunk co-presenter arrived out of the blue. He wasn't due to be filming, but was holidaying in nearby Did's Bay and had decided to come over and say hi.

He was also a very sweet, genuine man, who had quite clearly remembered Nell's obvious upset when he had said those three magic words to her, 'barking to buy'. In all his time on the *Grand Openings* team, he had never seen someone look so mortified at such a slant being put on their hopes and dreams. He had a huge soft spot himself for Cornwall and holidayed here every year. He could totally understand Nell's desire to make a home and a life for herself here, and had suffered several sleepless nights at the thought that he had played a part in denting her confidence.

After hellos and handshaking with the crew, he made a beeline back to Nell, who was watching shyly from the kitchen.

'It's just a gimmick, you know.'

'What is?'

'The barking-to-buy slot. I think you've made a great decision buying this place.'

'You do?' Nell asked hopefully.

'Absolutely. It may look a total mess at the moment, and that would put an awful lot of people off, but it has such potential, any idiot can see that,' and then he leaned in and whispered conspiratorially, 'Any idiot except the idiots

I work with. Do you know, I'm not blowing my own trumpet here, but I'm the only person on this show who actually knows anything about property, and I think you've made a sound investment. Good luck, Nell.'

When they had all gone, with a sigh that was a mix of relief and not so happy anticipation at the cleaning ahead of her, Nell took some time out and sat down on the floor with her back to the wall, contemplating the dust-laden room with its peeling paint and old-fashioned furniture tarnished from years of neglect that was now her future.

Ange sat down next to her and offered her a bottle of beer.

'Look what I found in my handbag.'

'And most girls just carry lipstick.'

Nell took it and they clinked their bottles together.

'To you,' Ange toasted her, taking a swig from the frothing neck.

Nell waited for her to finish before adding, 'To us.'

'To us,' Ange echoed, 'and to Ye Olde Tea Shop. You know, Ye Olde really doesn't work on something that for you is all brand new. Are you going to change the name?'

'I think I should.'

'Ye Newe Tea Shop,' Ange joked.

Nell smiled and raised her own bottle to her lips.

'Did you ever think you'd end up doing this?'

Nell shook her head. 'Nah, but I never thought I'd end up working in banking and spending five years of my life in a relationship with an idiot either.'

'Another toast, then: no more crap boyfriends and no more bitchy bosses.'

'To both of the above.' Nell raised her drink. 'And to long days in the kitchen making food. Heaven. At least it will be when I've got it cleared and cleaned.'

'We.'

'Sorry?'

'When *we've* got it cleared and cleaned.'

'Oh Ange, thanks.' Nell sighed, leaning her head on her friend's shoulder. 'You don't know how great it is to hear that *we*.'

'You don't think I'd let you do all of this on your own, do you?' Ange leaned her head against Nell's. 'You can pay me in cake. So, now you have the job of your dreams, is next on the list to find the man of your dreams?'

Nell's eyes widened at the thought. 'Well, seeing as I normally dream about Max Beesley, Ewan McGregor and occasionally Tom Cruise, I think that might be a bit of a tall order.'

'Why?' Ange blinked. 'Are you saying you're not good enough for Max Beesley?'

'That's exactly what I'm saying.'

'There are plenty of famous people who've married normal people with normal jobs. We're all human, you know.'

'Yeah, just some more than others. Besides, I'm hardly likely to bump into someone like Max Beesley working in a tea shop in Cornwall, am I?'

'Don't forget you now *own* a tea shop in Cornwall.' Ange nudged her. 'And lots of famous people holiday here. It is quite possible that one day Max Beesley will walk in, come up to your counter and tell you what lovely baps and buns you've got and how he'd love to sink his teeth into them.'

Nell burst out laughing.

'It's not so daft. You're forgetting, Nell, this place might be famous itself soon, once it's been on *Grand Openings*. Talking of which, you're going to have your first famous person through that door any day now.'

'Well, I suppose Tam McCavin has to come and film his bits sometime.' Nell sighed.

'Ooh . . .' Ange pulled a lustful face, 'love that phraseology, Nelly Belly. Wish I could—'

'Don't say it, Ange.' Nell held up a hand to stop her.

'Me and Tam McCavin and a video camera. Would you just picture that?' Ange smacked her lips in appreciation of this thought.

'Celebrities aside, what about you?'

'Me?'

'Man?'

'Ah.' Ange nodded thoughtfully. 'I've been thinking about that. I think I might try and find myself a pirate.'

'A pirate?'

'Ah ha.' Ange nodded, doing an impression of what she thought a pirate might sound like.

Nell laughed. 'I think you've been watching too many Johnny Depp movies.'

'Perhaps, but isn't it nice to dream sometimes?'

'Fantasise more like. Aren't they pretty much extinct now anyway?'

Ange shook her head. 'Bunch of them stole a huge freighter not so long ago. It was on the news and everything.'

'Oh yeah, I remember hearing about that, but it was miles away, Asia or something. I don't think you get pirates in England any more.'

'Sure, but if there are going to be pirates left anywhere on this old island it'll be in Cornwall.'

'Perhaps.'

'Hope so.' Ange grinned lasciviously. 'Think, Nell, all that hair and leather and bad attitude.'

Nell's brow knitted into a puzzled frown. 'Can't see the appeal myself. I know you like a bit of rough, but that's *all* rough. Can you imagine what his breath would be like, all that rum and no toothbrush?'

And then, despite being banished, the door swung open and Maud looked around the edge of it waving a white dishcloth.

'Am I allowed back in if I promise not to try and polish anything?'

She had brought with her a contingent of the LLs all in aprons and sporting matching pink rubber gloves, and once again an awful lot of new hairdos and bright lipstick, obviously hoping the camera crew would still be *in situ*.

'I'm just going to sit in a chair and order people around,' Maud insisted when Nell tried to send her back to bed again. 'Just the tonic I need. Besides, there are several rather elderly people here who will catch my cold quite easily, and you know I always say that the best way to get rid of a cold is to give it to someone else.'

The LL's were raring to go, polish fingers twitching, hoovers revving. There had been some disappointed faces when they realised that the *Grand Openings* team had gone, but they pitched in with gusto none the less.

Nell was so grateful for their help. They were like a Chanel-scented tornado whisking through the tea room, taking the dust and debris with them, restoring order from the chaos.

After five hours, what was once a homage to dirt was now a sparkling advert for clean. Things Nell had thought were too dulled ever to be revived shone as brightly as the sun, which had emerged for the afternoon.

As they collapsed in the rickety chairs gratefully drinking restorative tea, a small scream escaped the lips of the youngest LL, the pretty and prettily named Maris, who had unfortunately married a man called Mr Piper. She shrieked in a very girlie fashion, and then instantly covered her mouth with her hand and flushed with embarrassment as the man who had caused this commotion by sticking his head around the door winked at her broadly.

It was Oliver Gold come back again, looking for Nell.

'I forgot my jacket, which in itself is not the end of the world, but it just happens to have all my worldly goods in the pocket, which at this precise moment in time include wallet, holiday cottage front door key, and most important of all, bag of dog biscuits. By the way,' he added, as a hairy face pushed its way past his knees, 'this is the disgruntled owner of said dog biscuits, Boris. Is he allowed in, because I think he's decided he's coming anyway.'

Boris the dog was as funny looking and funnily endearing as his master, as round as a barrel, with stumpy legs and the ugliest and yet sweetest face Ange had ever seen on a dog. She had to literally put her hand over her mouth to stop the comparison jokes coming out in floods.

But despite this, he was soon feeling the warmth of the fussing hands of an awful lot of women, as the LLs surrounded him making ooh and aah noises.

Oliver watched him with affectionate envy. 'Boris has this effect everywhere he goes,' he told Nell. 'Just wish some of it would rub off on me, but all I ever get is stray dog hairs. And this is why he's so tubby,' he added as Maris fed Boris half a scone. 'Women just seem to want to feed him up.'

'He's very cute. What is he?'

'A dog.' Oliver nodded wisely.

'What kind of dog?' Nell grinned, resisting the urge to stick her tongue out at him.

'A very lucky one.' Oliver sighed as Ange knelt down to fuss Boris and he pushed his big brown head eagerly into her cleavage.

'Oh, I'm sure she'd let you do that if you asked her nicely.'

When they had finally finished fussing Boris, the LLs were reluctantly shepherded away by Maud.

'We've got to go, darling. Fund-raiser tonight,' she said to Nell. 'Sponsored sleepover at the wild fowl sanctuary; they're trying to raise money to build a new pond.'

'Don't you overdo things.'

'I'm being given money for charity to go to sleep . . . not exactly strenuous . . .'

They were closely followed by Oliver, who collected his jacket, and said reluctant goodbyes.

Only to return minutes later.

His taxi had gone.

'I did ask him to wait, but I don't suppose he reckoned on Boris adding a few more members to the fan club. I've been a bit longer than I thought I'd be.' And then he simply shrugged. 'Oh well, fate steps in. Don't suppose you girls fancy coming down to that pub in the harbour for a drink with me? A holiday on my own to recharge the old batteries seemed like a good idea at the time, but a man can only cope with so many roaring fires and bottles of wine with just a farting dog for company.'

'Sounds good to me.' Nell nodded. 'Ange? Do you want to go to the pub?'

'Are Barbie's boobs plastic?'

'Jolly Rogering it is then.' Nell nodded enthusiastically, and then, as Oliver started to look too keen, added quickly, 'Sorry, that's the pub, not an offer.'

'Although the night is still young,' Ange added with a wink, taking his arm.

They started off in the Jolly Roger but they didn't stay there long.

Marge was in one of her moods.

As soon as they walked in, Tony Junior spotted them and started pointing at his stepmother and making cutting motions across his throat with his hand. London Tony was quivering in the cellar doorway, balanced on one big foot on the tiny top step, obviously poised for flight, and the twins and Beth were nowhere to be seen.

'I'll put up with her moods when I'm working,' Ange whispered, looking both narked and fearful at the same time, 'but I don't have to when I'm not. Shall we go somewhere else?'

'There's a nice pub near my cottage,' Oliver suggested.

'Are you inviting us back to see your etchings?'

'Unfortunately I don't actually have any etchings, but Boris has a rather fine collection of rubber balls if you want to see those.' He grinned, and Ange burst out laughing.

'Rubber balls, eh? I once had a boyfriend with a pair of those. Definitely over to Did's Bay, then. Shall we taxi?'

Nell shook her head. 'I'll drive. I can't get drunk tonight, I'm starting on the flat tomorrow and I don't want to struggle through cleaning that with a hangover.'

With Oliver and Ange in the back and Boris riding shotgun with his head out of the car window and his tongue lolling out of his mouth, they drove the winding coast road to Did's Bay. It was smaller than Polporth but just as quaint, and despite the fact that it was half the size it actually had two pubs instead of just the one: the Drunken Monk, which was down by the beach in an old fish factory and was more like a cellar bar, and the Fisherman's Arms, further up in the village, which was a proper village pub.

Having heard that the Drunken Monk could get a bit wild, they decided to go to the Fisherman's Arms, where they found Beth and the twins hiding out in the bar, the twins ensconced in a far corner, chatting to a friend.

'What are you doing here?'

'Same as you, probably. Did you go in the Roger?'

'Went in and came straight out again.'

Beth nodded, her lips pursing. 'Poor old Dad. He's a total martyr to Marge's moods.'

'The Martyr and the Tartar,' mused Nell. 'Hey, maybe you should change the name of the pub.'

'Maybe Dad should change his wife,' Beth muttered, looking guilty as she said it.

'Why did your dad marry Marge? He's such a sweetheart,' added Ange, ordering drinks.

Beth sighed heavily. 'To be honest, I think he was on the rebound from Mum. He really loved her and she broke his heart when she left; he was like this big old mess of blancmange someone had dropped on the floor, and Marge kind of came along and scooped him up and put him back together again. She was so good to him when he really needed someone. And I have to say that she was good to me and TJ too, fierce maybe, strict, no hugs or cuddles, but she did all the proper stuff like making sure you did your homework and ironing school uniforms and always making sure there was a decent meal on the table. I think she just used up all her sweetness and light fixing him. It took a long time, you know.'

'Oh, poor Tony,' sympathised Nell.

'I think she's always felt second best,' Beth continued with a shrug and a wry smile. 'More like cook, cleaner, babysitter than wife. He loves her, but he's not really *in love* with her, and that's what she wanted more than anything.'

'Oh, poor Marge.' Nell switched camps, her own heart breaking at the thought of being in love with someone who could only give you a little bit of their heart back. 'How awful. I don't think I could be in a relationship like that. I know it's a bit idealistic, but I really want someone who's going to be head over heels in love with me and me with them.'

'Yeah,' Beth nodded, 'everyone wants the cliché, don't they, comes from having Cinderella and Sleeping Beauty rammed down your throat when you're little.'

Oliver shook his head. 'I don't think it's just the influence of fairy stories. I can hardly say that my mum and dad read me to sleep every night with tales of love and romance, and yet I'm still looking for someone special to share my life with . . . the yin to my yang . . .'

'Every Barbie has her Ken,' agreed Beth, smiling shyly at him.

'There's just something in all of us that from an early age feels the need to find someone else to complete them, that perfect partner, The One,' Nell said.

The three of them sighed.

'Utter cobblers,' Ange tutted, knocking back her cider. 'Anyone want another one?'

'You don't believe there's someone out there for all of us?' Nell queried in surprise.

'Of course not. The thought that just *one* man could make me happy beggars belief really. This one special person, and if I don't find him I'll never truly be happy? Just setting yourself up for a fall, really . . .'

'That's so cynical.' Beth pouted.

'Not cynical, just realistic. What if your one special person lives in Outer Mongolia or something?'

'Then fate would step in,' Beth said, closing her eyes dreamily.

'That's so sweet,' Oliver said with the same expression on his face, only it wasn't aimed at the ceiling; it was aimed at Beth.

'If you want something, you can't just leave it to fate, or you could be waiting for ever.' Ange, who was convinced that you made your own destiny, was horrified at the thought. 'I'm sure there are loads of people out there who give up waiting, and settle, or who marry someone they think is The One to start off with and after a while realise that they're the one they want to divorce, or the one they want to strangle and dump in the river, and if you think of the logistics of it, it would be so hard to meet The One that there would be tons of unhappy relationships out there . . .'

She trailed off when she realised that all three of them were looking at her as if she'd just proved their point for them.

'That's the thing, Ange, there are, that's what started this whole conversation: Tony and Marge.'

'They're not unhappy.' Ange shrugged.

'They're not totally happy either,' Beth said.

'And Beth would know.' Nell backed her up.

'Sure, but isn't not being unhappy quite good in a world where misery prevails? Why does everyone have to strive for the ultimate best of everything? Why can't we all settle for a bit of mediocre and be happy with that, hence lots more people being happy just because they're trying less hard to be happy.'

Now Nell knew that Ange was just toying with them.

'Go and get the drinks, idiot.'

'Idiot?' Ange pretended to look hurt. 'I remember a time when you were so polite to me I'm surprised you didn't call me Miss O'Donel.'

'That was the old Nell. Doormat Nell. Now the only thing matt about me is the paint on the tea shop walls!' Nell joked.

'Hear, hear!' everyone chorused, crashing empty glasses together.

'You know that was very sincere, but it would have worked better if these actually had some alcohol in them,' said Beth, peering into her empty glass.

'Hear, hear again!' said Nell. 'Miss O'Donel, it's your shout: to the bar with you, post-haste!'

An hour later, the twins had left to join the rowdier crowd at the Drunken Monk and Nell, Ange, Beth and Oliver were comfortably ensconced in a seat in the bay window, eating pork scratchings. Oliver was regaling them with scurrilous stories about Z-list celebrities, Beth rapt with attention.

Ange, noticing the way she was looking up at Oliver like a spaniel gazing at her master, nudged Nell.

'Is she star-struck or do you think she just fancies him?'

'Both.' Nell nodded. 'She told me in the loos that she thinks he's really cute; she said he reminds her of Mark Owen.'

'Beer goggles!' Ange rolled her eyes.

'She doesn't need those.' Nell shook her head. 'He's a real sweetie.'

'Yes, my lovely Nell, he is, but is that what you want from a man?'

'It's better than an ignorant, egotistical arsehole.'

'Oh, absolutely, but tell me this, do you find Oliver sexy?'

'I think Beth does.'

'Sure, but do you? Don't you want a man in your life that you just look at and go, *Phwooar!*'

'Sure I do, but that fades after a while anyway. Isn't it better to get someone you'll actually *like* after a few years, when the sexual magic is down to a sprinkling of fairy dust rather than a whole wand with a phoenix feather?'

'Contrary to popular belief, desire doesn't have to fade with time, you know. You can actually have a long-term relationship with someone and still want to bonk them after you've spent a few years together. For example, attractive man at six o'clock.'

Nell dutifully followed Ange's direction.

'Yeah, I have to admit he's attractive.' She nodded her agreement.

'Sure.' Ange nodded. 'But that's not enough. Now let me see . . .' She began to scour the room. 'Ah yes, attractive *and* sexy man at ten o'clock . . .'

'What?' Nell, who wasn't sure where Ange was going with this, had bent down to feed some pork scratchings to a slavering Boris. As Ange didn't actually reply, Nell had no choice but to look up and follow her gaze again, and much to Boris's waggy-tailed delight she dropped the whole bag on the floor.

There was a group of men at the bar. They were all pretty tasty, actually, so Nell wasn't sure which one Ange was referring to, but just as she was about to ask, she saw him.

And that was when she dropped the pork scratchings.

Ange, who had actually been pointing out someone else entirely, saw Nell's jaw literally drop, and suddenly had to hand it to fate after all. Lust at first sight, not quite as rare as love, but still good going for something she didn't actually set much store by.

And then he glanced over and caught Nell watching him, and for a moment he looked straight back at her, and rather than turning away in embarrassment, it was as if both their gazes were trapped, locked within the other, and they had to keep on looking, and then he smiled at her, slowly, almost in wonder, and Nell actually managed a glimmer of a smile back before letting her face drop and her hair fall in front of it to hide her.

Ange watched her with a knowing smile on her face, and counted the heartbeats in her head, *one, two, three*. And then on cue Nell looked back up and he was still looking, and her smile widened and she laughed, and so did he, and then as if by mutual agreement they both turned back to the people they were with, and Ange just knew that they would immediately want to talk about each other to them.

'Oh my God, Ange, is that the guy you meant?' Nell was almost breathless.

Ange wasn't going to lie to her. 'Well, he wasn't actually the one I was pointing out to you as my example of fit *and* sexy, but he bloody well should have been. You should have seen your face . . .'

Nell immediately covered it with her hands.

'Did *he* see my face?'

'Course he did. Why do you think he was smiling at you?'

'He was smiling, wasn't he? It wasn't laughing, was it?'

'Well, he's looking over again, so judge for yourself.'

It was a definite smile. A gorgeous, sexy smile on a gorgeous, sexy face.

And then her view was obscured by the barmaid, who had come to the table to collect their empty glasses. She tried to look round her, only for the girl to move again, and short of shouting to get out of the way, Nell could do nothing but wait for her to leave.

But what Nell saw as obstruction, Ange saw as opportunity.

She put a friendly hand on the barmaid's arm. 'You see that man over there?'

The girl nodded, guarded.

'Well, my friend fancies him . . .'

Nell choked on her drink and tried to hide behind a bar menu.

'. . . so we want to know who he is, what he does, where he lives, in fact absolutely everything we can possibly find out about him.'

The barmaid's eyes narrowed. 'His name's Hal. Anything else you want to know I think you'd better ask him yourself, don't you?'

Two minutes later, Nell fell out of the front door, laughing, mortified.

'My friend fancies him . . . What are we, Ange, twelve?' Nell gasped, as Ange followed her out.

'Well, you don't ask, you don't get.'

'And we didn't get. Did you see that woman's face!'

'I know.'

'Maybe she fancies him too!' Nell shrieked with laughter.

'So you're not denying it, then?'

Nell attempted to look coy, and then just gave up and shrugged.

'What the hell . . . He's gorgeous, Ange. Yes, your friend fancies him.'

'You're full of surprises, Miss Everson.'

'I'm surprising myself. I'm normally a personality-first kind of girl, and I don't even know him.'

'But you'd like to get to know him?' Ange asked, already planning to drag Nell back in and make her go over.

But Nell's attention was directed elsewhere, over Ange's shoulder, back at the pub.

'Talking of getting to know someone . . .' she squeaked, beginning to grin again.

She indicated through the illuminated window by which they had been sitting, where they could clearly see Beth and Oliver still at the table, kissing.

'Well, at least someone's pulled,' Ange announced in delight.

And then the front door of the pub swung open, letting out the light and the laughter and the music, and also the group of men who had been standing at the bar, one of whom had so captured Nell's attention.

They were heading for the car park, and as they passed, smiles were exchanged by all until he and Nell drew level, and he almost stopped but not quite, hovering, like the negative side of a magnet above metal.

'Hi,' he said.

'Hi,' Nell repeated.

And then both Ange and his companions started laughing knowingly.

'Aren't you going to ask her if she comes here often?' called back a wag getting into an Audi.

'Oh, it's our first time, but I think we'll definitely be back,' Ange called back with a come-hither smile on Nell's behalf, as Nell herself was looking a little bit like a kitten trying to hide under a car.

'Fisherman's Arms virgins!' yelled the wag in the sports car.

The guy glanced over at his loud friend and shook his head apologetically. 'Sorry,' he said, and when he smiled, Nell noticed it went to his eyes. Which were a greenish grey. A gorgeous greenish grey, with little lines at the sides that crinkled when he smiled.

'No worries,' she managed to murmur back.

'Well, bye.'

'Bye then.'

'See you again . . .'

Nell nodded, no longer actually able to speak.

Ange looked at her in amazement. She had never seen a man have this effect on Nell. Not even Marcus when they were in their loved-up stage.

'Want to follow them?' she asked as the men got into two cars and drove off, a distinctly lingering backwards glance coming from the passenger seat of the Audi, where the man with the grey-green eyes was sitting.

Nell nodded firmly. 'Of course not.'

'But you just nodded.'

'My head's being an idiot, my mouth's being sensible. What's just happened to me, Ange? I feel like someone's just rewired me so everything works backwards.'

'I think it's what you call lust, Nelly Belly. The point I was trying to make in the pub so beautifully illustrated and with such perfect timing too.'

'I think maybe it's best if we just go home, you know. I suddenly have this strange desire to lie down . . .'

Ange banged on the window and made driving motions at Beth, who was still kissing Oliver. She opened her eyes long enough to give a thumbs-up, and wave them to go without her.

'Jolly Rogering it is after all then for the lovely Oliver.'

'She wouldn't.' Nell shook her head. 'He's lovely, but she barely knows him.'

'Sometimes, my friend,' Ange said happily, slinging an arm around Nell's shoulders and helping her back to Cyril, 'that's the best way.'

15

When Nell woke up the following morning, she could still see his face.

Even when she had her eyes tight shut in embarrassment at the memory of how like a gauche schoolgirl meeting him had made her.

She couldn't even blame it on the alcohol because she hadn't actually had any.

She had acted like an idiot because she was one.

But he had been just her type. She'd never really known what her type was before, but now she knew exactly.

Short brown hair, a little bit pepper and salt, but in a way that really suited him, strong face, broad shoulders, firm thighs, eyes that sparkled with light and laughter.

Nell was almost drooling in the way she did when she was thinking up new recipes.

What had the barmaid said his name was?

'Dream of Al last night?' was the first thing Ange asked at breakfast.

Al, that was it, Nell mused, and Ange immediately laughed, not at Nell, but at how amazing it was to see her friend so blindsided by her emotions.

Ange dragged her back to the pub that evening, but apart from the extremely unfriendly barmaid, there were no familiar faces, and Nell certainly wasn't going to ask her if she thought that her mystery man with the grey-green eyes and the seriously sexy smile might be back any time soon.

It was a good job she had the tea shop to keep her occupied.

The clean-up downstairs had been in preparation for Nell's team of workmen to move in and start the refit, and it was currently going full steam ahead.

Her plans to move into the flat above the tea shop as soon as possible had been thwarted somewhat, however, by the fact that the flat itself had been completely wrecked by the squatters, who had quite literally pitched a tent in the middle of the sitting room, and then, because all the power was disconnected, lit themselves a campfire outside the tent flap to light their evenings and over which to cook their supper.

'It used to be so lovely up here,' Maud sighed, kicking at the charred floor with the toe of her wellington boot. 'Claire and Elizabeth had it set up like a Moroccan kasbah, with beautiful silks and cushions and rugs, Claire's paintings, Elizabeth's pottery . . . They used to have music and poetry evenings, where everyone was encouraged to contribute with verse or song . . .' Maud's eyes fluttered shut as the evocative power of memories took over from real life.

'If you breathe in deep you can still catch a faint whiff of patchouli oil.' Ange winked at Nell.

'Maybe we should have a music and poetry evening,' Nell mused, trying to picture from Maud's imagery.

'Yeah, you playing the mixing spoons and Maud on the maracas whilst I recite Irish drinking songs,' Ange chortled.

Maud's eyes snapped open. 'You may mock, but I had some of my best times in this flat.'

'That's nice to know, Auntie Maud.' Nell slipped an arm through her godmother's. 'Makes me feel more at home here.'

'It's strange to think that you'll be living here now.'

'Strange odd or strange odd but good?'

'Strange odd but good.'

'There once were two girls from the city,' began Ange with a wicked smile, 'who moved into a flat that was shitty, had an evening of song, with a beer and a bong—'

'And some bad poetry more's the pity,' cut in Maud, slipping her free arm through Ange's. 'Come on, girls, let's go and have some supper. We'll worry about tackling this flea pit tomorrow.'

In a way, it was nice not to have to leave Maud's. They were both more than comfortable there, Nell in her childhood and teenage angst room, Ange in the first room she had had to herself since, well, for ever. Ange was particularly fascinated by the view of the sea from her bedroom window. She had been a city girl her entire life; even when she lived in Dublin she was on the wrong side of the city to see any water.

Nell did, however, recognise the fact that the tea rooms would be up and running far more quickly if she were on site to chivvy the workforce and take deliveries, and as nice as it was, she couldn't languish at Maud's for ever.

Getting the flat cleaned was slow going without the LLs to help out, but they managed it between the three of them, Nell a constant, the other two fitting shifts of scrubbing between work and play and other commitments.

'I don't have a life,' Nell chastised herself one evening as the other two departed, Ange to work at the pub, Maud to drink at it, having a long-standing date with a male friend who lived further up the coast.

Her evening ahead was filled to the brim with the exciting prospect of painting her bedroom.

'I have a date with a paintbrush,' she announced, trying to feel and look forlorn about this fact, but when she actually got in to her room with her pot of Dulux Polar Flame and her brushes and rollers, she couldn't help but smile.

It was a tip at the moment, the same as the rest of the place, but it had two sash windows overlooking the edge of the cove and the hillside up to Maud's, not that she could see Maud's cottage, but it was a lovely view. It also had a real fireplace. Nell had always wanted a bedroom with a real fireplace, even if it was one that needed rubbing down, repainting, retiling and by the looks of things a bloody good sweep too.

But she wasn't put off by the seeming enormity of the task; in fact it only served to spur her on. Nell's previous job had all been about projected this and forecasted that; to actually see what she was achieving with her own hard work brought her huge pleasure, and so she worked like a maniac, hardly stopping for a break or to sleep or eat.

By the time Maud and Ange came back to join her the following evening, Ange to tackle the woodwork with her gloss white, Maud determined to re-cement the open fire in the sitting room, Nell had finished her bedroom, and then, feeling invigorated by how good it looked, had set to and sanded and buffed the wooden floors throughout the entire flat.

She'd done a brilliant job, although even when she had finished you could still see faint charring in the middle of the sitting room where the squatters' fire had been.

Nell had spent three hours working diligently on that part of the room.

Maud watched her scrutinising this one blemish with a faint smile on her lips.

She knew what Nell was like. The rest of the floor looked amazing, but this one flaw would have to go, even if it meant taking up the whole floor she had just spent a day working on.

'She's going to have that up before you can say DIY.' Maud nodded to Ange.

'Do you think? She's chilled out a bit since we've been living in Cornwall.'

'Sure,' Maud conceded. 'But is a bit enough?'

'Tenner on it?'

'Deal.'

They shook.

After surveying it for another five minutes, Nell turned to Maud and Ange, who were staring at her as hard as she'd been staring at the floor.

'I'll buy a rug,' she eventually announced, and as she walked past Ange and Maud, she leaned in and stage-whispered to Ange, 'And you can buy me a drink with that tenner you just won.'

When the day actually came to move, Nell was reluctant to leave Maud. Her flu had lingered and suddenly the self-titled tartar seemed very vulnerable.

'It's so easy to forget how old she actually is,' Nell had sighed to a sympathetic Ange.

Unfortunately Maud had overheard this comment and taken total umbrage. By the time she had finished raging at them about age being totally relative, Nell and Ange had packed everything into the back of Cyril Junior and escaped down to the flat above the tea shop with a sigh of relief.

Maud had watched them wheel-spin away from her wrath down the road, blown her nose into her thousandth tissue and allowed her furious frown to segue smoothly into a self-satisfied smile.

That was the thing with youngsters nowadays: sometimes they just needed a little push along the right path. And the right path was certainly not hanging around her place because they thought she would suddenly fade away without them.

Maud had lived alone for long enough to be able to manage quite well without them, thank you.

Not that she wouldn't miss them.

But it wasn't as if she was going to melt into a heap of sodden loneliness now that they were gone, despite the fact that this was what Nell was so obviously worried about.

That girl thought too much about others.

Sometimes in life you had to be selfish.

Nell's parents had taught her to be practical and thoughtful and obedient, and yet hadn't taught her that sometimes it was okay to put herself first, to take as much care of herself as she would afford to others.

It was only when Nell returned several hours later with a timid smile and a bottle of Maudlyn's favourite single malt whisky, purely for medicinal purposes of course, and was greeted with a radiant beam and her usual hug that she realised Maud's cunning, but of course by then it was too late. Maud had achieved her aim, and Nell and Ange had been booted from the nest they had grown a little too accustomed to over the past few weeks.

Maud just hoped and prayed they now had the brains and the stamina to spread their wings and fly.

Nell actually slept like a log the first night in her new flat, aided perhaps by the one and a half bottles of champagne she and Ange had sunk between them to celebrate, but it was undoubtedly one of those places that had a great feel to it, warm and welcoming.

Nell's room was all fresh and light and New England, with a touch of shabby chic in the embroidered bedspread and the painted gauze curtains.

Ange had painted her room dark purple and stuck a fake-fur throw on her bed.

Like the two girls, the two rooms couldn't have been more different.

Both had wondered if moving in together properly would change the dynamic of their friendship, but all they had found thus far was that they shared an even stronger sense of camaraderie. Although they had only had one night so far at the flat, sharing a bathroom with Ange at Maud's had already been a revelation for Nell, one that would in ancient times have been heralded by the prophets of doom, rather the blithe spirits bringing joyful tidings, but still, a bathroom share with Ange, no matter how dire, was better than an office share with Nasty Nicolette any day.

And a flat share with Ange . . . well, Nell had a feeling it would be anything but boring. But the best thing that Nell had found since moving down to Polporth was that she had stopped hunting desperately for a better future, and was actually beginning to allow herself to enjoy the present.

It took another two and a half weeks to get the tea rooms ready for opening. The delay was mainly down to the fact that Nell had chosen to replace the old chiller cabinet serving counter with a new one, as they had discovered that this was the source of the sour milk smell, and that no amount of scrubbing would make it disappear.

But finally the walls were repainted, the broken tables and chairs replaced, the kitchen equipment updated and the loos refitted, and they had a beautiful blank and spotlessly clean canvas upon which to work some tea-room magic.

'I want the room itself to look good enough to eat,' Nell had announced, upon pulling a swathe of material covered in cherry print from one of the trunks in Maud's attic, and having a flash of inspiration. So the tea cups were painted with cupcakes, and the proper china teapots were designed to look like fat round puddings, the lids the custard or the icing and the little round knobs on top in the shape of strawberries or cherries or sweet little knobbly raspberries. The sugar bowls looked like fairy cakes.

They were absolutely gorgeous. They had been Nell's idea, and after hunting high and low to find something she thought suited, she had commissioned a local potter to make them for her. Everyone loved them so much, Ange had suggested that they sell them in the shop, and so the old wooden dresser they had inherited with the place had been scrubbed up and turned into somewhere to display them.

'See,' Ange had said proudly, throwing an arm around Nell's shoulder, 'you're already diversifying.'

As a final touch, Ange had gathered driftwood from the beach, which she placed on the deep slate window ledges, and then Nell had added fir cones and fat cream candles. Little tea lights in coloured glasses were scattered on the tables. Although everything clashed it worked wonderfully in a shabby chic kind of way, but the overall theme of the room was uniform: it had ended up appropriately enough being food.

The whole effect was far removed from Nell's original vision of sleek and contemporary, but it had a warm and welcoming feel to it, like the comfortable sitting room of a favourite aunt who couldn't decide if she was old fashioned or trendy. Come to think of it, it looked rather like Maud's sitting room minus the clutter; perhaps this was something to do with the fact that most of the items in the room had been borrowed from Maud's house.

Nell stood, hands on hips, head on side, and surveyed their handiwork.

'What do you think? Is it too chichi?'

'Wasn't that a giant panda?' Anged teased. 'It looks great, mate,' she said, hugging her sideways. 'There's only one problem that I can see.'

'What have I missed?'

'A name. You're not sticking with Ye Olde, are you?'

'Well, that wasn't the plan, but I might have to, seeing as I haven't come up with anything else. Don't suppose you've got any ideas?'

'Nelly's Deli?' Ange suggested.

'We're not exactly a delicatessen.'

'You're going to sell stuff, aren't you?'

'Apart from the pottery? The odd pot of home-made jam, and if I'm feeling adventurous I might even try some chutney.'

'Well, you already sell cakes. You could do Maud's honey, some home-made pasties, add in some olives and some cheese and you're almost there . . . oh, and bread, you could make your own bread too.'

'I rather like the idea of the bread and olives and stuff, but I'm afraid the name's not doing it for me.'

'You can't have a place without a name.'

'I know.' Nell frowned.

'With me working here sometimes, you could call it Hot Stuff.' Ange grinned, plumping up her cleavage. 'Don't you just love double entendres?'

'Prefer double vodkas.' Nell winked. 'How about Pastyche.'

'Clever.' Ange nodded in admiration.

'Too clever,' Nell backtracked.

'Cream Tease.'

'Good but terrible all at the same time.'

'A bit like eating a whole Easter egg in one go . . . Sweet Tarts?'

'Almost as awful but not quite. How about if I just hang a couple of cupcakes outside, you know like a pawnbroker's balls. You don't need a name when you have a sign like that.'

'Yes, everyone knows what a pair of balls stands for.' Ange sniggered. 'Hey, how about hanging a pair of old tarts instead?'

'Okay, so let's forget that idea. Moving swiftly on . . .' Nell grabbed a piece of paper and a pen. Sitting down at one of the tables, she scribbled quickly and then held it out to Ange.

'Here you go, this is the final decision.'

Ange beamed in surprise. 'You mean you've actually come up with something?' She reached out for the paper.

Nell watched her deflate with disappointment as she read what was on the other side.

'Ye Olde Tea Shop. Oh Nell, I thought we'd agreed that change is a good thing.'

'Well, I think I might be changed out at the moment, 'cause I can't think of anything better. If it was good enough for this place for the last twenty years, it'll do for me for now.'

Ange's frown deepened.

'And at least I don't have to pay out for a new sign.'

'Oh well, if we're talking good business sense here instead of total lack of imagination, then that's totally acceptable.' Ange rolled her eyes. 'Talking of being totally acceptable, are your parents coming down for the opening party?'

Nell almost visibly whitened at the question. 'I doubt it.'

'You're kidding, aren't you? This is your big day. Don't tell me they turned you down.'

Nell bit her bottom lip and looked guilty.

'I dare say they might have if I'd actually told them about it.'

'You haven't told them? I can't believe that, Nell, and you're normally so up front and honest about everything . . .' Ange teased.

'Don't start. As far as Justin's concerned you're still engaged, but you haven't seen him for two months.'

'Okay, so maybe I'm a big fat pot calling you out, but I'm going to do it anyway. Justin is a little tiny corner of my life that is filled with dirt and cobwebs. At the moment I'm ignoring it, but one day very soon it'll be swept out and away. Your parents are another matter entirely. No matter what happens in life, they will always be your mum and dad and there's nothing you can do about that.'

'Don't remind me.'

'You don't fool me; you love 'em to bits, we both know that.'

'I know. Doesn't mean they don't drive me round the bend, though, and you know that, so why are you asking?'

'Rule of life number forty-three: don't allow hypocrisy in others, but it's bloody useful for yourself.'

Nell shook her head and laughed, as she did every time Ange mentioned her life rules. She was certain she only told her about them to make her smile, and she was also certain that she made them up as she went along. Sometimes Nell felt like writing them all down to see if Ange could remember them, or if she sometimes overlapped or changed them to suit.

'I don't want them to know just yet, and that's that as far as I'm concerned.'

'Ooh, Nell's standing up for herself, fabulous. Life rule number one hundred and seventy-eight: if you think you're right, hold your ground. Proud of you, Nell. Right, so I'm staying out of it, but what about Maud?'

'She won't tell if I ask her not to. She knows what they're like. Do you know,' Nell frowned, 'in a way I'd really like them to come, but I'd feel far worse if they did come and spent the whole time telling me what an idiot I've been for jacking in my job and buying a business that will really only trade in the summer months. And if I don't tell them I had an opening party they won't feel like they've missed out.'

'Ignorance and bliss?'

'Exactly. And they'd give Maud grief too, and she doesn't need that. They've already been on the phone chastising her for luring me down here.'

'They blame Maud? That's not fair.'

'I know. They don't really approve of her "influence" over me. Me being here, well, in their minds I've gone over to the dark side.'

'In that case, can you use the force to come up with a name for this place?'

'I think I might delegate that one.'

'Who to?'

Nell smiled hopefully at Ange.

'Me?'

Nell nodded.

Ange looked doubtful. 'You haven't exactly been impressed with anything I've come up with so far.'

'I always think you should give people a second chance,' Nell joked.

'Um, okay. How about . . . Nice Baps! No, I can see by your face you don't like that one. Let me see . . . mmm . . . yes, I know, what about Firm Buns?'

'I can see a theme emerging here, Ange.'

'Okay, okay, serious head on.' Ange bit her lip as she tried to think. After at least three minutes of agonising silence, she blew out a sigh. 'No, sorry, it's been so long since I used my serious head that it's not actually working any more.'

'Well, Ye Olde it is then.'

'No!' Ange wailed. 'Anything's better than that; not Ye Olde, anything but Ye Olde.'

'Then come up with something better, otherwise Ye Olde Tea Shop it is,' Nell teased.

'Okay,' Ange said defiantly. 'I'm going to brainstorm here so they're just going to come raining over you like a hailstorm. Are you ready? CupCakes, Tea Cups, D Cups, Old Tarts, Tickle Your French Fancies, Fondle Your Fondants, Butter Your Baps . . .'

'Oh shut your cakehole, Ange.' Nell guffawed with laughter, walloping Ange over the head with a cherry-print seat cushion.

Then they both fell silent and looked at each other.

And they both began to grin as they realised they'd just found the perfect name. 'The Cakehole.' Nell sighed happily and a delighted Ange nodded her approval.

17

'I think your godmother's got herself a toy boy,' Ange announced at breakfast the next morning.

'That's nice,' said Nell.

Ange blinked in surprise at how unfazed Nell was by this announcement.

'I'm being serious. I've seen this bloke heading up the cliff road quite a few times since we moved out. The lane only leads to Maud's house, doesn't it? Well, I've seen the same car going up there at least twice this week, and three times last week as well.'

'What car?' Nell asked, wondering if she too might have spotted something. After all, she wouldn't put anything past Maud, not even having a toy-boy lover.

'This posh silver jeep-type thing. I think it might have been one of those really big BMWs.'

'No.' Nell shook her head. 'Not seen it myself.'

'Well I have, yesterday being the last time. I popped back up to raid the attic, 'cause I saw this fabulous forties dress up there when you were looking for material for the tablecloths and I was going to ask Maud if I could recycle it, and he was driving down the lane, and when I went in and asked who it was that had been there she said it was the gardener. Maud hasn't got a gardener, has she?'

'Hence the toy-boy theory?'

Ange nodded, grinning.

'Well she did say something to me about having someone in to help out occasionally. The garden's got a bit much for her recently.'

'Sure, but did you ever see a gardener when we were staying there?'

Nell shook her head. 'No, but we were there to help then.'

'Maybe so, but have you ever seen a gardener who wore a suit to work before?'

'You saw him?'

'Only from a distance and through a car windscreen. But it definitely looked like a suit and tie job, and it was a pretty posh car for a humble dirt-digger. Those aren't the things that made me most suspicious about the gardener story, though. It was the fact that half an hour later she was telling me he was the plumber.'

'Well, that would explain the flash car, the amount plumbers charge . . . Hang on a minute, did she say he was the gardener or the plumber?'

'That's what I'm saying, Nell, she said both, you know, at different times: told me he was the gardener and then later said something about him fixing her pipes. Which is why I came to the toy-boy conclusion, because why lie about anything else?'

Nell nodded. 'What is she up to?'

'So you agree she's up to something?'

'She normally is.'

'Maybe he's not for her, and she's actually lining *you* up a new man,' Ange suggested, smiling lasciviously at the thought.

Nell wasn't so impressed. 'I've only just got shot of the old one!'

'You don't want another?'

'I'm not exactly saying that,' Nell replied, thinking of the gorgeous and yet still maddeningly elusive Al, who despite the fact that Ange and Nell had been to the Fisherman's three times since had yet to be seen again.

'Well, if you don't want him, can I have him?'

'I thought you wanted to find yourself a pirate, not a gardener.'

'Oh, I could take a Mellors if a Jack Sparrow doesn't show.'

'Can I suss him out first and then decide if I want to pass him on to you?'

'Your leftovers, eh?' Ange grinned.

'Actually no. From what you're saying, he's Maud's leftovers . . .'

'So you'd go with the toy-boy theory?'

'I wouldn't actually put it past her, to be honest. She has been out with much younger guys before.'

'In that case, what we need to find out is whether Maud is the kind of girl who'll share her toys,' Ange joked.

'Was he hot?'

'Hard to say a definite yes from what I saw of him . . .'

'Well if he is Maud's toy boy he'll probably be gorgeous. She's got great taste in men. Did she ever show you a picture of Monty? No? Well he looked just like George Clooney . . .'

Nell had always been a live-and-let-live kind of girl; it was Maud who had taught her that, so she felt kind of hypo-critical taking a trip up to the cottage just to check up on Ange's story. Instead she invented a legitimate reason to go there, choosing to bake Maud's favourite cupcakes as a tester for the old Aga and an excuse to visit.

Maud was knocking up a chilli when she got there.

'Perfect timing.' She offered Nell the spoon. 'Taste that for me, tell me if it's hot enough.'

Nell did as she was told. 'Could do with a little bit more of a kick.'

'Another chilli?'

'How about a splash of Tabasco?'

'Ah yes, your favourite tipple.' Maud winked, referring to her parting gift to Marcus, the story of which she had listened to with much amusement, pride and the urge when Nell had finished to applaud. 'Talking of which, have you heard from him at all?'

Nell shook her head. 'He's obviously missing me as much as I miss him.' She smiled, putting a reassuring hand on Maud's. 'Don't worry about him, Maudie, it just makes me realise even more that I did the right thing in calling it a day. Now, how about one of these . . .' and she offered up the cupcakes as a sweetener to her next topic of conversation, waiting until Maud had exclaimed in delight and then claimed a large pink one as a pre-dinner treat.

'I've heard you've had a visitor.' Nell tried to say it casually, but of course when you're trying to be casual it never really works.

'Mmm?' Maud pretended not to know what Nell was talking about and bit into her cake.

'A man. A handsome young man actually,' Nell embroidered in order to try and gauge Maud's reaction. 'Been spending a fair bit of time up here, according to local gossip.'

'The local gossip being Angelina, I presume?'

'Well, she might have mentioned something about a man in a silver BMW coming up here rather a lot.'

'A silver BMW?' Maud mused, as if she were totally at a loss as to what Nell could mean. Then she allowed some fake realisation to dawn on her face. 'Oh, she must mean Harry Fox. He's not really a visitor. He came to fix my creaking pipes.'

'You told her he was the gardener.'

'I did? Well, I suppose a better description would be handyman; he's very good at most things.'

Nell struggled to read Maud's face, which was difficult, despite how well they knew each other, but the very fact that she remained so inscrutable when she was usually so open with her made Nell suspicious. And there was a definite avoidance of eye contact.

'Really? That's interesting. Maybe I could get him down to the tea rooms. There are an awful lot of DIY things that need doing that I can't actually D myself.'

'Well you could but it might be difficult. He's very in demand, being so . . . er . . . so . . .'

'Handy?' Nell offered with a wry smile.

'That's the word.' Maud beamed insolently. 'Now, are you stopping for dinner? Yes? Lovely. In that case, phone Ange and tell her to come up and join us, and whilst she's on her way she can detour via your fridge and bring us some pudding. The same little bird that seems to have been twittering about me also told me you were making cheesecake yesterday.'

And as she abandoned her cupcake and turned her attention back to her chilli, Nell knew that conversation was dismissed. However, it had been enough of a conversation for her to realise that there was every possibility that Ange was right. Maud was definitely being cagey. Perhaps she did have a new man after all.

Despite the fact that Ange had seen him heading up or down the coast road several times as she walked back-wards and forwards from the Jolly Roger, it was still another few days before Nell actually met Harry.

She had woken early to the tuneful sound of Ange snoring in the bedroom next door after a late shift at the pub, and when she couldn't rouse her, she decided to walk up the cliff road to have breakfast with Maud, who had seemed a bit peaky the other day after dinner. Either that or she was quiet because she didn't want to answer any more questions.

It was a beautiful morning, the air heavy with the promise of summer soon to come. The sky was blue, huge white clouds drifting like tankers on the water, and the sea breeze coming in off the water was playful and gentle, lifting Nell's hair like a lover's caressing fingers.

It was one of those days and one of those views where you just wanted to suck it all inside of you with a great lungful of air that would inflate your spirits and your smile.

Nell was carrying a basket of fresh-baked chocolate croissants, and had to resist the sudden urge to skip up the hill singing 'Oh, What a Beautiful Morning'; well, at least at first she tried to resist it, the tune playing over and over in her head, and then she started to hum, and before she realised she was singing out loud, and the further she went the louder she got.

And then she saw the big silver BMW on the drive.

She immediately fell silent.

The mystery man was actually here.

For a moment she considered giving Maud the privacy she obviously sought, but then curiosity overcame her and she let herself quietly into the house, laughing inwardly at the situation as she tiptoed through to the kitchen, from where she could hear the radio playing softly.

What did she expect, to catch them at it on the kitchen table?

He was actually at the kitchen table, but the most decadent thing he was doing was drinking a cup of tea. He had his back to her, but even from that angle he certainly didn't look like a handyman; in fact he was far too smart, in blue chinos and a grey cashmere jumper over a pinstriped shirt.

Maybe he was a con man and not a handyman, here to fleece a vulnerable old lady. Nell shook her head. Maud was most definitely not a vulnerable old lady, and any man who tried to take advantage would no doubt be sussed out and caught out and immediately thrown out, probably over the cliff. But no way was this man here to do DIY.

Unless of course he was a *gay* handyman.

Gay men were usually so impeccably dressed, Nell had found, at any time of day in any given situation. Perhaps this was the gay man's version of an overall?

Well, there was only one way to find out.

'Good morning. You must be Harry.'

At the sound of her voice, he dropped his tea cup back into its saucer with a clatter. Nell almost laughed, and then, as he hurriedly got up and turned to face her, she remembered her manners.

'I'm sorry, I didn't mean to make you jump.' She extended a hand. 'I'm Nell, Maud's god-daughter. She might have mentioned me.'

'Only about once every five seconds,' he said, reaching out to take her hand.

And then as their hands met, and folded into each other, they just kind of stuck there, as both parties finally took a proper look at who it was they were introducing themselves to.

'You,' they both said in unison.

There was a heartbeat of silence, hands still held, and then he managed two more words.

'You're Nell?'

She nodded.

And then she smiled broadly. 'And you're the guy from the Fisherman's Arms.'

It took a few moments for them both to realise that they were still holding hands.

It was too late to shake, and so there was a kind of awkward shuffle before they both dropped and stepped away.

'Um . . . is Maud about?' Nell finally managed to ask.

'She's upstairs getting dressed,' he said, and then instantly clamped his mouth shut, in the way you do when you know you've said something without thinking about it *at all*.

'She . . . er . . . she . . . um . . . she got kind of muddy in the garden . . . needed to change.'

He's lying to me, thought Nell, her smile slipping. 'Bit early for gardening, isn't it?'

'You know what it's like, early bird catches the worm . . .'

'Have I?' Nell replied without missing a beat.

He looked at her for a moment.

And then he couldn't help himself. He began to laugh.

Despite his obvious discomfort, it was such sweet, genuine, infectious laughter that Nell couldn't help but catch it, and found her smile again.

And then Maud came into the room.

'Ah, good morning, Nells Bells. I see you've met Harry. He's been cleaning my windows for me, bless him.'

Nell managed to smother her smile with her hand, but it was still obvious that he'd spotted it.

'Well, it was great to finally meet you, Nell,' he said hurriedly, 'but I must be off. Places to be . . .'

'Windows to clean, gardens to dig.' Nell nodded sympathetically, biting her bottom lip to stop herself from laughing out loud.

When he had gone, Nell looked at Maud with a cocked eyebrow and waited.

'What?' said Maud a touch tersely.

'Who's Harry, Maud?'

'I told you already, lovey, he comes round to help me with the house.'

'Well, he just told me he'd been gardening, and you just told me he'd been cleaning your windows.'

'And?'

'And who was telling me the truth?'

'Hasn't it occurred to you, my darling, that we both might have been? Maybe that's why Harry is so handy: he's the first man I've ever met who can multitask. Now,' she lifted the cloth from Nell's basket and peered inside, 'have you brought me something nice?'

Harry got in the car, drove down the road as quickly as a sense of decency and safety would allow, and then pulled over to the side of the road, because he was actually shaking. He felt like a kid who'd been caught scrumping for apples.

So that was Nell. *She* was Nell. No wonder Maud had wanted to keep him away from her.

'She's beautiful,' had been Maud's exact words, 'inside and out, so keep away from her, Harry, we don't want any added complications to our dangerous liaisons now, do we?'

And he had laughed at the audacity of it.

Now he began to laugh again, but this time at the irony of it.

And then he stopped abruptly, rested his head against the steering wheel, and, though he was a man who rarely swore, said with great feeling, 'Oh fuck.'

'I can't believe you didn't even ask if he was single.' Ange shook her head in amazement.

'I know.' Nell laughed. 'But I was kind of sidetracked by Maud; you know how good she is at changing the subject.'

'You think she's lying about him?'

'I don't see why she would be.'

'Because he's her toy boy.'

'Maud wouldn't hide a fit toy boy; she'd parade him proudly.'

'Is he still as gorgeous as you remember from the Fisherman's Arms?'

Nell closed her eyes and sighed. 'Oh, Ange. More so.'

'Well then, there's only one thing left to do.' Ange posed, *Charlie's Angels* style. 'Send in the Ange.'

Half an hour later, and Ange was letting herself in through Maud's kitchen door.

Maud was at the table, drinking a cup of tea.

'Morning.' Ange nodded. 'Just came round to borrow a . . .' she cast her eyes about the room in search of inspiration, 'teapot,' she blurted, her eyes lighting on Maud's collection of china on the huge wooden dresser.

Maud narrowed her eyes in suspicion. 'Ange, darling, you are very welcome to borrow a teapot, but when you live in a tea room that has thirty of them, it confuses me a little as to why you might need one of mine.'

'To remind me of you.' Ange beamed disarmingly. 'I miss you.'

'Well, that's very sweet, but rather scary, so I'm pleased that I know you're lying to me.'

Ange tried to do an innocent, 'who, me?' face, and then gave it up as a waste of time. 'Okay. I'll stop beating around the bush. You've had a good-looking young man coming to see you.'

Maud nodded.

'*Very* good looking,' Ange added knowingly.

'Oh, absolutely.' Maud's lips twitched as she held back a smile. Ange's curiosity was killing her.

'He seems to be coming round an awful lot.'

'Are you watching my house, Ange O'Donel?'

'Yes.'

'And why would you want to do that?' Maud cocked an eyebrow in amusement.

'Because I want to know who Harry Fox is.'

'I told Nell, he's my handyman.'

'Pull the other one, it's got bells on.'

'I've no intention of pulling anything, young lady. You either take my word for it or you don't.' Even though she was only pretending, and they both knew it, fierce Maud was kind of scary, and so Ange backed down . . . and backed towards the kitchen door, bowing as she went.

'Won't say another word . . .' she said, until she was far enough away, when she added, 'for now.'

'Angelina!' Maud thundered, and Ange gave up the backwards worship walk and shot out of the door like a dog who's just been caught stealing supper.

Maud nodded in satisfaction. She might be getting old and decrepit, but she still had it. But then, undeterred, Ange stuck her head back round the door and did her best Arnie impression:

'I'll be back . . .'

*

When Ange had gone, Maud, suddenly weary, sank down into a chair at the kitchen table, and tried to suppress a huge yawn. Harry had come so early today. She far preferred it when he called later in the day. She was worn out; perhaps she should go back to bed for another hour or two.

Alone, she added to herself, allowing a small smile to play about her lips.

She could understand why the girls were so curious about her handsome visitor, and she hadn't really minded Ange's obvious information-gathering session too much; it had actually cheered her up on what so far had not been the best morning. But it was going to become a problem if they continued to hunger for detail at such a ravenous level.

Maybe she should tell them; heaven knows, it was difficult enough not to. Harry wanted her to, kept telling her she should. He wasn't the kind for lies and deceit, but then again he hadn't had to do an awful lot of lying yet, just a certain amount of avoidance. But she had made her decision, thinking it for the best, and to be honest, if it wasn't for the girls' obvious and rather understandable interest in the lovely Harry, she wouldn't even be contemplating changing her mind.

Maud yawned. She'd sleep on it. One should never make important decisions with a tired mind.

True to her word, Ange was back the following day. She had an excuse: she was delivering a prize, a bottle of whisky, that Maud had won in the pub charity raffle, drawn the night before, but it was pretty obvious that she still had the same agenda, so Maud decided to cut the crap and get straight to it. She had also decided yesterday that she was going to stick to her original decision of keeping her business with Harry exactly that. *Her* business. And so, after pouring them both a cup of tea with a drop of the new whisky added for warmth, she asked Ange, 'Why are you so interested in Harry Fox?'

Ange was always one to appreciate the blunt approach. 'Truth?'

'Would be nice.'

'It would, wouldn't it?' Ange replied pointedly.

Maud chose, equally pointedly, to ignore this, merely taking a pleasurable sip of her alcohol-laced tea.

'Okay,' Ange conceded. 'Because Nell fancies him, and he seems lovely, and I thought it might be nice to do a bit of matchmaking . . . That's not what you're doing, is it? You're not matchmaking, are you, Maud? You're not lining yourself up a prospective godson-in-law?'

'Oh, goodness, no!' The exclamation was so rapid and natural that Ange knew this one was the truth.

'Why not? Keeping him all for yourself?' Ange teased.

Maud actually blushed.

It was like seeing the Statue of Liberty bend over and scratch.

It was all Ange could do to stop her jaw from falling open at the sight of it.

'Well . . . erm . . . of course not, no, half my age, and in fact I do believe he's married, actually, yes I think he's married, or if not married then very involved. Now, you forgot your teapot yesterday. Which one would you like, or would you prefer to borrow some spoons, so you can do a bit more stirring?'

When Ange got back to the Cakehole, Nell was painting the bathroom. They had scrubbed the existing bathroom suite and tiles until their arms ached, and then given in and got it redone. Nell hadn't budgeted for a new one, and so she was recouping the costs by not hiring painters and doing it all herself. She was pleased to report that thus far she was doing a pretty good job of it, and had even consoled herself with the fact that if her new venture didn't work out, she could always set herself up in the painting and decorating business.

'Bad news, Nell: he's married, or if not married, very involved with someone.'

Nell, who knew that Ange was repeating Maud verbatim, couldn't help but smile, despite feeling a weight of disappointment that was far too overwhelming considering the level of her acquaintance with the guy.

'Who?' She pretended not to know who Ange was talking about.

'Hotty Harry.'

'Oh, right, then it's bad news for Maud, you mean,' she said, determined not to show any upset to Ange, who would leap upon it like a big cat on prey.

'Nope.' Ange grinned. 'You. Don't tell me you no longer find him fiendishly attractive.'

'Yeah, sure, but wouldn't every woman with a pulse?'

'That's true.' Ange pursed her lips and nodded. 'So if he's not Maud's new toy boy – although there is always the possibility that she's lying to cover her tracks, but she did seem pretty convincing, and you know me, Nelly Belly, I can sniff out deceit a mile away – if he's not some pretty thing to be played with, then what is he doing at our Maudie's?'

Nell grinned at the 'our Maudie'. She loved the way that Maud and Ange had just clicked straight away, new friends like old friends in moments.

'She told us, Ange, he's the handyman.'

'Yeah, and I'm Madonna,' said Ange. 'Maybe,' she mused, eyes sliding sideways as she thought about it, 'she's running a marathon and he's her personal trainer. She does always seem knackered after he's been round there.'

'That's probably the hot sex wearing her out.' Nell tried flippancy and found, like the Triple Berry paint she was slapping on the walls, it didn't really suit her colouring.

Ange grinned broadly.

'Or,' Nell shrugged, 'maybe he is exactly what she says he is, and he's just fixing things up for her. The house takes a hell of a lot of upkeep, and I've noticed that Maud has been struggling a little bit lately to stay on top of things.'

'Mmm,' Ange mused, 'she does keep complaining about her aching joints.'

'And saying she's tired, and Maud doesn't moan about stuff like that normally.'

'Well that's it then, there's our answer. Mystery solved.'

'It is?'

'Yeah.' Ange laughed wickedly.

'You think he is her handyman now, then?'

'No.' Ange shook her head so hard her dark curls bounced with the vigour of her denial. 'I think he's a masseur and she's getting him to rub her stiff bits for her.'

'Do you think he can come round and do mine?' Nell grinned.

'Sure,' said Ange, sticking her finger in the paint and drawing a heart on the wall within which she wrote 'N 4 H'. 'But I get the feeling you'd much rather do his.'

The Cakehole opened for business on the first of June. The Grand Opening.

Nell preferred to think of it as her first day in her new job. This dumbing-down of the occasion gave less expectation, less height to fall from if, as Nell often dreamed, waking up in a panic, nobody bothered to turn up, not for the opening party, nor for the rest of the year.

Whilst driven by her enthusiasm and her excitement most of the time, in her darker moments she still wondered what on earth she had done.

She'd had a really good job, pension, benefits, long-term prospects, and she'd given it all up and embarked on this, something that might not work, that might even take everything she had worked so hard for over the last eight years, chew it up, and send it out with the trash, leaving her broke and disillusioned.

Still, as Maud always said, nothing ventured means you're a lazy sod. And she was so busy that she didn't have an awful lot of time to dwell too much on the what ifs.

On the day itself, Nell got up stupidly early, pretending to herself that she had slept for more than two hours, showered, dried her hair and then put on her carefully chosen outfit, marvelling at the hours of agony that had gone into the simple combination of blue jeans, blue T-shirt, and red-striped butcher's apron.

Thank heavens, however, that she'd actually have some clothes on, and the opening-the-tea-rooms-naked dream was one at least that would not be coming true.

To her amazement, Ange was already up and dressed and in the kitchen doing a frightening impression of a Stepford wife.

A bacon sandwich and a cup of tea were sitting on the table waiting for her, and Ange was already washing up the frying pan.

'Where's my Ange?' Nell joked. 'You know, the one who thinks that kitchens are God's reminder to go out and get a takeaway?'

'Replaced just for one day by considerate Ange, who knows that her best friend has enough on her mind and her proverbial plate as well as her physical plates without having to worry about the mundane.'

'I'm your best friend?' Nell said, aware that she sounded pretty pathetic, but so happy that she didn't really care.

'I made an executive decision to promote you to that position the day you slammed on your brakes and unlocked your car door, yes. Most people would have seen me in their rear-view mirror galloping after them and put their foot down.'

Aware that she didn't have the stomach to eat a thing, but eternally grateful for the kindness, Nell sat down and valiantly tried to chew her way through what was probably the worst bacon sandwich she had ever come across.

She was saved by the bell. The Alexander Graham Bell to be precise, which rang three times in a row.

The first call was from Maud to say that she was on her way down. The second was from London Tony at the Jolly Roger to tell them that Beth was on her way up but that she had forgotten to leave the cellar keys and so could they ask her to come straight back. The third was from a researcher from *Grand Openings* to let them know that the crew were on their way but had got stuck in traffic and so would be a little late, and could they possibly hold fire on the cutting of the *Grand Openings* Gold Ribbon until they got there?

'What are people supposed to do?' Nell grumbled, having passed this information on to Ange. 'Duck under it?'

'They could always limbo.' Ange grinned. 'Fun way to start proceedings, don't you think? Did they say if Tam was coming? You'd think he would be, wouldn't you, seeing as this is the actual Grand Opening and he hasn't filmed any sections yet at all.'

'They didn't mention him.'

'Probably Sidekick Oliver again.' Ange rolled her eyeballs. 'Do you know, I really think they only have him on that programme to highlight just how gorgeous Tam is.'

'Aw, don't be mean,' Nell exclaimed. 'He's lovely.'

'I know, he's fab, but would you shag him?'

Nell had pondered this question before. 'Possibly, but I think I'd have to fight Beth first. They still seeing each other?'

'Well, not seeing, logistics, but I gather there's been an awful lot of texts and e-mails flying back and forth. She's really hoping he'll come.'

'So am I,' Nell told Ange with a defiant grin. 'I'd much rather have Sidekick Oliver here than Tam McCavin. Then again . . . I suppose it would be good for business if he did come; might draw a few more people.'

'You don't need him for that, Nell,' Ange said confidently. 'They'll be queuing up outside to get in.'

'Outside where?' Nell said in a small voice, peering out of the window. 'It's certainly not outside here.'

'There's another half an hour to go.'

'Which means nothing. You know what the people in this village are like: they'd queue up for the opening of a public toilet if it meant freebies.'

When the clock said five to eleven, they hugged, and then Nell, who really couldn't wait, turned the sign from Closed to Open and then stood back and looked hopefully at the door. When it opened moments later, Nell and Ange clung together in excitement, only to see that it was just Beth, stooping to get under the huge *Grand Openings* ribbon that cut through the middle of it.

'Where's the party, then?'

'We thought you were it.'

'Well, I thought I was going to be early,' Beth looked at the clock on the wall, 'but it obviously took me longer to get here than I thought it would.' She frowned in puzzlement, as did Nell.

'Yeah, you and everybody else.'

'Am I the first one here?'

'You're the only one here, apart from us, of course.'

'I knew it!' Nell wailed, sinking into a seat. 'No one's coming, it's going to be an absolute disaster!'

Thank heavens for Maud, who arrived with the entire contingent of the LLs once more in tow.

'Thank you so much for persuading them all to come.' Nell hugged her in relief as the LLs, thirteen of them in total, spread themselves about the room to make it look fuller.

'They didn't take any persuading, my darling. Mention tea and cake to this lot and they move faster than a greyhound after a stuffed rabbit. By the way, did you know your clock's fast?' she said, indicating the clock over the mantelpiece with her head. 'By fifteen minutes, actually.'

Nell banged her forehead with her fist.

'Oh, I'm so stupid, of course it is. I changed them all so I wouldn't be late, and then I forgot.

'So we were early, and,' Maud paused and looked at her watch, 'it's now a few seconds off eleven o'clock.'

As if on cue, the church clock began to strike the hour.

They all looked at the door expectantly.

It swung open.

They held their breath.

And then Maris rushed in, all apologies for being later than the rest of the LLs.

Fifteen minutes on, and they had been joined, albeit briefly, by London Tony, Marge and the twins, who had come up to support Nell by wolfing down four cups of tea and four pineapple tarts in about four seconds flat before apologetically having to rush back to open up the Roger having collected the cellar keys from Beth.

'It's not exactly buzzing, is it?' said Nell dejectedly after they had gone and all that was left was themselves and the LLs, who had all consumed far too much tea to be able to do anything much other than queue for the ladies'.

'People will come, Nell, they're probably just avoiding the initial rush.'

'What rush?' Nell looked around her and wrinkled her nose.

'Well, it's like you never go supermarket shopping on a Saturday morning 'cause you think it will be packed, but if everyone else thinks the same, then the supermarket will be empty, but that's not because people don't actually want to go,' Ange said, smiling hopefully at Nell.

Nell stared back at her.

'I'm just trying to make you feel better.'

'I know. Thanks. But it's not working.'

And then a strange thing happened.

The camera crew finally arrived, and ten minutes later it was as though the entire village was in the tea shop, drinking tea, eating pineapple tarts and home-made eclairs, and surreptitiously flicking fingers through fringes and checking out reflections in the windows.

'What did I tell you?' Ange nudged Nell, who was surveying the full room with a huge smile.

And then Beth squeaked with happiness as the door swung open and Oliver walked in. 'I thought you couldn't come!' she cried, hurling herself across the room to hug him. Nell noticed as they embraced that Beth was a good two inches taller than Oliver, even in her flip-flops.

'I couldn't, but I wouldn't have missed this for the world.'

'Nell, can we just have a quick interview, please.' Lisa and the camera crew, who had been outside filming the queue of people going in and out when Oliver arrived, had spotted an opportunity and rushed in after him.

'Oliver, seeing as you're here, I don't suppose you'd do this to camera for us, rather than Seamus just asking the questions from off screen?'

'Of course,' he replied, smiling reassuringly at Nell. 'It'd be my pleasure.'

'Lovely. Right, Seamus, if you'll just mike Oliver up . . . great . . . as quick as you can, Seamus . . . Are you done? Yes? Lovely, and cameras rolling, and action in five, four three . . .' she fell silent and mouthed the rest, 'two, one . . .' and Oliver took over like the pro he was.

'Well, here we are back in Ye Olde Tea Shop in Polporth with the gorgeous Nell, and I have to say that since we've gone from "you'd have to be barking" to "heavenly baking", I'd be happy to bet that we have another *Grand Openings* success story on our hands . . .'

M aud reclined wearily on her bed and watched Harry sorting himself out in the bathroom.

He had his back to her, was washing his hands in the sink. As his hands twisted together, forming lather from soap, she saw the muscles of his back moving beneath the cotton of the shirt he was wearing.

He really was a fine figure of a man.

After the opening, once the villagers had been evicted, there had been a private party where tea was swapped for champagne, courtesy of Maud, and after a few glasses a slightly tipsy Nell had asked her about Harry. She had sidestepped the questions as neatly as usual, but Nell was tired and half cut and definitely not on form, and Maud wasn't sure how much longer she could keep on avoiding them.

If circumstances were different, he was just the kind of person she would love Nell to get together with, but that wasn't something that was going to happen . . . at least not whilst things were the way that they were between Maud and him.

Just then she heard the sound of a car and dragged her eyes away from Hal to the window, only to see Cyril Junior making his sporty purple way up the cliff road and into the driveway.

'Oh my lord, it's Nell!' she exclaimed.

Harry swung around, his hands still wet and dripping suds, his eyes as wide as Maud's at the sight of Nell's car.

Maud had always been one for thinking on her feet . . . or on her back.

'Well, I'm far too knackered to shift myself yet. We'll have to tell her you've been in fixing the plumbing,' she said quickly.

Hal hesitated for a moment, and then, as he couldn't think of a better excuse himself, nodded.

They heard the slamming of the car door as Nell got out of the Mini and then the bang of the front door as she let herself into the house, followed by her cheery call of 'Maudie!'

'Up here, darling.'

Harry threw her a pained look.

'What else could I do, pretend to be out?'

'Well, if you think I'm going to escape through the bedroom window, young lady, you're very much mistaken.'

Maud loved it when he called her young lady. 'Quick, take your top off!'

'Take my top off?' Harry exclaimed, eyes widening further.

'Well, you'd hardly be fixing the plumbing in a Savile Row shirt.'

'It's not Savile Row, Maud.'

'Really?' Maud reached out and fingered the cotton. 'It's an excellent material and cut, you'd really think it—'

'Um, Maud, Nell . . .' Harry urged, his eyes darting to the door as Nell's footsteps came ever closer.

'Yes, yes, of course, shirt off, come on, Hal, be quick.'

'You just want to look at my chest.' He laughed, unbuttoning none the less.

'Oh, absolutely.'

Harry was joking.

Maud was not.

Young people thought a libido was something you exchanged in return for a bus pass and grey hair, but Maud got as much pleasure out of watching Harry remove his shirt as Nell did walking into the room and finding him shirtless, with a hastily grabbed wrench in his hand, and the Marmite from Maud's morning toast smeared across his bare chest as fake oil (Maud's handiwork, of course), bending over the sink in Maud's en suite and looking busy with a tap.

Whilst they had thought of an excuse for Hal being in Maud's boudoir, they hadn't exactly come up with a reason why exactly Maud was resplendent on the bed in her best nightgown watching Hal supposedly change a washer with the wrench that she normally used to bash the reluctant sash window catch until it opened.

Fortunately Nell, totally blindsided by the sight of Harry's bare torso, didn't ask any questions, not then at least. She fetched them all a fresh cup of tea, and then sat on the edge of Maud's bed to drink it and make helpful suggestions to Hal about how best to replace the shower head that had fallen off after he had hit it a touch too enthusiastically with Maud's wrench.

When she got back to the tea shop she asked Ange instead.

'Why would Hal be fixing Maud's en suite plumbing at nine in the morning whilst Maud is still in bed?'

Ange just shrugged, and pulled a 'who knows' face.

'You don't think it's a bit weird?'

'What's the definition of normal nowadays?' Ange said philosophically.

*

This was the only response Nell got until later that day, when in the hour between the tea shop closing and the pub opening, she and Ange shared a moment of respite, with a cup of tea and a cake apiece.

'You know, the more I think about it, the more convinced I am that Hal is Maud's toy-boy lover.'

Ange often had a habit of coming out with something during a period of companiable silence that blew Nell's mind; this one was no exception, especially as she appeared to be deadly serious.

It took Nell a while to think of an answer.

'Lucky Maud,' she sighed, and for once Ange didn't pick up on the wistfulness in her voice.

Ange nodded her agreement vigorously, and added, 'If he's a handyman then I'm a prima ballerina. He's the worst handyman I've ever met.'

'A handyman who isn't handy.' Nell nodded. 'I have to agree, this is looking even more suspicious. So you think that the only other explanation is that he and Maud are, well . . .'

Ange nodded again.

'But Maud? Really? You *really* think so?'

'Why not? What woman wouldn't? Don't say it hasn't crossed your mind . . . don't tell me *you* haven't tried to imagine him naked and reclining on your double duvet . . .' and she bit into her cream and jam doughnut and closed her eyes with the pleasure of its taste. Either that, or she was doing exactly what she had just accused Nell of.

Nell had to confess that she had often imagined him naked, but certainly not with Maud in the picture, or more to the point in the bed, next to him.

'Okay . . .' she said reluctantly, her face screwing up with discomfort at the image that was now in her mind, 'I get your point, but still . . . Maud . . .'

'Yes, Maud. She's not just your godmother, you know, she's a person in her own right, a woman, and she only has to be what? Fifty-something . . .'

'She's sixty-two.'

'You're kidding me!' Ange exclaimed, making a mental note to check out the face creams on Maud's dressing table the next time she visited. 'She looks so good for her age, doesn't she? But anyway, fifty-something, sixty-two, twenty-three, thirty-four, there isn't this special particular age where your libido just switches itself off. We're not all stamped with some use-by date, or best-before. Come on, Nell, be honest, if you were Maud, would you?'

'If I were me, Maud or any woman with a pulse, I would,' Nell admitted with unexpected frankness. 'But particularly if I were Penelope Cruz. I think I'd stand a good chance of actually getting somewhere if I were Penelope Cruz.'

'You stand a good chance of getting somewhere being Nell; you don't have to be a movie star to get laid around here. Trust me, I know what I'm talking about.'

'You could be a movie star,' Nell protested immediately.

'Yeah, *Free Willy*. Anyway,' she added before Nell could protest at the comparison, 'what I'm saying is if you like Harry you should just go for it.'

Now Nell was confused. 'I thought you were telling me that Maud should go for it, that Maud is actually already going for it.'

'No, I'm telling you that you should.'

'If he wasn't sleeping with Maud, that is.'

'He's not sleeping with Maud, though, is he?' Ange shrugged matter-of-factly.

'After such a convincing argument that he is!' Nell exclaimed.

'I was only saying we'd be wrong to just assume that it *couldn't* be that.'

'Um . . . so the phrase "Hal is Maud's toy-boy lover" was a point for discussion and not an actual statement?'

'Couldn't have put it better myself.' Ange grinned.

'You're a devious bugger, Ange O'Donel.' Nell pouted, as she realised what Ange had just done, but underneath the pout Ange could see that she was struggling not to smile.

'Well, you've been making enough excuses already not to pursue him; didn't want to add another one to the list.'

'What, as well as being married or heavily involved?'

'He's not married, Nell.'

'Maud said he might be.'

'Maud is fibbing. You need to ask him for yourself.'

'Oh yeah.' Nell rolled her eyes and put on a silly voice. 'Excuse me, but are you married?'

'Why not? I think it's about time we stopped dealing with the cheeky monkey and went straight to the hopefully huge organ-grinder.'

A t the end of the first week, Nell totted up her accounts and decided that business, whilst not exactly booming, had been steady enough for her to feel like the Cakehole actually stood a chance of working. She had always known that trade would be seasonal, and it wasn't quite the summer season yet. If things were ticking along nicely now, then the school holidays should be the boom time that she needed to boost her profits in order to survive the winter.

One of the things she had decided to do to make her profit margins higher was to make and sell nearly all her own produce.

And so on Monday morning, between breakfast and lunch when it was quiet, she decided it was time to give it a go.

All of Nell's baking was done in an old Aga that she had uncovered in the kitchen from a mound of grime. She had fallen instantly in love with it, but she still hadn't quite got the hang of it. It was an electric one, so that kind of made it less scary, but it still had four ovens. One was a fan oven, one conventional, one a slow-cook and the other a grill. So far she had only used the fan oven because that was what she was used to cooking with, and the grill for the odd toastie when the sandwich-maker was on overtime, but today she was feeling adventurous and her bread was baking in the conventional oven.

It smelled wonderful.

Fresh bread and fresh coffee permeating the air like aphrodisiacs.

Her old office used to smell of sweaty feet and photocopiers.

When she pulled the tray from the oven, the bread looked perfect, round and gleaming brown like a ripe conker.

It took all of her self-control to leave it alone to cool.

How sad that I'm excited over something so simple, she thought, and then chastised herself. Turn that around. How lovely that I can be so excited about something so simple.

After twenty minutes she could wait no longer.

'Right.' Since she had started working on her own for the majority of the day, Nell had found that she spent an awful lot of time talking to herself. 'Proof of the pudding is in the eating, as they say, although in this case it's the proof of the loaf . . .' and picking up a carving knife, she brought it down and across the shiny brown surface with a little regret at defacing something that looked so flawless.

The knife snapped and so did her wrist, both of them pinging alarmingly, the broken knife flying across the kitchen and landing in a bowl of cake mix. Gingerly holding her wrist, Nell prodded the loaf with a finger from her good hand. It was rock hard, like she'd mixed it from concrete instead of flour.

'What the . . . ?' She frowned in confusion.

There must be something wrong with the oven. A bad workman blames his tools, she told herself, but she went to look at the oven anyway.

It was still on, so she opened it carefully. Despite the fact that the dial said one hundred and thirty, the temperature in there was more like a furnace. Funny, she thought, it had seemed okay when she opened it up to get the bread out, but then she had been so excited at the sight of her first loaf looking so perfect that she hadn't really taken much notice.

She switched it off. Then turned it on again.

Nothing happened.

Off, then on. Off, then on. It wouldn't even turn on now. She tried the other ovens – thankfully they all seemed to be working – and then she realised that her wrist actually really hurt.

As she was peering gingerly at it, Maud arrived. 'Hello, darling, how's it going?'

'Well, I've hurt my wrist on a loaf that's harder than an Einstein equation and my oven's playing up.'

Without a word, Maud took Nell's hand and gently examined her wrist. 'You've hurt yourself. You should go to the doctor.'

'It's nothing,' Nell said. 'Besides, I don't have time.'

'It's not nothing. Your wrist's all swollen.'

'I'll be fine.' Nell gently drew her hand away.

'So you won't go to the doctor?'

'Not unless he can fix my oven.' Nell smiled stubbornly.

Maud wrinkled her nose. 'I'll ask Harry if can come down and see you.'

'Can he fix ovens?'

'He can fix most things, darling, although not everything.'

'I thought he was fiendishly busy.'

'Well, yes, he is, but he's coming to mine later to . . . chop some wood, so I'll ask him if he minds calling in on you on the way.'

*

How could she be so excited about someone coming down to look at her oven?

Normally happy to chat to any customers well after closing if they were of a mind to stay on, Nell ushered the last two lingerers out bang on five, with apologies and a bag of cookies to take with them. Then, in anticipation of his arrival, she decided to make herself look a little more presentable. She'd brushed her hair, and was just rummaging in her handbag for a lipstick and some mascara when the bell heralded the fact that the door had been opened, and her involuntary yelp signalled the fact that she'd hastily shoved her handbag under the counter with the wrong hand.

'Hi.' He'd obviously heard the yelp. 'Are you okay?'

'Well, that depends. Can you get repetitive strain from slicing bread?' Nell joked, wincing as she pushed her bag further under the counter.

'Maud said you'd done something to your wrist. Here, let me take a look.'

'Thought you were here to see the oven.'

'Sure, but let me take a look at you first,' he said, reaching out for her.

His hands were firm but gentle, the skin softer than she would have expected from someone who supposedly spent his days fixing plumbing, gardening and chopping wood for people, but she was so fazed by his touch and the way he glanced up at her and smiled as he was examining her wrist that any leading questions that had begun to form in her mind just slipped away like the condensation on the inside of the tea room windows when she lit the fire.

'Nothing broken, fortunately,' he finally said. 'Strap it up, buy ready-cut loaves, and you should be as right as rain in a few days' time.'

Her raised eyebrows were question enough of the credibility of his diagnosis.

'I know a bit about this kind of thing. Maud's probably told you I'm a jack of all trades . . .'

Nell was frowning at him, so he threw in some truth as balm to the irritation.

'I've done the odd first-aid course, that kind of thing.'

She nodded.

'In fact, if you have a first-aid kit I can have a go at strapping it up for you.'

Nell nodded again and pointed to the cupboard just behind him.

She watched as he weaved the gauze about her wrist, marvelling at the skill and complexity that went into something so simple, watching his hands move with a rhythm that was almost mesmeric. And then he caught her gaze and for a moment they both just stopped and looked at each other, like they had in the Fisherman's Arms, until he literally shook his head and, pulling his eyes away, speeded up.

'Do you know,' she said, testing her wrist gingerly as he finished tying and stepped away, 'that feels better already. Let's hope you can work wonders with my oven too.'

'Ah, yes. The oven.'

'Can I get you a cup of tea whilst you take a look?'

He shook his head. 'Thanks, but everywhere I've been today people have very kindly offered me cups of tea.'

'Something else?'

'Why don't I just see what I can do with this thing?'

She could have been imagining it, but he suddenly seemed anxious to get on with it and go, heading straight over to the oven, where he opened and twiddled and prodded and flicked, all with a frown on his face that didn't really hold out much hope for his ability to fix her oven as well as he had fixed her wrist.

'Any joy?' Nell asked after five minutes of sighing, expecting the negative that followed.

He stood up and shook his head. 'Sorry. Ovens aren't really my forte, and as for Agas, well, they're a foreign country completely.'

'Thanks for coming to take a look, though.'

'No worries.'

'And at least you've managed to fix something.' She waved her bandaged wrist at him. 'What do I owe you?'

He look horrified. 'Don't be daft, you don't owe me anything . . . I mean, I didn't fix anything, did I?'

'Maybe not, but it's still taken up your time. I mean, I know it was mainly on fixing my wrist, but . . . well, Maud said how busy you are.'

'Honestly, don't worry about it, please,' he said, backing towards the door. 'Although I do have another appointment, so I have to . . . go now.'

'Okay, thanks.' Nell nodded, and then, summoning up every ounce of courage she had, called after him.

'Maybe I could buy you a drink sometime to say thank you.'

He paused and turned back to face her, his teeth biting into his bottom lip, and then he nodded slowly.

'I'd really like that, Nell,' he said, and she knew from his face that he meant it.

When Ange arrived back from her shift at the Jolly Roger, Nell was pulling a tray of cookies from one of the ovens that still worked.

'Oh wow, they look good.'

Nell offered them up. 'Mind, they're still hot.'

'Thought you were baking bread today?'

'Oven's busted.'

'Not the only thing, by the looks of it.' Ange indicated Nell's wrist. 'What happened to you?'

'Had a fight with a loaf of bread.'

'And then a fairy cake came along and made you all better?'

'Hal strapped me up.'

Ange just about managed to avoid the obvious innuendoes by literally biting her tongue. 'Harry was here?' she asked in surprise.

'Maud sent him down to see if he could fix the oven, but he ended up fixing me.'

'So I see. And did he?'

'Did he what?'

'Sort out the oven?'

'No.' Nell blinked, and Ange thought to herself for a moment that if she didn't know that Nell was as bright as a hundred-watt bulb, she would have thought her pretty gormless. 'He didn't, actually.'

'Did he even look at it?'

Nell sort of shrugged, and then nodded.

'What happened, Nell?'

'I offered to buy him a drink sometime to say thanks.'

'And what did he say?'

'He said that he'd really like that.'

'Great! So when are you going?' Ange asked excitedly.

'I don't know. We didn't actually get to that part.'

'Oh.' Ange deflated.

'But it was obvious he really meant it when he said that he'd like to.'

'Right. So you're not going out for a drink and the oven's still not working?'

'Nope.'

'And the baking-your-own-bread thing didn't exactly go according to plan either?'

'That's putting it mildly.' Nell laughed and indicated the offending article.

Ange picked it up.

'Wow, this thing weighs a ton. What did you use, Nell, flour or cement?'

'I don't know what went wrong.'

'Apart from the oven,' Ange reminded her.

'I think it's called a cottage loaf because it's made out of stone.' Perfectionist Nell shook her head. 'Total waste of time and money.'

'Oh, I don't know,' Ange mused, picking up Nell's cottage loaf again and turning it in her hands. 'We could varnish this and use it as a novelty doorstop. Either that . . .' she slung it into one palm and raised it back over her shoulder, 'or a shot put.'

The following morning, Ange practically locked a protesting Nell in the flat, insisting that she take a break and give her wrist a chance to heal, and that it was quiet enough before lunch for her to handle the place on her own for a couple of hours.

After the usual queue of people picking up their lunch on the way to work, Ange did four cream teas for a quartet of ramblers, and when they had gone and the place was empty, she found a pot of varnish left over from the refit and was happily painting Nell's loaf with it when a voice interrupted her.

'Forty pasties, please.'

Ange looked up to see a tousle-headed man with a Noel Gallagher accent and Liam Gallagher eyes standing on the other side of the counter, smiling at her.

She crossed her arms across her chest. 'Pull the other one.'

'Why, does it make your face light up with a smile?'

For a moment she looked furious, and then she began to laugh like a drain.

He began to smile and then he realised she was taking the piss out of him.

'Oh my lord, does it make my face light up? How hilarious, how original, I'm swooning.'

To his credit he took it in good stead, even managed a smile himself whilst waiting for her to run out of sarcasm.

'Great. The woman is silent. Now you've got that out of your system, can I have forty pasties, please?'

'You were being serious?' Ange frowned.

'Er . . . yeah.'

'No can do, I'm afraid.'

'You don't want to serve me?'

'On the contrary, I'd love to serve you. I just can't do hot. The oven's on the blink.'

'And if your oven was working, would you heat me my pasties?'

'Sure.'

'Then show me the way.'

'To what?' Ange frowned.

'The oven, of course.'

'You fix ovens?'

'I fix ovens,' he said and winked at her.

When Nell finally plucked up the courage to break the Ange-induced curfew and gingerly made her way downstairs, she found Ange dancing round the empty tea shop with a duster.

This in itself was extremely unusual, but Ange was also smiling so hard, Nell instantly looked at the pineapple tart tray to see if there were any left or if she'd eaten them all. She'd had two. Either that or sold two. So the smile wasn't a sign of a sugar high.

'What?' Nell demanded, as Ange greeted her not with words but a one-hundred-watt beam.

'What!' she repeated even louder and with an added squeak as Ange grabbed her by the waist and danced her round the room.

'I have a date tonight,' Ange sang, spinning Nell back to rest against the counter.

'You do?'

'His name is Niall, he's gorgeous in a grungy trainers and anorak kind of way, and he fixed your oven for you.'

'He fixed my oven!'

'And I have a date.'

Nell shot over to her beloved Aga. Sure enough, when she turned the conventional oven to On, it hummed quietly into life.

'I don't know, I leave you here on your own for an hour and a half and you've mended my oven and pulled in one fell swoop.'

'You should have mornings off more often.' Ange nodded.

'So where did this mystery oven doctor suddenly appear from?'

'He came in for forty pasties.'

'Ooh, a man with an appetite to rival yours. Could be a match made in heaven.'

21

Nell was in the kitchen on another early-morning baking session when Ange came back from her date.

'Ooh, the dirty stop-out finally returns,' she teased. 'I take it from the fact that you didn't come home that you and Niall, um . . . *hit it off* really well. Did you have a good night?'

'I had a great night. Amazing.'

Nell looked at Ange's miserable face and frowned. She certainly didn't look as though she'd had a good time.

'Are you going to see him again?'

Ange shook her head. 'He's just passing through. Him and a group of friends are down here for the week on a stag do.'

'Doesn't mean he can't come back,' Nell said sympathetically.

'Well, the fact that he's the stag might mean he doesn't.'

'Oh, Ange.' Nell's mouth opened in horror. 'I'm so sorry.'

'Yeah, well, don't be, because I found out when I answered his hotel bedroom phone to his fiancée. Now he's sorry enough for all of us.'

Nell wrapped Ange in a hug.

'You don't think they're all arseholes, do you, every single one of them?' Ange mumbled into Nell's shoulder.

Nell sighed. She had never seen Ange so vulnerable. 'Probably.'

'I just feel so sorry for the girl he's left at home, with her plans for the wedding, and her hopes and dreams of their future together all shattered by a stupid one-night stand.'

'It wasn't your fault, Ange, you didn't know.'

'I know, but when you don't normally let your conscience have much say in your life, it's kind of hard to deal with when it does kick you up the bum with all the force of a shire horse on steroids.'

Nell offered solace in the best way she knew how.

'*Dirty Dancing* on DVD and a pineapple tart?'

'Yes, please,' Ange croaked pathetically.

'Well, I'm just icing them now. You pop up and get yourself comfortable on the sofa and I'll bring one up in a minute.'

'Thanks, Nell.' Ange walked slump-shouldered to the door marked Private.

When she got there, she paused and turned back.

'Oh, Nell . . .'

'Yes, love?'

'You couldn't make that four pineapple tarts, could you? I definitely think this is a four pineapple tarts situation.'

A few days later Harry Fox stood outside the Cakehole, contemplating whether or not he should go inside, the slight confusion registering on his face nowhere near an indicator of the inner turmoil.

He really felt like he shouldn't be here, but Maud had asked him to help her out. Surely this justified a follow-up? He would just call in for thirty seconds, check that everything was in working order and go; no one could grumble at that.

He took a deep breath and walked purposefully up to the door, pushing it open before he could change his mind. At the sound of the bell ringing, Nell popped up from behind the counter, a welcoming smile on her face, a smile that he saw drew noticeably wider when she saw who it was that had come in.

Her hair was pulled back in a ponytail, and she had no make-up on. She was dressed down in skinny jeans and a yellow vest, with a red apron tied around her waist. Despite the fact that the kitchen was steamy, she looked as fresh as a daisy and as pretty as one too, and he instantly knew that he'd been a fool to come, but the fool still wouldn't make his excuses and turn around and leave.

'Just came to see how you were doing.'

'Me or the oven?' Nell smiled.

'Both.'

'Well, I'm happy to report that my wrist is almost perfect, and my oven's fixed.'

'Your oven's fixed? That's good.'

But then her face fell. 'Well, yes and no. The chap who fixed it, well, he broke something else when he did it.'

'Something important?'

Nell nodded solemnly. 'Ange's faith in mankind.'

It would have been rude not to stay and hear the story.

From feeling as if he shouldn't be there, it was amazing how quickly he felt so comfortable, just sitting next to her at a table, drinking a glass from the bottle of wine she had tucked away at the back of the fridge.

'You wouldn't think it to talk to her, in fact she'd deny it if you asked, but deep down, I mean *really* deep down, she's an old romantic at heart,' Nell was saying, shaking her head. 'It's always the lies, you know. You tell a girl the truth, no matter how awkward, and at least she has the choice. If he'd said to Ange, look, I'm just out for a final fling, she might have said to him, okay, I'm your girl, but he didn't, he just took something from her. False purchase. It's wrong.'

'What if your feelings are as honest as they get, but your circumstances mean that you can't tell the truth?' Harry found himself saying before he could stop himself.

She looked at him quizzically.

'Is there something you need to tell me, Harry Fox?'

His question and her directness in her response surprised both of them, and he had to think on his feet.

'Um . . . just that I've heard so much about you, but we don't really know each other.'

It was a clumsy answer, but she let him get away with it; simply laughed and replied, 'Well, you're at an advantage, because Maud has been distinctly tight on the details as far as you're concerned.'

'What do you want to know?' he asked her, and his tone was teasing.

Nell paused for a moment to gather her courage so that she could answer him honestly, and then, biting her bottom lip in the way that he found so appealing, she tilted her head and looked at him sideways. 'Everything.'

It was the way her mouth moved when she said it.

At that moment in time, nothing – fire, flood, earthquake or something as simple and yet as complicated as a promise – could have stopped him from leaning in towards her, and as he leaned towards her so she did towards him, both pulled by something they couldn't and didn't want to fight.

And so they fell into a long, slow, perfect kiss. One of those kisses where you don't think, you don't worry if you're doing it right, if you cleaned your teeth after you had that cup of coffee, where your noses don't clash. One of those kisses where the feeling spreads from your lips through your entire body, where your eyes stay open and lock so tight it's almost as if you can see inside each other.

And then he pulled away, broke away from her suddenly and somewhat violently, as if he'd just been stung instead of kissed.

Nell blinked in surprise at his abrupt departure.

It had been a mutual thing.

A shared look, both leaning in together.

Both kissing each other.

She hadn't thrown herself at him.

Had she?

And now he was looking apologetic. There was nothing worse than someone kissing you and then looking sorry about it afterwards.

'I'm really sorry, Nell, it's not that I don't . . . because I do . . . It's just that I . . . well I can't . . . not right now, it's complicated you see, well you don't see, of course you don't, why would you . . . Look, I really had better go. Sorry . . .'

And then to a mortified Nell's utter surprise, he took her chin in one hand and leaned in and kissed her again, briefly but firmly and very purposefully on the lips, his eyes holding her own, and then he smiled, again briefly, and left.

'What the . . .' Nell frowned in confusion, her gaze following him as he literally sprinted out of the door and to his car.

Okay, so they had just fallen into that first kiss, but the second kiss had been a pre-considered thing on his part, a choice, a decision, not a spontaneous action like the first.

Spontaneous and irresistible.

Irresistible and disturbing.

Tell her they shouldn't and then do it again?

Talk about confusing.

What did the man want from her?

Well, that was a question she definitely couldn't answer, so instead Nell tried to stick to her new resolution and look at things from her own point of view rather than somebody else's. So what did she want from Harry? She didn't want a relationship right now anyway, did she?

'I don't want a relationship right now,' she said to herself out loud, as if to reaffirm this feeling.

'Sure, but I bet you wouldn't say no to a shag.'

Nell almost jumped out of her skin at the amused Irish-brogue-tinted whisper in her ear. 'Ange!'

Ange smirked and waggled her eyebrows.

'I thought you were upstairs. Where on earth did you spring from?'

'You know me, omnipresent.' She grinned broadly. 'So, how do you rate him, then?'

'What?'

'The kiss.'

'How did you . . .'

'I was watching through the door.'

'You were what?' Nell exclaimed, laughing despite herself. 'Honestly, Ange, I know you have a different set of life rules from the rest of us, but doesn't not spying on people come under the heading of common decency?'

'Oh, I decided a long time ago that a very *basic* sense of common decency would do me nicely; anything too finely tuned and you miss out on so much.'

'I see you're feeling a bit better now.'

'I forgave myself,' said Ange, though if truth were known, it was the sight of such a soul-searching kiss that had healed the hurt. It didn't matter that he had bolted. You couldn't kiss someone like that without it being the beginning rather than the end of something.

If a kiss like that could happen, then anything was possible.

She had been witness to something wonderful.

Ange had hope again.

Some flowers arrived later that day. A huge bouquet delivered by old Dougie from the florist's. Old Dougie, five foot four and not quite seven and a half stone, was actually staggering under the weight of them: lilies, orchids, birds of paradise, enough to fill two vases.

'Think this might be your apology,' Nell said, handing the unopened card to Ange.

Ange handed it straight back. 'Not when it says "Nell" on the card.'

Nell frowned as she opened it. 'I'm so sorry. Can you ever forgive me for being such an idiot?' she read, as she pulled the card from the envelope.

'Harry.' Ange nodded. 'For kissing and running.'

'You think?' Nell said, beginning to smile, and then she revealed the signature.

'Love, Marcus,' she said flatly.

'You're kidding me.' Ange snatched the card from Nell so she could read it for herself.

'What the . . . Why now? How many weeks have you been gone, and the guy suddenly realises he's the biggest dipstick this side of a monster truck rally?'

'Do you think he misses me?' Nell frowned.

'Er . . . do pole dancers have thighs of steel? Of course he misses you, Nell, you're bright, beautiful, warm, funny, loving, you've got the brains and balls to make something of your life, and that big idiot let all of that walk out of *his* life. I'm just surprised it's taken him this long to realise, that's all. And I'm totally gobsmacked that he thinks a big bunch of flowers is the thing to fix it! Shall we bin them?'

Nell pouted. 'I've already binned the man. Shall we give the flowers a reprieve?'

Ange looked doubtful. 'You're not . . .' she began, but Nell shook her head; she knew what Ange was going to ask.

'It's nice to know that he finally understands the reasons why I left, and might be feeling a little bit gutted about it. But trust me, Ange, it would take something pretty major to make me even think about getting back together with Marcus Bennet.'

22

It was the day of Polporth's much-feted fete.

Midsummer Madness.

The name said it all.

Polporth didn't just do your run-of-the-mill fete with a tombola, a kids' fancy dress, a few home goods stalls, and perhaps a donkey or two; Polporth did Midsummer Madness.

'A mix of flower festival, Mardi Gras and mental institution,' Maud had described it the previous week when they were gathered at hers for afternoon tea.

'Why? What does it involve?'

'Well, there's a Midsummer Market: lots of stalls, you know, the usual kind of thing, bric-a-brac, books, cakes, cheese, cider, spells and potions, paintings, hand-made clothes, sweets and chocolates . . .'

Ange and Nell looked at each other, amazed at the way Maud threw spells and potions in amongst the mundane as if it were a perfectly normal thing to have at a village fete.

'Elspeth Towan runs that one,' Maud added, as if this explained it all.

'I thought she owned the posh dress shop on the high street?'

'She does, but she also fancies herself as a bit of a

Harriet Potter on the side . . . Don't knock it till you've tried it, kid.' Maud nodded solemnly as Nell started to laugh again. 'Her rosemary and radish poultice totally got rid of old Mrs Treventhan's unwanted facial hair, and London Tony's Beth swears it was one of Elspeth's potions that finally put paid to an unwanted admirer . . .'

'Yeah, she slipped it in his beer and poisoned him,' Ange whispered to Nell, who started laughing again.

'And then there's the garnishing,' Maud continued with a fond smile.

'Don't tell me,' Nell hiccuped as she struggled to stop giggling, 'someone runs round throwing lettuce, chopped tomato and cucumber slices at people . . .'

'No, darling.' Maud winked at Ange as the girl poured her another cup of tea and then added a drop or two of the Irish, as she always did when Nell wasn't looking. 'That's the flower part of the festival.'

'Festival? I thought it was a fete?'

'Fete, festival, farce, fracas, utter folly.' Maud shrugged. 'It's actually really hard to categorise.'

'How come you've never been before?' Ange frowned at Nell.

'June. Not a school holiday,' Maud answered for her, her voice deep and her lips pursed in an awful impression of Nell's dad at his strictest. 'Besides, Nell would never have been allowed to attend something so uncouth and debauched.'

'Probably still wouldn't let me now,' Nell joked. 'Not that I've ever been down this weekend before. The traffic's usually so horrendous it's not even worth trying to get here.'

'Uncouth and debauched. Two of my favourite words.' Ange beamed. 'Sod the traffic. I'd be here every year.'

Being a founding member of the LL, Maud was a Midsummer Madness aficionado.

She went on to explain that the event was also a competition, a heavily fought one at that, with the various local organisations competing to see who could raise the most money. And yes, there were actually donkeys, but not just one or two; there were thirty, all kitted out in racing colours for a beach Grand Prix.

And the finale of the evening was apparently the crowning of the Midsummer Madness Goddess – yes, Goddess, not Queen – who would apparently be worshipped as a deity by all Polporthians until the following year, and who would also, according to Maud, have flowers strewn at her feet by a minion chosen especially for the job whenever she walked down the high street.

'Any time she walks down?' Nell asked, her eyes wide at the thought of crunching her way down to the paper shop on a path of daffodils.

'Any time.' Maud nodded.

'No matter what time of the day?'

'Absolutely. It's a bugger of a post to fill; at least it was until Neville Ross moved here last year, you know, the little bald chap who runs the post office. He actually jumped at the chance, but I wasn't totally surprised by that.' Maud leaned in conspiratorially, her tongue loosened by the nip that Ange had added to her Darjeeling. 'You see, a couple of weeks ago, I heard from Sandra Wright up at Polporth Farm that he has a bit of a . . . well, you know, a bit of a *subservience* thing.'

'He does?' Ange's eyes were on stalks at this.

Maud nodded solemnly. 'Not that I'm given to village gossip, but Sandra's sister Beryl heard from Mildred Trenance at the fishmonger's that he once asked her cousin Bevan, who he was seeing at the time, if he could borrow her pinny and scrub her kitchen floor.'

'Well, that doesn't necessarily mean he's subservient,'

Nell said, her mouth sliding into a grin. 'He might just have a fetish about cleanliness; maybe Bevan's floor was a bit grim . . .'

'Perhaps.' Maud nodded with the half-smile of someone who knew otherwise. 'Except for the fact that he was stark naked but for the pinny and he wanted her to smack his backside with a carpet beater and call him a dirty slut whilst he beavered away with the scrubbing brush.'

Nell choked on the tea she had mistakenly put to her mouth.

'I'll never be able to lick a stamp from that shop again!' she exclaimed once she'd regained control of her breathing, mainly thanks to a timely, if slightly heavy-handed, thump on the back from Ange.

'Anyway, so the goddess has her very own toadying minion in the form of Neville. She also never has to queue in any Polporth shop . . . that will include the tea rooms, Nell, so remember that one; it's very frowned upon if you don't adhere to the rules.'

'You get to queue jump?' Ange, fed up with the mile-long queue that usually formed outside the fish and chip shop on a Friday night, was obviously impressed by this.

'Oh yes, and no one complains, because it's tradition. You also get to commandeer the lifeboat any time you feel like it, regardless of whether they've been called out for an emergency, even if it's just because you fancy a jaunt up the coast.'

'You're kidding us, aren't you?' Nell's mouth dropped open at the thought.

'Afraid not.' Maud shrugged matter-of-factly. 'Person-ally I've always thought this one was a tad OTT, especially since the 1996 goddess used to get them to ferry her to St Ives every Tuesday for a jazz evening at the Harbour

Hotel, so woe betide any surfer, ship or swimmer who got into trouble on a Tuesday . . .'

Nell frowned at Maud, eyes narrowed, trying to work out if she was on a huge wind-up or not. Maud liked to play jokes on people, and this tale sounded typical of her mischief, but her face was totally deadpan as she continued.

'You also get a free flagon of ale from the Jolly Roger every Friday evening – oh, and you can command any man to fall at your feet and worship you and he will. Well, he should, though not everyone sticks to that one, which is perfectly understandable, especially when it's raining.'

'Sounds awful,' was Nell's comment, but Ange's eyes lit up in a dreamy 'if only' kind of fashion.

'Personally I've always wanted people falling at my feet, other than when they've had too much scrumpy at the pub, that is. How do you enter?'

'You don't.' Maud smiled cryptically. 'You get entered. You can't nominate yourself. There's been a box in the village hall for the past month. Anyone can go in and write down the name of the girl they think should be this year's goddess, and post it in. Whoever gets their name written down most times wins the crown . . . well, it's not actually a crown, it's this weird garland thing made out of shells and bits of dead seaweed, but you are supposed to wear it on your head, so I suppose crown is right in an odd sort of way.'

'Box in the village hall . . .' Ange mused.

'Yes, but voting's closed now. The box will be in the safe hands of the trusted Midsummer Marauders treasurer . . .'

Ange's face fell. Dreams of a dawn raid with one of Nell's order pads filled with the name 'Ange' shattered as Maud spoke.

'Midsummer Marauders?' Nell queried.

'The committee in charge of the Madness. Convened all year round, they are. It's a permanent commitment planning for each year.'

'So you're being totally serious?' asked Nell, who had started to think Maud was making it all up. 'Where on earth did all of this come from?'

'Well, the Madness has been going since the late forties. It was started by a local landowner, Hugh Tregunning, to celebrate the end of the war. All the rules and regulations were drawn up by him. He was a little bit mad, by all accounts . . .'

'Just a little bit?' Ange snorted.

'If the stories are true, he supposedly dressed up as Queen Victoria every year and rode around the village on the back of his manservant Harold, handing out pennies to any child at the fete who came dressed as Winston Churchill.'

'Well, that explains an awful lot.' Nell crossed her eyes in mirth and derision. 'And people listened to this lunatic?'

'Things were different in those days.'

'Lairds and serfs.' Ange nodded. 'You had to do as you were told back then, even if it meant stripping down to your bloomers and painting yourself purple.'

'But that doesn't mean you have to continue the Madness now, so why does it still go on?'

'For one simple reason, my darling girl: it may be completely and utterly bonkers, but it's deliciously good fun.'

As she did every year at Midsummer Madness, Maud was manning the fancy goods stall. Ange had been fascinated by this phrase. Fancy goods. She had joked that perhaps they would be selling frilly knickers and fluorescent dildos, and had been rather disappointed when Maud had explained that it was actually more likely to be padded coat hangers, lavender bags and crocheted doilies.

Nell's contribution had been to make a ton of fairy cakes, cupcakes and her special pineapple tarts for the cake stall, which was one of the numerous food stalls in the Midsummer Market, set up around the harbour. She was also only opening the Cakehole for early breakfasts, and then closing for the rest of the day in order to give the charity stalls a monopoly on food sales.

Ange's contribution had been to watch her whilst she baked and then to taste-test everything. Maud had tried to persuade them into opening a kissing booth, but had failed dismally.

Nell couldn't contemplate that anyone would actually pay to kiss her.

Ange, who probably would have been up for it, was working all day.

It was the Jolly Roger's busiest day of the year apart from New Year's Eve, when everyone apparently went just as insane as they would today, the whole village erupting in a riot of fancy dress. According to Maud, last year everyone at the pub, including Marge, had dressed up as Elvis.

This was what had started it all off, Maud saying that she was in charge of fancy goods and suggesting the kissing booth, followed by Ange's announcement that she was working. Hal had been at the house when this conversation was had. He had been there when Nell and Ange arrived, banging about in the kitchen, fixing a leaking tap or something.

He had smiled, she had smiled, and there had been a nervousness in this exchange but not a discomfort. Nell had wondered how she would feel when and if she saw him again, and was surprised that the overwhelming feeling was of pleasure. It was a thrill. Although she did her best to act as normal as possible.

As did Maud, who, determined not to let them think that they had caught her and Hal out again, made them all tea and got out the cakes and, before they could question her, turned talk to the fete the following week.

When Maud and Ange said what they were doing, Nell had commented ruefully that she might not go as she'd be on her own, and what fun would it be on her own, to which the other two had told her not to be so daft, and then, as they were leaving, Hal had said straight out that he was thinking of going and maybe he would give her a call.

Nell had been utterly, mortifyingly embarrassed by how delighted this simple sentence had made her. She had hoped desperately, but at the same time had known she had no hope, that this delight didn't show on her face.

She had already confessed to Ange that she had a huge crush on Harry Fox.

Now a crush wasn't such a bad thing in itself, as long as it was controllable, and you recognised it for what it was and didn't get hung up so much on it that it turned into an obsession, but to be perfectly honest, she hadn't been looking for something like this. Far from it.

And now she knew exactly why.

Breakfast was over and the Cakehole was now closed as promised.

Ange had gone to work, Maud would no doubt be manning fancy goods, both in the thick of it so to speak, and Nell was still at the flat . . . staring at the telephone. Which hadn't rung. Well, strictly speaking it had, twice, but the first time it had been Maud to say see you later, which had been her way of saying make sure you come, and the second time it had been London Tony for Ange, asking if she could come in half an hour early. It had not rung for Nell. And it had not been Harry Fox ringing.

Now Ange had gone to work and Nell was on her own.

She kept trying to do things – after all, there was plenty to keep her occupied – but whilst her hands were busy, her mind could only think of one thing.

'There's nothing worse than waiting for your phone to ring,' she announced to the empty room.

The best thing would be to just go out, but it was sod's law that if she went out, he'd call and she'd miss him. But at least that would be better than sitting by the phone and him not calling at all.

A watched pot never boils, her mother would always say.

A watched telephone never rings was far more apt, because a pot would inevitably boil sooner or later but a telephone could sit solidly silent for days.

Then again, all he'd said was 'Maybe I'll give you a call', and here she was like a teenager sitting on the bottom of the stairs, staring at a handset.

On this thought, Nell pulled her jacket off the hook, kicked on her shoes and strode out of the door.

23

She felt instantly better outside in the sunshine. The village was thronged with people. Maud had already told her that the Madness attracted thousands of visitors every year, but she had never imagined a crowd on this scale. There were people everywhere, and the garnishing was obviously already in full flood. It was like the sixties had come alive in Cornwall. Everyone seemed to be wearing garlands of flowers, and one woman had so many hung about her person she looked like a walking bouquet.

There were Morris men dancing in the high street. Nell resisted the urge to slide down a back street, and squeezing behind the gathered crowds managed to avoid being pulled into a dance by hiding behind Mrs Staveley, the rather rotund schoolmistress.

Her plan had been to go into the Jolly Roger and see if either Ange or Beth were on a break. Unfortunately this plan failed on a technicality, since she couldn't actually get *in* the Jolly Roger. Not without sharp elbows and possibly a bit of ankle-kicking. People were spilling out of the door, sitting on the steps, doubling up at the few tables Tony had put out with a thumb on the nose to the parish council, who'd told him he couldn't. And so she decided to go down to the harbour and see if the LLs needed a hand on one of their stalls.

Down in the harbour, the market was buzzing. Stalls lined the harbour walls so closely it was amazing that the people manning them managed to stand behind and serve without falling in the water.

As she was scanning the market looking for Maud, Lizzy, the receptionist from the dentist's surgery, danced past and threw a string of what Nell thought were freesias around her neck.

'Sweetpeas for a sweetheart,' she called with a wink, before dancing off.

The smell was sweet and made her sneeze.

'Bless you.'

Nell spun round to see Harry standing behind her.

He smiled. And then, after a pause that was a heartbeat, added, 'Sweetheart.'

Nell, who had never blushed before in her life, who in fact thought that blushing was a terrible cliché, resisted the urge to pat her reddened cheeks before she turned.

'Nice flowers.' He nodded to the garland. 'I think you might have a fan.' And then when Nell looked confused, he added, 'You do know that Lizzy likes women?'

'Well, that's lovely. I like women too, we're rather wonderful people.'

'That's not what I meant and you know it.'

'I know. But in answer to your question, no, I didn't know that Lizzy likes women, but now that I do, I'm rather flattered.'

'You are?'

'Of course. Compliments are like cheques. It doesn't matter where they come from, you should always take them with good grace and a thank you, and then bank them before they become invalid.'

'That's a Maudism, isn't it?'

'How did you know?'

'I've been spending an awful lot of time with Maud in the last few months.'

'Yes, you have, haven't you?' Nell said it so quizzically, he knew it was a question.

'You know what it's like, old houses, always something else to do.' He shrugged, and then rapidly changed the subject. 'I called earlier to see if you were coming, but I'd obviously missed you.'

'You did? You called?'

'Yeah, about ten thirty.'

Considering the scream was silent, it was still pretty deafening.

'To be honest, I thought you might have forgotten.'

'Of course not.' This was the truth. He had thought of nothing else since he had inadvertently blurted what he was thinking, without thinking. The look Maud had given him when he'd said it and the lecture afterwards had both led him to call as he'd wanted to, but when he thought she might already have left for the Madness. A compromise that hadn't really worked for anyone, but at least left his conscience a little clearer.

'And you're not avoiding me?'

'Of course not.'

'Liar.'

They both knew she was right, but as she was also smiling as she said it, he didn't turn and run.

'If you're embarrassed about the kiss, don't be, it was just a kiss.' No beating about the bush there, then; Nell was almost proud of herself.

'Was it *just* a kiss?'

She looked at him in surprise. Unless she was very much mistaken, he was flirting with her. The way he had sprinted off, she hadn't expected him to be flirting with her again. Nell needed to know. 'Harry, can I ask you something?'

He nodded cautiously.

'Well, Maud said that she thought you might be married . . .'

He smiled at this. Amused. 'I'm not married.'

'But you are in a relationship?'

The pause was pretty long.

'Kind of,' he eventually answered. 'It's complicated.'

Nell nodded. 'Okay. Fair enough.'

He was amazed at how easily she accepted such a vague answer; most women in his view would have held out for a far more intricate explanation. But for Nell complicated was not on her menu this year. No matter how much she fancied Harry for lunch, dinner and, even more so, full English breakfast.

To Harry, though, it wasn't fair enough. It wasn't really fair at all, because now she had the wrong idea about him. Truth was that he liked Nell, really liked her. He liked the way she tilted her head when she listened to someone talk, and she really listened, in a way that not many people actually managed. He had liked the way her tongue tasted of honey when he had first kissed her, and the surprise in her big golden eyes when he had then done so for a second time. He liked the hint of promise that the looks and the conversations and the electricity that so obviously crackled between them held.

What he didn't like was the fact that he wasn't free to follow any of this through, and even more so the reasons why he wasn't.

He hadn't been lying when he said he was in a relationship. It just wasn't the kind of relationship that Nell probably thought it was.

And then a little girl of about seven or eight, with her long dark hair in a thick plait, came running up to them, grabbing his hand, swinging from it.

'There you are! I've been looking for you all over the place. Mummy said you were going to meet us at the cake stall. We've been there three times already. I had two pineapple tarts and a doughnut, and I'm going to go back and get some fudge later.'

'Well, good morning to you too, young lady.'

His smile to Nell was apologetic.

'Can we go and see the donkeys now?'

'I'm just talking to Nell. Nell, this is Jasmine; say hello to Nell, Jasmine.'

'Hello,' said the girl, looking suspiciously at Nell, and then she turned to Harry and the beseeching smile returned. 'Can we go see the donkeys now, pleeease.'

'In a minute, Jaz.'

'But I've been waiting all morning.'

'Patience is a virtue.'

'I thought it was a game of cards.'

'You always have an answer for everything.'

'Which is why I always get gold stars at school.'

He raised his eyebrows at Nell. 'Kids,' he said, as the girl let go of his hand and danced away from him, urging him with her own footsteps to move in the same direction.

'*Your* kid?' Nell asked.

He shook his head. 'As good as, though . . .'

Nell thought he was about to explain further when she came running back to him and grabbed his hand. 'Come on. Mum said you're such a slowcoach!'

He looked at Nell and shrugged apologetically. 'I'm so sorry, I've been summoned. See you later, yeah . . .'

Nell watched them weave their way through the crowd

towards a woman who was obviously waiting for them.

She was a beautiful girl with long dark hair like her daughter.

When she saw that Nell was watching her, she smiled uncertainly at her. Nell sent the same kind of smile back.

They were obviously both thinking the same thing.

Who are you and what are you to Harry?

Or was Nell imagining it?

When Harry reached the woman, she smiled and slipped her arm through his, and then for a moment leaned her head on his shoulder in such a proprietorial fashion that Nell was left with little doubt that whatever they were to each other, it was something more than friends.

The question was what?

He had said his situation was complicated. Maybe Nell herself was what was complicated about it. He had after all said that the girl was 'as good as' his own child. Maybe her mother was the 'kind of' relationship he was in.

'Break time,' said a cheery voice, and an arm slipped through Nell's as Ange came alongside her. 'Which is a bloody good job, 'cause I'm ready to murder someone. No wonder they call this thing Madness; it's insanely busy in the Roger. London Tony's selling tickets just to get to the bar. Was that hunky Harry I just saw you with?'

'Yes,' Nell said, still looking after him, and Ange, who despite the fact that she normally chose not to use it, *was* actually blessed with some tact, said nothing further about it, simply looked, saw, and like Nell wondered. And then, as Nell was still staring after them, she tugged on her arm.

'Come on. Let's go and have a look at Maud's fancy goods. I could do with a new Rampant Rabbit.'

It had the desired effect. Nell burst out laughing and

managed to tear her desirous eyes away. 'Maud keeps telling you, Ange, that's not what fancy goods means.'

'I know, but wouldn't it be wonderful if she were lying?'

'I suppose a girl should always live in hope.'

'Too right,' Ange said, giving her such a pointed look that Nell was left in no doubt about what or rather whom she was referring to.

Much to Ange's disappointment, fancy goods was, as Maud had tried to tell her, nothing more exciting than an assortment of hand-embroidered handkerchiefs, home-made perfumes, pomanders, and other items of that ilk that wouldn't go amiss in a lady's boudoir.

Maud was in the thick of a scrum of LL girls who were manning three tables in a row. Fancy goods in the centre, home-made jams and pickles and other preserves to the right, and cakes to the left.

She was obviously having a wonderful time, the general commanding her troops. She was wearing so many garnishes she looked like one of their pomanders, and her clothes were streaked with pollen.

'You must buy something, girls!' She pounced upon them the minute they came into view. 'The Lifeboat Crew Wives beat us by two pounds thirty-five last year with their hand-knitted Aran jumpers, and it's not going to happen again, although they've been extra sneaky and added hats and scarves this year without declaring them at the last Midsummer Market meeting. I will not have them smirking at us again this year ... All of yours are gone,' Maud added as she saw Nell surreptitiously looking at the cake stall. 'Sold like hot cakes – pardon the awful pun – which was fantastic for our profits and also a wonderful opportunity for lots of shameless plugging for the tea rooms.'

'Are you here all day?'

Maud nodded. 'Most of it. This part of the market closes at five, although the food stalls stay open until midnight most years. As you can imagine, they do a roaring trade when Tony shuts up shop for the night.'

'How about we all meet up in the pub at six?' Ange suggested.

'You're kidding, aren't you?' Nell crossed her eyes.

'Oh, the crowd will have thinned by then. The outsiders will have been evicted. They're not allowed to stay for the crowning of the goddess, only residents. Rumour has it that this was because the crowning used to be followed by a good old-fashioned orgy, but I don't know how much truth there is in that one,' added Maud as Ange began to nod and grin in delight.

'London Tony told me that one too. Said it's tradition for the pub landlord to crown the goddess and then "initiate proceedings"; said that he'd happily play Caligula, only Marge apparently said that tradition is all well and good, but this particular one is a tradition too far.'

'I bet she didn't phrase it quite like that.' Maud smiled. 'You know, I do think Tony's a little bit scared of Marge.'

'Everyone's a little bit scared of Marge.' Ange laughed. 'Including me. You know, I don't think I've met many people who intimidate me, but she could, you know, if she wanted to. Just one look from her and Tony's like a chastised schoolboy. Maybe Neville Ross isn't the only one who enjoys a bit of dominating now and again.'

'Ange, you've got a one-track mind.'

'Yeah, and it's a dirt track, although right now,' Ange looked at her watch, 'it needs to be a race track. I'm due back at the pub in five and I need to stop and buy myself an Aran scarf on the way.'

'Don't you dare . . .' Maud warned in a low growl as Ange began to move backwards away from them and closer to the Lifeboat Crew Wives' stall, but Ange flicked out her tongue and delved in her pocket for a five-pound note, which she threw at Maud's adversaries before whipping a scarf from a hanger and winding it defiantly round her neck as she ran off cackling and throwing victory signs at Maud.

'That girl!' Maud exclaimed. 'Impudent madam!' She was trying to sound cross, but there was love in her voice.

'You really like her, don't you?' Nell grinned.

Maud dropped the unconvincing angry act and nodded vigorously. 'She reminds me of someone I used to know.'

'Who?'

'Me.'

'Give or take two foot in both height and hair, and an Irish accent.'

'She's a good friend, Nell, you're lucky to have her.' And then Maud uncharacteristically caught hold of Nell's hand and clung on to it. 'Cherish your friends, Nell. Life could be very bleak without them.'

Nell frowned in concern. 'Are you okay, Maud?'

Maud, pulling herself together, nodded again.

'Do you miss Mum?' Nell asked gently.

'I miss the person your mum used to be before she married your father,' Maud replied briskly. 'Now, what are you going to do with yourself for the rest of the day?'

'Not sure. I was wondering if you needed some help?'

'Oh, that's great, I'm so pleased you've offered, because I've kind of volunteered you to help out with something already.'

'Okay. Great.'

'You don't mind?'

'Not at all.' Nell shrugged. 'As long as it's not a kissing booth.'

'Oh no,' Maud shook her head, and coming out from behind the stall, took hold of Nell's arm, 'it's definitely not a kissing booth.'

24

'No way, Maud. Absolutely no way!'

When Maud had announced somewhat coyly to Nell that she had put her down for the Polporth Donkey Grand Prix, the kissing booth suddenly didn't seem so bad, but Maud was employing her none too inconsiderable powers of persuasion to stop Nell from running. 'Oh darling, please. As you can see, none of us are exactly fit for it, all a bit too long in the tooth, apart from Meryl of course,' Maud indicated one of the younger members, whose leg was in a cast, 'though as you can see, she can't even get on a bus at the moment, let alone a donkey, or perhaps Maris, but she's so allergic to them she'd be suffering for weeks. Go on, Nell, you used to ride when you were younger.'

'I know, but I used to ride horses, not donkeys. Big difference.'

'Take it for the team.'

'Auntie Maud, please . . .'

'Come on, Nell, the Polporth Twitchers and Ramblers beat us in the Grand Prix last year. We haven't heard the last of it since, and it didn't help that we came second in absolutely everything else as well, which isn't very good considering the motto we picked at last year's task force meeting for the Madness was Polporth LL, Second To

None. Now we're called Polporth LL, Second To Everyone.'

'Personally, I think LL stands for Load of Lunatics.' Nell pulled a 'Help!' face, as she saw Beth heading their way.

'That's what most people call them,' Beth nodded, 'apart from Dad, who says it stands for Liquid Lunchers, or . . .' she glanced at Maud, and then leaned into Nell and stage-whispered, 'in certain cases, Luscious Legs.'

'Your dad has a crush on Maud?' Nell asked in amazed delight.

Beth held up her hands and pretended to look coy. 'Don't ask me stuff like that. I'm just here to straddle a donkey.'

'You're riding in the Grand Prix?'

'Absolutely. Do it every year.'

'I thought it would be a bunch of kids.'

'Big kids more like. You have to be over eighteen to enter.'

'Poor donkeys!'

Beth shook her head. 'The Polporth donkeys are a special breed, Nell. This race has been run since the forties, and they breed them almost solely for it. They're more like race horses than donkeys nowadays. Come closer, say hello, they won't bite . . . well actually they might, but you know what I mean.'

As they got closer, Nell realised that they were indeed the biggest, sleekest donkeys she had ever seen, nothing like the cute little donkeys she remembered as a child on the beaches of Norfolk.

The LLs' donkey was of course sponsored by a local independent brewery, typical Maud, and was therefore called Half Pint. It was the most inappropriate name they could have thought of, Nell thought. They should have called him Full Flagon, or even Huge Tankard, seeing as he was the size of a small shire horse.

'You want me to ride that?' Her eyes widened in fearful amazement.

'Isn't he a beauty?' Maud nodded proudly.

'That is the biggest donkey I have ever seen in my life.'

'I know, look at the legs.'

'Almost longer than yours,' grinned Lola, Maud's deputy.

'Built to run,' Maud said, running a hand down the donkey's sleek flank. 'We're going to win this year, girls, I can feel it in my whisky,' and she turned to look beseechingly at Nell. 'If we can just get ourselves a decent jockey.'

'What would you have done if I wasn't here?'

'Well, the plan was always for me to take the reins, but as you know . . .' Maud paused and coughed pathetically, 'I haven't been feeling that wonderful lately.'

'Emotional blackmail,' Nell hissed at her.

'I know.' Maud leaned in. 'Is it working?'

'Unfortunately, yes.'

'Hurray.' Maud turned to address the gathered LLs. 'We have our donkey jockey.'

'I've never been called that before,' Nell muttered, but couldn't help smiling at how delighted all the girls were.

'Right. Kick-off in ten minutes. Hat, please, Lola.'

Lola handed Maud a riding hat.

'Socks and boots, Maris.'

Socks and boots followed.

'Coffee beans.'

'Coffee beans?' Nell's eyes crossed in confusion.

'They're for Half Pint.'

'The donkey eats coffee beans?'

'They're his favourite treat, and I swear the caffeine gives him a bit of an extra kick, so to speak, when it comes to running. Now, who's got the vodka?'

'The donkey likes vodka too?' Nell's eyebrows shot up into her hairline.

'That's for you,' Maud laughed, handing her a hip flask. 'A little rocket fuel to help you go as fast as him.'

It was a sight to behold, thirty donkeys in a row, all backed up behind a line of multicoloured bunting. It wasn't exactly like the start of a proper horse race, where the horses prance and wheel and whicker with excitement, whilst the jockeys stay calm, keep control. For a start it was a touch too static: donkeys stood solidly, some looking asleep almost, all four hooves planted so firmly in the sand it was hard to imagine that they would actually be moving anywhere in the next few minutes, let alone reaching the finish line half a mile down the beach. Secondly, the jockeys were anything but calm and controlled. They sounded like a flock of chattering birds, laughing, talking, calling each other out, yelling challenges.

Nell was amazed at the people who were taking part. Practically all the Jolly Rogers, Beth, TJ, Liam and Ben, were riding, as were most of the pub's regulars, from eighteen up to eighty. Arthur, the owner of the Good Cod, who must be in his sixties at least; Melanie Praze, who ran the yoga class at the village hall, and who had taken to popping into the Cakehole every lunchtime for a tuna baguette and a pineapple tart; most of the Polporth lifeboat crew; Beattie Williams from the newsagent's, who was forty-three and four foot eleven; old Dougie who delivered the flowers for the Polporth florist; Davey Penrithen, stocky and handsome, from the fishmonger's; even Neville from the post office in actual silks and proper breeches, his knee-high boots polished to within an inch of their lives.

Nell had started to go from feeling like an idiot to feeling nervous. These people might be laughing and joking, but they were deadly serious about winning this race; you could see it in their faces.

The woman next to her, who Nell knew to nod to because she lived in one of the cottages on Crantock Lane, near the Cakehole, was staring at the finish line and chanting to herself, 'Visualise winning, Mona, visualise winning!' over and over.

The twins, who were just beyond her, were laying a bet with each other, each adamant that they would win. The girl on the other side of Nell, who was racing for the Ramblers and Twitchers, was being given a pep talk by her team.

'You can do it, Lowena, you've been training hard for this for months . . .'

'Oh my God,' Nell groaned to herself, closing her eyes.

'. . . you're ready, Rocket Robin is ready and raring to go, you're a winning team.'

'Think someone needs to tell Rocket Robin that he's raring to go,' said a quiet voice full of laughter at Nell's side. 'I think he's actually asleep.'

Nell looked down in surprise to see Harry standing at her stirrup.

'Hi.'

'Hi.'

'Big donkey.'

'Huge.' Nell couldn't stop herself. 'But size isn't everything.'

He laughed. 'What are you doing up there, Nell?'

'Maud.' The one-word answer was enough explanation.

'The things we do for love, eh? Well, good luck . . . I'd say break a leg, but under the circumstances . . .'

Nell burst out laughing.

'That's better,' he said, starting to walk away again, as the linesmen moved into place. 'You stay as tense as you were, if you fall off you'll shatter.'

He was challenging her.

Nell rose to it. 'I won't fall off,' she called determinedly after him.

He turned around and just looked at her for a moment. 'Very glad to hear it,' he finally said, then winked and walked back into the crowd.

Nell exhaled slowly. Okay, so now she had gone from not wanting to take part at all to actually wanting to win the bloody race. She wasn't sure if this was a good mental shift or not, especially when the most sensible option would probably be to get off right now and leg it in the other direction.

She had been a good rider when she was young, won rosettes even, but this was different. For a start, Half Pint felt nothing like the rubber-ball ponies she used to ride, tubby and sleek with springs in their legs. The only thing she could liken it to was being on top of an extremely sturdy greyhound, with his narrow withers, high backside and long, long legs.

Like the other donkeys in the line-up, Half Pint stood stock still, but his ears were twitching like crazy. Nell knew that meant that he was taking in everything around him.

'Okay,' she found herself talking to him, 'Maud says you're the fastest thing on four legs since Shergar, and you're obviously brighter than your pals here, so what do you say, HP, feeling saucy?'

'You know talking to them doesn't make them go any

faster, Nell?' yelled Liam from two donkeys away.

'That's not what your last girlfriend told me,' teased his brother.

'Shut up, you tosser, at least I can get a woman into bed. The most intimate relationship you've ever had is with your right hand.'

'Piss off, you bastard ... everyone knows I'm left-handed.'

The two boys began to throw good-natured punches at each other, before one of the linesmen yelled at them to pack it in or be disqualified, as they were about to call the start.

The twins stopped their banter, suddenly deadly earnest, intent on winning.

The first whistle blew and the whole crowd fell silent.

All you could hear was the sound of the sea.

And then the second whistle blew and the bunting dropped.

Immediately the sound flooded in again like a tidal wave.

People began to cheer and call out.

Nell expected a big surge forward, but several of the donkeys didn't move at all, another group headed in the direction of the Biggest Vegetable competition, the animal on the far end turned around and began to eat the straw hat of the nearest linesman, and a few of his friends trotted down to the sea for a paddle in the water.

For a moment Nell thought that Half Pint was joining the stationary crew, but then to her delight he sprouted coffee-coloured wings and shot off towards the finish line like Schumacher in a Ferrari. They were closely followed by both twins, Neville from the post office, several of the lifeboat crew, Lowena, the girl who was riding for the Ramblers and Twitchers, and the vicar's wife Tulip, whose arms and legs were going like a windmill.

It was like *Chariots of Fire*, only with hairier legs.

As they galloped along the sand, Nell could almost have sworn she could hear the theme tune, until she realised that some wag was actually playing it over the tannoy system.

They lost some more runners along the way.

Tulip and her steed Holy Smoke veered madly to the left and ended up at the Lifeboat Wives' knitted clothing stall, where Tulip had the softest landing ever in a pile of stripy socks when Holy Smoke slammed on the brakes and calmly began to chew on a rollneck sweater.

The lifeboat crew were doing well until their beepers went off, at which point they turned their steeds en masse towards the lifeboat station and galloped that way instead like a small cavalry charge, the crowd cheering them as they went.

So now it was just Nell, the twins, Lowena on Rocket Robin, and Neville from the post office in his oh so shiny boots and racing silks bringing up the rear.

By this point Nell was laughing so hard it was amazing she could even hold on, but this didn't deter Half Pint. Unbeknownst to anyone that day except the breeder, Bernie, Maud had taken on the final stages of Half Pint's training herself. Discovering one day when eating a picnic lunch with Bernie that as well as coffee beans, Half Pint also had a fierce fondness for Nell's pineapple tarts, she had taken to leaving a pile of them on a rock a hundred yards on from the finish line on training days. When Half Pint realised that if he was the fastest donkey down that beach he'd get to shovel eight pineapple tarts down his neck he'd been the first donkey from Bernie's stables across that finish line every single time.

Today, with more donkeys behind him than usual, which meant more competition for his favourite tarts, he was running like a thoroughbred race horse.

Nell and Half Pint thundered past the finish line fifty yards ahead of the rest of them.

Unfortunately, with Half Pint intent on his hidden stash of treats, they didn't actually stop. Or not until they reached the rock, where Half Pint slammed on the brakes, hoovered up the tarts and then, as if carried away by his outstanding victory, began to bray and then buck like a bronco.

Nell, who had clung on gamely all the way, finally lost her grip.

Was this, she wondered for a moment, as she sailed majestically through the air back towards the finish line, what it felt like to fly?

The only problem with flying is that at some point you have to land.

The wet sand was as hard as Nell's first loaf.

Harry was the first to reach her, running so fast he crossed the finish line before several of the donkeys. A fact that was noticed by more than one woman in the watching crowd.

As he neared her his heart quickened as he thought he heard her crying, but when he reached her he found that she was actually laughing her head off.

When Nell saw Harry, she managed to hiccup the laughter to a stop and looked rather sheepish. 'I fell off,' she said. It was an admission. A pretty obvious one, but an admission none the less.

'So I see.' He smiled down at her, a mixture of humour and sympathy. 'But you won, so the triumph kind of negates the humiliation, don't you think?'

Nell nodded uncertainly, and he crouched down next to her and looked deep into her eyes. For one mad moment, Nell thought he was going to kiss her, but then he held a finger up in front of her face and began to move it from side to side, watching closely as Nell, obviously confused by his actions, let her eyes follow it.

'Good, no concussion,' he announced. 'Now, where does it hurt?'

'Everywhere,' Nell replied.

'Then why are you clutching one body part in particular like you think it might drop off?' he said, indicating where Nell's left hand was holding on to her left butt cheek. 'Want me to take a look?'

'No,' Nell said petulantly.

'There's blood on your fingers, Nell, let me see . . .' he coaxed her, gently taking her hand away.

'Blood?' Nell wasn't that keen on blood.

'Don't panic, there's not much, but I just need to take a look, okay, assess the damage. Do you mind . . . would you roll over for me?'

Nell resisted the urge to say 'Any time' and reluctantly shifted so that he could see.

'I must admit, it feels like I've been stabbed by something.'

'I'm afraid that's because you have.'

'I've been stabbed?' Despite telling her not to panic, that was of course the first thing she did.

'By a seashell. It's still there . . .'

'A seashell? I've got a seashell stuck in my arse?'

He nodded, his mouth fighting oh so hard to stay in a straight line.

'It's gone right through your shorts, but don't worry, I can get it out for you . . . if you just keep still a second . . .' There was a sharp pulling pain. 'There we go. Now, I've got a couple of plasters in my pocket. I'll just cover the wound, okay . . .'

'I think I preferred it when you were bandaging my wrist,' Nell joked weakly, so embarrassed she would have been happy if the tide had swept right in and washed her away. 'I can't believe this is happening.'

'Er . . . what exactly *is* happening here?'

They both turned at the sound of the woman's voice.

More people were coming up the beach, but the first to arrive was the girl Nell had seen earlier with Harry. She didn't look very happy.

'Um, Annie, this is Nell. Nell, this is Annie, Jaz's mum.'

It was not the most appropriate time for a formal introduction.

'What's going on, Harry?'

'Nell kind of got . . .' He looked at Nell and smiled an apology, knowing full well that she was already dying of embarrassment, 'well, she got stabbed by a seashell when she fell off.' He held up the offending article for both of them to see; it was long and pointed, like a thick needle. 'A needle whelk, aptly named,' he said, smiling at Nell in sympathy. 'Very pretty, but kind of nasty if you suddenly land on one.'

Nell and Harry shared a smile, and suddenly Nell felt as if she was being stabbed again, by Annie's glare.

'Well, whilst you've been doing your good doctor bit, Jasmine's had an accident. She's been kicked by one of those bloody donkeys you promised she could see.'

'Is she okay?' Nell asked in concern, but Annie ignored her.

'Is she okay?' Harry repeated.

'She's asking for you, Harry, *crying* for you.'

He looked at Nell.

'Are *you* going to be okay?'

'I'll be fine. The cavalry's nearly arrived now anyway.' She indicated Maud and the LLs, who were almost upon them.

The LLs practically carried Nell to the Jolly Roger. They were so ecstatic they would have paraded her there on their shoulders if she hadn't been trying to hide her embarrassment in the midst of them.

Her legs still felt like jelly, and her body ached in places she'd forgotten she had, but the LLs' tidal wave of joy was sweeping her through the streets towards the pub when all she really wanted to do was go home. It was as though they were Arsenal and Nell had just scored them the Premiership-winning goal. Although to her it felt like she'd done it naked with ten million people watching.

'Just relax and enjoy the adulation,' Maud whispered when people started to clap as they went past, and Nell visibly stiffened. 'You're a hero now.'

'For riding a donkey?'

'Don't knock it, Nell, you won the Grand Prix. In Polporth that puts you in the ranks of Michael Schumacher. Do you know, the year before last, nobody even managed to get across the finish line. The Bells and Spells donkey Hurry Trotter was in the lead and decided it was going to the Jolly Roger for a swift shot, and the others followed it. Marge was chasing them all up Lanyard Alley with a carpet beater.'

Nell laughed and Maud smiled softly.

'What I'm trying to say is that you don't have to worry about making an idiot of yourself in this village, because it's full of them already; in fact it's practically a prerequisite for being accepted into the community. What you've done might feel stupid to you, but to these people, well, they'll look at you in a different light now; you'll be one of them, not the new girl any more. You wait and see.'

Ange, who had heard the news on the village jungle drums, was waiting outside for them, ready to escort them through the throng into the pub.

'What happened?' she called excitedly.

'Oh, you should have seen her go!' Lola clapped her hands with joy.

'It was just like *National Velvet*,' sighed Maris. 'Except Nell wasn't pretending to be a bloke.'

'No, I shall be pretending to be someone else after the race instead of during, to try and avoid the embarrassment.' Nell cringed.

'Don't be embarrassed, you were great.'

'She was great,' the rest of the LLs chorused happily.

'I fell off!'

'After you'd won,' Maud said, hugging her and then letting go as Nell cried out in feeble pain.

'I had a shell stuck in my left butt cheek.' Nell pouted. 'I'm going to have a bruise on my arse the size of my head, and a bruise on my head the size of my arse and a bruise on my ego the size of both of those two put together.'

'Don't worry.' Ange slung her arm around Nell's waist. 'Let's get you inside. A few vodka and tonics and you won't feel a thing . . . Make way, make way, Grand Prix winner coming through . . .'

*

Nell was just telling Ange about Harry and how he had removed the shell from her left butt cheek, and then how Annie had arrived shooting daggers, when they were interrupted by Tony's voice booming through the outside speakers so that those who couldn't fit inside could hear. It was time for the Midsummer Madness prize-giving.

There were prizes for various different things.

Fancy dress, a whole plethora of prizes for the largest or the strangest-looking vegetable, raffles, painting competitions, guess the weight of the fattest person in the village, best home-made wines, jams, pickles. It took an age to get through them all.

Nell beamed with surprised delight when she won best cake for her pineapple tart. She hadn't even known that Maud had entered her, and was amazed and delighted to find that it was a village vote that had got her first prize, but it was when she was called to collect her cup and a magnum of champagne for the Grand Prix that the whole pub erupted into applause and cheers, and despite being as red as a ripe cherry, she actually found she was smiling even harder.

People were reaching out to pat her back as she passed them on the way up to Tony, who hugged her so hard he lifted her off the ground, and on the way back to Maud, who was almost bursting she was so proud.

And then everyone roared with laughter as TJ snuck up to the music system and started to play 'I Believe I Can Fly', and Nell's cherry colouring turned into an overripe tomato and her smile to outright laughter.

And then Marge turned the music off again and London Tony began banging a swizzle stick on the side of a pint glass.

'If I can have your attention, everybody, please . . .'

The pub hushed in anticipation, this moment obviously well known to them.

'Now. Our treasurer tells me that the totals have been tallied . . .' He paused for effect, and everyone around Nell, all the various groups who had been competing so hard to make the most money for charity, leaned forward, breath held, waiting for him to go on, hands gripping hands in nervous, excited anticipation, 'And the Midsummer Madness Master Moneymakers for this year . . .'

Maud held on to Nell's hand so hard her knuckles went white.

'. . . who managed to raise the amazing total of one thousand three hundred and twenty-four pounds and eighty-two pence on their own . . . bringing the grand total of today's Madness to the incredible sum of forty-two thousand six hundred and nineteen pounds, are . . .' He paused again, and Maud's nails dug in deeper, '*the Polporth Lunching Ladies!* Now, as agreed at the last general meeting of the Midsummer Madness Marauders, all proceeds will be divided between the Lifeboat Association and—'

But Tony's words were drowned out by the screams of delight of the LLs, who all started jumping up and down and hugging each other; well, all of them apart from Maud, who flicked a none too surreptitious Churchill at the leader of the Lifeboat Crew Wives, who was looking like someone had just put some very bitter lemon in her gin and tonic.

'Calm down now, please . . .' Tony held up his hands for peace but was completely ignored.

'Calm down, please!' He tried again to no avail.

'Quiet!' thundered Marge in a voice that you wouldn't have thought could come from such a thin woman . . . or a woman at all, come to think of it, it was so like one of those Satan arrives moments at a seance.

The whole pub fell silent.

'Thank you,' said Tony, to both Marge and his now silent clientele. 'I just wanted to say a huge thank you to everyone that's been involved this year. Every year we say we can't beat the last and every year people just dig deeper. This is an amazing village and I for one am so proud to be a part of it.'

'Hear, hear!' The cheers became deafening, particularly as Tony paused to wipe away a genuine tear, and then he held up a hand and this time was afforded instant silence.

'And now, my wonderful friends and neighbours, for the moment you've all been waiting for, the culmination of Midsummer Madness, the highlight of our tradition . . . The result of the village vote for this year's Goddess of the Sea is finally in, and it's—'

'Orgy time!' yelled a wag at the back, who was instantly mown down by Marge's gunfire gaze.

Despite hearing the same thing every year, Tony still managed to laugh heartily. 'Sorry, folks. Although we do now get to ogle a beautiful woman, she will unfortunately be keeping her clothes on.'

'Not like the 2002 goddess, then,' Maud murmured to Nell. 'As soon as she was announced, she ripped off her dress and streaked through the back lanes until Marge felled her with a rugby tackle and made her get dressed again.'

'Liam, the envelope, please.' Tony's son passed his father a very large gold envelope, which Tony made a show of opening before sliding the piece of card from within, reading it, and then looking up with a huge smirk on his face.

'Without further ado . . . I am delighted to announce that our new Midsummer Madness Goddess of the Sea is . . .'

London Tony paused for dramatic effect, and Nell had to resist the urge to drum-roll with her fingers on the table. TJ, Liam and Ben, however, were not so restrained, and the threatened drum roll materialised as they grabbed snooker cues and began to tantivy them on the pool table.

'. . . our very own bombshell of a barmaid, Ange O'Donel, the best pint-puller in Polporth!'

Ange's jaw clanged to the floor. Nell could have sworn she heard it echo as it hit the wooden floorboards.

'Me?' Ange rasped, her voice suddenly lost. 'Me?' she squeaked again, her voice returning halfway through this second attempt, so that the E of it was like the bray of a donkey.

And then everyone was on their feet, cheering and clapping, and Ange had turned a strange colour like a stain made on a white shirt by the juice of a ripe blackberry.

'Me?' she mouthed again, her voice taken away by the shock.

A beaming Nell gently handed Ange her drink, and after a mouthful of vodka and tonic she regained her usual colour and composure and only needed a slight shove in the small of her back to sail regally over to where London Tony was waiting for her with open arms, the Goddess of the Sea crown of shells and flotsam and jetsam clutched in one of his big meaty hands.

'I crown you, fair maiden, our Goddess of the Sea, and everyone shall bend to ye,' he announced in a horrendous take on a Cornish accent.

There was a chorus of wolf whistles as a still blushing Ange bent her head to receive her crown and flashed her cleavage.

'And she wonders why she won . . .' Maud said with a wink.

Ange was then hoisted on to the broad shoulders of the

Jolly Roger rowing team and carried out of the pub. Everyone surged outside after them, following them down the winding cobbled street towards the harbour, the procession accompanied by a rowdy chorus of clapping and singing.

And then suddenly this impromptu music was rudely interrupted, as with hollers and catcalls, whoops and yells, a gang of men erupted from the shadows, falling out of darkened alleyways and doorways.

'Pirates!' Nell mouthed in disbelief.

A few people screamed, and then the whole crowd seemed to hold its breath, as though they were watching a key scene in a movie, which seemed to involve a rather fierce battle between the Polporth rowers and the interlopers, before one of the interlopers pulled the leader of the rowing team's jersey over his head, grabbed Ange from him, and ran off with her.

Maud had carried on walking when the pirates swooped whilst Nell had stopped to watch in wonder, so she tugged on the sleeve of the next person to pass, who just happened to be Elspeth Towan, owner of the dress shop and self-styled Harriet Potter, who was wearing so many garlands she looked and smelled like a walking pomander.

'What the hell's going on?'

'Oh, them's just the lads from the Penmorvah Manna.'

'The what?'

'Penmorvah Manna, the Drunken Monk in Did's Bay. They do this every year; it's tradition, they always run off with the goddess. Don't you worry, my lover, they'll bring her back in the morning.'

'In the morning!' Nell exclaimed in concern. 'What on earth are they going to do with her all night?'

'Well, that I don't rightly know, but I wish I'd had a

chance to find out when I was younger.' Elspeth winked and then, grabbing Nell's hand, urged her to 'Come on or we'll miss it all.'

They caught up with Maud just as the ruffians had reached the end of the harbour.

'Did Ange know this was going to happen?' Nell rasped, breathless and more than a little concerned.

'Are you worried about Ange, or are you worried that you're missing out?'

Nell burst out laughing. 'Maybe a bit of both.'

'Well, I wouldn't worry about Ange. She certainly doesn't look like she minds very much.' Maud grinned broadly.

Maud was right as always. Despite the fact that her ride to the harbour from the point of her 'kidnap' wasn't exactly an easy one – instead of being carried aloft like a queen she had been thrown over the shoulder of the largest of the ruffians – Ange was indeed grinning like a pussy in a field full of catnip.

Even when they reached the harbour wall and threw her none too gently into a large rowing boat, the smile stayed firmly in place. And then they began to row away into the distance, until the lights and laughter could be seen and heard no more.

26

Nell was asleep and dreaming, the weirdest kind of dream. Harry was kissing her, which in itself wasn't weird – in fact it was really rather wonderful – but then he stopped, to tell her that he shouldn't be kissing her and he couldn't have a relationship with her because he was married to Half Pint. He was just about to kiss her again, despite telling her that he really shouldn't because Half Pint was watching, when her mobile phone began to ring. 'Hadn't you better answer that?' said dream Harry, his face segueing smoothly into Marcus's as Nell leaned in closer to kiss him again.

'Yes, you should answer that!' snapped Half Pint, who despite still having the hairy body of a very tall donkey, suddenly looked just like Harry's mystery brunette.

Nell awoke with a jolt. The phone was ringing. For a moment she didn't recognise the voice, it was so distorted, and then she realised that it was Ange.

'Nell, we're on Polwest beach.'

Well, that explained the rushing sound on the line; it wasn't interference, it was the sea.

'What are you doing there?'

'A party. An all-night party.'

'It's three in the morning.'

'Like I said, it's an all-night party, we're going to drink too much . . .'

'I think you might already have done that bit,' said Nell at the sound of the slur in Ange's voice.

'. . . dance around the fire like savages, and then watch the sun come up over the sea.'

'Who are you with, Ange?'

'The drunken monks, they're lovely.'

'So you're okay?'

'I'm more than okay, I'm bloody wonderful, and I'm a goddess, Nell, a living, breathing goddess.' Her voice was all over the place, high-pitched on 'living' and 'breathing' and then deep as a man's on 'goddess'.

'Want me to come and get you?'

'Oh no, oh nononono, I want you to come and join me. The party dances on, and I want you to come and dance with me. Live a little, come and have a ding-dong, Nell, come out to play, pleeease . . .'

Nell went, but more out of concern for Ange, who was obviously way beyond her usual drunk, than a desire to start partying at three in the morning when she'd been happily snoring in bed since eleven thirty.

She could see the flickering gold and red flames of the beach fires long before she could see anything else. She could hear music and voices, acoustic guitars being strummed, someone singing, a female voice, sweet and vibrato, and then a male joining in, and then another, until a chorus of song was washing like waves on the shore.

Despite the fact that the only light was starlight and firelight, Ange could clearly be seen in the middle of this musical group, dancing, kicking up the sand with her feet, arms swaying above her head as if she was trancing.

When Nell got closer, she could see that Ange was

covered head to toe in sand. It was in her hair and the creases of her clothes, sparkling like stardust in the firelight. She looked hedonistic, and very, very happy.

She also amazingly seemed to have sobered up a little since the phone call, and was now just very drunk rather than verging on incoherent.

As soon as she spotted Nell, she staggered over to her, arms outstretched, and fell upon her in an embrace. 'Nell! Hooray! I was just thinking that all I needed to make this a perfect night was you here to enjoy it with me.' Then she dropped her voice to a whisper. 'Do you know, I think I've fulfilled about eight lifelong fantasies in one evening. I got abducted by pirates . . .'

'I know, I saw them carry you away. I'm here to rescue you. Come on, Ange.'

'Come on?' Ange crossed her eyes in confusion.

'Home.' Nell held out a hand. 'I think I should take you home.'

Ange staggered backwards. 'No way, Nell. We can't leave the party halfway through. And you're not going either; you're going to loosen up, lighten up and have some fun for a change. When was the last time you had fun?'

Ange had a point. Nell was struggling to remember.

'We have to stay at least until the sun rises. Please, Nell. Purlease . . .' Ange was staggering backwards as she spoke, holding out her hands to Nell, urging her to take them and join her in the short journey across the sand back to the party lounged around the bonfire.

'I want you to meet someone wonderful,' she slurred, leading her over to a man who was sitting cross-legged on the ground. 'This is Nell, my bestest friend,' she slurred, throwing an arm around Nell's shoulders and swaying about her like a drunk around a lamppost. 'Nell, this is Captain Jack I'm Hung Like a Marrow.'

After this introduction Nell didn't know where to look, especially as Captain Jack was clad in nothing but a pair of sawn-off jeans.

'You must be freezing,' was all she could think of to say to him.

He burst out laughing.

He had a laugh like gravel going down a waste disposal unit.

And then he held out a hand.

'Welcome to the party, Nell.'

With hair to his shoulders and a goatee beard, he certainly looked like a pirate. His Cornish accent was the softest of inflections on a rasping voice. Nell didn't know whether this was his usual voice, or whether his vocal cords had given up because he and his friends were all so bloody drunk.

It was a friendly group comprising of the original gang who had 'stolen' Ange, and some of the younger regulars from the Jolly Roger, including Beth, who it turned out was the girl that Nell had heard singing when she first arrived.

Nell was introduced to everyone, and the singing resumed, some still dancing round the bonfire like savages. Then someone produced a didgeridoo, heavens knew where from, although it made Nell giggle to speculate, and they all sat down and began to sing Rolf Harris songs.

Someone else handed her a stone flagon, telling her it was Cornish cider.

Nell took a sip.

It was nothing like the frothing sweet drink she was used to; it was heavy and fairly flat and head-swimmingly strong from the very first mouthful.

'I'm so glad you're here.' Ange rested her head on

Nell's shoulder. 'I'm so glad I'm here . . . not just here . . . but *here,* and I wouldn't be here or here if it weren't for you, Nell. Thank you, thank you so much. I love you, Nell.'

'Love you too, Ange.'

'Let's watch the sun rise together, Nell. You and me. We'll watch the sun rise on a new day and give thanks for our new lives.'

Nell didn't have the heart to confess to Ange that she had fallen asleep shortly after, and had only woken up moments after everyone else had watched in awe as the sun had shaken herself from slumber and risen dripping molten rays from the depths of the ocean.

By some miracle, Ange was still awake, awake and dancing with Captain Jack, who was whispering in her ear as they writhed in the sand.

'I love this place, Nell,' she called over on seeing Nell watching her.

'I can tell.'

And then her smile slipped into something serious. 'No, I mean it, I really, really mean it . . . You see, in London . . .' she paused to hiccup, 'I said in London, I'm a beached whale, Nell, a beached bloody whale. Here I am a goddess, a *goddess*. If only I'd known before that having a sexy body is nothing to do with diet and denial, it's just a matter of geography.'

And then she fell face forward into the sand.

Beth and Captain Jack helped Nell half carry, half drag Ange to Cyril Junior. Beth slipped into the back seat for a lift back to Polporth, and then Nell and Jack kind of half pushed, half folded Ange into the front.

As Captain Jack slipped the buckle on Ange's seatbelt into place, he leaned back out of the car but not completely, and Nell noticed him pull back the sleeve of Ange's sand-covered top.

'What are you doing?' she asked in concern as he took something from his pocket and pressed it against her flesh, and then she realised that it was a pen. He wrote his phone number in a large scrawl on a comatose Ange's forearm, winked at Nell and then stepped back and pushed the car door shut.

'I think she's pulled,' Beth giggled as Nell got into the driver's side.

'As long as she spots it before she has a shower.'

'Maybe we should copy it down for her?'

'Maybe we shouldn't.' Nell pulled a face at Beth in the rear-view mirror.

'Jack?' Beth asked in surprise, glancing out of the window to see him wave as they drove off. 'He's a nice guy, Nell, honestly. Just because he looks like a member of Motley Crue doesn't mean he acts like one.'

'Don't judge a bloke by his tattoos, eh?'

'Well, in Jack's case, yeah, but I wouldn't always say that. Did you meet Adam, the guy with the curly blond hair, the one who kept chucking Becca into the sea? Well he has this huge snake tattooed on his shoulder blade, and he's—'

'A total snake?' Nell offered, but Beth shook her head.

'He's got the hugest, biggest, most massive . . .' she began, her eyes wide with wonder, and then before she could finish, Ange jerked awake and began to sing.

'My ding a ling, my ding a ling, I wanna play with my . . .'

It wasn't the hangover that bothered Ange the following day; it was the fact that she'd had a shower whilst still half asleep and washed off Captain Jack's number.

A phone call minutes later, however, and any thoughts of Captain Jack were washed away as easily as his scrawl. 'He's coming, he's coming!'

'Well, it's summer,' Nell smiled indulgently as her overexcited friend bounced into the tea rooms, 'so I know you're not talking about Santa.'

'Tam McCavin,' Ange almost shrieked his name with pleasure, '*finally* is gracing us with his presence.'

'*Grand Openings* are coming down again?'

'Yep. They want to film the transformation scenes now, you know, the "a few weeks later" section: have they succeeded or haven't they, is it still gorgeous, has the lame bird they turned into a swan managed to fly, or has it come crashing to the ground . . .'

'When?'

'Today,' Ange said, doing a little dance of joy.

'Today!' Nell shrieked. 'Oh my lord! They could have given us a bit of notice. I mean, they've had to come all the way down from London, it's not like they're just popping up from Truro. A telephone call to say they were on their way wouldn't have killed them, would it?'

Nell stopped talking as she realised that Ange was unusually quiet, and turned around to find her looking sheepish.

'They did call, didn't they?'

Ange nodded. 'Lisa called last week. I'm so sorry, Nell, 'cause there was so much going on with the Madness I totally forgot until this morning.'

'You forgot Tam McCavin was coming here?' Nell asked incredulously.

'Oh no.' Ange shook her head vigorously. 'They only told me that bit just now when they phoned to confirm they were on their way and what time they thought they'd get here.'

'Which is when?'

'Well, they were at Exeter.'

'Exeter! They're already at Exeter?'

Ange bit her lip and looked guilty as Nell glanced panic-stricken at first her watch and then the clock on the kitchen wall.

'That means I have about an hour to do everything I normally do on a Monday morning *and* get the flat clean and cleared.'

'Sod the flat . . .'

'Sod the flat?'

'Yeah, the flat's fine.' Ange waved a dismissive hand around the semi-tidiness that was their home. 'It's you that you need to sort out. Get some lippy on, and do something with your hair, Tam McCavin's coming!' And with this last exclamation of happiness, Ange danced into the bathroom, slamming the door joyously behind her.

The next thing Nell heard was the shower, and Ange singing 'It's Raining Men'.

'Sod the flat' was easy for Ange to say; *her* mother

would be watching the show with her friends and neighbours and a bottle or two, going 'That's me daughter so it is, that's me beautiful Ange, I always said the girl would be a star so I did, a star I said.' She wouldn't be watching the show and tutting at every speck of dust, every cobweb, every unwiped plant leaf, every bit of clothing flung instead of hung. She wouldn't be phoning afterwards to say how she couldn't face the neighbours because she was so mortally embarrassed by the state of her bedroom.

Something Nell's mother had drummed into her was that cleanliness was next to godliness; an untidy home showed an untidy mind; the milkman would think you were a slut if you didn't rinse out your milk bottles before putting them out for him.

She had managed to wean herself partially off this unwanted obsession since moving away from her parents' house, but even after all these years it was still a work in progress.

Especially now that she and Ange were cohabiting.

Whilst Nell was a human Dyson when it came to cleaning, Ange was a human dynamo when it came to making things messy.

The kitchen was as always immaculate. Aside from her mother, Nell had this irrational fear that although the tea room kitchen was so clean you could eat off the floor, Health and Safety might one day announce that they wanted to inspect the living quarters too.

Nell looked around her bedroom. Despite the new carpet, the freshly painted walls and her beautiful if slightly eclectic mix of furniture, to her it was still a complete dump. Yesterday's clothes were in a heap on the floor by the bed, there were two old coffee cups on the bedside table, one from yesterday evening, and heaven forbid the other from the day before, the duvet was thrown back from when she had got up that morning, the embroidered quilt that usually lay neatly on the end of the bed had somehow settled itself into a heap on the floor.

Nell was just about to make the bed, berating herself for being so lax, when a freshly washed Ange, swathed in towels, stuck her head round the door.

'Wow, thank heavens it's so neat and tidy in here; might detract from the cesspit that is my room. Still, I suppose we could always say we saved mine as a "before" shot.'

Quivering inside at what she might find, Nell followed Ange back to her room. It was as though her suitcase had exploded scattering clothes everywhere. The only uncluttered expanse was Ange's duvet, although there was an empty cereal bowl perched in the middle of it, spoon in milk, tipping dangerously.

'You at least need to clear a trail to the bed so that Tam McCavin can find his way there,' Nell said, trying not to look or feel disapproving as she surveyed the junk yard that was Ange's bedroom, and then she hurriedly backed out before she turned into Monica from *Friends* and tried to suck the whole lot including Ange up with the hoover.

Half an hour later, Ange danced into the kitchen of the tea room, where Nell had retired to polish the chrome.

She had drawn rings of kohl around her grey eyes and loaded her lips with her favourite lipstick, aptly entitled Passion. Her curls were newly glossed with Frizz Away; her push-up bra was entering a weight-lifting contest and trouncing the competition. She was smoking and smouldering harder than a forest fire in a drought. She looked great – for a nightclub at midnight. It wasn't exactly a mid-morning in a tea room kind of look, but then if anyone could carry it off it was Ange.

'Lisa just called,' she said, practically floating on a cloud of her own excitement. 'They'll be here in twenty minutes. Can we please have a double skinny latte and a plate of something sweet waiting the minute they walk in the door. Apparently it's been a bit of a journey and Tam's blood sugar is too low.'

'In other words, he's in a bad mood.' Nell smiled wryly. 'Sounds like a bit of a diva, placing his orders before he even gets here.'

'I like divas.' Ange smiled wickedly. 'Especially muff divas.'

Tam McCavin walked into the Cakehole half an hour later and instantly made the large room feel small. Six foot two, with the physique to carry it off, he was strikingly handsome in the flesh, even more so than in his publicity shot.

A veteran of many a home makeover show, Tam possessed an Irish charm that had female hearts melting from Land's End to Lanarkshire, but Nell got the impression he hadn't been particularly charming on the way down to Polporth.

He had a face like a toddler on the verge of a tantrum, and the lovely Lisa looked totally frazzled.

Nell immediately handed her the latte and cakes she had prepared as instructed.

'For Tam?'

Nell shook her head. 'For you. You look like you need it more than he does.'

'Oh you're a sweetheart, Nell, but trust me, as soon as he's fed and watered he'll be sweetness and light, so the sooner I get this down his neck the happier I'll be.'

'Is he a nightmare?'

'Can be. But he doesn't mean to be really. He's like a cashmere jumper . . .'

'He shrinks if you put him on a hot wash?' Nell joked.

Lisa laughed. 'Every girl should have one, and they're as soft as a baby's bum, but very high maintenance to keep that way.'

Nell didn't do high maintenance. Not in that way, anyway. She was happy to work at a relationship, but she had a feeling that keeping Tam McCavin happy was a full-time job that required more than just one employee.

Ange, on the other hand, had decided that the looks and the physique far outweighed the personality.

'He's totally gorgeous, isn't he?' she whispered just at the moment Nell had decided he was too good looking to be good looking.

'If you say so.'

'You don't think?'

'Not my type.'

'Which leaves the field clear for Ange O'Donel, hawk of love, to swoop upon her prey,' Ange jested, making claws with her fingers. 'Give us a pineapple tart, Nell, he looks hungry.'

She sashayed across the room, pineapple tart held aloft on one of Nell's pink plates, like a cocktail waitress delivering something sinful and alcoholic and presented it to her idol.

'You look like a man who needs his sugar. Fancy a nibble on something naughty?'

'Go, girl,' Nell whispered, trying not to laugh at the fact that within seconds the previously grumpy Tam was smiling like crazy and practically falling into Ange's cleavage, mesmerised like a snake by the charmer's music, by the physical symphony that was Ange's bosom.

'Wish I had me a pair of those,' Lisa said, raising eyebrows at Nell.

'Me too, although I'm not sure I'd get a licence for them.'

'Lethal weapons?'

'Only to be operated by trained personnel.' Nell nodded.

He was whispering something into her ear now. Nell couldn't make out what he was saying, but Ange's response was loud and clear. 'Want to come up and do a voice-over in my room?'

Tam's laughter rang out.

The two cameramen nudged each other and rolled eyeballs.

Then he bit into Nell's pineapple tart.

Suddenly it was as if Ange's cleavage had lost its magical powers, as his eyes closed in sybaritic bliss and he pushed every last crumb into his mouth as though someone was going to come and steal the rest away if he didn't eat it fast enough.

'Oh my lord,' he said when his mouth was empty enough to actually speak. 'Did you make that?'

'No,' Ange said reluctantly.

'Nell did,' piped up Lisa, putting her hand in the small of Nell's back and pushing her forward gently.

Tam looked at her as if he was seeing her for the first time, which Nell thought actually he probably was. He hadn't taken much notice of anything other than his own displeasure when he had first arrived, and since then he'd been alternately hypnotised by cleavage and cake.

'Nell?' he said, moving over towards her.

Nell nodded.

'You made that tart?'

She nodded again, and Tam chastised himself for not noticing her before. She really was remarkably pretty.

'You're a genius. That was amazing. So light and fresh and sweet . . . and the pastry, absolute heaven.'

Ange sighed. She knew only too well the power those pineapple tarts could have on a person, but had never thought that even they could compete with the man-magnet that were her 40 DDs.

Tam had been her hunk of the month for a long time. She'd even had a Tam McCavin calendar pinned next to her office planner for the past three years usually stuck at August, where he was normally to be found, spade in hand and tanned and shirtless. And now she was sure he was looking at Nell, pastry queen, as if she was the pineapple tart and he wanted to devour her.

'Would you like another one?' Nell offered.

'Another tart? Oh definitely, yes, please.' And he gave her his best smouldering smile, the one guaranteed to melt women faster than butter in a microwave.

Nell didn't melt. She didn't even wilt a little; she simply turned to her friend and said, 'Ange? Do you want to get Mr McCavin another tart?'

Ange nodded gratefully at Nell for giving her another opener, and shot into the kitchen.

'Would you care to join me?' he asked, lifting the smile up a watt or two.

Nell shook her head. 'Thanks, but I have things I need to do. You know, ovens to scrub. Dough to knead, that kind of thing.'

'Surely you're not too busy for a tea break?'

'You'd think, wouldn't you, that in a tea room it would be a prerequisite to have a tea break, but I just don't have the time, sorry.'

She was making excuses.

She was making excuses. He had to repeat it to himself for it to sink in. It had been such a long time since someone had turned down the chance of his company that Tam wasn't too sure what to do with himself, but then Ange returned bearing a cake stand groaning not only with pineapple tarts, but Nell's coffee eclairs, her feather-light fairy cakes, her cherry-rich fruit cake, and her triple chocolate and raspberry cheesecake.

His ego dented but his mouth watering at the sight of such a feast of sugar, he trotted obediently after her to a corner table.

'He loves his food,' Lisa commented as he hovered hungrily over the selection, not knowing where to plunge his teeth first.

'Should get on well with Ange then.' Nell laughed.

'It does look that way already.' Lisa nodded, indicating with her head to where Ange was ripping a coffee eclair in half so that they could share.

'What about the rest of you? Do you love your food too? Fancy something to eat?'

'Love to, but I'm afraid we have a filming schedule to keep to . . .'

'I don't think you're going to be doing much filming for a little while at least . . .' Nell said as Ange loaded Tam's plate with a slice of cheesecake. 'He's already had a pineapple tart and a coffee eclair. If he eats the cheesecake on top of that, he won't be able to get out of his chair for at least another half an hour.'

'It's that heavyweight?'

'Plain, milk and white chocolate, mascarpone cheese, double cream, chocolate biscuits, butter, and the secret ingredient in the raspberries is a very large shot of vodka.'

'I'll take a piece of that then, please.' Lisa grinned and

plonked herself down at the nearest table. 'Don't suppose I can get it with extra vodka?'

By the time Tam had finished eating he was almost soporific, and when it came to filming his views on the Cakehole, he was as lyrical as his fellow countryman James Joyce with his praise.

'Welcome to the Cakehole, a hidden haven of hot and cold, a man-sized morsel of melt-in-the-mouth manna, a paradise of pastries, a veritable cornucopia of cake. My soul has been sold for a slice of succour to the senses, such is the wonder of the delicious Nell Everson's ultra-bankable, supremely consumable baking. Will the Cakehole be a business success? No it will not . . . it will be more than that: it will be a sugar-coated, jam-stuffed, ice-topped triumph! In fact,' he made a show of sitting down at one of the tables, 'I am going to claim this chair as my own from this day forth.' He picked up a knife from the table and, much to Nell's horror, used the blade to scratch the word 'Tam' into the wood. 'Because I am a sucker for succour, and here I have found an edible Garden of Eden that it would take God himself to evict me from. Come and join me, and taste a touch of hedonistic heaven . . .'

He paused and held his final pose until Ella the director shouted, 'Cut.'

'You know that is the best piece to camera we have ever done with him,' Lisa whispered to Nell. 'I think you must have sweetened him up for us, pardon the pun.'

'I think that was Ange's handiwork.' Nell laughed.

'Perhaps.' Lisa smiled enigmatically, and nodded. 'But I've seen him with that look on his face before, and it's not just when he *eats* something delicious. I'd say he definitely has something other than cheesecake on his mind.'

*

Tam looked around at the smiling faces and knew that he had done well and was being appreciated for it. He had been inspired today.

He had always loved an audience, and he had always needed to feel adored. And over the years he had got far more than his fair share of adoration.

Until today.

Today he had met someone who was different.

Someone who was indifferent.

Nell was very pretty, that part was plain to see, but it had been the reluctance in her eyes that drew him to her, the way she stepped away when he got close instead of trying to get close to him herself. The way that when the camera crew were in the tea room she had always tried to stay out of shot rather than get into it.

When he first broke into showbiz he had loved the way that women had thrown themselves at his feet.

Now easy was getting boring.

Something a little more challenging would be fun.

The friend, the enthusiastic one, a fellow Dubliner, with the big grey eyes and the even bigger boobs, now she would usually have been more his type; he would have taken one look at those beautiful come-to-bed boobs and dived on in there head first. But now . . . well, it was his thirty-sixth birthday soon, and although he was nowhere near that in his own mind and his mirror, it did somehow make forty seem so much closer, and to be honest he had got to the point where Tam McCavin the man, rather than Tam McCavin the celebrity, wondered if he still had it in him. If he weren't famous, would they still want him so badly?

Now Nell . . . well, she was obviously not impressed by all the razzmatazz, had taken a bit of persuading to let them film, according to one of his researchers. She was the kind of girl that all of this would mean nothing to, the kind of girl who would give his ego the real boost it needed, because she would be put off by the trappings of his celebrity, not encouraged and excited by them. If he could pull Nell, then he'd know that Tam was still the man.

28

Nell was in the Cakehole kitchen doing her morning bakeathon. Ange was sitting in her favourite spot by the window. She was on the phone, and from the sound of things was chatting away happily to Lisa the researcher.

Sometimes Nell envied the ease with which Ange made friends, but when she had mentioned this to Ange, she had simply told her her life rule number thirty-seven.

'Friends are like boobies, Nell. They may all look full of filthy promise but it's only when you squeeze them hard that you know if they're real or not. I can count my real friends on the toes of my left foot, and as you know, I lost one of them in a rather traumatic roller-skate accident when I was five.'

'Am I on that foot?' Nell asked.

'You're the little toe.'

'The *little* toe?' Nell pretended to pout.

'Without you I'd fall over,' Ange had replied.

Now she flipped off the phone and getting up strolled over to Nell and leaned nonchalantly on the counter. 'Did you know that Tam McCavin is still in Polporth?'

'Really?' Nell tried to feign interest.

'The camera crew packed up and went home this morning. He didn't go with them. According to Lisa, he said he wanted a holiday for the first time in six years.'

'Six years? Well, in that case he definitely needs one.'

'You don't think it's a bit weird?'

'That he wants to stay here? Not really, considering we know all too well the powerful lure of Polporth on us London-dwellers.'

'I don't think it's the powerful lure of Polporth, Nell.'

'You don't?'

'Uhuh.' Ange shook her head. 'I heard it's the powerful lure of your pineapple tarts.'

Nell burst out laughing. 'They're good, but they're not that good.'

'Okay, so how about if I told you it was the powerful lure of . . . well, you?'

Nell laughed even harder.

'I think you might have got that the wrong way round, Ange. It was you he was falling all over yesterday.'

'It's true,' Ange insisted. 'Lisa told me that he wouldn't shut up about you at breakfast this morning, and then he announced that he was staying on.'

'You're kidding me?'

Nell looked so utterly horrified that despite her disappointment, Ange couldn't help but laugh.

'You're really telling me that you don't find him the least bit attractive? He's gorgeous, he's famous, what more do you want . . .'

'Ange, you know I'm not that shallow. I want an even, stable relationship. I couldn't be with someone who has an ego that fragile. Can you imagine what it would be like? He'd need it stroking constantly. His ego, Ange, his EGO! Besides, I really don't think the guy wants a relationship; I wouldn't imagine he has them, just a whole line of conquests.' Nell flung an arm into the distance to signify exactly how long she thought that line would be. 'No,' she said firmly, more to herself than her friend. 'No matter how attractive or charming he might be, I do not want a relationship, whatever that might mean, with Tam McCavin.'

'You could always just shag him,' Ange said hopefully.

'Tell you what,' Nell slung an arm around Ange's shoulders. 'Why don't you do it for me?'

'If only,' Ange sighed. 'So you don't fancy a fruitless fling with a handsome hedonist, then?'

'Like I said, not my type.'

'I thought Tam McCavin was every woman's type.'

'Oh, I'm sure there are a few who are immune.'

'You're going to tell me you don't fancy Brad Pitt in a minute.'

'Well I don't, actually.'

Ange sucked in her breath, loudly, her hand flying to her heart in not quite mock shock.

'What is wrong with you, woman!' she pretended to thunder. 'You don't like the god that is Brad, and when I tell you that Tam McCavin, *the* Tam McCavin, man voted on *This Morning* as Britain's sexiest ever TV presenter, fancies the pants off you, you turn your nose up.'

'He doesn't like me, Ange, you're imagining things.' Turning her attention to the fairy cakes she had baking in the oven, Nell wondered if she dared check on them or if opening the oven door might make them sink.

'You think? Then why is he heading for here as we speak?'

Nell laughed.

'I'm being serious,' Ange insisted.

The bell rang as the door opened, but Nell didn't turn around. She wasn't even going to look and give Ange the satisfaction of laughing at her.

'Um, Nell, someone's here to see you.'

'Yeah, pull the other one, Ange, it makes my drawers drop off.'

'Two pineapple tarts, please, and a double skinny latte, please,' said a voice behind her that sounded a touch too familiar.

Nell spun round to see Ange grinning broadly at Tam McCavin, who was leaning his six-foot-two frame on the glass counter top.

'Um, yeah, sure, of course. If you want to take a seat, I'll bring that over to your table.'

'Assuming you can walk with your knickers round your ankles,' Ange stage-whispered.

'Oh my God!' Nell rolled her eyes, mortified, as Tam went over to a table in the corner and picked up a newspaper. 'Do you think he heard?'

'No, I don't think so.'

Nell sighed with relief until Ange added: 'I *know* he did.'

Nell thrust two pineapple tarts at Ange and then, drawing off a latte at the machine, handed her that as well.

'You take it to him.'

'Don't be such a wimp.'

'Please, Ange . . .'

'Okay, okay,' Ange said with as much reluctance as she had had enthusiasm the last time Nell had asked her to serve him. 'But,' she leaned in, 'he likes you, Nell, and you can't avoid that or him for ever.'

Ange was right.

When he'd finished his tarts and his coffee he brought the cup and plate back to Nell himself and leaned on the counter, determined to talk to her.

'You're an amazing pastry chef, Nell, are you trained?'

Nell shook her head, as Ange, who was helping out

behind the counter by peeling some apples for a tarte tatin, began to smirk knowingly.

'Wow, I'm surprised.'

'Thank you.'

There was a moment's awkward silence and then he tried again. 'I think what you're doing with this place is absolutely fascinating.'

'It's just a tea room.' Nell shrugged self-deprecatingly.

'Well, it was just a shell before; you've done wonders in such a short time. It looks great, very welcoming, very . . .' he paused and looked about himself appraisingly, 'very *appetising* actually.'

Nell looked at him in surprise, with in fact a little renewed respect.

'That's exactly the look I was aiming for.'

'Well, you've certainly achieved that. I really think this is one of *Grand Openings*' big successes, especially as you started off in the "barking to buy" section. Do you know, we sometimes do a special, where we do follow-ups on some of our more interesting businesses. I think the Cakehole would be a fabulous candidate for that, genuinely. I'd love to discuss it some more. What do you say to perhaps having a chat over dinner tonight?'

'I don't think—'

'Maybe I could give you some ideas for publicity and marketing?'

'Well, I'm not really—'

Nell felt a furious dig in her ribs and turned to see that Ange was nearly exploding.

'Would you excuse me for just one second,' Nell said politely, then, turning, she grabbed Ange by the shoulders and bundled her out through the fire door and into the courtyard. 'What is it?' she asked in a harsh whisper.

When Ange opened her mouth, it was like the valve on

an overfilled balloon being opened. The words came out on a rush of the air she had been holding in.

'You've been asked out to dinner by a bona fide celebrity, Nell; you have to go, even if it's just for something to boast to your grandchildren about in thirty years' time.'

'But it's you that likes him, Ange, not me.'

'I know, but he's not going to ask me out, and asking you is the next best thing.'

Nell still looked exceedingly dubious, so Ange went for her weak spot.

'What's more, he's bound to take you somewhere decent and you can steal their lunch menu and nick all their best ideas for here. He might even take you to the Plover . . .'

It was like waving a pineapple tart in front of a wavering Slim-U member.

The Plover Hotel, on the outskirts of Polporth, opposite and almost level with Maud's cottage, so you could see it in the distance from Maud's garden.

Five-star accommodation, Michelin-starred restaurant, celebrity chef in residence. Nell had gazed upon it from Maud's sunloungers with all the longing of the Romans looking across the English Channel on a clear day. Viewed with awe by the villagers as a bastion of poshness, its hallowed halls were trod mainly by Cornwall-loving celebrities and rich people from smoke-filled cities in search of the civilised side of the seaside.

The hotel was owned and run by Nadia Tomelli, daughter of the original owners and wife of a once famous but now retired opera singer. Its restaurant was never used by locals because it was far too expensive, but because of the celebrity chef who ran the kitchens, it had enough of a cachet with holidaymakers to allow it to be mentioned on the local news at least once a month, and have a waiting list as long as Maud's legs.

Nell had been dying to take a look inside its hallowed halls. Not least because the chef, the handsome and down-to-earth J.P. David, who was one of the most reclusive celebrity chefs in existence, was also one of her culinary heroes.

'And what's more,' Ange added, waving her words like a carrot, 'if you go to dinner with Tam McCavin, it's going to be all over Cornwall in next to no time.'

'And?' Nell queried, frowning, not at all certain this was an incentive.

'Well, it really wouldn't hurt certain people who express an interest and then back off like you've bitten them to know that you have other men panting to get in your knickers.'

'I don't play those kind of games, Ange.'

'No, old Nell didn't play those kind of games; maybe new Nell should give it a go. Go on, Nelly, why not? Live a little, stir things up, take a chance.'

'You're going to break into song in a minute, aren't you?'

'If you don't say yes to Tam, then yes, definitely.'

'Oh, okay!' Nell gave up. 'I'll go, I'll go out for dinner with him.' She marched back inside to Tam, who was still hovering by the counter. 'Okay, yes, thank you, dinner would be lovely.'

'Fantastic!' He looked so genuinely delighted that Nell immediately felt awful for making such a meal of her answer. 'I'll send a car for you, shall we say about seven? If it's okay with you, the place I'm staying at has a fairly decent restaurant, not really London standards, but more than passable I suppose. Perhaps we could eat there? Place on the other side of the bay. You might know it. The Plover.'

*

Nell had been poured into one of Ange's slim-into dresses, a sexy – all of Ange's slim-into dresses were sexy – dark green silk that showed off her slender figure and dark hair and eyes to perfection.

'God, that's an amazing dress.' Ange shook her head in a mixture of appreciation and envy. 'I wish I could fit into it.'

'You'd look wonderful in it.' Nell nodded her agreement. 'It would really suit your colouring.'

'Shame I'm never going to wear it then, isn't it?'

'Why on earth not? You'll fit into it soon, Ange, if you lay off the pineapple tarts.'

'Sure, but I won't wear it 'cause it won't be mine any more.'

Nell frowned in puzzlement at her friend.

''Cause I'm giving it to you,' Ange explained.

'You are?'

'Oh absolutely. Have you seen yourself, Nell? That dress belongs to you because it belongs *on* you. You look amazing, gorgeous.'

'You think?'

'If I was a lesbian I'd so be trying to pull you right now.'

Nell laughed. She had to admit she was actually excited, and although she swore to Ange that this was just because she had been longing to eat at the Plover since they had arrived in Polporth, if pushed she would have had to confess that she was fibbing just a little bit.

It had been so many years since she had gone on a first date, and she had forgotten what a buzz it was.

There was a bit of a hoo-hah when a chauffeur arrived to pick Nell up. He was bearing a gift of two dozen deep pink fat-headed roses and was driving one of those big

American jeep things with a low flat roof, humbugs Maud called them.

'Feel like I'm being picked up for army manoeuvres!' Nell muttered, going pink with embarrassment as curtains up and down the street began to twitch, no doubt because the throb of the massive engine was making their bits rattle.

'Well I think he's planning a military operation to get you into bed, so it's pretty apt.' Ange grinned, and then pressed something into Nell's hand as she hoicked up her skirt and hoisted herself into the car.

'Little pressie for you.' She winked, before stepping back to wave Nell off.

Nell looked down in her hand to see a pack of three. 'Oh, Ange!' she sighed, hurriedly shoving them in the inside pocket of her handbag.

'Better to be safe than skanky,' Ange called after her.

The Plover had originally been the private home of a rich local landowner, and was a huge old house set in grounds overlooking the sea. It was hard to tell its age as it had so many add-ons, but it was a beautiful place despite its indeterminate heritage.

Nell's jaw dropped in awe as she was helped out of the car and up through the entrance portico into reception.

She had been expecting Chinese patterned wallpaper, thick swirly carpet, neoclassical columns inside as well as out, Ming vases, and chairs as elegantly legged as Maud. Almost as if she had stepped back in time.

It was, however, a sumptuous feast of contemporary.

Modern art, suede wallpaper, ambient lighting, wood floors, and Tam McCavin lounging on a scarlet chaise longue by a roaring fire, a bottle of champagne in an ice bucket next to him.

Nell was given a glass without actually being asked if she wanted one, which she didn't really mind as she had always adored champagne.

But she also hated assumptions.

Looking back, she could see that that was when she and Marcus had started to go downhill, when he began to make assumptions about her. Like he knew her better than she knew herself. It had been small things at first, like not asking her what she wanted to drink when they went to the pub, just ordering her the same things every time he went to the bar, even if she fetched something different when she went; and ordering for her in a restaurant if she'd popped to the loo or something, assuming she'd want the chocolate fudge cake because he knew she liked it, when actually that evening she was in the mood for honey-roasted figs and ice cream.

Making decisions on her behalf without actually asking her, like the time that Ange had sent a message through Marcus asking if Nell wanted to join her on a sponsored walk for a local dog rescue charity. His immediate response had apparently been 'Oh, Nell won't want to do that', when the truth was that if only he'd asked her, she would have loved to have given it a go.

Nell shook her head as if to clear her mind.

Why on earth was she sitting here thinking of Marcus?

Oh well, at least it would make her determined to enjoy herself.

She looked across at the man sitting opposite her, smiling at her as he sipped his own champagne.

He was very handsome, Nell decided, looking shyly at him over the rim of her champagne flute, although – she peered a little closer – was he still wearing make-up from the shoot earlier? He was! He had mascara on, and she was certain she could see a faint trace of eyeliner around those striking blue eyes.

Normally Nell would have been put off him instantly. A man in make-up smacked so much of vanity, a trait she couldn't really cope with in someone else, having so little of it herself. But the new Nell told herself not to be so judgemental. Women wore make-up to enhance their features, didn't they, so in these days of equality, why couldn't men?

She could also give him the benefit of the doubt and say to herself that it wasn't intentional, that he probably just hadn't cleaned everything off properly from the morning, if only it didn't all look so perfect and barely there.

Nell felt the comers of her lips twitching. Perhaps they could swap make-up tips. After all, his was the hardest kind of face to do, the 'is she wearing make-up or isn't she?' face.

At this one, the snicker of laughter escaped.

Fortunately whilst Nell had been off in her own little world, Tam McCavin had chosen to break the ice by telling a joke, a long and convoluted one that had been incredibly funny when told by the person he heard it from but which he had turned into something slightly rambling and not nearly as coherent.

To see that Nell was laughing made him extremely happy, so much so that he leaned forward and liberally topped up her glass of champagne, despite the fact that only ten minutes previously he had berated the poor waiter that they were daring to charge more than three times Oddbins' price for a bottle of the same vintage.

'You must have been really excited when you found out the *Grand Openings* team were covering Ye Olde Tea Shop for the programme,' he said, knowing full well that she hadn't been.

He had a habit of testing people sometimes to see how genuine they were. It was a hazard of the world he lived in to come across disingenuous people.

Nell fortunately lived up to the impression he already had of her. She frowned and then confessed a little worriedly, 'To be honest, I wasn't too keen. Not really my cup of tea, all those cameras, people watching you on TV.'

'So why say yes?'

'Well, it sounds daft, but for Ange really, she was so excited about it. I didn't have the heart to let her down.'

'For your friend? That's sweet. And can I ask, why did you agree to come tonight? Was that for your friend too?'

He was obviously joking, fishing too, Nell could see it in his eyes, but she didn't have the heart to confess to the real reasons she had been persuaded to say yes: for a chance to see inside the fabled Plover – that seemed calculating – and also because Ange had asked her to do this as well. Neither of them were exactly compliments to him.

And so she said that yes, in a way it was for Ange, who had been keen for her to come – and that wasn't a lie, now was it? – but that mainly she had, she confessed, intended at first to say thank you but no thank you, and then thought instead, why not? And thankfully he accepted this without further question, simply moving his enquiries on to her.

'So what is Nell short for?'

'Nothing,' Nell lied.

'Eleanor?' he suggested. 'Helena?'

Nell frowned. She hated it when she said that her name was simply Nell and people still tried to guess at something else anyway. 'It's just Nell,' she persevered.

'Okay. Middle name?'

'Elizabeth.'

'Nell Elizabeth . . .' He paused, waiting for her to fill in the gap.

'Everson.'

Another reason she would never confess to being Penelope. Her parents really hadn't given it much thought when they had chosen her names as a baby. Penelope Elizabeth Everson. The worst thing had been when you were supposed to put your initials on your school stuff. Penelope had become Nell pretty rapidly after she left playschool and joined the ranks of the self-aware at primary.

'What about you?' She turned the tables before he could press further. 'Is Tam short for anything?'

'Well, no, it isn't,' he said, leaning back in his chair and crossing those long, muscular legs. And then his voice slipped from faint Irish burr to strong Dublin drawl. 'It was meant to be Tom, so it was, except me mammy could never spell to save her loife.'

Nell laughed, and he laughed too, in delight at such a genuine reaction. She was even prettier when she smiled; in fact he thought she looked a little bit like a young Liz Hurley. He'd once met Liz at a celebrity party and had suffered a huge crush on her ever since.

From this point on he determined to make Nell smile as much as possible. He would usually do this by regaling his victim with stories of life in the celebrity fast lane. Every girl he'd ever been out with wanted to hear about his life now, the people he knew, the parties he'd been to. Only this time he determined not to. He wanted to win her over with his personality, not his contacts, and so he told her tales of growing up in Dublin. Charming stories, witty, sometimes touching, and the more he made her laugh, or sigh in sympathy, the more he felt he was winning her over and she was falling for him, the real Tam.

As far as Nell was concerned, however, it wasn't that she was falling for Tam; it was that the more he talked, the more he was losing his celebrity air of mystique, which she quite honestly found a little intimidating, and was coming over as just a chap. A chap who was actually rather nice, albeit a bit self-deluded, a bit up his own bum, as Ange would probably have put it, so far up his own bum in fact he could tickle his tonsils.

It seemed that life for Tam both pre- and *après* celebville was all about Tam. But she supposed that wasn't really his fault. When you were the centre of attention all the time, with people pandering to your every want and whim, it was bound to turn your head.

The maître d' and the waitresses had all been falling all over him, people had sidled up for autographs, girls at other tables were looking jealous: everything you needed to make you feel as if you were a superstar.

And all of those envious eyes looking her way would never have guessed that the high point of the evening for Nell had not been basking in the attention of Tam McCavin; it had been that the restaurant was as amazing as she'd hoped it would be, and the food even more so, and that J.P. David had come out of the kitchens to personally pass on a recipe for a chocolate fondant cheesecake she had tentatively asked if she could have as it was so wonderful, and talked enthusiastically to Nell about baking, not even noticing the fact that she was sitting with someone so famous, so intent was he on discussing the delights of cooking.

It wasn't as if Tam was boring company; he was actually quite delightful, and if he hadn't been so self-absorbed – well, despite the fact that he was so self-absorbed – Nell could have found herself warming to him. Apart from one thing. Every time she decided she liked him a little bit more than a moment ago, every time she moved herself on in her head from enduring dinner to enjoying dinner, from thinking she really wouldn't want to to perhaps she might, to picturing that perhaps she could, there was something, one thing, that always pulled her back.

It was no good.

Nell smiled softly at him, gently. 'Well, it's been a lovely evening, but I have such an early start, I'm afraid I really must say thank you and take my leave.'

'You seriously want to go?' His disappointment was obvious.

'I should.'

'Perhaps, but do you want to?'

It was the sudden hand over hers, the inflection of the voice and the come-to-bed eyes that gave this question its true meaning, and just in case it hadn't been made clear enough, he added a rider.

'How about coffee . . . up in my room?'

Instantly Nell thought of Ange's parting gift blushing away in her handbag zipper pocket. If she had been serious about indulging in a fling or two, then here was the perfect opportunity.

Like her dinner . . . on a plate.

And it was with the presentation of this opportunity that she finally admitted the truth to herself.

If Harry Fox were here, looking at her like that, suggesting what Tam McCavin was suggesting, then she wouldn't even still be sitting in her chair; she'd have grabbed his hand and dragged him upstairs when he'd uttered the first Y of 'You seriously . . .'

29

Ange was working at the Jolly Roger. Nell had promised to report straight back to her, and so, despite feeling ready to go home and curl up under her duvet, she got the chauffeur to drop her at the pub.

Ange had been looking out for Nell all evening. Well aware that she had been reluctant to go, she had been half expecting her to walk into the pub long before now, and so the minute she did walk in, Ange shot straight over to the other side of the bar, looking all perky and interested, like a dog who knows you've got a biscuit in your pocket.

'So?' she asked, eyebrows moving up and down like a yo-yo in anticipation of the answer to such a short yet loaded question.

Nell headed over to her and sat down on a vacant bar stool. 'So?' she queried back.

'Did you shag him?'

'Oh yes.' Nell nodded, pursing her lips in amusement.

'You did!' Ange's eyes expanded to twice their usual size.

'Oh absolutely, several times, several different positions, forwards, backwards, sideways, upside down, hanging out of the window, on the restaurant table. We even had a go in the restaurant kitchens but he kept burning his backside on the griddle.'

Ange huffed and looked affronted. 'Sarcasm's my designer outfit, Penelope, and it doesn't suit you at all.'

'Well what do you expect? I went for dinner with a guy I don't really know; of course I didn't just jump his bones. Although . . .' Nell added, looking at Ange sideways mischievously, and letting the last word hang in the air like the tempting scent of a cooking loaf.

'Although . . .' Ange urged her excitedly.

'I could *so* have if I'd wanted to. Only I decided I didn't.'

'Details!' Ange exclaimed. 'Details, now.'

'Okay.' Nell settled herself more comfortably. 'Get me a vodka and tonic and I'll tell you all about it.'

Harry had been up to see Maud. She had been his last call of the evening, and he had ended up staying on and chatting for several hours. Although they had drunk endless cups of tea, she hadn't been in the mood to eat, and his stomach was complaining about this fact. He had been so busy recently he knew the cupboard at home was bare, and it was so late he couldn't be bothered to cook for himself anyway.

Annie had left a message on his mobile asking if he wanted to stop in and have supper with her and Jasmine, but she had been a bit funny with him lately, clingy. He hesitated to say the word because it wasn't appropriate, but it was appropriate to how she'd been. A bit of distance would probably do them both good, and he knew full well that Jasmine went to bed at eight, so he also knew that the invite was actually supper for two, not three.

He therefore determined not to even call her back. He would ring in the morning and apologise, say he'd been working till midnight and got her message too late to call. He wasn't the kind to lie, but he knew that if he called her she'd be so insistent, verging on upset, that he wouldn't have the strength or the heart to turn her down. And he couldn't deal with her, not tonight.

He'd heard that Polporth had an excellent fish and chip shop. He'd stop there, get something to eat and go home and sleep. Heaven knew it had been a long day.

Knowing better than to try and park in the car park by the harbour, he left his car on the edge of the village and began the walk down, relishing the feeling of the night air, the way it tasted of sea salt and the way it had already begun to help clear his head. His conversation with Maud had been pretty heavy, and he needed something to wash away the feeling of unease that had settled over him since.

As he passed the Cakehole, he couldn't help but look up at Nell's flat. The lights were all off. He looked at his watch. It was after ten. Perhaps she had gone to bed already.

He had to fight a very strong urge to go and knock on the door anyway.

He seemed to be fighting his feelings for Nell an awful lot at the moment, sometimes far more successfully than others. To be honest, it was really starting to get to him that he had to. Especially since Annie had started in on him after the Madness. Who was this Nell? What was she to him? At which point he'd had to gently but firmly remind her that whatever Nell was to him it really shouldn't matter to Annie. And she'd started to cry, and of course he'd hugged her, and then she'd tried to kiss him, and he'd pushed her gently away, and she'd cried even harder and started to ask the same old questions. Why? Why didn't he want her? He'd tried to reassure her, to tell her how beautiful she was, and how bright and funny, and how any man would be happy to be with her. Any man but him. And of course this made it worse.

Being with Annie, well it just wasn't what he wanted.

She couldn't understand that, and it was frustrating for both of them.

But the most frustrating thing of all was that at this moment in time he couldn't have what he wanted, and he'd just have to live with that, do as he'd promised and keep his distance.

For now.

The call of the Jolly Roger waylaid him on the way to the Good Cod. After the day he'd had, he really needed a drink. Hell, after the month he'd had, he could do with a few drinks, but he was tired and he was driving; he'd just have one, relax for ten minutes, then he could get his food and head home.

As he pushed open the door and went up the three narrow steps into the body of the room, he heard a group of lads at the window table talking in hushed tones.

'Go and speak to her.'

'I can't.'

'Coward.'

'She's with *Ange*.'

'What, you mean *with* Ange?'

'No, not like that, you dirty bastard.'

'Then what's your problem?'

'Ange is scary.'

'Scary good or scary bad?'

'Oh, definitely scary good, but still scary.'

'Wimp. Just go and talk to her, you know you want to.'

It was the mention of Ange that caught his ear, and so when he got to the bar he followed their gaze. They were staring at a girl at the other end of the bar. She had her back to them, but even from the rear, it was obvious that she was extremely attractive.

She was wearing a green dress that fitted like a glove,

the shine of the silk skimming over her body, highlighting the delicious curve of her backside, cut low to show off a slender back, luminous skin. Her dark hair shone in the spotlight of the overhead bar lights with a sheen to rival the silk of the dress.

There was something about her that was familiar. 'Nell?' he called uncertainly.

She turned and smiled and he actually caught his breath, swallowed it so hard it almost hurt.

She looked gorgeous. She always did, even in her usual uniform of jeans and T-shirt, with her hair knotted into an uneven plait and her face scrubbed clean, the only enhancement on it a smile. But today . . . It was as though someone had taken an already delicious-looking cupcake and added frosting.

Harry felt his heart sink and lift at the same time. It was a very strange sensation.

It was all very well staying away from Nell himself, but how on earth could he get other people to stay away from her as well? Especially when she looked like that.

'Going somewhere?'

She'd actually jumped at the sound of his voice, a mixture of pleasure and surprise crossing her face.

'Oh, the dress?' She looked embarrassed, as if she'd been caught doing something seedy. 'A bit OTT for the Jolly Roger, isn't it, but I've been out to dinner somewhere quite posh, so . . .'

'With Tam McCavin,' Ange announced loudly, nodding as if to say 'There you go then, Mister Hot and Cold, look what happens when you turn about like the tide'.

'Oh, I see.'

'At the Plover,' Ange added.

'Are you two . . . ?'

He was ashamed at how delighted he was at the rapidity with which she shook her head, eager herself to dispel any doubts that she and Tam McCavin were an item.

'He wanted to talk to me about the Cakehole.'

'Yeah, and I'm Mahatma Gandhi,' cut in Ange.

'Can I get a beer here, please, Mahatma?' called a regular at the other end of the bar. 'Or is it against your religion to serve alcohol?'

Ange reluctantly went to pull pints and Harry took the oportunity to move over to Nell's side.

'You look beautiful.'

This elicited a small smile.

'I only called in to see Ange on my way home. I wouldn't normally come in here dressed like this. In fact,' she pretended to yawn, embarrassed, 'I'm pretty shattered, should probably head back.'

'I'll walk you,' he said, with such alacrity that even Ange lost her frown and found a smile.

It had been a beautiful day, but the evening air was chill. As soon as they stepped out of the warmth of the pub into the dark of the night, he automatically took off his jacket and put it around her shoulders. It was the jacket and not the cold that made Nell shiver. It smelled of him. Made her close her eyes briefly and drink it in.

'So did you have a good evening?'

'It was okay. The food was amazing . . .'

'I've heard many women say the same thing about the company you were keeping.'

'Tam?' Nell smiled. 'He's a bit like a designer handbag: every woman would love to be seen out with one on her arm, but as soon as you got home all you'd want to do with it is put it back in its bag and stick it in a cupboard.' She laughed softly. 'Actually, I don't mean to be cruel. He's really rather nice, just not . . . not . . .' She wanted to say 'you', but ended up simply shrugging and saying, 'for me' instead, and then adding, 'Oh, I wanted to ask you . . . the little girl you were with at the Madness . . .'

'Jasmine.'

'Yeah, Jasmine. Is she okay?'

'She's fine. A bruise to rival yours, but she's wearing it like a trophy.'

'Do you mind if I ask . . .' she began.

'Her mum?'

Nell nodded.

'Annie . . . well, we're friends. I look out for Jaz.'

'So are you and Annie. . .'

He shook his head. 'We're not together. We were once, for a couple of years, not living together, just dating, but I got pretty close to Jasmine in that time. Her dad's a total waste of time, poor kid, remembers she exists when it suits him, which isn't very often, so when her mum and I didn't work out, I couldn't bring myself to just walk out on her completely.'

'That's understandable, commendable.'

'I don't expect a pat on the back for it. She's a nice kid. I enjoy spending time with her. It's just awkward some-times . . .' He trailed off, unsure of how to explain without getting in too deep, but Nell nodded, understanding immediately.

'It gives her mum the wrong idea?"'

'I think a clean break would have been easier for her, but she knows how important it is for Jaz to have some continuity.'

'Why did you break up? You know, if she still wants you to be together . . .' but then Nell shook her head apologetically. 'I'm sorry, I'm so nosy, it's absolutely none of my business.'

'She's bright, articulate, beautiful. I enjoyed her company, we had a good relationship. She just wasn't . . . The One.' He looked up at Nell, and she could see that he felt foolish. 'Does that sound insane?'

'No. Of course not. It makes perfect sense actually.'

They walked on in silence until they reached the Cakehole.

'Well, this is me.' She shrugged, feeling stupid because that was so obvious.

His hesitation on the doorstep made her bold enough to ask, 'I don't suppose you fancy a cup of coffee and a ham and cheese toastie? I know I've been out to dinner, and the food was wonderful, but it was one of those places where they give you enough to leave you wanting more . . .'

She stopped talking for a moment and bit her lip, unnerved by his silence, the way he was looking at her. 'No, of course you don't. I'm sure you're totally knackered and ready for bed—'

'I'd love to,' he interrupted her. 'If truth be known, I'm famished.'

The first thing he noticed were the three bouquets, hastily shoved by Nell into vases, still in their cellophane.

'Beautiful flowers?' he said as she made them coffee and sandwiches.

It was a question.

Nell laughed at how much she liked the note of jealousy not very well hidden within the curiosity in his voice.

'They're from Tam . . .' she pointed to the roses, 'and those, well they're actually from my ex, the guy I left in London. He's . . .' She paused as she thought how best to explain, both to Harry and herself. 'I think he must have decided we have unfinished business. That's the third lot he's sent . . .'

'And do you agree?'

'Do I agree?'

'That you and this ex have unfinished business.'

Nell shook her head. 'My leaving him may have been abrupt,' she said, coming to sit down next to him, 'it was probably a shock to both of us, but it was the right thing to do.'

'You know for sure?'

'I don't miss him. For me that says it all.'

'I think he might be missing you.'

'Well, you know what they say: you don't know what you've got till it's gone, and he had no idea that I was going.'

He nodded his understanding. 'Maud told me about your moonlight flit.'

'It was a morning flit,' she corrected him, as though this detail were vitally important. 'I'd slept on it.'

His mouth quirked into a smile, and Nell flushed, not at her own pedantry but at the fact that at that very moment all she could think was how much she'd like to kiss him.

'Do you sleep on everything?'

'Oh my God!' She burst out laughing, and he joined in, embarrassed, but delighted to see such genuine amusement.

'I didn't mean it like that,' he protested. 'I just thought . . . I mean to say . . . that is . . .' and then he stopped as he realised that they had once again fallen into each other, shoulders touching, cheeks close, and he had to literally pull himself slowly away from her, as if she were holding on to him and he couldn't get loose.

He sighed so heavily Nell could feel his breath fanning her face, and then the laughter fell away from him and he suddenly looked sorrowful. 'Oh Nell, I'm so sorry. I really shouldn't have come here. I'd better go ... I'm really sorry, I don't want to, but ...'

He went to get up, but an emboldened Nell reached out and took a firm hold of his wrist, stopping him.

He looked down at her hand on his arm, and then up at her eyes. Uncertain, hopeful, scared. 'Nell, please. I shouldn't be here. I really shouldn't.'

'Harry, why ... what on earth is going on?'

His face said more than words could. Anguish, apology, and in a strange way such utter honesty.

'Okay.' She nodded, and released his arm. 'If that's the way it has to be, then fine. But just tell me one thing before you go. Am I imagining ...' She paused, unsure of how to say it, and then the perfect word came to her quite clearly. 'Us. Am I imagining us?'

He reached out and touched her face, the merest whisper of a touch. It started as an apology, but when his fingers met her flesh he found that they couldn't disconnect, that they pressed closer, her eyes shutting as his thumb brushed so slowly across her slightly parted lips until his hand was gently cupping her face, and then it was only right and natural that his mouth should follow.

It was a long, slow, sweet, delicate kiss, until they drew against each other, finally as close as both had ached to be for such a long time, and then her arms slid about his waist, his own going over and around them to hold them there, to hold her there, and he knew now that he was going nowhere, no matter what the consequences.

Despite her promise to Nell to try and quit, now that they were geographically closer Ange had got into the habit of sneaking off to the harbour last thing at night to have a cigarette. Only when she wasn't working. When she was working, she would share her guilty secret and her Marlboro reds with London Tony round the back of the pub, behind the wooden structure that covered the steps down into the beer cellar, so no one could see them. They would puff away, cigarettes hidden in palms in case anyone came out, eyes swivelling left and right furtively, not a word exchanged, just a hurried fumbling of packet and lighter, then sounds of relief and pleasure mingled with exhalation.

London Tony had promised to quit as well.

Marge would turn him into a Ruby Murray if she knew he still hadn't, but Ange couldn't refuse him: he was like a puppy begging for scraps when she got her lighter out. Besides, it would be the pot calling the kettle black if she told him not to smoke when she hadn't quite managed it herself. Despite her conversation the previous week with Nell.

'It's a vice. Everybody has them; I just happen to have one that was the coolest thing ever when it first came out and then by the time we discovered it could kill you we were all addicted,' Ange had replied, when Nell had mentioned gently that she was concerned that Ange still relied on the dreaded weed as a form of recreation and release.

'I think that information might just have been available when you first decided to put match to tobacco.'

'Okay, so maybe you're right,' Ange had looked as coy as it was ever possible for Ange to look, 'but what would you do if you were halfway through the best chocolate fudge cake you'd ever had and some government science bod suddenly announced that chocolate cake was the angel of death. Would you stop eating?' Ange leaned closer and raised her eyebrows in question. '*Could* you stop eating?'

It had taken Nell a few moments to escape the penetrating gaze and answer. 'I get your point, but . . .'

'There's always a but.' Ange leaned back and crossed her arms, defiant.

'There's normally several in this household,' Nell joked, trying to lighten the atmosphere, 'usually stubbed out in empty Coke cans.'

Coke was Ange's other addiction. For her, a cold can in one hand and a fag in the other, with time to enjoy both and no one nagging her not to, was utter heaven. She had however recently seen one of those television makeover programmes where a woman had ruined her teeth by drinking too much Coke, and what with sneaky cigarettes and flashbacks to a mouthful of rotted stumps, she now spent the rest of her time between vices vigorously cleaning her teeth.

Ange was a person who didn't have fears but tended to get a rational thought and focus on it so much as to make it slightly irrational. She was very aware of this and was convinced it was a form of mental OCD, but she was usually so focused in the rest of her life that she allowed herself this particular personality hiccup without too much self-chastisement. She was also as tenacious as a terrier's teeth in a postman's bum, even when she knew she was wrong, sometimes just *because* she knew she was wrong, and this was one point she wasn't giving in on without a fight.

'So would you, Nell?' She had turned the penetrating gaze back on her friend, and leaned in towards her like Father O'Mally, her mother's priest, when he was seeking confession. 'Would you give up cake?'

Nell thought for a moment, and then came back with one that always blindsided Ange.

Altruism.

'I'll give up chocolate cake if it means you give up cigarettes.'

And knowing how genuine this offer was, Ange had had no choice but to agree to try.

Sometimes she just tried harder than others, that was all it was.

She'd cut down an awful lot.

One day she would quit completely.

But it would be when she decided to, not when someone else told her that she should. No matter how well-meaning that person might be. And yes, maybe this was cutting off her nose to spite her face, but Ange had never liked being told what to do. Even by someone as lovely and genuine as Nell.

Today Ange had only had one cigarette, and as she walked home from her shift at the Roger, she was starting to feel that familiar itch in her spine that was the first acknowledgement of a growing craving.

'Be strong, Ange O'Donel,' she urged herself as she neared the Cakehole. 'You don't want a cigarette, the cigarette wants you, and you know you hate being told what to do by anybody.'

But then, as she opened the front door, quietly in case Nell was asleep, and began to make her way through the door marked Private and upstairs, she heard voices. She turned around and crept back downstairs, grabbed a jacket and a torch from the hall and let herself out again.

She had recognised Nell, of course, but she also knew who it was she was talking to. Harry.

Harry was still there.

Now Ange really needed a cigarette.

There was a deep shadow thrown from the harbour wall by the lamplight in the corner beyond, and it was here that Ange would lurk and puff away furtively until she was down to the filter, when she'd dispose of the evidence by flicking the butt into the sea, shoving a Polo in her mouth, and then spritzing herself liberally with the bottle of Febreze she had stashed behind the rain butt outside the Jolly Roger.

Tonight the night was dark and tempting and so was her craving. The usual one turned into an unusual two, the second long and savoured, and the church clock was striking midnight before she thought of heading back. But just as she was about to turn and leave, a sound brought her to a standstill again. It was the soft chug of a diesel engine, a boat engine.

A shadow at the harbour mouth, moving steadily and quietly. Ange's eyes narrowed. She had never seen a boat come into harbour at night, this late and with no lights on, and her curiosity was immediately aroused. Instead of leaving, she stepped back into the shadows to watch.

A lone man steered the small ship into dock, hopped on to shore and tethered it secure and safe with ropes. Then he stood as still as Ange, as still and poised as a cat about to pounce, and peered towards the town, almost, Ange felt, looking directly at her at one point. She held her breath, but then he went back on to the boat and returned carrying a large box. He jumped lightly on to the harbour again and began to quietly tiptoe towards her.

He looked so furtive that mischievous Ange couldn't resist.

'Stop or I'll shoot,' she said, flicking on her torch and shining it in his face.

He jumped, held up his hands and dropped the wooden crate.

Ange didn't know whether to laugh or apologise, but seeing as she had a tendency never to do the latter, she burst into bubbles of laughter instead, at which the man immediately looked furiously aggrieved and bent down to retrieve his box, scowling. 'Cigarettes or alcohol?' Ange asked, completely unperturbed by his obvious annoyance.

'What?'

She indicated the dropped crate.

'Well, that's what people normally pop across the Channel for; either that or I've just stumbled across a major drugs cartel and my tombstone will be engraved with the epitaph "Here lies Ange, she shouldn't have been so bloody nosy".'

For a moment he just looked at her, then the scowl intensified, and to Ange's pleasure the tense face broke into a smile and he too began to laugh.

'It's not drugs, well not in the illegal sense, although I have to confess my trip was driven by an addiction.'

He bent down to the box and pulled off the lid.

Ange peered inside. 'I still don't know what it is, but from the way it smells, I think it might just be a mutilated dead body, in which case all of my instincts now are telling me to run, run, as fast as I can . . .'

His smile deepened. 'As much as I like the imagery, I'm afraid it's not quite as exciting as a mutilated body.'

'Dead animal?' Ange offered.

He shook his head.

'Well what on earth can smell that bad and still be alive?'

'Cheese,' he replied.

'Cheese!' Ange exclaimed, her disappointment palpable. 'You're smuggling cheese?'

'Well, Cornwall does have a long tradition of smuggling, and it's important to keep up tradition.'

'Even if it is just cheese?' Ange looked back up at him, her mouth quirked into a twisted smile of amusement, and it suddenly struck him what a pretty girl it was who had accosted him. With her dark eyes, flame-red curls, creamy skin, ruby lips and Rubenesque hips, she looked as if she'd stepped out of a Pre-Raphaelite painting.

'Oh let me assure you, this isn't *just* cheese,' he said, allowing his own smile to grow.

'It isn't?'

'This is the finest cheese France has to offer.'

'And you have to do a midnight maraud to get it? You can't just nip to your local Sainsbury's?'

'Well, I could ...' He laughed. 'But where's the adventure in that?'

'You like adventure?' Ange tilted her head to one side, her eyes lighting with interest.

'There's nothing worse than life becoming too predictable.'

Ange's eyes blinked wide and she became a little breathless. 'My thoughts entirely,' she said, suddenly noticing what a sexy, husky voice he had, and how tall and beautifully built he was.

'And may I ask what you are doing lurking in the shadows?'

'Well, I'm kind of smuggling too.' Ange waved her cigarettes at him. 'My friend and flatmate is an evangelist for tar-free lungs.'

'Can't blame her,' he said, shaking his head in gentle reprimand. 'Filthy habit.'

'Perhaps, but I have other filthy habits that make this one look angelic.' Ange blinked slowly and deliberately at him, giving him a few moments to wonder what these filthy habits could possibly be, and then continued. 'Besides, too much cheese is just as bad for you, all that fat and cholesterol, clogs the arteries, stops the blood . . . *pumping*.'

'It's always the things that are bad for you that you crave the most,' he agreed, his voice dropping to an even huskier level as he stepped a little closer.

'Like chocolate.' Ange nodded.

'I *love* chocolate.'

'I love a man who loves chocolate,' she rasped, thinking how sexy the fan of lines around those laughing eyes made him.

'And red wine . . .' he continued. 'What are your thoughts on a man who likes red wine?'

'Full-bodied,' was all she said in return.

'The man or the wine?'

'Both.'

'I have wine in the next crate . . .'

'Cheese *and* wine?'

'Absolutely. If I produced a baguette from my pocket, we could have a picnic.'

'If that's *not* a baguette in your pocket I'll be far more impressed,' Ange purred, looking quite purposefully at his crotch.

'Now what on earth would you say if I started looking at your chest and talking about nice baps?' he pretended to admonish her.

'I'd invite you to butter them,' Ange retorted.

With an animal snarl they pounced upon each other.

31

When Nell woke up Harry was gone.

For a moment she wondered if it had all been some erotic dream. Heaven knows she had fantasised about him often enough; perhaps her mind had just taken things one step further than usual and made a dream seem like reality. But then she turned to the other side of the bed, the empty side of the bed, and sitting on the pillow in the dent where his head had lain was a seashell.

The seashell.

The one he had so delicately removed from her backside.

He had kept it.

He had wanted to stay with her. To watch her sleep. To watch her wake. To make love to her again, to hold her for a very long time, and yet he knew that with the morning light would come questions, questions he couldn't yet answer.

And so he had left and walked the beach, watched the sun come up over the water, waiting, waiting until it was a reasonable enough hour to call on the other woman in his life, the one who meant that Nell was off limits, should have been off limits. It was time to come clean. To both of them. To let each know about the other. And although he knew there might be hell to pay, he would just have to take it on the chin and deal with it as best he could.

When he got there, she was in the kitchen, looking at a piece of toast, not eating it, just looking at it, a strange expression on her face.

She looked up as he entered the room, didn't seem at all surprised to see him there.

'How are you?' he asked gently.

'So-so.' Maud waved a dismissive hand.

Her mood was obviously irascible. It probably wasn't the best time to broach a subject that she had made quite clear was one she didn't really wish to discuss. And so he left it for a while, made small talk, hoping that she would come round a little.

'Why are you here, Harry?' she interrupted as he tried to talk to her about her roses, a subject usually guaranteed to soften. 'Don't you have someone else to go and annoy today?' she asked.

'I need to talk to you, Maud.'

'Not now, Hal.' She shook her head. 'I'm tired.'

He nodded. But as he reached the door she called out to him, and when he turned her smile was apologetic.

'Come back later. Have tea with me.'

He nodded again, returned her smile, and left.

Ange slid in through the door, shoes in hand, hoping to get to her room before Nell saw her so that she could pretend she hadn't been out all night. If truth were told she was bursting to tell Nell everything, but she had a feeling after hearing Harry's voice coming from the sitting room last night that Nell might have a story of her own to tell, and for once Ange was going to be the one who listened.

Nell was already up and in the Cakehole. She had got up early to bake yet again, and was in the tea room kitchen, freshly showered, hair tied back in a ponytail, pinny on, hands scrubbed and kneading a bowl full of oats, flour, honey and sultanas into cookie submission.

There was nothing unusual in this sight; Nell often got up early to bake. What was strange, though, was the fact that she was singing.

Ange went and leaned on the counter behind her. Waited until she'd finished the final verse and then applauded quietly.

'If I'd known you could sing that well before I quit my job I might have offered you a contract.'

'Thanks, but I think I'm happier making cakes than records. Tell all, then. Where have you been?'

'You first.'

'Me?' Nell asked, all innocent.

'Yes, you. What were you up to last night, Miss Everson?'

Nell's smile spoke volumes. 'How do you know I was up to anything?'

'Because when I came back after work, Harry was here.'

'Ah, so you did come back then. If only for a little while. Did you catch up with Captain Jack again?'

Ange shook her head.

'So you weren't with him?'

'No!'

'So . . .' Nell employed the Maud tactic of ask and wait. It didn't work.

'So . . .' Ange queried back at her.

Their stares locked, but Nell, who wanted to have her night with Harry all to herself for just a little longer, had an ace up her sleeve, or rather a pineapple tart on a plate.

'Trade you,' she said.

It took Ange half a second to make the decision. 'I met

a man down in the harbour. The sound of the sea in the background, a crate of cheese on the floor between us . . .'

Nell frowned in confusion.

'Then we took a walk on the beach, and it was just like that scene in *From Here to Eternity*.' Ange sighed, picking up the tart and chewing thoughtfully. 'Except it was dark . . . and the tide was so far out we couldn't be bothered to walk out to the shoreline.'

'You mean you just met the guy and you . . .'

Ange nodded happily.

'I'm still picking sand out of my—'

Nell held up a hand.

'Too much info, Ange.'

'Life is for living, Nell,' Ange said, sensing disapproval. 'Men are for—'

But Nell held up the other hand. 'Like I said, too much info, although there is one thing you can tell me. What's his name?'

Ange stopped chewing and blinked slowly. Then she frowned, and shrugged.

'Do you know, I never thought to ask.'

When Harry went back at four, Maud was in the garden, in her favourite spot at the wrought-iron table under the apple tree.

'Can I come in? Or rather out, that is.'

'Of course, young man, always a pleasure.'

He pulled a face at her.

'Okay, so it's nearly always a pleasure. Sorry about earlier, you know how it is.'

'That's the thing, I do.' He came over and tried to take her hand, but she drew it away from him.

'Don't be nice to me, Harry Fox, you know I don't like it. Take a seat and take a cake.'

She poured him tea without asking, then, when he hadn't taken anything from the laden cake stand, pushed it across the table towards him. 'I'd recommend one of those to start,' she said, pointing to a Cherry Bakewell.

Hal took the pastry and bit into it, knowing as soon as he did that it was one of Nell's, so sweet and light and mouth-watering you just wanted to go back for second helpings, even before you'd finished the mouthful you were eating.

'Nell's, of course,' Maud said with pride. 'So why did you want to see me, other than for the usual?'

She counted to thirty before he actually managed to answer her, pretending to chew on his cake when she knew he could devour it in two bites if he so chose.

'It's about Nell, actually.'

'I thought it might be.' She nodded.

Maud wasn't stupid. She had seen the looks, felt the air positively crackling with the spark between them.

'I really like her, Maud.'

'I know. I told you that you would, didn't I?'

He nodded.

'But I also told you to keep your distance.'

'I know. But what if I find that I don't want to?'

'Well, we can't always have everything we want, can we, young man?' she replied archly, and then her face softened.

'I'm sorry, Harry. But it's for the best. I know you two have a thing for each other, and under normal circumstances I'd be meddling to get you together, not trying to keep you apart, but think about it: you couldn't be honest with her . . . and if she finds out you've been lying to her, and especially what you've been lying about, she may never forgive you. If you like her as much as I think you do, then it's best to keep away, to give you both a decent chance. She can't know you too well until . . . until . . .' Maud couldn't bring herself to say the words. For a moment she lapsed into silence, and then Harry saw her physically and mentally draw herself upright again, the same proud, determined, kind-hearted woman he had come to know and in truth love over the past few months. 'She can't know you too well right now. I know it's another huge ask, Harry, but if you get close to her now . . . well . . .' Maud hung her head by way of apology. 'The truth will out in the end, as they say, and my secrets and lies might just be the end of you before you've even had a chance to begin.'

He nodded, knowing the truth of her words, no matter how much they weren't what he wanted to hear.

'So, tell me you've kept to your promise and not told her.'

'I have.' He answered her truthfully.

Now Maud reached out and took his hand. 'Thank you. But there's just one more thing, Harry . . .' and she turned to look him in the face, in the eyes. 'I know you like her very much, but tell me, are you in love with her?'

She wanted to hear a denial. He could see it in her, feel it from her. She wanted . . . no, the right word was *needed* . . . she needed to hear him say a firm and emphatic no. And right now, what Maud needed, and not what *he* needed, had to be paramount.

And so he shook his head as firmly as he could, and saw her positively melt with relief.

'Good.' She let go his hand, patted it as if he was a child. 'Love is a wonderful thing, Harry Fox, but boy is it complicated, and right now we don't need that, do we . . .'

*

When Nell got into bed that night, she could still smell the glorious scent of him lingering there. She closed her eyes and breathed in deeply. In a way she hadn't been surprised to wake and find Harry gone. But what she was surprised about, what was killing her right now, was that he hadn't come back.

32

The next morning, on her way out to meet the milkman, Nell found a box on the doorstep. 'There's
something here for you,' she said, going back inside and
holding it out to Ange, who was sitting at the counter
drinking her first latte macchiato of the day.

Ange took the box warily. 'To the flame-haired
temptress of the harbour.' She read the label aloud. 'How
the hell do you know that's for me?'

'Well, it was on our doorstep.'

'The operative word being "our",' Ange replied.

'Well, if it had said "To the greasy-haired skivvy in
the kitchen", I might be tempted to think it was mine.'
Nell grinned. 'But seeing as it was you, my flame-haired
friend, who seduced a pirate in the harbour, I think it
would be a pretty safe bet to assume this particular
delivery is yours.'

'I suppose you could be right,' Ange conceded with a
cheeky smile, and with no further ado she took the spoon
from her coffee and used the pointed end to slice through
the tape that held the lid of the box closed. Reaching in,
she pulled out a large round item wrapped in what looked
like a waxed cloth.

'What is it?'

'It's a cheese,' Ange replied, her voice wreathed in

smiles and as delighted as if she'd just announced it was a winning lottery ticket.

'Well, I've heard of say it with flowers, but I've never heard of say it with cheese.'

It looked like a big creamy Brie, its insides ripe to the point of collapse, but there was something different about it.

The white skin had burst at one edge where the cheese was fighting to get out, and to Nell's surprise she could see that the creamy insides were flecked with tiny black specks.

'Pepper?' She frowned, peering closer, then took the large stinking article from her friend and, feeling very brave, held it to her nose and inhaled deeply.

'Truffle,' Ange announced proudly once Nell had managed to stop coughing.

'Wow.' Nell nodded, impressed, as Ange reclaimed the cheese and held it reverently aloft for further inspection.

'Truffle,' Ange repeated, like Homer spotting doughnuts. And then, after a pause in which to admire, 'It's the nicest thing that anyone's ever given me.'

'It is?' Nell couldn't hide her incredulity.

Ange nodded slowly.

'Diamonds, holidays, car keys?' Nell questioned.

Ange shook her head solemnly.

'The man learns quickly,' Nell said, turning and smiling softly at her friend. 'The way to an Ange's heart is through her stomach.'

He hadn't said that he would come, but Ange wallowed in a scented bubble bath, where she plucked and shaved and buffed and conditioned until she arose from the steam feeling like Cleopatra anticipating Antony.

And at eight on the dot, the doorbell rang.

'Onward Christian Soldiers'. Just the first three words of the hymn. That was the ring. Maud had said they should get it changed, but both girls had refused. They must have heard it a hundred times since they moved in, but it still made them fall on each other's shoulders in fits of laughter.

'Shall I get that?' Nell called from where she was curled up on the sofa, pretending to flit between a magazine and some reality show where Z-list celebrities were being made to look like idiots for the benefit of several worthy causes.

'Don't worry, it's for me,' Ange called back from her bedroom, with such certainty that Nell didn't even think to question how she could possibly know this, since neither of them was expecting anyone.

Of course it was him, standing on the doorstep looking slightly nervous, despite everything, despite the night before, looking as if he wasn't sure he should be there or even if she'd want him to be.

'You look . . .' he said, and then trailed off.

'I do.' Ange nodded. 'I look at a lot of things,' and she smiled and he smiled back and managed to stop stepping backwards with every hop from foot to foot.

'Did you get the cheese?'

Ange nodded.

'Bit unconventional, I know. Maybe it should have been flowers.'

'I like unconventional.'

'I thought so. I hope you like conventional too,' he added with a sheepish smile, and pulled from behind his back the most beautiful bunch of red roses Ange had ever seen. Most beautiful simply because they were for her. The first bunch of roses anyone had ever bought her. The first bunch of flowers anyone had ever bought her.

'So . . .' he started uncertainly, 'would you . . .'

'Yes,' Ange said, making it simple for him. 'I'd love to.'

And he realised that the straightforward, sarcastic, funny, feisty girl he had met last night was still the same girl on the doorstep this evening, and that she hadn't morphed in daylight into someone he didn't feel as instantly at home with, as instantly attracted to, as instantly crazy about . . . Did he really just think that? Yes. He did. He suddenly felt his nerves fall away and a broad smile grow steadily across his face.

'So where should a pirate take a girl on their first date?'

'I didn't think pirates did dates. I thought they just wantonly raped and pillaged.'

'Well, seeing as we've already done the wanton part,' he said, smiling coyly at her, 'I thought we should probably do the—'

'Pillaging?' Ange interrupted hopefully.

'If you like. Although I was probably going to suggest a drink or dinner. Where do you go around here to pillage?'

'We could always raid the Cakehole and steal Nell's pineapple tarts.' Ange nodded behind her.

'Cheese and pineapple tarts: real pirate me, eh?'

'Trust me, Nell's pineapple tarts are better than any gold you could steal.'

He looked thoughtful for a moment. 'You could come back to the boat.'

'Is that where you live?'

'Sometimes.'

'And the rest of the time?'

'I've got a cottage at Merryn, just down the coast. But I rent that out sometimes to holidaymakers, so I decamp to the boat when I need to.'

'Other people in your home?' Ange wrinkled her nose.

'If I rent it out to holidaymakers in the summer, I can get a thousand pounds a week for it.'

'Now I know you're a real pirate!'

'It's the going rate.'

'Sounds like a rip-off to me.'

'It's a lovely place. Sea views and everything. Maybe I should show it to you sometime.'

'Well, I'd rather like to see what the "everything" is.' Ange fluttered long dark eyelashes at him. 'As long as it doesn't cost me a thousand a week.'

'I wouldn't charge you, but we could talk about an exchange.'

'You mean barter?'

'If you like.'

I like, Ange thought, looking into his light grey eyes, I like very much.

'Is it rented at the moment?' she asked, a suggestion, not a question.

He shook his head.

'So why can't we go back there?' She shot him a sideways look that he struggled to read for a moment, until she added quietly, 'Don't tell me, the wife's in tonight.'

He smiled gently at the first hint of insecurity in a woman who he already knew laughed at the word.

'No, but my brother and *his* wife are.'

Ange looked at him quizzically.

'Molly's been ill. They needed a break; I told them they could have Pebble Cottage for a while.' He shrugged, looking away as if slightly embarrassed.

'You kicked yourself out of your own house so your brother and his wife could have a holiday?'

'Yeah, well . . . you would, wouldn't you?'

'Well, actually, no, not everyone would, which means that you're a nice man.'

'Oh, right,' he said, looking deflated.

'That was a compliment.'

'Are you sure? I thought you wanted a pirate. Pirates aren't exactly renowned for being nice.'

'No, maybe not, but you'll find that in a lot of the movies, a heart of gold is as much of a requirement as a chest of gold.'

Jarrad laughed, and Ange smiled back at him.

'So what do you actually do?'

'What, apart from sail the high seas plundering foreign shores for stinking cheese?'

'Yep.'

'I'm a chef.'

He said it as if he was expecting her once again to be disappointed, but Ange instantly melted. A man who could cook! Heaven.

'You're a chef.' She had to double-check just to make sure she wasn't dreaming.

He nodded, unsure as to whether she had suddenly gone breathless because she was excited about this revelation or because she was getting ready to run from the nice man who was a chef, the nice boring man who was a nice boring chef.

But she hadn't moved.

Yet.

Instead she asked him another question. 'Are you a good chef?'

'I'm not a *bad* chef.'

'Well, considering another thing I've learned about you in the past five minutes is that you're modest, that means you're bloody brilliant.' Ange sighed with pleasure. 'Oh how bloody brilliant.' And stepping out into the street, she linked an arm through his. 'I've always wanted a man who could give me orgasms in the kitchen. How about you take me back to your ship and show me your galley?'

'And I've always wanted a girl who could make a simple sentence like that sound so disgustingly rude.'

'Then we're both ludicrously happy. What do you think? Ship ahoy?'

'I couldn't think of anything nicer.'

'Then lead the way, Captain.'

He made her seafood linguine that had her demanding seconds, and then he made her come twice on the narrow galley table, after which they clung to each other in happy amazement, and she christened him Captain Cock, which made them both laugh so much they fell off the table and decided that bed would be a better place to continue the evening. And so they went to bed and left the dirty dishes in the sink, which to Ange, having lived with über-tidy Nell for the last few months, was almost as satisfying as the sex.

Ange woke early the following morning. The earliest she had woken since arriving in Cornwall and deciding that any part of the day before ten a.m., unless you'd met it coming the other way past midnight, was a complete waste of living.

It was warm in their little cabin. The morning sun was streaming in through the portholes, casting its light over their naked bodies, highlighting Ange's bum, which after their fall from grace the previous night now looked like a bruised peach. She prodded it and winced, but revelled in how tender it felt and how purple it was, like a trophy to keep, if only for a little while.

And as the sun slowly continued its path across the little room, it left Ange and crept across Jarrad, like a lecturer with a laser pen pointing out the finer bits of some stupendous architecture. Ange followed its progress with a growing sense of wonder, marvelling at the long, lean contours of his muscles, until the light reached his face, his lovely face, and then travelled across his head, picking flecks of colour from his shaggy dark red hair and making it shine like gold.

And Ange had one for the first time in her life.

A revelation.

That's it, she thought, that's how it feels. *This* is how it feels. Love. And as she settled back under the duvet and snuggled into the warm back of him and closed her eyes, her final thought as she drifted back to sleep was, at last.

Ange and Jarrad had sat together on the beach all morning in the sunshine, and barely exchanged ten sentences. When this kind of thing had happened in a relationship before, it had been because they had nothing to say to each other any more. This was different; this was that wonderful, comfortable kind of silence that came with coy glances, smiles, touches, sighs of happiness and kisses the only communication needed.

They had just met the day before yesterday and they had already become a couple; not only that, but the kind of couple Ange would usually make fun of. Heavens, they'd be wearing matching pullovers and anoraks next. Ange had a vision of the two of them strolling the beach in Aran jumpers, and was surprised to find that it made her wistful rather than nauseous.

As if he could read her thoughts, Jarrad turned to her. 'Is this for real, Angelina? Tell me you feel it too.'

And without hesitation or humour she nodded.

She took him back to the Cakehole, supposedly for lunch, but in reality to meet Nell. She was surprised, however, to find that Nell wasn't there and Beth was behind the counter.

'Where is she?' Ange asked, suddenly furious with herself for being so wrapped up in her new romance that she had left Nell on her own since the previous day. 'Is she okay?'

'Well, she was fine until *they* arrived.'

Beth nodded to a huge vase of multicoloured tulips on one of the window ledges.

'Marcus?'

Beth, who knew the story, nodded. 'Yep. More flowers from the ex. Looked a bit disgruntled when she read the card, I can tell you.'

Ange could imagine. She'd bet any money Nell thought they might have been from Harry. To find out they were yet again from Marcus would have been a blow.

'What did it say?'

'See for yourself.'

Beth handed her the card.

'Is there a chance for us?' Ange read out loud, her nose wrinkling in disgust. 'Yeah, *no* chance.'

'Then those ones turned up.' Beth pointed to a bucket on the kitchen floor, in which sat a monstrous bouquet of pink roses clouded with gypsophila.

'Who from?' Ange asked keenly.

'Tam.' Beth laughed.

Ange sighed. Not from Harry, again.

'And would you believe, almost the same wording as the ex's? And then *they* arrived.'

This time she pointed to the bin, which was now home to a display of orchids.

'Tam again. With an invitation to dinner. That's when she really lost it. Said she was going into town to kill the florist and asked if I could cover. Do you know, I've never seen someone get so pissed off about receiving flowers before.'

'Was she okay?'

'Yeah, I think she just wanted to clear her head really.

Said she wouldn't be long, as long as she didn't have to chase him to shoot him, and if you came home to ask if you'd wait here for her, she'd be grateful, wants a word.'

'Oh right, well in that case, we wait. Um, Beth, this is my . . .' Ange hesitated and turned to look at Jarrad. 'This is my . . .'

'Boyfriend, soulmate, other half, husband to be . . .' Beth offered with a grin.

Ange could have gone and hidden in the fridge. Why did friends have to be so embarrassing sometimes? But then Jarrad simply smiled and took Ange's hand, and replied, 'All of the above, and probably in that order too.'

Ange felt herself melt. If it were at all possible, she liked him now even more than she had ten seconds ago.

'Beth,' she said, smiling up at him, 'this is. . .'

'Hi, J,' said Beth, grinning.

'Hi, B.' He smiled back.

'You already know each other?' Ange frowned.

Beth nodded. 'I used to waitress for him when I was younger.'

Jarrad nodded. 'Bloody useless she was too.'

The pair laughed.

'Of course you know each other. We're in Cornwall. You're probably related.' Ange shrugged, shaking her head.

'Nah. Just friends,' Beth said. 'Although I've always told him he looks old enough to be my dad.'

'Well, I was quite friendly with your mother before she moved back to London,' Jarrad teased her with a wink.

Ange was pleased when he excused himself to go to the loo so she could pump Beth for information.

'He's one of the nicest guys I've ever met.' Beth shrugged.

'And?'

'That's all I need to say.'

'No skeletons in the closet?'

'Not even a bone in a box.' Beth smiled. 'You're a lucky girl, Ange O'Donel. He's one of the biggest catches in our little harbour. Talking of which, do you mind holding the fort till Nell gets back?' She suddenly looked coy. 'Oliver's coming down for a few days and I said I'd pick him up from the airport. . .'

'Oh lord, yeah, of course, have a great time.'

Beth paused at the door. 'Is she okay, Nell? She seemed a bit, you know, distracted. . .'

Ange shrugged. 'Beth, what do you know about a guy called Harry Fox?'

Beth frowned. 'Quasimodo,' she said after a moment.

'You what?'

'You know, the name rings a bell.'

'That's it?' Ange frowned in disappointment.

'I've heard it somewhere before, definitely.'

'But you don't know him?'

'Know *of* him, but honestly for the life of me can't think where from.' Beth shrugged apologetically. 'TJ knows everyone within a ten-mile radius. Leave it with me. I'll see what I can find out. If you want me to . . .'

The 'if you want me to' was Beth's way of asking why Ange wanted to know without actually asking why she wanted to know.

'He's just a friend of Maud's . . . we were curious,' Ange hedged, unsure if Nell had confessed all to her or not.

'Doesn't the fact that he's Maud's friend tell you everything you need to know? She doesn't suffer fools, you know . . .'

'Good point. Thanks, Beth. See you later, yeah?'

Thirty seconds after Beth had gone, Nell burst through

the front door and slammed it hurriedly behind her, collapsing back against it as it closed. She had been running and her heart was beating so fast she could swear you could see it thumping under her coat.

'I'm being stalked by a celebrity!' she exclaimed in breathless disbelief. 'He's just followed me all the way up from the harbour. He was trying to be inconspicuous, but that's a bit tricky when people keep recognising you and asking for your autograph.'

'Are you sure he was following you, and you didn't just happen to be going in the same direction?'

'Well I did wonder, so I went round in a circle three times, doubled back on myself twice and walked up and down Lanyard Alley four times.'

'And he stayed with you?'

'Like chewing gum on the heel of my shoe.' Nell nodded unhappily.

Ange's big grey eyes widened even further.

'When people talk about celebrity stalkers, it's usually people stalking celebrities, not celebrities doing the actual stalking.'

'I know,' Nell wailed unhappily. 'What should I do?'

'Hmmm.' Ange put her chin in her hand for a moment whilst she thought long and hard, and then she looked back up at Nell and smiled.

'Well, it's a toss-up between *Heat* magazine and the *News of the World* for me.'

'Ange! I'm being serious!'

'So am I. They'd pay you a fortune for a story like this . . . I'm joking, Nell. Look, he really likes you. Isn't that even the tiniest bit flattering?'

'Well, it would be if he wasn't freaking me out so much.'

'Want me to have a word?'

'What on earth would you say to him?'

'Stop following Nell around, you're freaking her out?' Ange suggested.

Nell looked at Ange in surprise. It was the first time since she'd run into the flat that Ange had actually said anything remotely sensible. 'You think that might work?'

'Well, I don't think he's a total head case; at least he didn't come across as one the times I've met him, just a bit . . .' Ange struggled to think of the right word, and came up with a phrase instead, 'out of touch with reality. You know, these stars are really overindulged, they can have pretty much anything they want, and we know it was a shock to his system when you turned him down about staying over. I mean, you were probably the first woman ever to say no to Tam McCavin, so perhaps it's just turned him a little bit . . . um . . . obsessive . . .' she said the word gently so as not to scare Nell further, 'about you, and a quiet word might be all that's needed to make him see sense. It's not as if people normally dare to tell him he's wrong, is it? It might shock him back to normality.'

'I'm not sure, Ange, not if it was me telling him no in the first place that made him like this. I don't think he's ever heard the word in his entire life.'

'If only I'd known.' Ange rolled her eyeballs in mock regret. 'Then again, I suppose he's got to ask for me to refuse, and he didn't do that, did he?'

'Think yourself lucky.'

'Oh, I do,' Ange said with such a soppy look on her face that Nell really had to resist the urge to tease her by pretending to barf.

'Do you know what you look like right now?' she said instead.

'Smug,' Ange replied, looking the epitome of the word. 'It's going well, then?'

'You can ask him yourself,' Ange replied, looking

beyond Nell and going all gooey again. 'Nell, this is Jarrad.'

Ange looked at Nell in surprise as she began to beam broadly and, stepping forward, held out her hand.

'Mr David. J.P. How lovely to see you again. I so wanted to thank you for that cheesecake recipe you gave me, it was absolutely amazing!'

Lunch lasted two hours.

Nell and Jarrad were chatting like old friends, Jarrad insisting on tasting every single one of Nell's home-made cakes, full of compliments and offering tips and advice.

Ange for once was lost for words.

She simply sat back and watched them with a stunned smile on her face.

Jarrad, her Jarrad, was J.P. David, celebrity chef.

But the most amazing thing about that, she realised, was that she didn't care. He was quite simply *her* Jarrad. It wouldn't have bothered her two hoots if he'd worked in McDonald's frying onion rings.

When he finally and reluctantly, on the part of all, left, Ange asked Nell, ever so casually, what she thought of him.

'He's absolutely great.'

'You would say that.'

Nell shook her head. 'I'm not talking J.P. David here, Nell, although he's an absolute star. I'm talking Jarrad. He's amazing. You're a very lucky girl.'

Her voice was wistful.

Ange reached out and put her hand over Nell's. 'Have you heard from him?'

'Who?' Nell joked back weakly.

'No, then?' Ange said gently.

Nell shook her head, sighed, then tossed back her hair

and tried to look resolute. 'But I'm not going to let it get to me, Ange. Absolutely not. Life isn't all about Harry Fox. I have other options, as you can see.' She waved a hand around at the Garden of Eden the Cakehole had become. 'And you know the song, that one about when you can't be with the person that you love . . .'

'Love Tam McCavin?'

Nell laughed as Ange had hoped she would, but then Ange finished the song properly.

'Love the person that's available? It's a nice line, Nell, but not one I can see you living your life by . . .' and then she paused as the most relevant word of the whole sentence finally hit her.

Love.

If you can't be with the one you *love*.

It hadn't just been lust at first sight that Ange had witnessed all those weeks ago in the Fisherman's Arms.

It had been love.

Nell was in love with Harry.

Ange had struggled to sleep, but now, at breakfast, Nell looked like the one who'd been up all night. She looked tired, weary, drawn and down, and all Ange wanted to do was give her a big hug and make it all better.

But she wasn't the one who could do that. And the person who could, Harry, for reasons unknown, couldn't.

Complicated, my arse, Ange thought, battering the top of a boiled egg. When a man told you his situation was complicated, you could bet your boots it meant another woman on the scene.

Well, Nell might have been prepared to accept half-truths and excuses, but Ange wanted answers and she wanted them now. But how? She had a feeling Maud knew everything they needed to know, but getting answers out of Maud at the moment was like wrestling with an eel that was already in jelly.

And then Ange's phone rang.

It was Beth.

'Ange, it's me . . . Look, you know you asked me if I could find out who Harry Fox is . . .'

When they had finished speaking, Ange pulled on her shoes and jacket.

Maybe there was something she could do after all.

'I'm just popping out.'

'Down to the harbour?' Nell smiled at her, and Ange marvelled at the fact that even though her own heart was obviously breaking she could still take huge pleasure in Ange's happiness.

'Something like that. See you later, yeah?'

But instead of turning down towards the harbour, Ange cut through Lanyard Alley and set off up the cliff road.

Ange had always been a fan of killing two birds with one stone, so to speak, although she preferred her own analogy of spanking two cheeks with one hand; after all, whoever wanted to kill birds these days had to be pretty barbaric, either that or a poultry farmer.

Maud was in the garden. Usually to be found pruning or weeding, she was reclined upon a sunlounger, a copy of *War and Peace* in hand.

'Heavy going?' said Ange, indicating the book.

'I've always meant to give it a go,' Maud shrugged, 'but I'm not sure if I'm just wasting my time. It's hardly Jilly Cooper, and I do like a good Jilly Cooper.' She snapped the book shut determinedly and put it down on the floor. 'And to what do I owe the pleasure, Angelina?'

'I want you to meet someone,' Ange announced, all casual, although Maud could tell it was far from.

'Bring him to tea,' said Maud.

And so Ange took him to tea.

He sat on the edge of one of Maud's Queen Anne chairs for the first two minutes looking tall, even though he was sitting down, and uncomfortable and nervous, and then he spilled the tea in his bone-china cup all over his trousers, and he and Maud looked at each for a moment and then burst out laughing. After that he complimented her on her home-made Battenberg, made her laugh with his jokes, which was a rarity, as Maud's humour was on a different level to an awful lot of people's, and the two of them chatted for over an hour about life, the universe, the universe that was Cornwall and everything, without Ange having to help the conversation once. She simply sat back and enjoyed the show, not that it was a show: their rapport was real and genuine and frankly quite lovely to see. Ange had been nervous for Jarrad, and had also thought that Maud had been looking a bit peaky lately, and wasn't it fantastic to see her laugh? The time flew by. It took ten minutes to get from four o'clock to five o'clock, when Jarrad reluctantly dragged himself away because he was working at the Plover that night.

He kissed Ange a lingering goodbye at the garden gate and began to make his way down the cliff path to cross the beach back to the village and the harbour. Ignoring the chill, not quite able to turn away whilst he was still in sight, Ange stood and watched him.

It was only when she felt her jacket being put around her shoulders that she realised that Maud had joined her at the bottom of the long garden.

'So?' Ange asked.

'You don't care what I think,' Maud replied, both knowing full well this wasn't true.

'So?' Ange said again, more insistently.

'He's absolutely awful.' Maud turned up her nose. 'Don't know what you see in him.'

Ange grinned broadly. 'Knew you'd love him.'

'And it's pretty obvious you do too, so why seek an old girl's approval?'

Ange shrugged. 'Can't take him to meet the parents to see if he'd run a mile, so you're the next best thing.'

Maud was absurdly touched by this blunt statement.

'It must be difficult being so far away from your mum and dad.'

'Nah!' Ange wrinkled her nose. 'Love the folks, but

we've never been ones to live in each other's pockets. Besides, it's hard to get close to your parents when you're one of fifteen,' she added with a melodramatic sigh.

Maud grinned. 'Balderdash. I know for a fact you are the eldest of three, and that you have two younger brothers called Tristram and Byron. Fabulous names; do they have the faces to suit?'

'Mother's an old romantic.' Ange shrugged. 'And yes, they have the looks. There are a lot of broken hearts in Dublin over my two brothers. Byron even has the hair, all flowing dark curls.'

'And flashing dark eyes?' Maud asked eagerly.

Ange grinned and said, 'Hang on a minute,' and diving in her jacket pocket pulled out her wallet, from which she produced a photograph. She handed it to Maud.

'Delicious ruffians!' Maud announced in delight after studying it. 'Lovely. If only I were eighty-three years younger.'

'You don't look your age.'

'Maybe not, but I do feel it nowadays. So, your young man . . . who may I say has a fine head of hair himself. Do you know, I was very tempted to lean across and run my fingers through it? Like a fox's pelt, a damp dark fox; is it as thick and soft as it looks?'

Ange grinned broadly and nodded.

'Lucky girl . . . So, your young man, why bring him to me like a lamb to the slaughter?'

'Maybe I wanted someone as honest as I am to tell me that I'm not imagining it. I think I'm almost asking you to pinch me, Maud. He is wonderful, isn't he? He hasn't slipped something in his cooking that has me seeing him as this gorgeous, thoughtful, sensitive, intelligent, funny, wonderful man, when all along he's actually some gimpy idiot?'

Maud burst out laughing and then reached over and put a reassuring hand on Ange's.

'Trust me, darling, he's absolutely adorable, wonderful.'

'Really?'

'Absolutely. And you know it yourself, you don't need me to tell you.'

'It's just I never expected it to be so easy . . . love, that is.'

'Ah yes.' Maud nodded sagely, and bent to pull a weed that had dared to insinuate itself in amongst her hardy roses. 'I know what you mean. Everyone thinks that love should only be found after an angst-ridden ordeal, but I always think it's rather nice when you fall into it like a big comfortable bed. That's how it was with me and my Monty . . .'

'I thought that relationship was the queen of complicated.' Ange crossed her eyes in confusion. 'Nell said that you were in all sorts of trouble because he was older and had immense amounts of baggage and stuff like that.'

'Sure, but when we moved down here it was as if the rest of the world just fell away, like we shed an old skin and woke up bright and shining and new. If you truly look at the problems in your life, analytically and not emotionally, you'll often find that they are the making of other people.'

'And by shedding the other people you shed the problems.'

'Exactly. That may seem idealistic or impossible or even harsh, but what rule in life says that you should accept people in your life simply because *they* feel they have a right to it? My whole family told me I shouldn't be with Monty, that only unhappiness would come of it, but that man brought me nothing but joy. I never loved before him and I never loved after.'

Ange looked at her sideways. 'Talking of love and of foxes . . .'

'Which is a rather strange combination.' Maud smiled, plucking a single red rose and handing it to Ange.

'Thank you, it's beautiful . . . Talking of foxes . . .' she started again, 'what is it with you and Harry the Fox?'

Maud, who had bent back over another rose bush that she thought might have greenfly, snapped upright far too quickly, and clutched at her back and hip, which cracked in protest.

She had got used to Ange's forthright manner now, but this was one question that still caught her out. That was the thing about Nell: she was so damn polite you could count on her not to ask awkward questions. Usually as cool as a cucumber and yogurt dip, Maud found herself temporarily flustered, which wasn't good. To survive around Ange, one had to be as razor sharp as she was.

Her brain scrambled for her stock reply. 'Harry? He's such a nice young man, isn't he?'

'Sure.' Feeling bad that she had obviously caused some physical pain instead of simply mental turmoil, Ange gave her this one and steered Maud back towards the cottage, guiding her into one of the garden seats.

'You okay?'

'Old age,' said Maud flippantly, but her face was pinched with pain.

'Can I get you anything?'

'Large Scotch?' said Maud hopefully.

'I meant like a painkiller or something.'

'Best painkiller I've ever come across.'

Ange shook her head, but went to fetch Scotch and soda none the less, the plan of attack abandoned temporarily.

It didn't take her long to return to the fray, however.

She waved the tray she was carrying at Maud before putting it down on the wrought-iron garden table, and then: 'You okay?'

'Sure, just pulled my hip a little, I think. Too much gardening . . .'

It was so obvious that Maud was lying.

Too much guilt more like, Ange thought to herself. Don't know what's going on here yet, but there's definitely a secret being kept. I can almost hear Maud's brain rattling as it bangs around in there, threatening to escape at any moment.

Thinking that Maud needed a sweetener, Ange had hunted in the kitchen and found some of Nell's famous pineapple tarts. She had arranged these on a plate with some Jammie Dodgers. Maud loved Jammie Dodgers. Probably, Ange mused, because she was one. So far she had been very jammy at dodging questions. It was time to just go for the jugular. Bluntness, Ange had always found, was like a crowbar, kind of heavy-handed, but in certain circumstances it was the only thing that was actually going to work.

She gave Maud enough time for half a glass of her favourite tipple, a pineapple tart and most of a Jammie Dodger before she spoke again. 'Okay, so I'm just going to cut straight to the chase.'

'I thought you already had.' Maud shrugged, laughing lightly.

'And you pulled the old and injured card on me.'

'An old girl's got to do what an old girl's got to do.'

'And is this particular old girl "doing" Harry the Fox?'

Maud, who had just taken another mouthful of her drink, struggled not to spit it all out again and swallow it without choking, and then realised that a choking fit would actually be another pretty good diversion from Ange's inquisition and so began to cough instead.

Ange gave her plenty of time to recover, even tapped her gently on the back and offered her a napkin, but long after the actual coughing had subsided and the fake coughing was threatening to pull something else in Maud's body, she was still staring at Maud with that probing gaze of hers.

'So are you?' she said when Maud gave up faking it and collapsed back against her cushion with a sigh.

'Is that what you think?'

'Perhaps,' Ange lied, her theory being that if you accused somebody of something you were pretty sure they weren't doing, then you were more likely to get the truth about what they were actually up to.

'Of course I'm not!'

'I hope you don't mind me asking . . .' Ange said, fully intending to ask some more.

'To tell you the truth, it's actually very nice to know you think he might want to . . .'

'He's not the only fox around here, Maud Pemberton.'

'You're too kind, Ange.'

'No I'm not. I'm usually far from it.'

Maud shook her head vigorously. 'You are, you know. As much as you'd like to deny it, you're a lovely girl. You don't want too many people to know it, but I see through you, Ange O'Donel, and I couldn't wish for a better friend for my Nell. I'd like you to know that I'm very, very glad indeed that she has you . . .' Maud reached out and put her hand on Ange's, and for a moment they were both so shocked by her sudden outpouring of affection that they sat in a slightly stunned silence, until Ange stuttered:

'Well, that's the thing, you see . . .'

'What is, darling?'

'Nell.'

'What about her?'

'She's why I asked. About Harry. You see . . . well . . . it's . . .'

Maud looked at Ange in astonishment. In the months she had known her, she had never known her to be lost for words.

'It's what, Ange?' she prompted, suddenly concerned.

'It's just . . . the reason I wanted to know the lie of the land is that I think Nell's in love with him.'

This one made Maud pull the other hip.

'You think she's in *love*?'

'Yep.'

'Not just that she has a crush, or she fancies him, or she thinks he's rather attractive, or there's a whole dollop of lust going on? It's love? Actual love?' she asked, wide-eyed and worried.

'Yep.' Ange nodded firmly, secure in the higher knowledge that came with being Ange. 'That's what it is. Love. And I didn't know before because, well, I just didn't know . . . you know, much about what it actually is to feel it, not for real . . .'

Maud paused for a moment, biting her bottom lip until it turned white, and then, having obviously come to some form of decision, she nodded firmly.

'And you think Nell is feeling this for real too?'

Ange nodded firmly.

'And Harry?'

Ange sighed, and let her eyes slide sideways. Nell was her friend, she didn't want to betray a confidence, but there was something inside that told her that this was the right thing to do.

'They spent the night together,' she said simply.

She wasn't quite sure how she was expecting Maud to

react to this, but she hadn't expected a smile. A smile, though, was what she got. And then Maud laughed, and then to Ange's total surprise her eyes filled with tears.

'Oh goodness,' was all Maud managed for a moment, and then she pulled herself together.

'And I'm afraid there's something else I'm pretty certain Nell hasn't told you,' Ange added reluctantly. 'Marcus . . . well, he's been sending her flowers, apologies. I think he wants her back.'

'Oh goodness no, he's the last thing Nell needs to make her happy. The man was sucking the life out of her . . .'

'And one last thing . . .' Ange cut in.

'There's more?' Maud sighed heavily and shook her head in disbelief.

Ange nodded. 'I know who Harry Fox is.'

'You do?' Maud asked quietly, cautiously.

'I don't know what he is to you. But I know *who* he is.'

There was a moment of silence, and then Maud nodded slowly as if in resignation.

'Well in that case this is a whole different kettle of fish, isn't it?'

'It is? What is? What kettle are we talking about here, Maud, because up until now you've kind of been denying that there's been a kettle at all.'

'Oh there's a kettle, I'm afraid, Ange, and a pot.'

'A pot?' Ange echoed, frowning.

The poor girl looked so confused and so genuinely worried that Maud, used to putting on a front, could no longer hold it in place so firmly. And so she dropped her head into her hands.

'A great big black one.' She nodded, talking through her fingers. 'I've been so selfish . . .'

This was something else Ange had never seen before, Maud looking so defeated, so lost. Ange offered up her hand and Maud took it and clung on as if for dear life. Taking strength from the touch and the gesture of solidarity, she finally managed to regain control enough to talk.

'I'm a stubborn old fool who has to have things done my way right to the very last, but perhaps my way isn't the best way after all ...' She looked up, her brown eyes solemn. 'Now, Ange, I'm going to tell you something, but you have to swear on something precious that you'll keep it secret.'

'I swear,' Ange said, sitting upright.

'On something precious,' Maud urged. 'I know it sounds childish, but I'm afraid at the moment it's a need ...'

'The need to be childish on occasion, even when actually completely grown up, should never be ignored,' Ange finished for her.

'Rule number ... ?'

'Two hundred and forty-seven.' Ange grinned and then began to fumble in the lining of her voluminous purple shirt, pulling out a crumpled packet of Marlboro reds and putting them down on the wrought-iron table in front of Maud.

'They're not exactly precious.' She shrugged apologetically. 'Well, not in the right sense of the word anyway, but Nell would kill me if she found out, so now you have something on me. If I tell, you tell, and vice versa.'

Maud looked dubious for a moment. 'If you told Nell what I'm about to tell you, then I'd want to do more to you than shop you for smoking.'

'I won't say a word, I swear,' Ange promised.

'It's very important that you mean that,' Maud said quietly, and the tone of her voice was enough to extinguish any mischief from Ange's answer.

'You have my word,' she replied solemnly.

Maud nodded. 'Right, well if I have your word, then that's good enough for me. Okay, well you see, it's like this . . .'

Jarrad was on the *Blackguard*, packing up to go home. His cottage was finally empty of family, friends and sea-searching tourists, and he was looking forward to getting back there. He always did. The boat was great fun, but not exactly roomy, and there was nothing like sleeping in your own bed, and he wasn't even going to mention his luxurious en suite bathroom with the full-size rain shower. How many times, standing in the poky excuse for a bathroom on the boat, trying to scrub all six foot of him with a trickle of water and his elbows hitting the sides, had he dreamed of that shower? And then there was his kitchen. He really missed his kitchen, his big indulgence, the perfect chef's kitchen, with its stainless steel, its full-sized range cooker and every appliance a man who loved to cook could ever want. Oh how he missed his kitchen.

But this year was different, because in a way he didn't want to go.

A big way. Well, not so big, say about one hundred and forty-seven pounds, and a whole ton of attitude.

'Ange O'Donel.' Just saying her name made him grin like an idiot.

So not what he thought he'd been looking for, but everything he had ever wanted without knowing.

For some time now he had begun to think that perhaps

it was his destiny to be alone. He had turned thirty-eight last birthday, and relationships thus far had been like holidays on foreign shores: great whilst they lasted, but none yet where he had been in any way tempted to set up a permanent home.

Home is where the heart is had always been his grandmother's favourite saying. He finally knew exactly what this well-worn adage meant. And now, in returning to one home, he was leaving another, and it wasn't the boat, it was the girl. He knew the cottage was only another eight miles up the coast, but those eight miles felt like eighty. He had got used to her just dropping in whenever she felt like it, letting herself on to the boat and into his bed, sliding into his arms and – he felt daft even thinking it, but it was true – into his heart, like she'd always been there.

He was like a teenager with his first crush, walking on air, singing along to stupid love songs, smiling at people who usually annoyed him.

Only he knew without a shadow of a doubt that this wasn't a crush. This was it.

This was finally it.

When he heard the banging on his door, he knew it would be her and couldn't stop himself from smiling like an idiot. Dropping the clothes he had been folding in his haste to answer, anticipating her face, her voice, her touch, her smile as eager as a kid waiting for Christmas.

But when he opened the door, instead of her angelic face with its devilish grin, he saw a pale, tear-stained stranger, so unlike the girl he thought he knew he had to ask if it was definitely her. 'Ange?'

She fell into his arms and began to sob her heart out.

36

Nell was at a loose end.

The Cakehole had been quiet all day. Lots of people had been in for food, but it had mainly been for things to take away to eat on the beach. It was such a beautiful day, Nell couldn't blame them, but she really enjoyed it when the room was full of chat and laughter.

At the moment, especially, she needed something to take her mind off everything.

She hadn't seen Ange all day either. The last she'd seen of her was when she headed off up to Maud's to introduce her to Jarrad. She hadn't come home last night. Nell presumed she was with Jarrad on the boat. After all, he was moving back home soon, and they probably wanted to spend as much time as possible together before he went. Nell smiled indulgently, but it wasn't like Ange not to at least call and say she wouldn't be back.

And so she was really pleased when the phone rang and it was Maud. 'Hello, lovey, Auntie Maud's feeling a bit lonesome. Don't suppose you'd come and keep an old lady company this evening? We could have a bite of something lovely for supper and then watch an old movie, maybe.'

'Love to.'

'I'm not dragging you away from anything?'

'My plans this evening were either to clean the tea room oven or pluck my eyebrows.'

'Well, in that case I'll see you at six thirty sharp, and Nell, why don't you pluck your eyebrows anyway before you come? There's no excuse for being hirsute when we live in the age of tweezers and depilatory cream.'

When Nell got to Maud's cottage, eyebrows perfectly plucked, there was a note stuck to the front door saying 'In the garden, come on round'.

It was a beautiful evening. Maud had obviously decided to start them off with a favourite al fresco starter of a jug of sangria and some tapas.

Nell smiled at the prospect and made her away around the side of the cottage to the back garden, but when she got there, she stopped in her tracks and stared in wonder.

There wasn't a jug of sangria or dish of olives in sight.

The wrought-iron table had been covered in a heavy cream damask tablecloth upon which sat a silver candelabra with its candles lit and guttering slightly in the gentlest of evening breezes. The apple tree under which the table sat had been garlanded with coloured lanterns. Maud had cut some of her precious roses and they sat full-headed at the base of it, soft hues of pink and yellow and clotted cream. Her best china, silver cutlery and crystal glasses had been brought out of the overstuffed cabinet and the table was set for two. A bottle of champagne sat unopened in an ice bucket next to one of the chairs, and on the table behind the candles and roses sat a big silver salver covered in ice atop which was a feast of chilled seafood.

Nell looked at this vision of outdoor dining in astonishment.

What was Maud playing at?

Seafood, champagne, roses, and . . . she paused and listened . . . unless she was very much mistaken, there was music playing softly somewhere in the background. Jazz, Maud loved jazz.

What on earth was going on?

Had Nell forgotten something, an anniversary of some kind?

It certainly wasn't Maud's birthday. That was in November, she was a Scorpio, although Nell had always joked that someone had removed the sting from her tail, to which Maud always replied that the sting was a stealth weapon, well hidden but there to use if someone truly deserved it.

It wasn't the anniversary of Monty's passing either, that was Christmas time.

'Maud!' Nell called.

No answer.

'Maud!'

Hearing soft footfalls in the grass, she turned, expecting to see her godmother.

But it wasn't Maud.

Her stomach twisted at the sight of him. 'Hal?'

'Nell?' He looked and sounded as surprised as she did. 'What are you doing here?'

'Maud called and said that she needed me.'

'She asked me up for dinner.'

They just stood and stared at each other for a moment, and then he stepped closer, reached out and put a hand on her arm. 'I'm sorry I haven't . . . I've wanted to come in and see you so many times . . .'

'Then why haven't you?'

He didn't answer, but looked at the homage to romance under the apple tree. There were place names on the plates. 'Harry' and 'Nell' in Maud's distinctive spiky scrawl. She had set them up, had set this up for them. Did this mean that finally there were to be no secrets?

He showed them to Nell and she smiled quizzically. 'What's going on, Harry?'

He turned back to her and smiled softly. 'You mean you don't get the feeling we're supposed to have dinner together? We've been set up, Nell. I suppose this means we can take it that we have her seal of approval.'

It was as though he had stolen the smile from Nell, however, as her own face suddenly knitted into a frown. 'Is that what you were waiting for?'

Although he didn't answer, she could see by his face that she had finally asked the right question.

'Well is it? You needed Maud's *approval*?'

'It's not quite as simple as that, Nell.'

'Complicated?' she said flatly.

He nodded.

Nell shook her head. 'I'm sorry, but that doesn't wash this time, Harry Fox. Why is it complicated? What is your problem with me?'

'I don't have a problem with you, Nell . . . in fact I think you're amazing. It's just that I have a problem with . . .' He paused again, and then deliberately used the word that Nell had used when trying to define them, 'us.'

'You mean *Maud* has a problem with us?'

'It's not that, not really; in principle she thinks it would be great.'

'Oh, so you've sat and had a cosy little chat about "us", and for some reason nobody will tell me, Maud said no and you just said okay . . .'

'It's not like that, Nell . . . it's just that . . .' He shook his head. Nell was right. What was Maud playing at asking him to keep away from Nell and then organising this without even talking to him? He shook his head in concern and bewilderment. 'This wasn't a good idea. I don't know why Maud's done it, but—'

Nell interrupted him. 'The problem here isn't whether Maud approves of us being together or not, it's why it should matter that she does. What's going on, Harry?'

He was quiet for a moment, bit his bottom lip, looked at the grass, looked back up at her, shrugged. 'I can't say.'

'You can't or you won't?'

'I literally *can't*, Nell, at least not yet, not until I've spoken to Maud.'

'So you do need her approval?'

'Yes, and no. Not in the way you mean it, but yes, I do . . . Oh Nell,' he threw up his hands in despair, 'please trust me when I say it's complicated. I'm not just fobbing you off. Okay . . . let me talk to Maud and then maybe I can explain . . .'

Nell's phone began to ring.

They both looked at each other, and then at Nell's pocket.

'Should you get that?'

'I'd rather you finished what you were saying,' Nell demanded, ignoring it.

The phone switched through to voicemail.

Two seconds later it began to ring again.

'That might be important.'

Nell pulled the phone from the back pocket of her jeans and glanced at the screen in irritation. It was a local number, familiar, but not one she immediately recognised. And then she realised it was the phone number of the Jolly Roger.

Ange wasn't working tonight. Maybe they needed her, couldn't get her and so were trying Nell instead. Well they'd have to wait. She cut the call, put the phone down on the table in front of her and returned her gaze to Harry.

'I need to know what's going on,' she said, and then her phone began to ring again.

'Oh bloody hell!' She snatched it up and barked, 'Hello?' into the receiver.

'Nell?' It was Tony, but there was something wrong with his voice. 'I'm so sorry, love, you need to come down here. I'm so sorry, Nell . . .' And then Nell realised that he was crying.

Anything Tony had said after that had been incomprehensible, and then Marge had taken the phone from him and said, 'Nell, darlin', it's Marge. Where are you?'

'At Maud's,' Nell whispered, her own voice lost because her throat was suddenly so dry.

'You on your own?'

'No. Harry's here, Maud's . . . friend. What's happened, Marge?' Nell croaked, her voice rising an octave in distress.

'I'm afraid it's your Auntie Maud, love . . .'

'Maud? What's happened? Is she okay? Has she had an accident?'

'It's best if you come down, love, quick as you can.'

'Marge, for God's sake just tell me what's happened!'

'I can't, love, not on the phone.'

'What do you mean, you can't tell me . . .' Nell felt her panic rising like bile in her throat.

Harry reached out, took her hand, and gently took the phone from her.

'Hello, Marge? My name's Harry Fox. Perhaps you could tell me what's happened.' And his eyes flicked up to Nell, full of apology. 'I'm Maud's GP.'

37

It had all seemed rather surreal from that point on, like a dream, only one she couldn't wake up from, a nightmare that couldn't be soothed away by Auntie Maud with a cool hand and whispered words.

Because Maud was gone.

She had been at the Jolly Roger, having a drink with Tony and Marge. The ambulance was there for her when Nell and Harry arrived. Come to take her away. She looked as if she was sleeping, but when Nell touched her face it felt so cold.

As the ambulance drove away, all Nell could think about was that Tony was still crying.

Harry took her up to Marge and Tony's place above the pub. Sat her down in the living room whilst Marge made tea for them both.

Funny, even in her blind grief she still had time to observe that it wasn't how she expected it to be, as if focusing on the decor, the real, the mundane, could make this surreal news a nonsense.

After Marge had placed a tray on the coffee table in front of them and left, Harry, calm, focused, held on to her hands and tried to explain as gently as he could. Maud had been very ill last summer, an illness that lingered. Her own doctor had put it down to a virus. It was only when she'd demanded a second opinion and been referred to Harry that they found she had advanced coronary artery disease. Heart failure.

The day after Harry had told her, she had walked down into Polporth and painted 'Bugger the NHS' in big red letters on the side of the doctor's surgery.

That was the day that Nell arrived.

Maud had made the decision then that she wanted her life to be as normal as possible: no hospitals, just palliative care, and no one knowing. Not even Nell. Especially not Nell.

'Life is for living, Harry Fox,' she had told him, 'not waiting to die.'

Nell listened quietly, so quietly in fact that he wondered if she was taking in what he said or if she was in shock. It was as though she had just switched off.

But inside her head the same phrase kept repeating.

No lingering virus, no handyman, no Maud.

No Maud.

No Maud.

And then she just erupted, from her seat and with her voice. 'Why didn't you tell me!'

Hal stood up to catch her. 'I'm so sorry.'

'Why didn't you tell me!' This time louder, harsher, broken.

He tried to pull her close, to hold her, but she fought him all the way, balling up her fists and hitting him and then flattening her palms against his chest to push him away, but he was stronger, physically and emotionally. He held on to her until she calmed, pulled her gently against him, stroked her hair, pressed his lips against her forehead, waited until he could feel the thumping beat of her heart subside a little.

'I couldn't tell you, Nell. Maud made me promise that I wouldn't ... and even if she hadn't, I'm her doctor, I couldn't tell you no matter how much I wanted to ...'

'No,' she spat, wrenching herself away from him. 'No! No excuses! There's no excuses.'

And then she ran.

Ange found her two hours later up at the cottage, sitting in Maud's chair, curled up like a child, feet tucked under her.

Ange didn't say a word, just wrapped her in a hug and held her tight until they both fell asleep where they were.

Ange woke up at first light, cold and stiff.

Made tea, hot and sweet.

When she took it back through to the sitting room, Nell was awake. She was looking at a picture of her and Maud on the mantelpiece.

She refused the tea, but accepted another hug.

'You're frozen.'

'Maud never has the heating on in summer, no matter what the weather. Says it's sacrilege to burn oil when there's no R in the month.'

'Do you want to go home?'

'This is home, Ange,' Nell said quietly, and then she looked about her at the overstuffed room and shook her head. 'At least it was.'

She sat back down in Maud's chair, biting her bottom lip until all the blood drained from it. She was rocking back and forth with the tension of the pain. Ange felt the tears burning her own eyes and the back of her throat and fought to keep them from falling. How could she cry when Nell wasn't?

Instead she went over and sat on the arm of the chair and took Nell's hands, cold like blocks of ice, in her own.

'Harry wants to see you. He's worried about you.'

'I don't want to see him.'

'I know you need someone to blame right now, but it's not his fault, you know.'

'He should have told me.'

Ange shook her head. 'You know he couldn't.'

'Oh bollocks to that!' Nell exploded. 'Hippocratic oath, hypocritical oaf!'

'It's not his fault,' Ange repeated slowly, gently. 'He wanted you to know, but the only person who could have told you was Maud herself, and she chose not to. If you want to blame someone, blame her, blame her for choosing to spare your feelings, for choosing to spend the last months of her life with you enjoying every minute, not wasting what time you had left with her anticipating the end of it. You must understand that ... you must understand why she chose not to tell you ...'

Nell still wouldn't look up at her friend, but after a moment she swallowed a sob and nodded, and then said in a broken voice, 'But I never got the chance to tell her how much I loved her.'

'You didn't need to tell her that. You really think she didn't know already? Be honest, Nell, what was left unsaid between the two of you?'

Nell looked up at her friend, her eyes shadowed.

'Goodbye,' she whispered bleakly. 'I never got the chance to say goodbye.'

Ange and Jarrad took charge of Nell, Ange as a Rottweiler at the door to the constant stream of well-wishers, Jarrad as unlikely nursemaid tempting her to eat with a stream of amazing dishes that elicited nothing more than a faint smile and a polite refusal.

For two days Nell shut herself away in her room and listened to the world go on outside without her, refusing to eat or to see anyone. When Harry came she sent him away; when he came back the next day she did the same thing. Ange, the messenger, was gutted by the look on his face as she refused to see him once again, worried when the food they had prepared for her was rejected in the same way, and worried that Nell just looked shell-shocked, that she still hadn't cried a single tear.

Then, the next morning, it changed.

Nell got up to her alarm as usual, showered, put on some clean clothes, and re-emerged into a world that seemed slightly emptier than it had two days ago.

'Nell, what are you doing?'

Ange, having heard the flat door go, thundered down the stairs after her.

'I'm getting on with my life,' Nell replied, heading for the kitchen, where she began to switch on the appliances.

Ange caught up with her, put a hand on her arm. 'It's too soon.'

Nell stopped and turned around to face her. 'Would Maud tell me that? Would Maud tell me to lie in bed all day feeling sorry for myself, or would she tell me to get my arse out of that bed and get on with it? Well, which would it be?'

Ange nodded. And then she began to cry.

Nell sighed, blinked, swallowed as though there was something stuck in her throat, and then reached out and touched Ange's face, wiped away her tears, pulled her into a hug.

'It's okay, Ange,' she whispered, stroking her hair. 'Today will be a better day, just you wait and see, today will be a better day.'

She waited until the sobbing had subsided and then smiled determinedly at her friend.

'Now I need your help with something. And I don't want you to try and talk me out of it, because it's something I really want . . . I really *need* to do, okay?'

Ange nodded.

The many well-wishers who came by that day to leave flowers outside what they thought would be a closed shop were amazed to find the Cakehole open, jazz music blaring loudly from inside, and a hand-written sign in the window that read:

'In honour of Maud Pemberton the Cakehole will be *open* all day today. Please come in and help us celebrate her life in the way she would have wanted.'

'Whisky and cupcakes!' Ange didn't know whether to laugh or cry, and so she did both.

Nell's impromptu party seemed to have the same

effect on nearly everyone in the Cakehole that day. People coming to mourn had found a party going on instead. Loud music, lots of food and plenty to drink. Just the way Maud would have wanted it.

And the unexpected opening of the Cakehole started to have a rather strange effect on the rest of the village, as everything else there began to close. First the pub, then the florist, then the dress shop, then the fishmonger, and so on until everyone who was in the village was in the Cakehole. Tony, Marge and the boys, Beth and Oliver, the Jolly Roger regulars, the rowing team, the lifeboat crew, the Ramblers and Twitchers, and last but not least the entire contingent of Maud's beloved LLs, all alternately in tears of sadness then of laughter, dancing, crying, hugging, sighing, singing, spilling out of the shop and into the street, such were the numbers of the people who had loved Maud.

And Nell sat behind her counter dishing out cakes and alcohol, and found as the numbers grew that so did her smile.

And then, in the middle of this massive party, the most unexpected visitor of all arrived, stooping as he came through the low doorway, looking about the room at the massed people in amazement.

'Um, Nell, there's someone here to see you,' Ange said uncertainly.

But Nell had already spotted him and come out from behind the counter. 'Marcus?' she said uncertainly.

Had it been so long she had forgotten his face?

He looked so different somehow, so familiar and yet almost like a stranger.

And then he saw her, and smiled at her gently, that same familiar smile she had once loved so much it had made her heart melt to see it.

'I had to come. Your mum and dad called and told me what happened. I'm so sorry, Nell, I know how much Maud meant to you.'

And because he did, and because he fell into the category of old and familiar, and that was a part of what she was mourning, she allowed him to come over and to hold her for a long time. To stroke her hair and whisper words of comfort, to plant kisses on the crown of her head, until finally she opened her eyes and looked up to see him smiling down at her.

'It's okay, Nell, I'm here now. I'm here. You don't have to worry about anything any more. I know I let you down before, but I'm sorry, I'm so sorry, and I promise that from now on I'll take good care of you,' he said.

Nell was silent for a moment. And then she stepped carefully away from him. 'Marcus, oh Marcus . . .' She sighed and he smiled again, but Nell shook her head.

'That's the thing now, don't you see? I don't need you to take care of me, I don't need anyone to take care of me, because I've finally realised that I can take perfectly good care of myself.'

And finally, *finally* Nell realised something else: that when she had left Marcus and her job and London, she hadn't run *away*, she had run *home*, and only now, with Maud gone, was it truly time to start afresh.

'Please, stay, join in the celebration. I really appreciate you coming all this way, and you're very welcome, but right now there's somebody I need to talk to, and I've learned recently that if something is important, then you should never prevaricate.'

Ange, who had been watching Nell like a hawk the whole day without her realising, swooped down before she could make the door.

'Where are you going?' she asked in concern.

'There's someone I need to see.'

'Want me to come?'

Nell shook her head.

'This is something that I have to do on my own.'

And Ange, who had already guessed where Nell might be headed, nodded, and stepped aside.

Once outside, however, Nell noticed another visitor.

It was Tam.

He was standing outside the Cakehole, looking as forlorn and lost as a six-foot-two grown man possibly could, clutching yet another bunch of bloody roses.

Nell didn't know whether to hug him or brain him with them, but when he saw her coming towards him, his face lit up and Nell's heart went out to him.

'Nell . . . I didn't know whether to come. I don't want to intrude, but I heard what happened and I just wanted to make sure that you're okay.'

'That's very sweet of you. Thank you.'

'And I know it's not the time, but I feel such an idiot . . . I wanted to say sorry . . . you know, for coming on so strong with all the flowers . . . These aren't for you, by the way, well they are, but really they're for Mrs Pemberton . . .' He trailed off, looking mortifyingly embarrassed. 'See, told you I was an idiot.'

'That's really very kind of you.' Nell smiled gently, taking the flowers from him, 'Maud loved roses. Thank you so much.'

Taking hope from her kindness, he tried one more time. 'I think you're a very special person, Nell . . .'

Nell paused and bit her bottom lip.

'Oh, Tam. You're a really nice man. And one day you're going to meet someone who makes you feel like you deserve to be loved. But that person's not me.'

'What makes you so sure?'

Nell hesitated to say it because she didn't want to hurt him any more, but it was something that had been left unsaid for so long, she knew that the words finally had to come out.

'Because I'm in love with someone else, that's why. I'm madly in love with someone else . . .'

She didn't know how she knew he'd be there, but he was.

In Maud's garden. Pruning her roses for her.

'So you are a gardener after all,' Nell said softly.

He paused, but didn't turn to face her. 'She'd hate to see it go to ruin,' he replied.

'Hal . . . I . . .'

But he shook his head.

Nell fell silent. Waited. And finally he began to talk.

'My mum died when I was fifteen. She was ill for a long time, she had cancer. She was in so much pain but she never let it show. Maud was so like her. Feisty, funny, a real fighter.' As he turned around to face her, she realised that tears were streaming down his face. 'She wasn't just my patient, she was my friend. I loved her too, Nell. I loved her too.'

For a moment Nell's fractured heart plummeted further as she thought the forgiveness she sought for rejecting him so harshly was beyond him, but then he simply held out his arms. This time Nell didn't fight, she walked straight into them, wrapped her own around his waist, sighed long, low and heavy and leaned into the warmth and the strength of him. And finally the tears that had been so long held back they were filling her lungs and making it hard and painful just to breathe began to flow.

Typically of Maud, her last request was that she go up in a firework as part of the display at the next Midsummer Madness.

Nell had rather wanted to keep her godmother with her. Put her in her box on the shelf above the fire in the tea shop, feel like she was watching over her.

But then Ange had said that Maud wouldn't want to be shut away in a box. Nell knew she was right.

In fact she could picture Maud's spirit roaming free as a bird, happily haunting the villagers, and hanging around the tea shop counter criticising her cooking and her portion sizes.

'It's just so hard to let go,' she had whispered.

And Ange had just said nothing and hugged her, and then after a few moments had said quietly: 'You don't have to let go, Nell. Do you really think that Maud's going anywhere? I know it's a cliché, but she'll always be with you, even if it's just in here.' Ange had put her hand on Nell's chest, where her heart was. 'But I can guarantee you, wherever Maud is, she's going to make damn sure that she doesn't let go of you just yet either.'

Nell had nodded.

Unable to get permission from the relevant authorities or find someone who was actually willing to turn Maud's ashes into a giant rocket, they decided that the next best thing in Maud's book would be to do something she had always joked about and throw her off the cliff.

And so a week after the funeral, when Nell's parents had gone back to Norwich, they set off just before dusk, just the four of them, Nell and Harry, Ange and Jarrad, and headed up to the cottage and down to the end of Maud's garden.

'Should we say a few words, do you think?' Jarrad asked.

Nell shook her head. 'Let's just say "So long, Maud."'

But as she took the lid off Auntie Maud's temporary home and hurled the contents over the edge of the cliff, a freakishly strong gust of wind blew in off the sea and carried her back inland again.

They literally had to duck as the cloud of dark grey dust flew purposefully back inland and set off down the steep hillside towards the village.

For a moment they looked after her in shock.

Ange was the first to speak. 'Told you she wasn't ready to go just yet.'

'Think she's off to the pub before they can call last orders?' Hal smiled gently, slipping his hand inside Nell's jacket pocket and squeezing her hand.

Nell, who had been about to cry, burst out laughing instead. 'Well, she always did want to have a nose around London Tony's private quarters. Check for dominatrix outfits.'

'London Tony's *privates*, more like. You know, she once confessed to me that she found him rather attractive, in an uncouth kind of way,' Ange said.

'She told me that she thought he was the kind of guy who'd put the rough into rough and tumble.' Nell nodded, her smile broadening.

And in moments they were all laughing.

'Just the way she would have wanted it, kiddo.' Ange grinned. 'Everybody happy.'

'A happy ending,' Nell said, smiling softly at Harry.

Epilogue

Nell watched the little girl playing on the beach. She was building a sandcastle close to the tide's edge, and every time the sea washed in, the castle washed away, but rather than being discouraged, she would just chuckle in delight and then methodically start again with a cheerful determination that was both admirable and delightful to see.

It reminded Nell of Maud.

Then again, everything reminded her of Maud. She still expected to see her at every turn. Every time the phone rang, she thought it would be her voice. Every time she saw the LLs heading down the high street, she still expected Aunt Maud to be leading them with her long, liquid, graceful lope and her strident voice urging the stragglers to keep up.

She could see her now, her silver hair shining in the sunlight, her stern face ready to break into a smile as they passed the Cakehole. She could imagine London Tony hanging out of the front of the Jolly Roger just to catch a glimpse of the magnificent woman that she was, a glimpse that would make his day . . .

The sound of a horn brought her back to reality. Spinning round, she saw Harry's car turning on to the cliff road, and her poignant smile turned to one of sheer delight. It had been four years now, but still her heart began to skip like a lamb in spring at the sight of him.

'He's back,' she whispered happily to herself as the four-by-four made its way steadily up towards Maud's cottage, their cottage.

And then she looked back at the little girl, and held out her hand. 'Come on, Maudie, time to go,' she called. 'Daddy's home.'

little black dress

brings you fantastic new books like these
every month - find out more at
www.littleblackdressbooks.com

Why not link up with other devoted Little Black
Dress fans on our Facebook group? Simply type
Little Black Dress Books into Facebook to join up.

And if you want to be the first
to hear the latest news on all things
Little Black Dress, just send the details below to
littleblackdressmarketing@headline.co.uk
and we'll sign you up to our lovely email
newsletter (and we promise that we won't share
your information with anybody else!).*

Name: _____

Email Address: _____

Date of Birth: _____

Region/Country: _____

What's your favourite Little Black Dress book?

_____

How many Little Black Dress books have you read?_____

*You can be removed from the mailing list at any time

Pick up a *little black dress* – it's a girl thing.

978 0 7553 4715 5

THE FARMER NEEDS A WIFE
Janet Gover
PBO £5.99

Rural romances become all the rage when editor Helen Woodley starts a new magazine column profiling Australia's lovelorn farmers. But a lot of people (and Helen herself) are about to find out that the course of true love ain't ever smooth . . .

It's not all haystacks and pitchforks, ladies – get ready for a scorching outback read!

HIDE YOUR EYES
Alison Gaylin
PBO £5.99

Samantha Leiffer's in big trouble: the chest she saw a sinister man dumping into the Hudson river contained a dead body, meaning she's now a witness in a murder case. It's just as well hot, hard-line detective John Krull is by her side . . .

978 0 7553 4802 2

'Alison Gaylin is my new must-read' Harlen Coben

Pick up a *little black dress* – it's a girl thing.

ITALIAN FOR BEGINNERS
Kristin Harmel
PBO £5.99

Despairing of finding love, Cat Connelly takes up an invitation to go to Italy, where an unexpected friendship, a whirlwind tour of the Eternal City and a surprise encounter show her that the best things in life (and love) are always unexpected . . .

Say 'arrivederci, lonely hearts' with another fabulous page-turner from Kristin Harmel.

978 0 7553 4743 8

THE GIRL MOST LIKELY TO . . .
Susan Donovan
PBO £5.99

Years after walking out of her small town in West Virginia, Kat Cavanaugh's back and looking for apologies – especially from Riley Bohland, the man who broke her heart. But soon Kat's questioning everything she thought she knew about her past . . . and about her future.

A red-hot tale of getting mad, getting even – and getting everything you want!

978 0 7553 5144 2

You can buy any of these other
Little Black Dress titles from your
bookshop or *direct from the publisher*.

FREE P&P AND UK DELIVERY
(Overseas and Ireland £3.50 per book)

TO ORDER SIMPLY CALL THIS NUMBER

01235 400 414

or visit our website: www.headline.co.uk

Prices and availability subject to change without notice.